PRAISE FOR FEATHERED SERPENT

The setting for this novel is fertile and fruitful. Brusca provides a sobering history of Central American countries, an informed explanation of the archeology of the area, and appreciative rich descriptions of the cities and lush countryside. Odel Bernini's time there becomes a journey of self-discovery.
Arizona Daily Star/Christine Wald-Hopkins. Book critic (San Francisco Chronicle, Denver Post, etc.) and essayist; member National Book Critics Circle.

Reading Feathered Serpent inspired me to want to travel in Central America. The depictions of science, politics, history, and the inner workings of the CIA seem genuine and authoritative. The myth aspect is well handled, as the book is not a copy of The Odyssey but rather a nod to the trials of Odysseus. I enjoyed the trip with Brusca and Odel, and I believe readers with an interest in that part of the world will also enjoy the book. **Portland Book Review**

A capacious, multi-storied novel in the classical mode. The action moves seamlessly back and forth between the states and lush backdrops of Central America. As Dr. Odel Bernini plunges into the unknown, he is led not by equations and analyses, but is prompted by his dream visions of a dark, beautiful woman. By the time this odyssey is complete, Brusca seamlessly stitches . . . a satisfying tapestry of action and self-discovery. A wonderful and engaging writer, Brusca has produced an entertaining, touching hero's journey, an epic of the soul. **Mary Ellen Hannibal**. Author of The Spine of the Continent, Citizen Scientist: Searching for Heroes and Hope in an Age of Extinction, and others.

Brusca weaves bright threads of Latin American history, political angst during the Sandinista revolution, anthropology, marine biology, suspense, travel, and a series of heated romantic entanglements. The overarching spiritual journey of Odel Bernini keeps Feathered Serpent meaningful, poignant, and deeply human. I liked this book so much I bought copies for friends. **Jonathan White.** Author of Talking on the Water and Tides: The Science & Spirit of the Sea.

Feathered Serpent is a wonderfully unique novel; part explorations of marine biology and archeology, part illuminating the history of Central American politics in the 1980s), part international thriller, part love story, and part spiritual journey. You'll find touches of Steinbeck/Ricketts, your favorite thriller author, and Carlos Castaneda. It's a joy to see someone bring a wondrous new aspect of themselves to full fruition. And Brusca has achieved that here in spades...buckle-up! **Steven L. Meloan.** Author of The Shroud. Writer, blogger, musician, Steven Meloan has written for Rolling Stone, Wired, Playboy, Buzz, Los Angeles Times, San Francisco Chronicle, and many others.

This story, like the feathered serpent itself, moves through time and space to an era remembered by many Americans as one in which the U.S. government worked to destabilize Central American countries that were at odds with its politics. Prodded by his wife, the daughter of an American cultural attaché, Odel Bernini approaches the CIA to ask if they could fund his continued research in the region in exchange for "some silly things" he might do for them. Those "silly things" lead to funding from a private foundation to cover his travel—but with strings attached. Having sold his soul, he gradually undertakes more dangerous tasks on the CIA's behalf.

Author Brusca delivers modern man's Odyssey, both in scale and complexity. We are riveted to Odel Bernini's journey of self-discovery as he navigates the siren calls of a smart beautiful woman from his dreams, while his academic world slowly disintegrates. Brusca has an effortless style that quickly absorbs the reader, and he delivers a mega-novel that will resonate with readers drawn to sensually charged, clandestine storylines that run through dangerous political landscapes and treacherous jungle settings.
Chanticleer Book Reviews

Odel Bernini believed he had it all . . . But on a trip to Central America, everything changed. He will make hard choices, confront his demons and his virtues, and stumble toward a greater understanding of himself and the world around him . . . if he survives. In the Land of the Feathered Serpent is author and scientist Rick Brusca's ambitious reimagining of The Odyssey for modern times.

An epic tale of personal growth where Odel's romanticism is at once embraced and stripped away from him, and he begins to see those around him as true, flawed people, not just the archetypes he'd painted them as. The reader takes this journey alongside Odel, often a step or two ahead of him, but always rooting for him.

Odel is an Everyman worth cheering on . . . The book is incredibly engrossing. Experiencing Central America as a place, a complicated mélange of politics, choices, beauty, chaos, and potential, strips away the reader's false images just as Odel's illusions are similarly confronted, and those moments are powerful. Odel's struggles, the labyrinthine threads of his life that tangle and knot in peculiar ways, and the path he takes to the other side is an intriguing one, rich in color and character, vibrantly realized.

Feathered Serpent is quite unlike anything I've ever read. This is a multi-course meal to be savored, not devoured in one sitting.
Glenn Dallas, San Francisco (CA) and Manhattan (NY) Book Reviews

A prolific science writer, Richard Brusca has now written a fiction novel imaginatively spiced with love, adventure, magic, politics, and a very personal sense of humor. One can't stop reading this book and, when you have finished, it leaves you with a desire for a sequel *on the amazing life of marine biologist Dr. Odel Bernini.* **Omar Vidal.** Former Director-General, World Wildlife Fund, Mexico.

Sexually-explosive political intrigue, a sense of place worthy of Dan Brown, historical explorations à la Ken Follett, and philosophical musings à la The Prophet. *Feathered Serpent is a thoroughly enjoyable spy thriller about a spy who didn't know he was a spy. In fact, Odel Bernini is field researcher painfully unaware of what is going on around him and how deep he is into it, until it comes to bite him, hard. Set in Central America during the tumultuous 1980s,* Serpent *reminds us just how misguided U.S. foreign policy had become, and probably continues to be. But that's only part of a book with twists and turns that kept me reading.* **Gene Helfman.** Professor Emeritus, University of Georgia; author of *Beyond the Human Realm*

Feathered Serpent *is a superb read—I was truly dazzled. It takes only a few pages to get caught up in Odel's odyssey of self-discovery and his developing insights into the role of trust in relationships. The vignettes on Central America's political and social history, and culture of the period, provided a thoroughly credible framework, as did the insights into Maya history and culture. The underlying layer of magical realism is very appropriate for a novel about Latin America, as is Odel's mystical experiences and his coming to terms with the greater Latin acceptance of nonempirical knowledge. The book is beautifully written and nuanced and a real tour de force. This is a powerful book with much to say about the human experience. I've read it twice, the second time just to savor the prose, the characters, and the insights into human relations. I expect to read it many more times.* **Thomas Bowen, PhD.** Professor Emeritus in Anthropology, California State University, Fresno

An epic read! A mystery, a love story, and a historical drama—all wrapped together in a journey through the politics and culture of Central America in the 1980s. Odel Bernini, the naïve marine biologist who finds himself suddenly ensnared by the CIA in a situation that spirals out of control, is a character you won't soon forget. **Jeff Hartman.** Author of *Atkinson Exit* and *The End of the War.*

I highly recommend this novel—a wonderfully told story of Odel, a charismatic and culturally curious American biologist who, because he is driven by the need for research funds to continue his work in Central America, ends up working with the CIA during the Contra years. As he pursues his research (both biological and reconnaissance) he explores the area's archaeological history (and its enduring magic) as well as the mysteriousness of love. The book moves along, keeps you wanting to know more, and teaches a great deal about history, culture, and the basic human desire to know the other.

Sylvia D. Torti, PhD. Latin America scholar, and award-winning essayist and novelist; author of *The Scorpion's Tail* and *CAGES*. Dean, Honors College, University of Utah.

Our hero is a brilliant marine biologist who takes on what at first appears as a small risk to secure funding for his work. A bit of spying, what could that hurt? But as he descends deeper into the 1980s Central American geopolitical soup, he also must contend with the unraveling of his marriage and what turns into ultimately a romantic quadrangle. The magical realism all occurs in Latin America, a culture more open to the otherworldly than buttoned-down American academia. A satisfying ending leaves our somewhat scarred hero with less heart-churning passion but more comfort and wisdom. **Carolyn Niethammer**. Author of *A Desert Feast, The Piano Player, American Indian Food and Lore,* and a dozen other award-winning books

A wonderful, many-layered story. The author takes us on trips to Central America, gets involved with the CIA, and experiences powerful mind-altering experiences. And through the book is the meandering story of his intimate relationships with three women, which ends up being a large part of why one wants to read on. **Professor Elizabeth Bernays.** Regents Professor Emerita, University of Arizona; author of *Six Legs Walking* and many other books and essays.

A great thriller—rich with cultural history, geopolitical intrigue, and mysticism. **William Shaw, PhD.** Professor Emeritus and Latin America History enthusiast, University of Arizona

As the story moved along, it sucked me into real life memories of a particularly brutal era in Central America. I found myself wondering how Brusca was so successful in his efforts to pack so much accurate history and Maya culture into such a fast-moving story. Eventually, I realized that the story line actually follows true historical events. At the end I was struck with the realization that this is by far the best historical novel I have ever read. I urge you to read it, share the loves and adventures of Odel Bernini's odyssey, absorb the history, and contemplate the important lessons yet to be learned in our society. **Paul K. Dayton, PhD.** Professor Emeritus, Scripps Institution of Oceanography. George Mercer Awardee, W.S. Cooper Awardee, E.O. Wilson Naturalist Awardee, Ramon Margalef Prize in Ecology.

In the Land
of the Feathered Serpent

Richard C. Brusca

In the Land of the Feathered Serpent
by Richard C. Brusca

Quetzalcoatl Press/KDP Publishing
Tucson, Arizona

ISBN 9781794544727

Cover illustration and design, and Quetzalcoatl chapter divider
by Alex Boersma (alexboersma.com)

To learn more about the author, the novel,
and Central America
please visit: **www.featheredserpent.online**

For Wendy, who never stopped encouraging me to get this story out of my head and onto paper. And for Jeff and Linda, my writer's club amigos who provided sound advice, fine rum, and endless persuasion.

Contents

Preface

Maps

PART I. ODEL AND PENELOPE

PART II. CROSSING THE RIVER

PART III. INTO THE MYSTIC

PART IV. FINDING DESTINY

PREFACE

Most of this story takes place from 1981 to 1985—the first half of Ronald Reagan's two-term presidency, and when Nicaragua and Guatemala were struggling to emerge from four decades of bitter civil war. While Odel Bernini and his closest friends are fictional characters caught up in situations of the time, the other people, places and events in this story are true and accurate. The names of some people have been changed to protect their privacy.

Perhaps no other country in the world has been so extensively manipulated by the United States as Nicaragua, beginning with American occupation in 1912 during the era of the Banana Wars. American support of the ruthless Somoza family dictatorship from 1936 to 1979 fueled the country's forty-year civil war. After the Sandinistas finally toppled the Somoza regime in 1979, the United States consolidated former Somoza loyalists and various criminal elements as an invading CIA-trained "Contra army," based mainly in Honduras. Reagan's ill-fated Contra War of the 1980s took the lives of thousands of Nicaraguans, was fiercely condemned by the international community, destroyed the economy of Nicaragua, and was an utter failure.

Beginning in the 1930s, Guatemala's government and military began working closely with the U.S. State Department in the interest of American political and business concerns, especially in support of United Fruit Company. United Fruit had $600 million in assets in Guatemala, and it controlled the country's major railway and power companies. In the early 1950s the U.S. government, under pressure from United Fruit, ordered the newly created CIA to stop Guatemala's "communist revolt," which was, in fact, no more than a fair-labor and human rights movement. The U.S. State department and CIA chose extreme right-wing Colonel Carlos Castillo Armas of the Guatemalan Army to lead a 1954 coup d'état that deposed progressive president

Jacobo Árbenz Guzmán. During the Árbenz government's land reforms, United Fruit Company had become a primary target. From then on, a series of coups d'état and fraudulent elections assured that only American-friendly politicians (usually Guatemalan army officers) were installed as president.

For the next forty-two years, Guatemala was a client state of the U.S. Throughout this time, Guatemala's military held nearly absolute power, and paramilitary death squads roamed the country operating with impunity. The Guatemalan Human Rights Commission estimated 42,000 civilians were killed or disappeared between 1966 and 1974 alone. The murders continued into the 1980s, forcing the indigenous Maya People and other citizens to live in constant terror. By 1981, death-squad killings of forty people a day were being reported; almost all were Maya and showed signs of torture. It wasn't until 1994 that the United Nations stepped in to oversee a "peace process" in Guatemala. By the end of the civil war, it is estimated that two hundred thousand people (mostly Maya) had been killed and countless Maya villages massacred and burned to the ground.

The CIA was created under President Harry S. Truman, through the National Security Act of 1947. The director of the CIA is appointed by the president, confirmed by Congress, and serves at the pleasure of the president. Although similar in many ways to the Soviet Union's KGB (which was dissolved in 1991), it differs in that the CIA is forbidden by law from conducting intelligence and counterintelligence operations on domestic soil. William J. Casey was CIA director during the presidency of Ronald Reagan; it is widely acknowledged that he had little concern for human rights, had an inordinate influence on Reagan, and played an unconventionally large role in shaping U.S. foreign policy in Latin America.

MAPS

Mexico and Central America

Nicaragua

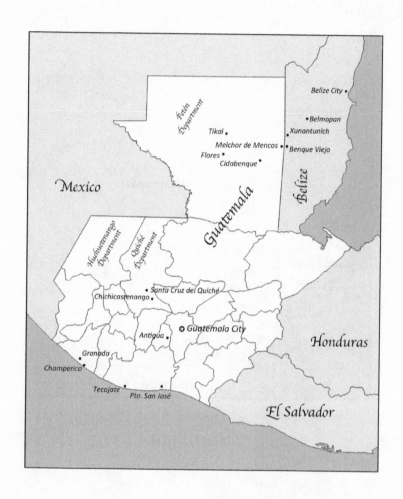

Guatemala and Belize

PART I. ODEL AND PENELOPE

It is a wise child who
Knows his own father.

Homer, *The Odyssey* (850 B.C.)

1

Cidabenque, Guatemala

Summer Solstice, June 1984

The dirty canvas tarp pressed lightly against my face. Aged and fatigued, it was loosely tied over the bed of a rusty '68 Ford pickup filled with firewood, a couple machetes, sundry jungle flotsam, and me. The history of the Petén emanated from the hot oiled canvas. I could smell the iron-based red muds of the tropical lowlands, the cooking fires and meat— even animal blood. At least, I thought it was animal. Dust danced in psychedelic streaks of splintered sunlight that penetrated through pinholes in the old canvas. I was hot, de-hydrated, and afraid to move.

As I lay there sweating, my baking brain rapidly alternated between the nauseating heat and claustrophobia of being under the tarp, and memories of my early childhood. My older brother and I were snuggled in our sleeping bags in an old oiled canvas tent that smelled much like this tarp. Our parents were asleep in a small house trailer that they towed behind their 1955 Oldsmobile Ninety-Eight, with its massive V-8 engine. We were camped in the high pines of Montana on summer vacation. Mom and Dad convinced us early on that we were the lucky ones, enjoying the sounds and smells of nature in our tent far better than they could inside their wheeled aluminum shell.

"You kids are so lucky," Mom would always say, "you're *really* camping! Daddy and I are just sleeping in a bed like we always do at home."

"Wow, thanks Mom," I heard my eight-year-old voice reply. "If you hear a bear or anything, just holler and me and Lorenzo will blast out of the tent and come to your rescue." I must have been thirty years old before it dawned on me why they really wanted us to sleep in the tent, giving them their privacy in the trailer.

I was born with a genetic condition known as hyperosmia—an acute sensitivity to odors in the environment. During the twentieth century, doctors didn't know much about this condition and my friends suggested it might simply be a consequence of my oversized Sicilian snout (there was a lot of real estate there). But early in the twenty-first century, as the field of molecular genetics was rapidly expanding, some gene mutations would be discovered that cause hypersensitivity to certain classes of odorants. In my early childhood, this condition caused my parents and me some consternation. But by the time I had reached high school age I'd gotten quite used to it, and as I went through puberty I discovered I rather liked my ability to recognize certain girls by their smells. I also discovered that boys who were troubled usually had a distinct and unpleasant odor; I could smell anger or fear on them. Some powerful odors I never overcame, and even as an adult I continued to find the intense acrid-sweet aromas of cinnamon, clove, and nutmeg overpowering to the point of nauseating.

As a biologist, I was well aware that our sense of smell, or olfaction, is the most primitive of all human senses. It's wired directly into the region of our brain known as the limbic system, which deals with deep memory and with pleasure. Thus, smells can quickly evoke both positive and negative feelings from the past. Odors get embedded in memory without a filter, and olfaction is the only human sense that bypasses the thalamus altogether to connect directly to the limbic system. Scents immediately register meaning and emotions in both our cognizant mind and our subconscious. For this reason, our earliest memories are typically smells—baby powder, the scent of our mother's cologne or our father's aftershave or pipe tobacco, or in this case the smell of oiled canvas that took me back to my childhood. Scent memories last a lifetime.

The childhood memories spilling into my head were split-second instant replays, alternating with the reality that I was now in the middle of the Petén jungle, in a small village called Cidabenque, where I increasingly realized I had no business being.

Cidabenque is an indigenous Maya community in northeastern Guatemala, isolated on the banks of the Río Salsipuedes, about a quarter of the way from Guatemala's border with Belize to the legendary ancient Maya ruins of Tikal. The village is two miles by dirt track off the road that connects Tikal to the border crossing. There is no reason why anyone in their right mind would want to visit Cidabenque.

The settlement is embedded in the largest expanse of intact Neotropical wet forest—aka jungle—north of the Amazon Basin. The families that live in this village are Maya subsistence farmers, each with a small plot of land where they grow their vegetables, raise their chickens, and care for their families. The Río Salsipuedes runs along the edge of the village, often flooding its banks to turn the dirt streets into a *pantanal*, a maze of muddy red-brown canals. The soil is poor here. So are the people. But in their wisdom, they know the land is their only real wealth. In 1984, about four hundred peasant farmers lived in Cidabenque, spread out over a few square miles. They rarely saw non-Maya, and it was usually bad news if they did. They virtually never saw gringos. No buses run to Cidabenque; instead, they drop locals at the turnoff from the main road that runs to the small town of

Flores, gateway to Tikal. It had taken me forty minutes to walk from the dropoff to Cidabenque's central plaza.

In these small Maya villages residents speak one of the thirty or so distinct Mayan dialects. I didn't expect more than a handful of people to understand my broken Spanish, and I absolutely did not expect to hear a word of English. The village, such as it was, comprised little more than the plaza with its small, whitewashed, one-room concrete church, intersected by some dirt tracks leading out to the various shacks and *milpas*—the small gardens where corn, beans, chiles, and calabash are grown. The truck was parked on the west side of the plaza, fortunately shaded by the church and its small steeple. I had been under the tarp for a half hour, but I felt like I'd already lost a gallon of water from profuse sweating. The heat and humidity of the Petén are stifling.

As I lay there, I considered how easy it had been to get to the village. The research ship I was stationed on, the RV *Double Helix* out of the Washington State Institute of Oceanography, was launched in 1956. She was a fine ship; 155 feet in length, clean, sleek and comfortable. The *Helix* carried an experienced crew of a dozen able seamen and a science crew of up to fifteen. The scientists' staterooms were spacious, each sleeping two on oversized "navy beds." We were laying over in Belize City for four days, taking on fuel and supplies. Our expedition had arrived nine days later than scheduled, due to delays passing through the Panama Canal and some interesting finds in the San Blas Islands that kept us there a few extra days. Most of the science crew were chemists, laboratory geeks with little interest in adventure or excitement. I was the token, but essential marine biologist for the expedition. I helped select the cruise track and the dive sites, and I was responsible for identifying all of the marine invertebrates we collected for chemical analysis. The lead biochemist, whose National Institutes of Health grant was underwriting the cost of the trip, was Dr. Simon Jolly. Jolly was a well-known and highly respected biochemist from the University of California at Berkeley.

The goal of Simon's expeditions was always the same—to find naturally occurring chemical compounds ("natural products") in marine organisms that might eventually prove to be a cure for the modern world's worst medical scourge, cancer. The silver bullet he called it. He was obsessed with exploring the unknown natural pharmacopeia of the sea. Simon loved scuba diving, but he was a terrible diver. I was one of few people willing to dive with him, given his proclivity for dangerous underwater stunts. I had been working with Simon Jolly, whose personality matched his surname, on these expeditions for years and we'd dived in some magnificent places, including Australia, Africa, and much of the tropical South Pacific.

Simon never gave me much advance notice when he needed my help. I'd get a cold call, and he'd ask if I was "busy next month."

"Odel, it's Simon Jolly here. How the hell are you? Are you available for a little expedition by any chance?"

"Well, your timing is impeccable, Simon. Spring classes just ended and I've got some free time. What's up?"

"Heading to the Caribbean in three weeks. We've got a great team put together for the trip. Marie is coming along to handle the seaweeds, and we need you for the invertebrates. Can you join us? We're going to dive and sample on the Mesoamerican Barrier Reef from Panama to Cancún."

"Fabulous—count me in. How long will the expedition be?"

" . . . Five weeks."

"Five weeks! Shit, Jolly, you can't expect me to commit to five weeks of fieldwork on three weeks' notice!"

"But we need you, Odel. You've got to join us for this one. The diving will be superb and I feel like this is the place we might find that magic molecule. You know there are

6

hundreds of species of tunicates in the western Caribbean—great potential for finding cancer-busting compounds."

I usually found a way to say yes to Simon. I loved the guy like a father. He was an absentminded but brilliant scientist, easy to work with though demanding, and the episodic expeditions we enjoyed together allowed me to collect my own beloved marine crustaceans in places I might otherwise never get to. And he often took along a charming Italian algologist, Marie Mare, who was, like me, more interested in the travel and having fun than in finding miracle cures in marine organisms. She was the only other member of the regular team who was willing to dive with Simon, and also like me she was a calculated risk taker. Marie's family was from northern Italy, near the border with Switzerland—the Piedmont region. She was short and had wild blond hair that seemed completely uncontrollable. And like most Italian women, she was uninhibited, gregarious, and delightful to work with. I was also of Italian ancestry, but Sicilian; tall, lean but muscular, with jet-black hair. I was, Mom always said, a spitting image of my father. Although Marie and I couldn't have looked more different from one another, Simon's science crew referred to us as the Italian Scuba Mafia.

Marie, Simon, and I routinely buddied up, especially for the deeper dives; absolutely no one else would join Simon for dives below 60 feet. He went too deep, too fast. He paid little attention to decompression protocols and no attention whatsoever to the "buddy system," thus ignoring the two cardinal rules of scuba diving. Once, near a mangrove-lined cay in The Bahamas, Simon went MIA for more than two hours. We all imagined a shark had gotten him. We had two inflatable Zodiacs out searching for him when the long gray hair on his head finally bobbed up near the Zodiac I was in.

"Simon, where the hell have you been!" I screamed. "We've been searching the area for you for forty-five minutes. I was ready to start writing your eulogy."

"Just sitting on the bottom, plucking these little tunicates off the mangrove roots and putting them in my goody bag. I think they're the same species we collected in the West Indies last year—the ones that were highly active against the liposarcoma cell lines we had with us on that expedition. I want to get enough material to work them up back in the lab at home." Simon was small of frame but strong. Underwater, he was methodic and deliberate, burning the air in his tank very slowly. He had been at a depth of just 15 feet, and you can indeed work in shallow water like that for hours without worrying about decompression or getting the bends.

Jolly had turned fifty-six just a few weeks before our expedition, but he was in excellent physical and mental shape. He was a youthful fifty-six and easily kept up with the younger divers. But his recklessness would eventually do him in, and years later he would come to suffer from an accumulation of "small bends," or tiny gas embolism events. The bends, also known as decompression sickness, occurs when a diver rises to the surface too quickly and dissolved gases (mainly nitrogen) in their blood come out of solution as tiny bubbles. Bubbles in your blood are not a good thing. They can affect just about any place in your body, including joints, lungs, heart, and brain. In Simon Jolly's case, they affected his brain in much the same way that accumulating minor strokes might, and by the time he was seventy, he started showing serious signs of dementia.

On board the *Double Helix* was a vast laboratory, with everything from microscopes to mass spectrophotometers. The ship cost twenty thousand dollars per day to lease from the National Institutes of Health, the ship's owner of record. This expedition was five weeks long—you can do the math. The NIH was investing heavily in the search for a cancer cure, the Holy Grail. The ship had departed from Seattle, but the science crew had boarded her in Panama City. Having traversed the canal, we were now working our way up the Caribbean coast of Central America, diving and collecting on some of the most pristine coral reef sites in the world strewn along the massive Mesoamerican Barrier Reef.

For our four days docked in Belize City, virtually all of the crew and chemists had opted to stay aboard the *Helix*. The city was a dump; they saw no reason to go ashore. Oh, some of the seamen probably slipped ashore late at night for some entertainment *con las dulces flores de la noche*, but we never heard about it. The chemists had plenty of work to do; catching up on several weeks of collecting, extracting compounds from sponges, bryozoans, and tunicates, and plating them out on the living tumor cell cultures growing in petri dishes aboard the ship. But I had made it clear from the start of the expedition that I planned to go ashore in Belize to visit the best-excavated pre-Columbian Maya city in the country, Xunantunich.

Jolly didn't get it. "Odel, why do you want to spend all day in a hot, steamy, uncomfortable, bug and snake-infested jungle looking at some old ruins when you could be in the air-conditioned comfort of the *Helix*, helping us measure cell growth on liver tumor plates?" He laughed heartily. "I think those purple sponges we collected at Roatán might be hot— just what we've been looking for!"

But archaeology was a hobby of mine, and I had an amateur anthropologist's love of the Maya civilization, both ancient and contemporary. And Simon knew that I took advantage of all opportunities to get off the ship anyway— whatever ship we were on, wherever we were. He would just roll his eyes. He was happier with his test tubes and centrifuges.

I wanted to see the ancient city of Xunantunich. How would it compare to the great Maya cities of Mexico's Yucatán Peninsula: Chichen Itza, Tulum, Uxmal, Calakmul, and the mysterious Palenque? And how would it compare to the magnificent ruins of Guatemala's Tikal, the "Manhattan" of the Classic Maya Period? Tikal's remoteness, buried deep in the heart of Guatemala's massive Petén region, assured it would likely never see too many visitors, though I had explored it several times. Only a fraction of it had been excavated, but it took only one visit to recognize the magnificent splendor and scope of the massive, ancient city sprawling over five thousand acres.

I woke before dawn on the *Helix* that morning, showered quickly, and threw some snacks and bottles of water in my daypack. On my way to the gangplank around six, I walked through the ship's main lab and noticed that someone had hung a new calendar on the wall. It was one of those large month-by-month calendars that flip up to reveal different color images on the top page, with the days of the month below. The calendar had been produced by Banamex—the huge Mexican banking conglomerate that had tendrils throughout Latin America and even in the U.S. The June image displayed was one of Carmen Lind Pettersen's wonderful paintings of a Maya village in the Guatemalan highlands, full of color and life. Those montane Maya villages had long been favorite haunts of mine, and the scene evoked strong memories. Looking at Pettersen's extraordinary scene, I could smell the sweet thick *copál* smoke and sharply scented pine needles of the Maya high country. The image was one of her most famous—*Market Day in Chichicastenango*. Chichi, as the non-Maya often call it, is one of the oldest continuously inhabited villages in the Sierra Madre of Guatemala, indeed, in all the land of the Maya. The painting captured it perfectly; women milled about in explosively colorful handwoven huipils distinctive to the area, their long silky black hair tied up and wrapped in woven *tzutes*, the finest of which are made of silk and colored purple using a dye from marine snails that occur along the Pacific coast of Nicaragua.

A few men also appear in Pettersen's Chichi scene, dressed in the complicated regalia that distinguishes lay helpers in the Catholic Church. In the background stands the pure white *Iglesia de Santo Tomás*; small but rugged, it was built in 1540. That the Spanish conquistadors built a church in the village of Chichicastenango in the mid-sixteenth century speaks to its importance among the Maya then, as now. And indeed, Chichicastenango holds the soul of highland Maya. On the steps of the church today, powerfully scented *copál* is burned to the glory of Maya "pagan" gods; but inside, traditional Catholic incense is burned to honor the Christian God. Among the highland Maya, there is no uncomfortable dividing line between the two. The pantheon of Maya gods is for the outdoors and for daily activities, while the Christian God lives and presides inside the church.

The Banamex calendar also noted it was the summer solstice—June 21, the longest day of the year. Unconsciously I thought, *Good, I might need as many hours of daylight as possible today.* I hoped the prearranged taxi was waiting on the dock. Simon was already at work in the lab, firing up the mass spec.

"Morning Odel. Off to Zuniland, or wherever eh?"

"Xunantunich," I replied, "spelled with an X."

"Well, have fun, Jungle Boy" . . . snort, chuckle.

Belize, like most countries in Central America, had a complicated colonial history. Originally part of the Caribbean coast claimed by Guatemala, it became a colony of the British Crown in 1862, during the era of British expansionism. It was settled through a joint effort of the British Government and English hardwood companies and given the name British Honduras. The Brits systematically removed nearly all of the country's large mahogany, Bahía rosewood, cocobolo, and other desirable timber. Although the colony didn't achieve independence from England until 1981, it had become a more or less self-governing territory and changed its name from British Honduras to Belize in 1973. The British "embassy," known as the High Commission of the United Kingdom, had just moved its offices from the old dilapidated capital of Belize City, to the shiny new capital of Belmopan. But even

11

in 1984, Guatemala continued to claim Belize as part of its sovereign land, and border tensions occasionally flared up between the two countries.

The taxi was on time, and I departed the central port of Belize City in a brightly colored but thoroughly rusted-out old Chevy sedan with four bald tires. The one-way fare had been negotiated the previous day. As we bumped and rattled and swerved our way out of the city on potholed roads, and the green jungle began to reclaim the land, I saw the large force of Harrier Jump Jets that the British kept stationed in Belize. This force was said to be the main deterrent preventing the well-equipped Guatemalan army from attempting to take back Belize's territory. The rows of gleaming metal war machines were a jarring contradiction to the soft, butterfly-winged morning and surrounding tropical forest. I knew that Xunantunich was an easy three hour taxi ride from the port by way of Belmopan.

Belmopan was founded as a planned community in 1970. Weary of the cyclical hurricanes that regularly devastated Belize City, the Belizeans finally decided they had to build a new capital on higher ground. But by 1984, Belmopan still had fewer than ten thousand residents, and it would hold the title of smallest capital city in the continental Americas well into the twenty-first century. As we sped straight through the new capital, the well cared for roads and light traffic stood in stark contrast to the crowded and tired old former capital on the coast.

I'd read about Xunantunich. The site is in the far western region of Belize, literally on the border with Guatemala. The ruins sit atop a high ridge of the western watershed of the Mopan River. From the tops of the great Maya pyramids in Xunantunich, one is witness to the vast green jungle of the Guatemalan Petén spreading to the west as far as the eye can see. Those high views of the Petén are stunning, with the mist rising from the jungle canopy in multicolored flashes of light filtered through the haze above a sea of dark green foliage.

Flocks of parrots and macaws rise like rainbowed clouds above the canopy, float a few hundred feet, and then disappear back into the jungle.

Xunantunich had a long period of habitation, from the Preclassic Maya Period all the way to the Postclassic—roughly 1000 BC to well after AD 900. It was a major ceremonial center during the Classic Period, when more than a quarter-million Maya lived in the region. The Mayan word *Xunantunich* loosely translates as "Stone Woman"—a reference to the ghost of a woman who has inhabited the ruins since at least the late nineteenth century. She dresses completely in white, has glowing fire-red eyes, and moves like a ground-cloud through the ruins of the ancient stone city. She often appears in front of the tallest pyramid—known as El Castillo—ascends the carved stone stairs, and then disappears into a rock wall. She was, according to my taxi driver, still present at Xunantunich, though likely to be seen only early in the morning, as the warming air pulls the moisture up from the damp jungle floor.

The first modern exploration of the site was conducted by Thomas Gann around the same time as the first reports of the appearance of the Stone Woman apparition. Though trained as a surgeon, Gann had moved from England to British Honduras in 1892 to serve as commissioner of Cayo District. And, like me, he had an amateur's zeal for archaeology and anthropology. Much later, in 1959, Professor Euan MacKie from Cambridge University led a large professional expedition to excavate the Xunantunich site.

During the Postclassic Period, when most Maya cities were deteriorating, Xunantunich managed to expand its power over other areas throughout the Mopan River Valley, and the city lasted at least a century longer than most of the other settlements in the region. Built on top of a hill, Xunantunich was a citadel, easily defensible. The core of the city contained more than two-dozen temples and palaces. I truly did want to see that important Maya site.

But, I was not headed to Xunantunich. Instead of turning north off the Western Highway to the ruins, my taxi driver took me straight to the Belize-Guatemala border, dropping me at the small border town of Benque Viejo del Carmen. There, using my U.S. passport, I crossed from Belize into Guatemala with the pretense of being a tourist on my way to visit the Maya ruins of Tikal. On the Guatemala side of the border is the village of Melchor de Mencos, and from there the road runs west to the town of Flores, where one takes a shuttle to Tikal. The Melchor–Flores bus route takes just over an hour. I made sure the bus I got on was a milk run. I got off at the turnoff for Cidabenque, twenty-five minutes after boarding. The bus driver raised his bushy salt-and-pepper eyebrows in surprise.

"¿Por qué querría visitar ese pueblo, señor? No hay nada más que gente pobre allí. ¡Ni siquier hay un restaurante o bar!"

"I am looking for the cousin of a friend of mine from Benque Viejo del Carmen. I have a message for him," I answered in my best Spanish.

It had taken me two and a half hours to get from the *Double Helix* to the Belize border, and another hour to cross it, find a bus, and begin hoofing down the dirt track into the village of Cidabenque. I thought, with any luck I should be able to wrap up this silly excursion in ten or twelve hours and be back on the *Helix* in time for the late dinner serving.

The morning had started off with gray skies and brisk offshore breezes. The captain's daily weather posting on the *Helix's* bulletin board forecast a tropical storm moving onto the coast, bringing thundershowers. I'd noticed storm clouds in the east, over the Caribbean, and could tell they were progressing quickly toward shore. As I walked toward Cidabenque, I could see the rain moving in fast as the skies darkened and stiff wind gusts began to snap branches of wet jungle trees back and forth along the roadside. The wind carried aromas of the tropical forest to me, odors piled upon complex odors, smells of green abundance. I wasn't cold—it's never cold in the Petén—yet I felt a chill and noticed goosebumps on my skin. I knew I must be getting close to the village, but I saw no one. Other than the sounds of parrots and the occasional scream of a howler monkey, the only background noises were the gusts of wind swatting the moist fronds of the *Bactris* and *Xylosma* palms along the sides of the road. No sounds of cars or trucks; no human voices.

The jungle here is so thick it's impenetrable. Shoulder-high ferns and broadleaf perennials crowded across a thick moss-carpeted earth. Massive spiny-skinned *árbol del dosel* and kapok trees, known locally as ceiba, have bladelike buttress roots that expand 50 feet from the trunk, making movement difficult. The ceiba is pollinated by bats, and both the bats and the tree are held sacred by the Maya. Human travel is largely confined to cleared paths and roads, and keeping them free of the encroaching vegetation is a full-time job. In cleared areas, such as roadsides, the light-gap-loving *Cercropia*, *Heliconia*, and *Gunnera* grow in profusion. The leaves of the latter, commonly known as "poor man's umbrella," reach two meters across and literally are used as umbrellas.

In this part of the world, only a fool travels without a machete. I didn't have one. And for the Guatemalan Maya, machetes also are their only weapon. Though hardly an adequate defense against a firearm, they keep their machetes sharpened and never leave home without one dangling from their waist.

Getting to Cidabenque had been easier than I had imagined. But it was not so easy now. I was sweltering, and it was dawning on me that I would not be able to stay under the canvas tarp much longer—it was simply too hot and humid. I felt queasy, as if I might pass out. I wondered what would happen if I did. Would the truck drive away with me prostrate in the back? Would a farmer come along and throw open the tarp and see me laying there—an unconscious gringo? *"¡Madre de Jesús, un gringo muerto en mi camión!"* Would I go into hyperthermia and die? This wasn't in the plan. Actually, there wasn't really a plan; I was responding to what I thought had been a simple request. I was supposed to just wander into Cidabenque and pretend to be lost on my way to Flores—a confused gringo hippie in search of the legendary Maya city of Tikal. I was to spend no more than a couple hours there, maybe have some frijoles and coffee, observe things, listen to conversations, and then leave. I would make my report, meager as it would likely be, at the U.S. Embassy in Belize City on my way back to the ship—or the next day if necessary.

But when I arrived at the plaza in Cidabenque, I knew something was amiss. There was no one in sight. The village was deserted. By then the skies had turned an angry black, and thunder was rolling across the landscape. A few fat drops of rain began to fall. I sat on a mold-covered concrete bench in the plaza, collecting my thoughts. The air was thick and heavy. I was hot and tired, and I suddenly just wanted to wrap this thing up and get back to the ship. I wondered how large this storm might be, as the thunder seemed to grow sharper and more staccato. My mouth went dry and a wave of nausea swept over me as I realized that it was not staccato thunder I was hearing in the distance but the angry retorts of M16s firing in the jungle. It was a sound I knew well—and didn't like. I could feel adrenaline rushing into my bloodstream.

The M16 had entered U.S. military service in 1964, and the following year it was deployed for jungle warfare operations in Vietnam. That madness of a war made the firearm famous. By 1969, the M16 had become the U.S. military's standard-issue service rifle. It had a bolt assist, chrome-plated bore, and thirty-round magazine that could be quickly switched out. It would still be standard issue at the turn of the century thirty-five years later, but it would be in its fourth generation and equipped with a removable carrying handle and Picatinny rail for mounting optics and other ancillary devices. The M16 proved to be such an excellent weapon—especially for jungle combat—that it was widely adopted by militaries around the world. It would become the most produced firearm of its caliber in history. The world was already awash with the weapon. The United States had been supplying the Guatemalan army with M16s for years. In the 1980s in Guatemala, tens of thousands of military personnel and paramilitary goon squads carried the rifle. And they had plenty of ammo, also supplied by the United States. The M16 was the gun that killed more Maya peasants in Guatemala every year than all other weapons combined—thousands of peasants, year after year, in a government campaign that approximated genocide.

Here, in the middle of the Petén, the sound of nearby M16s in a recently deserted Maya village was not what I'd bargained for. And when I'd heard approaching voices, I had quickly climbed under the canvas tarp of the old Ford pickup and tried not to move a muscle or make a sound. As I lay there, it began to rain hard. Although it cooled things down a few degrees, the humidity shot up from eighty to a hundred percent. I felt like I was trying to breathe water and an elephant was sitting on top of me. And I had a feeling things were about to go from bad to worse.

2

Looking for Research Funding
January 1981

The Seattle Museum of Natural History is the premier public museum of its kind in the Pacific Northwest. With two-dozen curators and over ten million expertly curated specimens, its research programs span the globe. It has extensive public outreach in Washington State and hosts nearly 5,000 K-12 school visitors annually. All of the curators also hold courtesy academic appointments at various universities in the area, through which they advise graduate students and teach occasional classes. I considered myself lucky to have snagged a job there, first as Curator of Crustacea, then later promoted to Chief Curator.

Sitting in my office at the Museum, I was struggling to come up with new ideas for funding my research in Central America. I'd become Chief Curator four years earlier, a position that included "supervision" of all the curators and collections. I still relished the job, as it provided me ample opportunity to follow my passion for marine invertebrates—those smaller creatures of the sea lacking backbones. I also taught an annual spring semester course on invertebrate zoology at nearby Northwestern Washington University, in Tacoma. I'd just wrapped up a four-year project funded by the National Science Foundation to document the rich marine crustacean fauna of Costa Rica, including the Caribbean coral reef at Cahuita National Park. The Cahuita coral reef is adjacent to the largest banana-growing region in the country, originally developed by American fruit companies who destroyed tens of thousands of acres of pristine coastal rainforest in the process. Over the years, coastal runoff from the plantations—including silt, fertilizers, and pesticides—had been gradually killing the reef and degrading the park. Costa Rica's National Park Service was deeply troubled by the reef's slow demise, but the American companies' corporate interests and political ties were powerful and influential, and little was being done to stop the pollution.

My project had been based out of the University of Costa Rica in San José, the country's charming but congested capital. For four years I made quarterly fly-in collecting expeditions, sampling both the Pacific and Atlantic coasts of the country. The University of Costa Rica was happy to assist with logistics, providing a van and inflatable skiff in exchange for training a number of their graduate students. I came to know Costa Rica well during that time, and I used my flights back and forth to lay over and explore some of my other favorite Latin American countries. The regional carriers— including Aeronica (the Nicaraguan flagship carrier), TACA Airlines (the El Salvador carrier), Copa Airlines (Panama), and LACSA (Costa Rica)—allowed passengers to "hop on/hop off" their flights in the capital cities they touched down in. I was fascinated in particular with the landscapes and cultures of Guatemala and Nicaragua, and I made a point of spending leisure intervals exploring one or both of those countries on every working trip I made to Costa Rica. The Sandinista Revolution in Nicaragua had succeeded in 1979, and the social and political landscape there was fascinating. I also enjoyed time with colleagues and friends at the National University in Managua.

My fieldwork in Costa Rica had led to the discovery of many new invertebrate species and laid the foundation for a large-scale monograph on Pacific Central American marine Crustacea. It was a project I desperately wanted to complete. The study of crustaceans, those hard-shelled marine invertebrates that include lobsters, crabs, shrimps, and a host of smaller carapaced creatures, had practical as well as academic appeal. I'd been fairly successful funding my work for the past five or six years. If I could secure a few more years of travel funds, I could gather the remaining specimens and data I needed from the coasts of Guatemala, El Salvador and Nicaragua. But funding was getting harder and harder to find, and I'd already milked the National Science Foundation, National Geographic Society, and several other private foundations for about as much as I could on this particular project.

My wife, Penelope, also did research in Latin America, but she was a political scientist with a specialty in economics. We'd met in 1975, when we were both completing our PhD work in Washington D.C. I was 28, she was 25. Penelope had been studying at George Washington University; her thesis topic was the history of banking in Panama City, which, by the mid-1970s had become the largest financial center in Central America. I was just completing my PhD at American University researching the crustacean fauna of the Greater Antilles, with a minor in Mesoamerican anthropology. Although working in entirely different fields, Penelope and I shared a deep interest in Latin America: hers was contemporary Latin American business practices and culture, mine were Mesoamerican landscapes (and seascapes) and pre-Columbian cultures.

We met standing in line at a cash bar one afternoon at a large conference for scholars of Central America, co-hosted by the American Association for the Advancement of Science and the U.S. State Department in D.C. She'd been standing in front of me, and I couldn't help but notice how attractive she was. She was slim and fair in complexion, with short blond hair, fiery blue eyes as clear and deep as the glass eyes of a child's doll, great legs, perfect posture and poise, and an assured air about her. At the bar, we both ordered *Cuba Libres*, sparking a conversation that led to marriage just a year later. Unlike my biologist friends, Penelope understood the genesis and meaning of the drink's name. It originated in Cuba during Fidel Castro's eventually-successful struggle to overthrow the repressive U.S.-backed dictatorship of Fulgencio Batista; the drink's name means, literally, "free Cuba." Rum and Coke, with a squeeze of lime—perfect for the Caribbean, where all three ingredients are invariably close at hand. And the mix goes down smoothly even without ice, which isn't always close at hand. Penelope seemed worldly, refined, and intensely astute. She listened carefully to what was being said in conversations, and when I told her about my interests in biology she was genuinely curious. When I told her about my travels in Central America and the Caribbean, she was enthusiastic and wanted to meet up later to talk about our experiences and shared interests.

Penelope's refinement was not pretentious—it fit naturally on her, like a favorite old sweater. And when she wanted to look downright beautiful, she knew how to do it. She would put on a low-cut dress that clung to her shapely little body and flattered her perfect curves. Her shiny blond hair would curl loosely around her ears and neck, not quite touching the spaghetti-thin straps of her dress; and in high heels her exquisite legs gave her a goddess-like appeal. She was just five feet, five inches, but in heels and a dress she looked like a runway model. She moved with practiced fluidity, and conveyed a sophisticated yet quietly seductive aura. A faint splash of freckles on her cheeks gave her a winsome look and a girlish appeal. Women found her as attractive as men did, and she had a deliberate way of connecting with them. When she talked with other women, she did so discreetly, almost privately, as they smiled at one another.

Admittedly, we'd rather rushed into marriage—the first for each of us—but I guess we were both ready. Our personalities seemed to jibe, and the sex was phenomenal. For me, it was the best I'd ever known or even imagined. I thought Penelope felt the same way. To my delight, Penelope's cultured savoir-faire in public was more than matched by her bedroom prowess. In fact, she was a virtuoso of the erotic. The first time we made love, it blew my mind, and it only got better from then on. I had the impression that Penelope was more experienced than me, but I wasn't sure. Our chemistry and open-mindedness seemed to be major factors elevating us to new levels of sexual awareness. We agreed that we had perfect "pheromone match." We were both at the point of launching our careers and decided that kids would not be in our immediate future. In fact, she wasn't sure she ever wanted to have children, though she made it clear that it was an option to keep on the table. That was fine with me; I loved kids, but didn't want to rush into it.

Although I'd always enjoyed nooky, I was not all that experienced. But I did love sex, from foreplay to endgame. For me, the bedroom was never a place to rush things, and the few women I'd known intimately appreciated what they sometimes called my "thorough approach." I never thought of it in those terms. I simply had an organic way about it all; perhaps because I was a biologist. I found it intriguing in every dimension—the different textures and colors of skin across a woman's body, their odors and tastes, the anatomical responses of a woman's flesh to my touch—and of mine to theirs. To me, sex was rather like a great meal, and I enjoyed the entire menu, from appetizer to entrée to dessert. I tended to linger on the appetizer, as I found that protracted foreplay usually led to a greater enjoyment of the remainder of the meal.

Not long before Penelope and I decided to get married—and certainly marking a high point in our premarital relationship—we found ourselves in the ultra-plush, newly opened, Sheraton Miami Beach Hotel. Penelope emerged from the ladies' room in the hotel's massive lobby with a wicked twinkle in her eye. Holding the door to the ladies' room partly open, she gestured provocatively, curling her index finger as a request for me to slip inside with her. Haltingly, I stepped into a well-appointed, large, marble-walled but empty women's washroom, with rattan fans slowly turning overhead and louvered mahogany doors on all the stalls. She entered one of the stalls and invited me to join her, whispering in my ear that the louvered doors allowed one to see out but not see in. She told me to stand on the toilet seat and enjoy the view through the louvers. I followed orders.

As she unzipped my pants, the first woman walked in, moving directly to the sink to freshen up. Then a second woman entered, took a stall nearby, and began to pee loudly—the blended bouquet of her floral perfume and urine creating an exotic aromatic dance around us. As Penelope began working her magic on me, we heard more sounds of the most personal nature, and watched women primping at the mirrors. The effect was intoxicating. Being hidden there as a voyeur, in a forbidden place, getting a surreptitious blow job from my extraordinary lover, with the subtle element of risk, aroused me wildly.

After we'd snuck out of the ladies' room, back into the lobby of the Sheraton, she suggested we have a drink at the bar to celebrate another first. Much later, I would wonder if she meant a first for us, or a first for her. Either way, I was thrilled. It eventually dawned on me that what I had taken as a look of arousal when she'd first opened the ladies' room door to beckon me in, was in fact just that—arousal from covertly watching other women through the louvered door of her own stall, the kind of arousal that comes through secrecy and voyeurism. As an enlightened enthusiast of sex, Penelope seemed almost too good to be true. It would be some time, however, before I was to learn what a harbinger that unexpected ladies' room event was.

We married without fanfare in a courtroom with only our parents as witnesses, settled into her place in D.C., and finished our PhDs. Our luck held, and soon after graduation we both got jobs in the Seattle area—Penelope as a professor in the Political Science Department at the University of Washington, and I as a research curator at the Seattle Museum of Natural History. Everything in my life had fallen into place—the perfect wife, the perfect job, a great city to live in. I felt certain about my future.

Penelope and I had both been raised to respect the privacy of others, including our closest friends and family. For her, privacy was one of the "Ten Commandments," and she made that clear from the outset. In my family, my mother gave my brother Lorenzo and me stern lectures growing up about the importance of respecting the privacy of others. Penelope and I vowed to abide by that credo in our marriage. With mutual trust, we assured one another, respecting the privacy of one's partner should be easy. We treated each other well, never argued, and seemed to be in unspoken agreement that courtesy between partners is even more important than it is between colleagues or strangers. At least, that's how it was in the beginning. We talked about rings, and even looked for something special, but never got around to buying anything. We wanted to, but it just wasn't high priority, and we were busy launching our professional careers. At the end of my first year at the museum, I was promoted to Chief Curator. Although I was "in charge" of twenty-three other research curators, the environment was egalitarian; my main roles were to help raise funds for research and to be the conduit between research activities and the museum's executive director.

We rarely visited our parents, though Penelope kept up with her dad through regular phone calls, usually a couple times a week. They were very close. After the wedding, we never tried to get our parents together again. They were from different worlds. Penelope's folks were sophisticated, cultured, world traveled, and rather stiff and formal. Her dad could be condescending at times and didn't hesitate to make a demeaning comment when someone said something he thought was wrong or foolish. But on the first anniversary of our marriage, Penelope's dad gave us a bottle of the famed 1961 Mouton Rothschild Bordeaux, and for months after that I was willing to forgive her father any transgressions.

On the other hand, my mom and dad were blue-collar, loud, boisterous, and anything but formal. They'd never heard of Bordeaux and drank what the family called "dago red" wine. Their one and only meeting—at our wedding—was a clash of patrician versus proletarian, the elegant versus the boogie. Oh, everyone was polite and courteous, each in their own way, and Penelope's parents had a thick veneer of civility that kept one from seeing what lay beneath. My parents were animated and wore their feelings on their sleeves. We were content to see our parents separately, once a year or so. And we were caught up with our own lives and our own fast-moving careers.

Although we loved being together, Penelope and I were at the same time fairly independent souls. We shared our work and other interests with one another, but we rarely traveled together for work purposes. My professional work took me to remote coastlines, and my avocational interests took me to distant villages and Maya ruins in Mesoamerican jungles and mountain forests. Penelope's work took her to the capital cities, where she elegantly schmoozed with high-level business people and politicians. Her research funding came mainly from the U.S. State Department and a couple of small private foundations. She had minored in Spanish and was fluent; my Spanish was funky, but I got by.

One Saturday evening over martinis as I bemoaned the dearth of funding sources for my research, Penelope, who was never short on creativity, suggested a seemingly wild idea.

"Listen Odel, with all the nonsense going on in Nicaragua these days," she said, "why don't you see if the CIA will support your research travel in Central America in exchange for some kind of 'insider' information. They might at least be willing to do so for your Nicaragua fieldwork. There must be some silly thing you could do for them in exchange for keeping your travel funding going for a few more years. I'll just bet they do that sort of thing."

I'd learned not to rush into responding to Penelope's sometimes outlandish ideas. As crazy as they often seemed—especially this one—they usually had merit, or at least some valuable germ worth contemplating. Her idea gave me pause. I was a socially liberal, though fiscally conservative Democrat; Penelope was a registered Independent and right-leaning middle-of-the-roader. When we disagreed politically, we did so with respect and thoughtfulness. She rarely swayed me much in my opinions, but she was patient and clever about showing me alternative ways of looking at things.

Ronald Reagan had just been elected president, after a quotidian and mundane single term by Jimmy Carter. Reagan was the first president the National Rifle Association openly endorsed. No one knew what to expect, but I wasn't happy about the election outcome. I hadn't been impressed by Reagan's governorship of California, and most of our university friends believed he should go back to acting. He was pretty good as the "The Gipper" in the 1940 Knute Rockne biopic—why couldn't he have just stuck to a screen career? Penelope, however, was not so negative about Reagan, suggesting that, in all fairness, we should cut him some slack and give him time—and that I should be more realistic about the world. I had to acknowledge that I thought Reagan might be a good man, an honorable man even, just terribly misguided. I didn't believe in his supply-side economics, I sensed he might be racist, and I was turned off by his disdain for student protestors. I was also outraged by his expressed desire to abolish the Department of the Interior;

although he failed at that, he appointed anti-environmentalist James Watt as Interior Secretary and Watt did everything in his power to eviscerate the department.

Obviously, however, most of America disagreed with me, as Reagan would end his second presidential term in 1988 with an approval rating of sixty-four percent, the highest in modern history and not to be surpassed until President Bill Clinton came along.

Three years after Penelope and I married, the Sandinistas took control of the government in Nicaragua, following a long and bloody civil war with the Somoza regime that had been in power since the 1960s. I was delighted, even enthusiastic. Penelope recognized the atrocities of the Somoza family's reign of terror and was glad to see the regime fall, but she had mixed feelings about the Sandinistas. To me, a beautiful thing had happened—the oppressed and tyrannized people of Nicaragua had taken back their country. The U.S. government—and the CIA in particular—had underestimated the Sandinistas, never expecting Anastasio "Tachito" Somoza to fall. For Reagan, who had an innate fear of communism, socialism, and all things left, the takeover of Nicaragua by socialists was intolerable, and as soon as he moved into the White House in 1981 we began to hear rumors of covert U.S. plans to topple the new leftist Sandinista government and put the "ruling class" back into power in the country. I was disgusted by the idea. Penelope didn't like it either, but she also didn't like the communist leanings of the Sandinistas' young and charismatic leader, Daniel Ortega. We had pointed but never acrimonious debates about the value (or lack thereof) of communism and socialism in the twentieth century, and in Latin America in particular.

"Odel, everyone knows the Somoza regime was corrupt and repressive, and it's a shame the United States supported it for so long, but how do you know the Sandinistas won't be

27

just as bad? Look at what Castro has done in Cuba. That country is now in bed with Russia, and the people are just as repressed as they were in Nicaragua under the Somoza family. You do remember the Cuban Missile Crisis don't you!" She liked to cut to the chase.

"I know, Penelope, but Daniel Ortega is different. He's no Castro. He's sincere and he's smart and I believe he truly has the best intentions for the people of Nicaragua. He has pledged there will soon be free elections."

"Socialists always promise free elections, and they always renege! And Daniel Ortega received his training in guerrilla warfare from the Castro government in Cuba. He is an avowed Marxist-Leninist. The first thing he did when he got power was start nationalizing foreign companies and redistributing their assets."

"That's more-or-less true. But he also launched national literacy and health care programs, and he's reached out to the United States for partnerships."

"And partner we did, with tens of millions of dollars in economic aid. Until Ortega began supplying weapons to the Leftist rebels in El Salvador!"

"Probably true—but Ortega and the Sandinistas have promised the new government will share authority and responsibility equally among the people of Nicaragua. That's something the Somoza family never did. There's no reason why it shouldn't work, and I'm willing to give them some time to prove themselves."

Penelope responded, "Ortega's promises might explain how the new government *could* work, but they don't assure it *will* work, or that it will be 'good' government."

We debated our points and, as usual, agreed that reality might be somewhere in the middle, in that murky gray zone where most of the world's power struggles actually take place. We both knew that nothing is black and white in the world of national and international politics.

As I contemplated Penelope's CIA suggestion, I thought about America's sordid history of disruption and control in Nicaragua.

I knew that U.S. intervention had begun shortly after Nicaragua had gained its independence from Spain in 1821. And I knew that by 1850 the United States had partnered with England to develop—without Nicaragua's consent—an interoceanic trade route from the Caribbean to the Pacific, using a combination of the San Juan River and the gigantic Lake Nicaragua, and from there, a short overland route to the Pacific. One of the main purposes for securing American eminent domain in Nicaragua had been to prevent any other nation from building a transcontinental Nicaraguan canal—an idea long deliberated in Europe. The U.S. was close to completing the Panama Canal at great expense, and it was in no mood to see any competition farther north on the continent. But the United States also had corporate interests in Nicaragua, notably the United Fruit Company's large and rapidly expanding banana business. In fact, Nicaragua was at the heart of the infamous Banana Wars. We hadn't hesitated to send the marines into the country, more than once, to help quell labor movements and populist uprisings.

Early in the twentieth century, the United States had begun installing puppet governments in Nicaragua, and by 1916 the country had become one of America's quasi-protectorate states under the Bryan-Chamorro Treaty. In the mid-1920s, a drift toward populism in Nicaragua led to another invasion of the country by U.S. Marines. On that occasion, however, a young man in his early thirties, named Augusto César Sandino, took up the cause against U.S. intervention. An impassioned and ardent revolutionary, Sandino built a guerrilla force in the mountainous region of the country. By 1933, Sandino's rebel army had the U.S. Marines in a stalemate. Sandino's guerrilla warfare made the occupation too costly for America, which was in the throes of the Great Depression, and President Franklin D. Roosevelt eventually pulled troops out of the country. Sandino became a hero throughout Latin America—a symbol of resistance to U.S. hegemony.

In 1934, shortly after the U.S. marines left the country, Sandino received an invitation to meet with the Somoza family patriarch, Anastasio "Tacho" Somoza Garcia, head of the Nicaraguan National Guard, for an alleged peace conference. But at the meeting, Somoza had him abducted and murdered. The assassination plot was said to have been cooked up by U.S. Ambassador to Nicaragua, Arthur Bliss Lane. With U.S. backing, Somoza went on to seize the presidency in a coup d'état in 1936, establishing a ruthless dictatorship and family dynasty that would control the country for forty-three years and through two generations of a father and his two sons: "Tacho" Somoza, his eldest son Luís Somoza DeBayle, and the younger son Anastasio "Tachito" Somoza DeBayle.

Alternately serving as head of the National Guard and as president, young Tachito would be the de facto ruler of the country from 1967 to 1979. He held the official title of president twice, making him the 73rd and 76th president of the country. In between presidential terms, Tachito commanded the thoroughly corrupt National Guard, through which he continued to control government and the populace by military intimidation and force.

Tachito was educated in the United States and graduated from West Point. In 1950, after his return to Nicaragua, he married Hope Portocarrero, an American citizen and his first cousin. Six years after the marriage, Tachito's father was assassinated. With U.S. support, his oldest son, Luís, assumed the presidency through a rigged election. In 1967 Luís had a heart attack (that eventually killed him) and passed the baton to his kid brother, Tachito. While Luís had ruled more gently than his father had, Tachito would tolerate no opposition, and his regime quickly turned to extreme oppression of the poor and working class. By the time Tachito was reelected the second time, in a rigged election in 1974, the Catholic Church had begun to speak out against his government. One of Tachito's fiercest critics was Ernesto Cardenal, a Nicaraguan padre who preached liberation theology and would go on to become the Sandinista government's minister of culture.

It was this background of oppression that led, in the 1960s, to the formation and rise of the Sandinista National Liberation Front, or FSLN, in opposition to the U.S.-supported Somoza family regime. Named in honor of the great revolutionary Augusto Sandino, the FSLN by 1970 had gained enough support among Nicaraguans to launch their first military effort against the Somoza government. Inspired by the campaigns of Fidel Castro and Che Guevara, the FSLN relied on guerrilla tactics.

Tachito Somoza's National Guard was highly trained by the U.S. military. Under the direct command of Somoza, they used torture, extrajudicial killings, and censorship of the press to combat the FSLN movement. By the late 1970s human rights groups around the world were condemning the record of the Somoza government, and support for the FSLN, or *los Sandinistas*, was growing both inside and outside the country.

Then, on the morning of December 23, 1972, an enormous earthquake struck Managua, killing more than ten thousand people and leaving a half-million homeless. More than half of the city's buildings were destroyed. The government's response was so feeble that opposition to Somoza flared, and the Sandinistas had a flood of new recruits. Somoza declared martial law in 1975, ordering the National Guard to begin razing villages throughout the country suspected of supporting the rebels. Human rights groups around the world condemned these actions as the country sank into disrepair and depression, but President Gerald Ford refused to break the U.S. alliance with Tachito.

In 1978 Pedro Joaquín Chamorro Cardenal, publisher of the country's main newspaper, *La Prensa*, and an open critic of Somoza, was gunned down. Over 30,000 people rioted in the streets of Managua, cars and buildings belonging to the Somoza family were attacked, and a general strike was called throughout the country. During the rest of that year, there were seven machine gun attacks and attempted bombings of *La Prensa*, which had fallen under the management of Chamorro's widow Violeta Barrios de Chamorro. In response to Chamorro's murder and Tachito's human rights violations, newly elected U.S. President Jimmy Carter finally cut off all aid to the Somoza regime. Then, on August 22, 1978, the Sandinistas pulled off their biggest success to date. Led by Edén Pastora, known as *Commandante Zero*, Sandinista forces captured the National Palace while the legislature was in session, taking two thousand hostages. It was one of the few Sandinista successes that were reported in the U.S. press, and it had led to some intense discussions between Penelope and me. Pastora demanded money, the release of Sandinista prisoners, and "a means of publicizing the Sandinista cause." After two days, Somoza caved in to the FSLN demands. By June 1979 the Sandinistas controlled all of the country except the capital, and the writing was on the wall.

On July 17, 1979, as the Sandinistas marched into Managua, Tachito Somoza resigned the presidency and fled to Miami in an old twin-engine Curtiss C-46 Commando plane that had been given to him by the U.S. Army. He took with him two caskets, containing the bodies of his father and his brother. He also took most of Nicaragua's cash, leaving the country with a $1.6 billion foreign debt, the highest in Central America at the time; it's claimed that the Sandinistas found less than $2 million in the country's treasury.

President Carter denied Tachito Somoza entry into the United States, forcing him to take refuge in Paraguay, where dictator Alfredo Stroessner took him in. Included in the deal was a bribe to Stroessner of an unknown amount. Stroessner ruled Paraguay with an iron fist for thirty-five years, making his repressive rule the longest in modern South American history. Birds of a feather. In Paraguay, Somoza bought a ranch and a gated house in Asunción, the capital, where he quickly earned the reputation of a wealthy and colorful socialite.

Tachito was assassinated near his home in Asunción on September 17, 1980. He was fifty-four years old. Published reports said he was ambushed by a seven-person commando team in support of the Sandinista cause; four men and three women, in what was known as *Operación Reptil*. The commando team was said to have had two Soviet-made machine guns, two Soviet AK-47 assault rifles, two Soviet-made automatic pistols, and a Soviet RPG-7 rocket launcher with four antitank grenades and two rockets. The team's leader was Argentinian Marxist revolutionary Enrique Gorriarán Merlo (code name Ramón). Paraguayan police counted twenty-five bullet holes in Somoza's body. In Managua, people danced in the streets and the Sandinista government declared a national day of celebration.

The Somoza family reign of terror from the 1930s through the 1970s had been propped up by the United States in large part to protect its corporate interests, such as United Fruit Company, Dole, and Standard Fruit Company, which had large investments in the country. But now, all eyes were on Nicaragua and Sandinista leader Daniel Ortega—the telegenic, charismatic hero of the oppressed people of Latin America. The Somoza regime had finally fallen, and Washington was nervous.

Ronald Reagan was fervent in his conservative anti-communist, anti-socialist views. He went ballistic when the Sandinistas came to power in Nicaragua. One of his first acts after being sworn into office in 1981 was to authorize the CIA—with a handful of dollars appropriated for interdiction of alleged arms traffic between Nicaragua and El Salvador— to assemble the remaining loyalists of the former Somoza dynasty's National Guard, along with former Nicaraguan death-squad leaders, and place them under the command of Argentinian military officers for training as a counter-revolutionary force. Thus was born the FDN, or Nicaraguan Democratic Force, later simply known as the Contras. With covert dollars from the CIA, training from Argentina's military, and weapons from the Israelis, the "secret" goal of the Contras was to topple the new Sandinista government and reinstall a more U.S.-friendly regime. It was the same old story. Money and arms for the Contras were funneled mainly through Honduras, but some also went through the hands of conservative private American expats living in Costa Rica. Many far right-wing Americans also contributed funds to the Contras, including TV evangelist Pat Robertson, as well as *Soldier of Fortune* magazine and the "Nicaragua Refugee Fund" (which was a sham creation of the FDN and CIA).

These were the particulars I ruminated on as I considered Penelope's idea. Perhaps she had struck upon a fruitful approach to funding my research travel, but the notion seemed unprincipled to me. And I knew I couldn't take the idea to my boss, William Harris, the museum's executive director. Harris had been hired by the museum's board of trustees only a few years back and I did not have a particularly warm relationship with him. No one at the museum did. At best, he would laugh me out of his office if I mentioned the idea of a grant from the CIA. At worst, he would threaten to fire me. Harris was not an easy man to work with, and he made a point of keeping considerable distance between himself and the "regular staff." Rather than being the down-in-the-trenches kind of leader we all had hoped for, he'd earned a reputation for remaining aloof, unapproachable, and opaque. I told Penelope thanks, but no thanks.

"Oh, honey, there's no harm in a simple inquiry. After all, you already know so much about the region from your travels.

And you've always been fascinated by the politics and people of Central America. Just drop them an inquiry. What could the harm be?" She could be so patient and at the same time so persuasive. She had a way about her, there's no doubting it.

"OK, Penelope, but given my political leanings and my two marijuana busts in the '70s, it seems pretty unlikely I'll even hear back from the CIA." I wrote a "To Whom It May Concern" letter and mailed it to the post office box address given in the government listings of the Yellow Pages.

And, indeed, nothing came of my inquiry. But the idea must have lingered in my subconscious because I began to have recurring dreams in which I found myself alone in the lowland jungle of Nicaragua's Miskito Coast, lost in a tangled world of strangler fig trees and thorny pejibaye palms, not knowing which direction to turn. Frequently in these dreams, a beautiful mulatto woman appeared on the opposite bank of a brown-water river, beckoning me to wade across and join her. Her voice was lilting, melodic, and irresistible. She wore only a white gossamer gown that undulated in a gentle breeze, her perfect hips, modest breasts, and dark erect nipples clearly outlined through the thin fabric. Her long hair, black as India ink, fell in waves to the middle of her back. I tried to cross the river to reach her. But every time I tried, my legs would move in slow motion, and I could barely pull my feet out of the mud. With each step I struggled to take, the river inched me farther downstream. As I watched her gradually fade into the distance, her bewitching allure and seductive voice pulled at me.

3

Odel and Penelope
April 1981

About three months later—much to my surprise—I got a call
in my museum office from someone named John Thornton.
He worked for the CIA; he didn't give his title, but simply
suggested he might drop by my office for a short chat. I didn't
hesitate to agree, and we set a date for our meeting. Oddly
Penelope seemed unsurprised, even amused.

"See, I told you so."

I told no one else about it, and I asked Penelope not to
mention it to any of our friends.

The night before John Thornton was scheduled to visit me
at the museum, it was the only thing I could think about. I had
no idea what I was doing. I was nervous and rambled on.
Penelope was cavalier about it all, making me feel a bit silly
for being so concerned. She wasn't as much of a talker as me,
not even when she was having difficulties at work. She was
the quiet stoic type, generally keeping her own counsel. For
Penelope, the more a personal issue worsened, the more
phlegmatic she became. She preferred to work things through

on her own rather than share her feelings with others. In fact, she often seemed somewhat aloof, like her parents. Some of her colleagues at the university had mentioned it to me, expressing the sentiment that she was "hard to get to know." I suppose, in some ways, we were rather different, although I, too, needed time to process conflicts before bringing them up with anyone.

Penelope was raised in Massachusetts in a refined, well-off, and well-traveled family. Her father, who worked as a cultural attaché for the State Department in Washington, D.C., was home only on weekends—when he was home at all. So she didn't see much of her dad growing up. But when he was home, she emphasized that things were always wonderful. It was a happy family. From what I was able to discern, her parents never argued (at least, not in front of her) and spent their leisure time visiting museums, going to local symphony and opera performances, and reading serious literature. Penelope knew every popular opera well, the story and the music.

An only child, Penelope loved both her parents deeply but had a special admiration for her father. When she was fourteen, her father's job took the family to Buenos Aires for four years, and then from there, the family moved to Costa Rica for three more years. She did her first two years of college at the University of Costa Rica in San José. Her Spanish was not only perfect, it had an urbane flair to it. She was, regardless of which language she was conversing in, a confident and adept woman. She went by Penny until she started college, at which point she decided to start using her full name. Her father agreed it was good decision.

I, on the other hand, had been raised in an Italian immigrant family in central Los Angeles. My father was working class and hot tempered. We scrimped and saved every penny and never even considered traveling beyond a few states from home. My parents had knockdown, drag-out arguments, although they were never mean spirited and they always reconciled with hugs and tears and declarations of love. My childhood had been emotional and exciting. However, like Penelope, I grew up a voracious reader, a habit instilled in me by my "Book of the Month Club" mother.

By the time I finished middle school, it had become clear that my given name was too burdensome. The other students, and even my teachers, had trouble pronouncing "Dangelo." Attempts to explain the pronunciation phonetically consistently failed, and all I got back was *dan-jello* or *dang-yellow*. In a grocery store with my mother one day, I saw a book of names for new babies. While Mom shopped, I studied the book. The closest sounding boy's name I found that I thought would be easy for people was Odel. And something about it rang true to me. That night I talked to my parents about it. They suggested I consider using Angelo as a nickname, but my mind was already made up. Dad admitted he'd had a similar problem with his given name—Laertes— and most people just called him Bernini. So, they were OK with it and told me I could "try it on for size." From that day on, I went by Odel.

My grandparents on my dad's side, Sardofino and Maria Bernini, along with their firstborn child and Granddad's brother, Paulo, emigrated to America from Sicily in the late 1800s to escape their Palermo mob family. They immigrated through New Orleans to avoid the better-organized record keeping of Ellis Island and also because some of the Bernini family had already settled in New York City and were establishing the family business there. In Sicily, the family had a vicious reputation. The four escapees made their way to Southern California, where granddad and his brother worked as laborers in the vast citrus groves southeast of Los Angeles. But our Palermo relations managed to locate them, and two fellows in dark flannel suits showed up from Sicily one wintery day to take Paulo "back home." They put twelve bullets into him in the middle of Via Roma, Palermo, making the point that one does not leave the family.

Granddad and Grandma Bernini, or Nonno and Nonna as we called them, managed to get away and hide out in the metropolitan labyrinth of central L.A. There they made a life and raised their children—nine in all. My dad, Laertes, was their seventh, and then came my Uncle Sandro and finally my sweet, beautiful Aunt Adriana. Adriana played the ponies, and she knew the history of every jockey and horse in the business. She bet scientifically, based on odds she calculated herself from track conditions and the backstories of the riders and horses. She knew reliable bookies and was remarkably successful.

After my father left home and got married, he went to work as a butcher. He never finished high school. We rarely visited his parents. I don't know why, but perhaps it was because Nonno was so difficult. He and Nonna knew minimal English—at least, they never spoke it around my brother and me on the occasions we did visit. And my older brother, Lorenzo, and I were not allowed to learn any Italian. Our branch of the Bernini family was in America now, and we were to forget about the past and integrate into American life.

Dad put Lorenzo and me to work in his butcher shop—Bernini's Fine Meats—when we were just thirteen or fourteen years old, giving us the dirtiest and most difficult tasks there were. It was his way of teaching us that we should go to college and get white-collar jobs. In fact, he pretty much insisted Lorenzo and I go to college, although he made it clear he couldn't pay for it. For our undergraduate degrees, we both went to state colleges in California, which were in those days essentially tuition-free.

Lorenzo chose California State Polytechnic College in San Luis Obispo, because he thought he might want to be a veterinarian. I chose San Francisco State College, because in the 1960s the Bay Area was the nucleus of a new music scene and the hippie movement in California. It was there that I met Bob Alcinous, who came to be my closest friend. We both fell in love with marine biology, ended up rooming together, and even dated some of the same co-eds. We were at the epicenter of an extraordinary new music scene, the civil rights crusade, and a social movement that came to be known as the "sexual revolution." We did our best to support all three efforts. The Grateful Dead played free concerts in Golden Gate Park and girls burned their bras. "The pill" had arrived, and women's rights activists heralded it as granting women sexual liberation and the ability to take charge of their own bodies. Feminists were encouraging women to reassess their roles in society and participate in (and enjoy) sex. In 1962, Helen Gurley Brown's *Sex and the Single Girl* offered young women advice on how to develop an active sex life while still unmarried. In 1964 the Supreme Court ruled that Henry Miller's *Tropic of Cancer* was not obscene, opening the way for books, magazines, and movies to begin describing and showing sex in explicit ways. And in 1967, James Salter, one of America's greatest writers, released *A Sport and A Pastime*; which, according to *The Guardian*, "set the standard not only for eroticism in fiction, but for the principal organ of literature—the imagination." Two detailed sex manuals by Masters and Johnson became best sellers and were translated into more than thirty languages.

I was attracted to Bob's mindful ways and philosophical approach to life—he was the most well read and thoughtful person I'd ever met. He once informed me, early in our friendship and with the greatest confidence, that all we need to know about such matters as happiness and the meaning of life could be found in Lao Tzu's poetic 6th century BC text, the *Tao Te Ching*, adding "as Lao Tzu instructed us, the Tao existed before anything, no one knows from where it came, and it is older than the gods." Bob had the build of a linebacker for the L.A. Rams, but he was one of the gentlest, kindest men I'd ever met. Together, we explored the emerging music scene in San Francisco and tidepools up and down the coast. For a few years we dived deep into LSD, psilocybin, and other hallucinogenic drugs as we explored

40

unknown trails deep in the dark, moist redwood forests of northern California. Late nights of delirious tripping, allowing the euphoria and recondite recesses of our minds to take us where they might, with Etta James, Miles Davis, Lou Reed, and Jefferson Airplane on the turntable. Bob was always the thoughtful one; I the impetuous one, eager to take chances, to lunge into uncertainty. We formed a bond that would end up lasting a lifetime. Bob went on to grad school at U.C. Berkeley, I went on to the American University in Washington D.C.

Although Lorenzo and I were raised Catholic, by the time I was a sophomore in college I'd become an atheist. I was convinced that organized religions were little more than con schemes, slick business franchises disguised as centers of enlightenment by using selected myths held together with rituals and financial extortion rooted in afterlife threats. Pomp, peer pressure, and guilt were devices used to manipulate and squeeze money from the congregation in support of the organization, particularly in support of the guys at the top. Yet people flocked to join, enlisting but never bothering to read the fine print. And many organized religions, especially Catholicism, Mormonism, the Southern Baptist Convention, and various cult groups like the American Amish are simply perverted, diminishing or outright preying on women and children, using liturgy and institutionalized patriarchy as a way to assure male dominance. Women are commonly condemned to submissive gender roles with limited free choice. Hypocrisy is rampant, and it was beyond me how anyone could believe the absurd stories that organized religions extoled. Even when I was young, going through catechism classes, the stories seemed absurd to me. It wasn't just the yet-emergent scientist in me; it was simply common sense. And of course, late in the twentieth century the Catholic priesthood would be revealed as a secret cult of sexual predators, preying especially on young boys. And in the early 2000s, investigative journalists would discover much

41

the same thing going on in the Southern Baptist and Amish communities of America's bible belt.

Religions, I would eventually come to believe, are the biggest shams on the planet—immoral and tragic fabrications peddled by priests, preachers, and other charlatans. Drifting away from Catholicism in high school wasn't instantaneous. I first tried on some other options for size. I joined a friend's Baptist church for about six months, mainly because I wanted to get to know his sister. It drove my parents crazy. I moved on to Rosicrucianism and took to practicing secret rituals in my room late at night with flickering candlelight. I can only imagine the conversations between my mother and father; but they patiently let me explore, not realizing that I would end up chucking the whole kit and caboodle. Lorenzo eventually came around to the same conclusion. Penelope wasn't quite as strident as me, and she claimed to be agnostic. But she too held disdain for most organized religions.

My college friend Bob Alcinous had a somewhat different approach to deciphering religions. He lumped them all together with other personal belief systems, arguing that whatever a person truly and firmly believes in becomes their personal reality, and people find ways to rationalize it and make that personal world order work for themselves, whether it is a Western religion, Eastern religion, a native belief system, or some other form of mythology. He argued that, in the broadest sense, even a strict adherence to science to explain the world could be viewed as a personal belief system akin to religion. But he also proclaimed, "So long as there are scientists and artists, there is no need for priests and cathedrals." Bob and I had endless discussions about this. He would state his core argument something like this: "These belief systems are simply people's ways of adjusting their personal reality to fit their psychic needs, to allow them to be comfortable in the world in which they find themselves."

For a while in college I participated in student debates in support of atheism. My argument was two-pronged. First, I

42

clearly distinguished between science and religion—the former being a fact-based belief system, the latter being a faith-based belief system. I argued that science is a *process of discovery*, a particular investigative method by which we obtain knowledge about the natural world. It involves a specific procedure of asking a question about the world, formulating a testable hypothesis, and then gathering measurable data through observation to test the hypothesis in an attempt to falsify it. Most scientific hypotheses are eventually falsified, leading to refinements, or to discarding them altogether. The longer a hypothesis stands up to testing, the more likely it is to be correct, to be the truth. Through this process of testing and falsifying hypotheses, we grow closer and closer to the truth. In science, long-supported hypotheses are said to be "highly corroborated." But they are always open to further testing—this is a fundamental precept of science. Scientific hypotheses can never be proven, only corroborated or falsified. If it cannot be falsified, it is not science. This process is known as the hypothetico-deductive method, and it has been a hallmark of science for more than a hundred years, most famously codified by the great Austrian philosopher Karl Popper in his 1934 book *The Logic of Scientific Discovery*.

This logical asymmetry in the scientific method—that hypotheses cannot ever be one hundred percent proven, but can be one hundred percent falsified—is a key attribute that distinguishes it from a faith-based system of understanding the world. The "black swan example" is sometimes used to illustrate how this asymmetry can play out. It goes like this. If a person sees nothing but white swans year after year, he might propose the hypothesis "all swans are white." The hypothesis may be corroborated for many years, but then a single observation of a black swan can happen and falsify it. The most elegant hypotheses are those that have been tested for many years, by many scientists, and not falsified, such as Darwin and Wallace's theory of evolution, Einstein's theory of relativity, Newton's theory of gravitation, and heliocentrism.

Faith-based belief systems are just the opposite. They ask a person not to question or test what they are being told but simply to accept it "on faith." Attempting to falsify a tenant of one's church or religion is anathema.

Falsifiability, then, is the principal criterion of demarcation between science and religion. My arguments were never that one or the other approach in life is right or wrong—but simply that they are profoundly different and should not be conflated with one another. Thus, the teaching of faith-based beliefs within science curricula—ideas such as creationism—would simply be inappropriate.

The second prong of my argumentation was that if faith is accepted as a basis for one's belief system, then there is no logical system at all—because a person can believe virtually anything on faith. One can believe in UFOs from the planet Uranus, or that the Earth is flat, or that Jesus teleported himself upon resurrection from the Middle East to Mexico to deliver sermons to the Aztecs (an embedded belief of the Mormon Church). Having no rational guideposts, such a system quickly devolves into logical absurdity. And, of course, most organized religions give their followers a set of beliefs that they are expected to simply accept, and, in doing so, those devotees and disciples forfeit their most precious human attribute—free thought and the right to question.

Until we graduated from high school and left for college, Mom and Dad took Lorenzo and me camping, hunting, and fishing as often as Dad could get away. I don't know how he managed those four-week-long summer vacations that allowed us to drive to Montana, Idaho, and Wyoming. On other, shorter camping trips, we went to Utah to hunt deer or to locations around Southern California and Arizona for bird hunting. I grew up comfortable in the wilderness, using guns,

44

eating wild game, home canning or smoking the salmon and trout we caught, and making venison jerky that we snacked on year-round. Dad worked hard and never traveled unless it was a family vacation. Our parents put everything they could into raising Lorenzo and me. Dad taught us to be good outdoorsmen, competent hikers and campers, and self-reliant. He taught us how to be mindful in the wild and how to be good observers—to understand the configuration of the shoreline in a stream to determine where the trout would be and to know what kind of clearing would be best to find game birds in. He instructed us in the stealth of deer hunting and taught us to keep our back to the sun so as to be less visible to a deer and, in turn, to illuminate our quarry all the better. These observational skills turned out to be favorable adaptations for me in adulthood—in more ways than I could have imagined.

We had a lot of guns in the house while I was growing up, and I never thought anything about it. Dad had three deer rifles and several revolvers. He and Mom had 16 gauge pump-action shotguns for bird hunting, and these were passed on to Lorenzo and me when they got new Remington 12 gauge semiautomatics. Lorenzo and I shared a .22 caliber revolver. On occasional Sundays we drove out to deserted stretches of Southern California's Mojave Desert for target practice. I was a good shot from the get-go—a "natural," my dad said. Before we left on our bird hunting trips, we always went to the trap and skeet range to polish our shotgun skills.

I favored bird hunting because it was more challenging than deer hunting and required greater skill. Deer were large, and they often stood still for you. I shot only one deer, when I was fourteen, and it left me feeling bad. It was such a beautiful, peaceful creature; I think it was looking at me, not afraid but simply curious, when I shot it. After that, I never pointed a gun at another deer, though I continued to go on deer hunting trips with Dad and Lorenzo because I loved the backcountry camping. But hitting a little white-wing dove in flight was completely different. It required one to not only be a good shot but also to judge the distance the bird was from you, how fast it was flying, what the angle of flight was relative to your own position, and even wind speed and direction. You had to lead the bird both ahead and above, estimating the speed of the bird and the buckshot and the effect of gravity on the shot. With enough practice, it became intuitive. And, unlike deer, if you hit a bird anywhere, it was likely DOA. I shot them, killed them, and stuffed them in my big, bloody bird-vest pocket. Later I plucked them and cleaned them and helped Mom fry them up in our gigantic cast-iron skillet. I loved the thrill of a pump-action shotgun, and I loved those fried dove and spaghetti dinners Mom prepared in camp.

The Palermo family business was never brought up in our household—such discussion was taboo. All of my aunts' and uncles' kids, save two, avoided a life of crime. One of my cousins was shot in the back and killed while robbing a liquor store at the age of sixteen. The other, one of Uncle Sandro's brightest boys who was a few years older than me, became a successful loan shark in L.A., and when I was older and thinking about buying my first car, Dad told me in no uncertain terms, "do not ever, ever take a loan from your cousin Marco." Of course, I did just that and borrowed money from Marco for my first car, a used '57 Chevy Bel Air. Marco and I were very close; we were pals and I trusted him. It all worked out fine, but Dad was never happy about it. And I never missed a payment.

Mom insisted I read books and learn proper manners. Dad taught me to be tough, but fair and honest. His butcher shop in central L.A. was a magnet for unsavory characters, and I learned early on where to find the right guy for a cheap stolen watch, how to play craps in the parking lot after work, how to play poker with the adults on Saturday nights after the shop closed, and, by the time I was sixteen, how to throw drunks and other troublemakers out of the store quickly without making a fuss. Dad taught Lorenzo and me basic tricks to disable mischief-makers, things as simple as grabbing one of their hands and pushing hard on the first bone of any finger, forcing it into their palm to create excruciating pain and submission—you can hold a mischief-maker's hand like that and walk him anywhere. Dad was also a bit of a pugilist, and he prided himself on his skills in that regard. Once or twice a year he'd come home after work all banged up. He always said it was because he had to "rough up some troublemaker" in the shop. But it was all good, and for being part of a lower-middle-income family Mom had some remarkably nice jewelry and even a couple of fur coats. When I was young, Dad's explanation for these items was always that they had, "fallen off the back of a delivery truck." Of course, I believed that story until I was about fifteen and my cousin Marco enlightened me, commenting on my naiveté (which was to become a theme in my life).

One of the most important urban survival lessons dad taught us was that there's no such thing as a fair fight. "When attacked, hold nothing back," he explained. "Disable your opponent quickly, any way you can. If you don't, you're going to get hurt. Maybe seriously hurt." Along with these words of wisdom came some rather ugly tricks to do the deed, including eye gouging and scrotum smashing. "If some big drunk SOB is about to kick the shit out of you, just rush right up to him and give him a big hug. It will completely throw him off guard. Wrap your arm around his neck until your hand reaches all the way around to his face, and then dig your finger or thumb into his eyeball as hard and deep as you can. He will be on the ground screaming in two seconds." I'd never had to use that trick, but I never forgot it either. Dad had Lorenzo and me practice these things passively until we understood them. "Fair fights," he would insist, "only happen in the movies. In real life, there is only one outcome to a fight—one person walks away, the other guy is on the ground messed up. And remember, the guy who throws the first punch is usually the one who walks away." I learned that last, acutely important lesson the hard way my first year in high school.

Even though we grew up in singularly different worlds, by the time we were both finishing our PhD programs Penelope and I seemed to have converged in lifestyles and intellectual matters. And we had definitely converged in terms of our sexuality. We were both enthusiastic and uninhibited, enjoyed creating and trying new positions, and had a panorama of sex toys selected by Penelope. Most importantly, we were both mindful lovers, paying close attention to how the other one responded, what they enjoyed, and the subtle nuances of lovemaking that elicited such different reactions. Penelope's orgasms were explosive, and when she was highly aroused, she could have a dozen O's in rapid succession. Sex was one thing we never argued about. We both dived in wholeheartedly, limited only by our imaginations. However, unlike me, Penelope's strict and conservative upbringing had prevented her from being an active participant in the sixties drug, music and student protest scene. I eventually came to believe that it was those crucial, conservative years of her maturation that deprived Penelope from having a more liberal, imaginative, and open mind. Except, of course, in the provenance of sex.

By the second year of our marriage Penelope had begun cultivating a penchant for covert sex in public places. At first I found it rather thrilling, but as she pushed for increasingly risky clandestine adventures I found myself growing wary. And when she began an offensive for stealth sex at corner tables in local restaurants I tried to draw the line. My reluctance disappointed her, and she let me know. I should have seen that as a forewarning, but for some reason I didn't.

4

John Thornton

May 1981

I expected John Thornton to match the stereotype of a CIA agent that I carried in my head: short-cropped hair, dark suit, simple blue tie, stiff and taciturn. I expected him to be young, new on the job, and getting his feet wet by handling the easy stuff, like interviewing nuts that wrote letters like mine to the agency. Or perhaps he would be old and almost over the hill, now taking on the easy assignments as he wound down into a cushy federal retirement. Either way, I planned to be completely open and straightforward with him. I knew a lot about Central America, particularly Nicaragua. I had a long history of travel in the region and knew a lot of people there. In exchange for sharing what I knew, I was hoping for a small travel grant to keep my fieldwork going for a couple more years. Of course, I also assumed the CIA already knew everything I knew about the region, so what I had to offer might be pitifully little.

Thornton walked into my office looking like a senior-citizen model for Tommy Bahama—khaki pants, boat shoes,

Hawaiian print shirt, mussed hair flopping down over oversize ears, and a big smile on his face. He was tall, handsome, loquacious, somewhere in his mid-sixties, and very relaxed. I opted for the "over the hill" hypothesis. Here was a guy who had put in his time and was now coasting into early retirement with great government bennies. He no longer had to do any long travel slogs or boring desk work. He was experienced enough that the Agency sent him out on these easy little tasks, interviewing probable dingbats like me, and he even got to have some fun and had an expense account.

"Ah, you must be Dr. Bernini. Very pleased to meet you. Thanks for your note. Say, you've got a swell place here." His eyes rolled around my office giving it a quick inspection. He sounded sincere. My office was filled with books and dust-capturing knickknacks from my travels in Latin America. Guatemalan huipils and San Blas Islands molas adorned the walls; Nicaraguan stone carvings and Mexican clay art served as bookends on the shelves.

"Mr. Thornton, pleased to meet you. And a bit surprised, I might add."

"Why would you be surprised? And it's John, please. Did you not write the Central Intelligence Agency offering some assistance with our efforts in Central America?" He spoke with a slight lisp.

"Yes, of course, I did. But I doubted you would be interested. After all, I'm sure the U.S. government has personnel all over Latin America, most probably more experienced in the region than I am."

"That's true, of course. But we do try to follow up on inquiries such as yours. By the way, you mentioned you had traveled quite a bit in Nicaragua, is that correct?"

"Yes, I have."

"And you must have many friends there?"

"Some, yes."

"Are any of them in the government?"

"Not really; most are academics."

50

"I see." (The *see* came out as "thee.") "And you mentioned you traveled on the coast a lot, is that correct?"

"Yes, as I stated in my letter, I'm a marine biologist and my field work takes me to coastal sites all through Central America."

"Have you ever seen a Nicaraguan soccer game?"

"A Nicaraguan soccer game?"

"You must know that old Nicaraguan joke, *¿Cuál es la diferencia entre el equipo de fútbol nicaragüense y una bolsa de té?*"

His quick switch to Spanish caught me off guard. "Sorry," I said, "what was that again?"

"Come on Dr. Bernini, you know the answer. *¡La bolsa de té suele permanecer en la copa!*" He chuckled loudly.

My brain caught up with my ears. I understood that phrase and intuited what I imagined the original question had been. I thought, *This guy in a Hawaiian shirt from the CIA has been here less than ten minutes and he's telling me Nicaraguan jokes in Spanish? What the hell!*

"How 'bout this one, *¿Qué sucede cuando un jugador nicaragüense pierde la vista?*"

"Uhhh . . . *se convierte en pintor?*"

"No Bernini! *¡Se convierten en un árbitro!*" Thornton roared with laughter. "Say, your museum has some nice exhibits down on the main floor. How about giving me a quick tour of the place?"

Thus we proceeded to spend the next hour looking at taxidermied birds and mammals, shell collections, and dioramas of Native American life. My guest seemed genuinely interested. I told him some of the backstories—how the museum acquired the objects, how many we had, that the "real meat" of the place was the research that two-dozen PhD curators undertook and the large research collections they managed that the public never saw.

When we were back on the elevator returning to my office on the third floor of the museum, I asked him about the possibility of the Agency providing a small grant to cover my travel expenses for a couple years. I suggested that, in return, I could visit some specific places they might not have good information on, or some such thing.

Thornton replied, "What makes you think the Central Intelligence Agency funds such things?"

"Well, I have no idea actually. In fact, in all honesty it was my wife's idea. But I thought it was worth an inquiry."

In a dry, matter-of-fact and perhaps slightly annoyed voice, he replied, "The CIA does not give grants, of any kind, for any reason."

"I see. Well, now I know."

Back in my office, we chatted for another half hour or so and when we said our goodbyes Thornton was back to his jovial self. He thanked me for the tour and said he could find his own way out, noting that he might spend a bit more time enjoying the exhibit areas before returning to his office.

When I got home that night and told Penelope how the meeting went, she seemed unsurprised. "Well, like I said, no harm in looking into it. At least he was a nice man."

So much for my brush with the CIA. *Nothing lost, nothing gained.* Or so I thought.

5

Antín Morales, the Patriot
Fall 1981

The weeks and months rolled by, and the first term of Ronald Reagan's presidency began to take shape. In El Salvador, inspired by the Sandinista success in Nicaragua, the *Farabundo Martí National Liberation Front*, or FMLN, launched a major offensive against the repressive Salvadoran government. The U.S. State Department issued a white paper claiming that Cuba and other communist countries were playing a central role in arming the Salvadoran insurgents. Reagan's forceful secretary of state, Alexander Haig, accused the Sandinistas of "exporting terrorism" to El Salvador, giving Reagan justification for terminating the economic assistance that President Carter had put in place for the fledgling new Nicaraguan government. The loss of U.S. financial support quickly began to cripple the new administration in Managua; thus Reagan began to sow the seeds of the "counterrevolution," or *Contra Revolución*. Many members of Somoza's former National Guard and scores of his sociopathic death-squad minions had escaped the Sandinista regime and gathered just across the border in Honduras. Under Reagan's direction, the CIA began working with them in earnest. Relying on covert funds from the United States, the Contras began to launch skirmishes on Nicaraguan soil. As Nicaragua's young socialist government came under attack from the CIA-sponsored Contras, and without financial aid from the U.S., they had little choice but to turn to Cuba and the Soviets for assistance in building their own military capacity. Escalation was inevitable.

However, Reagan's efforts to organize and strengthen the Contras met with opposition both internationally and from the U.S. Congress. So strong was the opposition in the United States that Edward Boland, chair of the House Intelligence Committee, would sponsor successful legislation in 1982 that specifically prohibited the use of U.S. funds for the purpose of overthrowing the new government in Nicaragua. But such efforts only forced Reagan and William Casey, director of the CIA, to more deeply hide their clandestine support for the Contras, which in turn forced the young Nicaraguan leadership to seek more and more assistance from Cuba and the Soviets.

Immediately after taking control of the country in 1979, the new Sandinista government launched a massive literacy campaign. They had such success in their first year that, in September 1980, UNESCO awarded Nicaragua the prestigious Nadezhda K. Krupskaya Award for its public education work. The revolutionary government also created a new publishing house, *Editorial Nueva Nicaragua*, and started printing cheap editions of books rarely seen by Nicaraguans under Somoza censorship, especially those authored by prominent Latin American writers such as Gabriel García Márquez, José Martí, Carlos Fuentes, Paulo Coelho, and the great Chilean poet and diplomat Pablo Neruda. Conservative groups in the United States launched a smear campaign, claiming the Sandinistas were censoring news outlets in the country and that they were targeting Jews for discrimination. Investigations by numerous international organizations, including the United Nations, proved those claims to be false.

By the summer of 1981, I had scraped enough money together for one more sampling trip; it would be to Nicaragua in November. My old college friend Bob Alcinous and his wife Beatriz, both of whom worked at the National University (*Universidad Nacional Autónoma de Nicaragua*, or UNAN), were sending me uplifting and optimistic letters. It was an exciting time to be in Nicaragua. In fact, positive things seemed to be happening all over Central America. Belize had even won its independence from Great Britain. I was looking forward to visiting Bob and Beatriz, hanging out with other friends and students at the University, and having a few weeks of fieldwork on the Pacific coast.

Things were also popping in the developed world in 1981. MTV was launched in the States, the first cases of AIDS surfaced in Los Angeles, and Pope John Paul II and President Reagan were both shot and wounded in assassination attempts. Reagan went on to nominate Judge Sandra Day O'Connor as the first woman on the U.S. Supreme Court. John Paul II went on to issue a statement that it was Our Lady of Fátima that kept him alive through his ordeal. The CIA claimed the Soviets were behind the assassination attempt on the Pope but offered no evidence to support the idea. Lady Di married Prince Charles, the wreck of the *Titanic* was found, and Ozzy Osbourne bit the head off a dove in a press conference. Perhaps tying with Ozzy for the most noteworthy event of the year, IBM released its first personal computer.

Penelope and I continued to debate politics and have crazy-great sex. Her work was soaring and her research papers were getting a great deal of attention. She made some good female pals on campus, other lady professors from the Political Science Department and some women from the Performing Arts Program. She would occasionally go to dinner with them or bring them over to our place for dinner. They were mostly divorced women, slightly older than us, bright and attractive. One of them, an artist-musician named Sonia Elatus, seemed rather odd to me, and I wondered what Penelope saw in her. I was never really sure what Sonia was trying to say, with her variegated thoughts and words. But she was an ace kayaker, and on occasion Penelope, or sometimes both of us, would go paddling on the coast with her. She was rather on the masculine side, as tall and nearly as strong as me, and she knew the best locations for kayaking. Sometimes, during a full moon, when the seas were calm, Sonia would guide Penelope and me on kayaks among the "big ships"—oil tankers, container ships, and navy vessels in the Seattle harbor. We were tiny ants floating among giants, drifting on a glass-like sea with only moonlight to guide our way. It was eerie and suspenseful and exhilarating. Sonia also introduced us to Jack Daniel's Tennessee Whiskey. Penelope took a liking to it, and it quickly became her go-to after dinner drink. When we paddled, Sonia always carried a flask of Jack.

One evening Penelope and I and another friend, Marjorie Agelaus (a political scientist and, unlike Sonia, quite sane), got a bit sauced and the subject of threesomes came up. Both of the ladies admitted to having experienced ménage à trois, leaving me a bit embarrassed to say that I'd not but would certainly be willing to give it a whirl some time—assuming my two dance partners were both women. Marjorie told us she had enjoyed a couple of two-women, one-man experiences, but Penelope, in her typically guarded way, declined to elaborate on her own experiences. That night, after Marjorie had left, giving us both enthusiastic sloppy-sexy kisses on the mouth, I asked Penelope why she'd never mentioned her threesomes to me before.

"Well, it's rather personal, Odel. I was actually a bit uncomfortable with that entire discussion. Besides—you'd never asked. I hope it doesn't bother you. It was years ago."

I told her it didn't bother me at all, but I went on to say, "You know, since we've been together, I've been so satisfied that I've not once considered sex with anyone else. I've assumed you felt the same way." For some reason, I suddenly felt the need to get that on the table.

"Oh, I do feel the same, Odel. I love you, and our sex is phenomenal. And I've not been the least bit interested in any other man, not since the first day we met."

That night our love-making was especially exuberant. Several of her favorite toys came out of the closet, and we slept in a seriously wet and delightfully aromatic bed.

On an unusually warm and sunny day in early September, I got a call in my museum office from someone named Antin Morales at the CIA. I was again flabbergasted. Mr. Morales suggested we meet at his office. We set a date and time, and he gave me directions to find him.

The eight-story nondescript gray concrete building was on the outskirts of Seattle, not far from Sea-Tac airport, in a semi-industrial area filled with similar nondescript gray concrete buildings. Most of the buildings seemed to be engineering and aerospace offices. All had well-manicured lawns in the front and large parking lots in the back. Displayed on the sides of the buildings or on tasteful lawn signs were the names of the companies. Apart from the signs, every building looked pretty much the same. But the one I was searching for, using the cross streets Morales had given me, had no signs or identifiers of any kind—just large address numbers over the entry doors. The parking lot was only half full. I pulled in, got out of the car, walked past a small lunch patio with scattered tables and chairs and around to the front of the building. On the front doors were painted the words, *United States Government. Controlled Access*, alongside the familiar seal of the United States—a bald eagle with one claw grasping an olive branch, the other a clutch of arrows. *E pluribus unum*, indeed.

The large foyer had two elevators. Between them a simple sign indicated what would be found on each floor. As Morales had told me, floors one through four were GAO offices, while five through eight were the Agency's offices. I was to go to floor five. On the fifth floor, the elevator doors opened to a small room with a few chairs along the wall and a receptionist. I gave her my name and told her I had an appointment with Antin Morales. She looked uninterested, but I saw several cameras around the ceiling, no doubt recording every millisecond of everything that transpired in that entryway. I wondered what I would have encountered had I tried to take the elevator to floor six, seven, or eight. She told me to take a seat and Mr. Morales would be right with me. I had an impulse to wave at the cameras but controlled myself.

I had only just sat down when Morales strode through an inconspicuous door on one side of the waiting room. He walked straight to me, shook my hand briskly as I stood up, and turned to walk away. I followed.

"Thank you for coming by, Dr. Bernini," he said over his shoulder. "I hope you don't mind if I ask you a few questions about your work."

"Not at all." What was I supposed to say!

We entered his sparse office. No photos of J. Edgar Hoover or Ronald Reagan hung on the walls. In fact, nothing hung on the walls. His desk was neat, with only one small stack of folders. The one window overlooked the parking lot behind the building. *This isn't a working office*, I thought, *it's an interview office*. As we began to talk, I noticed he was not taking notes of any kind. *OK, obviously this conversation is being taped.*

Unlike John Thornton, Morales was all business. I was fairly certain he was Mexican-American or Guatemalan-American, as he had a strong Maya Indian look to his features; the portmanteau figure with its distinctive blocky build and wide high cheekbones were pretty easy to recognize. I guessed his ancestral family roots were Maya-*mestizo*, probably Guatemala City, or perhaps from southernmost Mexico.

As if going down a checklist, he asked me about my job at the museum, my research program, and why and where I traveled in Central America. He zeroed in on Nicaragua, asking rather detailed questions about where I had been and when. I had to respond with a lot of generalities, simply because I couldn't remember the exact dates, or even years in some cases, and I had been to so many different areas in the country. I explained this to him and said I would have to check my field notes to provide answers to some of the specific questions he was asking. With that, he said, "You keep notes from your travels? How detailed are they?" I told him they were quite detailed, including sketches and maps and information that any careful naturalist would include in their field notebook. I had the feeling I was the first biologist he'd ever interviewed.

He asked why my birth certificate recorded my name as "Dan-Jello," but all my other official papers listed me as Odel. After getting over the surprise that he had seen my birth certificate, I explained that people who weren't used to speaking Italian simply couldn't get the correct pronunciation of "Dángh-el-oh," so, with my parents' blessings, I had changed it Odel. He looked at me curiously, but he didn't try to pronounce Dangelo again.

He asked about the people I knew in Nicaragua, but I avoided giving him specific names of anyone—instead referring to them only as "a professor at the National University who is a friend of mine" and such. The conversation went on for about forty-five minutes before I mentioned I would be returning to Nicaragua to collect crustacean samples on the Pacific coast that November. After I explained to him what crustaceans were, he asked where I planned to travel and I replied that I hadn't worked out a detailed itinerary yet.

"I'll certainly spend time southwest of León, in the Salinas Grandes area. And along the coast of Carazo Department, where there is good highway access to the beaches. And if I have time, I'll likely try to get south to the Rivas coast, just north of the border with Costa Rica."

He listened carefully. "Any interest in the Montelimar area?" he asked.

"Not really. It's pretty touristy, and those kinds of coastal areas are usually degraded and lack the biological biodiversity they once had."

But I saw an opening. "Of course, I could go to Montelimar if there was something specific you wanted information on from the beach area there."

"Well, that's up to you. But if you do find yourself there, I wonder if you might be willing to share your field notes with us when you've returned to Seattle. Especially if you come across any maps or sketches of that particular coastline."

"Look, Mr. Morales, I'd be happy to spend a couple days there, look for maps—though they likely don't exist—and make my own sketches of the coastline. That's not a big deal." I couldn't help wondering why the CIA would have an interest in that little dot on the map. However, it was one of only a few places on the west coast of the country where safe anchorage could be found, although in storm season it was not protected enough. The other main anchorages were the ports at Corinto and Puerto Sandino (called Puerto Somoza until the Sandinistas took the country), and the smaller covelike anchorage in the far south at San Juan del Sur. The Nicaraguan Navy, such as it was, had facilities at all three of these other sites, but they stayed away from Montelimar, leaving it strictly for the tourists.

"Thank you, Dr. Bernini. That could be helpful."

He walked me to the elevator, handed me a simple white card with nothing but his name and a phone number on it, and we said our goodbyes. Just before the elevator arrived, Morales said, "Dr. Bernini, you are a patriot, aren't you?"

I wasn't expecting that kind of a question, and I replied, "I'm not sure what you mean by that, Mr. Morales."

"It's a straightforward question. Are you a patriot?"

"Honestly, I'm not even sure what that word means."

"Dr. Bernini, it means that you truly *believe* in America."

I thought about it for a second, and replied honestly. "I believe America exists. And I believe it's a great country. Is that what you mean?"

He slowly shook his head back and forth and quietly said "yes." Then he turned and walked away. I could tell he found my response unsatisfactory.

Again, when I recounted the meeting to Penelope, she seemed unsurprised. "Well, he's just another federal employee doing what he's told to do and taking home a paycheck. He probably doesn't even know why his boss's bosses have an interest in Montelimar. Did you ask about the grant idea I suggested?"

"No, I didn't bring up the grant thing because John Thornton had made it clear the CIA doesn't do such things."

"Well, I wouldn't give up so easily. Maybe if you meet up with this guy Morales again, you should ask him about it."

That was the last I heard from Morales or anyone else at the Agency until late November after my return from Nicaragua.

6

Managua, Nicaragua
November 1981

My flight into Managua was uneventful. I used Aeronica out of Dallas-Fort Worth because it was cheap and I wanted to support the Nicaraguan government's airline. The food was good, the drinks were free, and the flight attendants were some of the best in the industry. The approach into Managua took our plane on a wide arc over beautiful Lake Nicaragua, an immense body of water that spans half the width of the country. The massive twin volcanoes of *Concepción* and *Madera* rise from the lake, forming steep islands of black basalt edged with green shorelines. They are but two of the thousands of volcanoes, large and small, that traverse the western rim of the Americas. In this part of the world, a series of great oceanic crustal plates beneath the Pacific Ocean move inexorably eastward like conveyor belts, slowly smashing and grinding into the American continental landmass. The plates capitulate and are forced downward to submerge beneath the land. A dozen miles down, the submergence creates so much friction and heat that it melts the subterranean rocks, turning them into molten lava that eventually finds its way to the surface of the Earth as a Vesuvian string of volcanoes that runs from Alaska all the way to Chile. The geometry of intersecting straight lines that our brain is used to thinking in is inadequate to understand these titanic events, and scientists still aren't certain how it all works.

An oceanic plate called the Cocos Plate has been submerging beneath Central America for millennia, creating volcanoes and earthquakes since long before the peopling of the New World began. Smoke ascended skyward from the cone of *Volcán Concepción* in the blue waters of Lake Nicaragua below me. The inhabitants of Nicaragua, and other countries of the Pacific Ring of Fire, have lived with active volcanoes and a trembling Earth beneath their feet since the first day they arrived in those places.

As I exited the baggage claim area, Bob Alcinous and Beatriz Eurycleia were waiting for me. They had big happy smiles on their faces. They were always a joy to see and hang out with. We had our big *abrazos* and they helped me schlep my excess luggage to a minivan in the parking lot. On the side of the van was the logo of *UNAN*—the *Universidad Nacional Autónoma de Nicaragua*. Bob and Beatriz both worked as biology professors there, although Bob had a half-time position and split his time with Columbia University in New York, where he also had a half-time professorship. They were both bright and highly respected in their fields. Bob had been a close friend since our undergraduate days in San Francisco; he was, like me, an invertebrate zoologist. But I was only just getting to know Beatriz, who was Nicaraguan, as they had been married only a few years. I liked them both very much. They had met when Beatriz was his graduate student at Columbia, studying coastal plankton ecology and ocean productivity. They dated secretly for a while, but once Beatriz was awarded her PhD they "came out of the closet." No one at Columbia was surprised or disturbed by it; in fact, it is a common theme in the university world, and many academic marriages had their roots in the classroom. And in the late 1970s Columbia University was, like the University of California Berkeley, one of the most liberal schools on the planet. When they got married a year later and came up with the idea of moving to Managua, Bob's friends and colleagues told him he was about to make a grievous and irrevocable mistake. His friends and colleagues were wrong.

Like me, Bob loved Latin America, and Beatriz wanted to be close to her family in Managua. She was also proud of her home country and wanted to work there to "help the cause" during the post-Somoza era shift to democracy. Bob relished the idea of living in the emerging democracy of Nicaragua, but he also valued his ties to the U.S. academic world, especially the availability of large government grants, which are not available in Nicaragua. Like most successful scientists, Bob relied heavily on research funding from the U.S. National Science Foundation, the Environmental Protection Agency, and other government sources. Hence, when he was offered a job at the National University in Managua, the split appointment arrangement was established. It had worked out well, and they felt it gave them the best of both worlds. They were two of the happiest people I knew. Penelope had met them only a few times, briefly.

Bob was 10 years older than Beatriz and that, along with the fact he was a liberal, intelligent American with good earning potential, made him a great catch in the eyes of Beatriz's mother and father. Plus, he was a righteous dude, and they recognized he was solid. However, the discovery that Beatriz could not bear children cast a gloom over her parents. She and Bob went through the blues, considered adoption, but eventually concluded that it might be for the best, given their complicated lifestyle and heavy professional demands. The happy couple had offered their spare bedroom to me for the days I would be in Managua, though I planned to spend most of my time at the coast. They had also arranged for my use of the university minivan. Good friends, good people.

Winding through the streets of Managua, the aftereffects of the massive 1972 earthquake and long civil war were still evident. Many buildings had rows of bullet holes from machine-gun strafings, and some blocks were literally demolished, with nothing left but piles of rubble. The city had a post-war look to it.

That night, over *Cuba Libres*, I outlined my collecting plan to them, asking for their advice on specific localities and places to stay along the coast roads. When I mentioned I might spend a couple days at Bahía Montelimar, Beatriz teased me.

"Ah Odel, using your museum's money to hang out in a swanky tourist resort drinking *Piña Coladas* and ogling the beautiful *Nicas*! What would Penelope say?"

In 1981, Montelimar might have been one of the nicest beach getaways in Nicaragua, but by U.S. standards it was far from swanky. And as for Penelope, she wouldn't care one bit if I ogled beautiful Nicaraguan ladies. In fact, she'd likely be ogling them too. But, I played along with the idea. "Well, I thought it might be a nice break from slogging around tidepools in the more primitive locations. Besides, I might get lucky and find some interesting mutant crustaceans living in the bay where all that raw sewage flows!"

Beatriz unfailingly had a sparkle in her eyes and a smile on her face. She was a beautiful woman, solidly built, slightly on the plump side, with large cheerful jiggling tits. She was proud of those particular assets and their fine, eye-catching qualities, and she dressed to present them to the world. In a tight-fitting, low-cut dress, Beatriz became voluptuous, her breasts heroic. Despite her mature figure, her face retained a young, charming, girlish look. She was self-assured, content, and happily married. Bob was similarly attractive: tall, large of frame, confident. Both of them were thoughtful people who could articulate their views easily. But whereas Beatriz spoke directly and clearly, Bob often couched his thoughts in a framework of wit and satire. They made a great couple. Beatriz's positive attitude toward life seemed to be a common trait among Nicaraguans, and one that I'd long been drawn to.

We talked at length about the situation in Nicaragua since Reagan's election. Of course, everyone there knew that the CIA was covertly organizing and arming a "Contra Army," but they didn't take it too seriously. The Nicaraguan people had just overthrown one of the longest running, most powerful and brutal regimes in all of Latin America. The entire country was behind the FSLN and Daniel Ortega. There was a "national high" from the deposing of Somoza and his family legacy. The people felt like international heroes—and they were, in the eyes of many. Keeping the Contras at bay would not be a problem. Oh, there were a few of the Old Guard in Managua who were disgruntled; the big businessmen who had benefitted from Somoza's way of doing things—bribes, secret deals, contracts awarded to relatives, intimidating the competition, and so forth. But, by and large, Nicaraguans were optimistic and excited about their new future. Nonetheless, Beatriz was more worried than Bob about the CIA-backed Contras.

"We have fought so hard for our freedom, for so long, I just want things to be peaceful now."

Bob turned his attention from a small fly floating in his drink to look directly at her, "Beatriz, those who complied or cooperated with Somoza had peace, but not freedom. Now all Nicaraguans have their freedom, but don't expect that to buy us peace. You can have one or the other, but you can never have both at the same time. At least, not for long."

By the fall of 1981, some things had already started to unravel for the Sandinistas, but few people had noticed. Long-time supporter and confidant of Daniel Ortega, Violeta Chamorro, had resigned from the ruling junta the previous year, in protest over its increasingly Marxist policies. And her family newspaper, *La Prensa*, which had long been strongly anti-Somoza, had begun to criticize the Sandinistas. Those events proved to be a portent of things to come.

Late in the evening, Bob opened a bottle of *Damiana* he'd picked up at a duty-free shop in the Mexico City airport on his last flight in from New York. We sipped the fabled philter, used as a medicinal herb since the days of the Aztecs, until our eyelids drooped, and then we stumbled to our beds and crashed. That night I dreamed again of the alluring mulatto woman beckoning me to cross the jungle stream to join her. I'd had the dream more than a dozen times, and each time it grew more detailed and more realistic. This time, the dream was astonishingly life-like, swallowing me completely, plunging me into a vortex of secrecy, and longing for something I didn't understand.

The young woman seemed a mix of Spanish, Caribbean-African, and Native American, perhaps Aztec or maybe even Maya. Again, her voice was irresistibly musical and had a seductive cadence. Her gown was so thin I could almost see through it, the outline of her hipbones and willowy thighs, her almond skin, and the shape of her modest bosom. She lured me toward her, but as before, with every step I took the rush of the stream carried me a bit further away. A large snake lay coiled on the ground beside her, its thick raised scales shining emerald green and cobalt blue. The snake's eyes shifted back and forth between the woman and me, watching, waiting. It tasted the air with its long forked tongue. The snake was a passive observer, showing no malevolence, simply an onlooker. As the woman's eyes locked onto mine she reached out with one arm, uncurling her long slender fingers, and called my name . . . "Odel, come to me" . . . and I awoke. For a few seconds, I wasn't sure if I was actually awake or still in the dream. I lay there stupefied, confused. I wanted to let myself slip back into the dream. Maybe it was the *Damiana*, but it was as if I had actually stepped into another world, a parallel universe, in my dream state. But the dream didn't come again that night.

The next day we all woke late. Over several cups of delicious dark Nicaraguan highlands coffee, I told Bob and Beatriz about my dream. That I'd been having the same dream for months, and it was getting a little too realistic for comfort. Beatriz looked thoughtful, and after a while she spoke. Out of courtesy to me she usually spoke in English, with the delightful accent characteristic of Managuans.

"*Maestro* Odel, I know you might think this is *loco*, but there is a woman on the outskirts of the city, in the east, in Barrio Nueva Esperanza, who is legendary for her ability to interpret dreams. Perhaps you should visit her."

Bob's eyes rolled up, but he didn't speak. Beatriz wasn't to be trifled with. "What do you mean, 'she interprets dreams'," I asked.

"She interprets them. You tell her your dreams, she asks you some questions, and she tells you what they mean. If they are dreams that make you uncomfortable, or that scare you, she helps you understand them and perhaps overcome the issue that is behind them."

I spoke cautiously. "Beatriz, speaking as a scientist, I'm not sure I believe dreams have meaning, or at least meaning that can be understood by anyone."

Beatriz replied, "*Por favor, mi amigo*, I too am a scientist. But just because Western scientists have not yet figured out dreams does not mean that some nonscientists have not done so. As a scientist, I understand your tendency to want to measure and quantify things, but perhaps sometimes it is better to just experience them, to feel their strength and promise. You know, someone once said your mind is like a parachute—it works best when it's open. There are ways of looking at the world outside the paradigm of science. I have heard amazing things about this woman. They say she is a *curandera*, perhaps even a seer. What do you have to lose?" Her patient persistence reminded me of Penelope.

Bob looked me straight in the eye, gave me a little wink, and said, "Yeah, what do you have to lose? You're already losing your mind." He chuckled.

My plan for the day was to unpack my bags, and repack into the van what I needed for my fieldwork. I'd brought along a lot of collecting material and snorkeling gear, but I'd not come prepared for scuba diving, thinking I'd keep things simple. I also wasn't sure I could get good quality air for diving, given the state of things in Nicaragua at the time. The packing would go quickly. I had time. "OK, let's go meet this *curandera*. I'm assuming you'd like to come along."

Beatriz hesitated. "I'm not sure. I have never been there, only heard of her from friends. In fact, I have never been to Barrio Nueva Esperanza. It is not a good neighborhood. But my friend Dolores can tell you how to get there."

I could tell from her voice that Beatriz wasn't going to have anything to do with this witch doctor she'd just referred me to. *What the hell!* I thought. Bob rolled his eyes again, and said "Shit man, I'll go with you. I'll check with Dolores while you get your things squared away. Maybe the doctor will be on call this afternoon or this evening."

A couple hours later Bob found me at the van, just as I was finishing up. "We're all set," he said. "Dolores talked to *La Señora* on the phone, and she can see you tonight at eight."

"Cool. Can't wait. Should be most enlightening. Not!" We both laughed.

We had a pleasant afternoon that included a stop at the university to visit some friends and a snack at a terrific Salvadoran *pupusa* café, after which I laid down for a short nap. Just ten minutes into my nap, I found myself back in the dream. The jungle was steamy, I was on some kind of quest, the river was an impediment, the beautiful mulatto woman was telling me, not in words but in gestures, that if I crossed the river to her I would find what I was searching for. I sensed the river was both a barrier and a connection. She beckoned me with her long slender arm and curling fingers. Beside her, the green and blue snake lie coiled, watching, but its scales were now raised, almost featherlike. Even the serpent seemed to draw me; a benevolent reptile with knowing eyes urging me to cross the river with its sibilant whispers. I awoke with a start, covered in perspiration and breathing heavily. *Shit. Enough already.* The idea of talking to a "dream specialist" was sounding better all the time.

On the drive to Barrio Nueva Esperanza that night, Bob said I seemed sort of wound up. I told him about the dream I'd had during my short nap. Bob just stared at me, not sure what to say. As we drove into the neighborhood, from somewhere deep inside, I sensed a shadow pass over me.

The streets in the *Barrio* were dirt and not well graded, so we drove slowly. There were few lights, mostly just the gas lamps of scattered street-food vendors and headlights of a few passing cars. We got turned around several times, had to stop for directions, and Bob complained, "Dolores gave me crappy directions!" But when he recognized an intersection with a used tire and battery shop he relaxed, knowing we were close. He flagged down two elderly women and asked if they knew where the house of *la mujer que ve* might be. The women shook their heads, quickly turned, and walked away. A half-block farther we asked a middle-aged woman with several children in tow. She stared at us intently. It dawned on me that we were two gringos, in a questionable part of Managua, looking for some *bruja*, and it might seem a bit odd to the locals. After a while, she pointed down the street, "*la casita azul, con los dos cedros.*" We parked in front of the house, walked to the door, and Bob knocked three times.

The woman who greeted us was dark skinned and looked to be in her late fifties. Her hair was salt-and-pepper, long but piled into bundles on her head, lengthy strands falling down here and there. She wore layers of bright clothing that seemed like patchwork. Looking beyond her, the house was so dark I could make nothing out. Unrecognizable, but not disagreeable odors wafted out the door. I mustered up my best Spanish, thanked her for agreeing to see me, and introduced Bob, who explained that he and his wife were friends of Dolores and so forth. She listened politely, and then invited us in.

"I am Circe," she said, "please sit." She said her name quickly, with an odd accent, and I wasn't sure I understood what she had said. The woman ignored Bob and stared directly at me. Her continence was strangely unfamiliar to me, though not unpleasant in any particular way. Her eyes were stunning; slightly oversized, black as coal but luminous—youthful and quite beautiful.

We sat on a tired and uncomfortable old sofa; she sat stiffly on an equally uncomfortable looking wooden chair. An ancient treadle loom stood in the corner, a half-finished fabric dangling out from behind and piling on the floor. The woman asked me why I wanted to talk with her. I explained that I'd been having a crazy dream, over and over, for months, and it was bothering me. I had been told she might be able to tell me what the dream meant, and why I was having it. She asked me a few more questions and said, "*Puedo decirle lo que significa su sueño*. But I cannot assure you that you will be happy with what you hear." And then, I realized she spoke the creole English of Nicaragua's Miskito Coast.

"Of course, *Señora*, I only ask that you share with me your gift of insight. Thank you."

She stood and told me to follow her into another room. She told Bob to "make himself at home," and that we would not be long. He settled into the old sofa and gave me a wink.

When she opened the door to her parlor, the smell of burning *copál* filled my nostrils. My acute sense of smell was usually a blessing, but on occasion it was bothersome. I knew the scent of *copál* well, but this wasn't the usual *copál* from the mountain pines. It was something far sweeter and more penetrating; perhaps one of the burseras, such as the Old World frankincense. It was powerful. The walls of the room had raw wood shelves, on which candles were burning. Hanging from the shelves were small bundles of herbs tied with old cords. There were no windows, and only candlelight illuminated the room.

She motioned for me to sit at the simple wooden table in the center of the room. As I sat down, I could smell the rich odor of the cedar furniture mingling with the *copál* in the air. On the table were a candle, a crimson porcelain cup, and a stack of uncommonly large, worn cards. There were perhaps four-dozen of the big, thick cards, each measuring about 6 by 9 inches. They were so aged, the white on them had begun to turn yellow. She went to a dark corner of the room and quickly returned with a teapot, pouring me cup of strong herbal tea, instructing me to sip on it while I tell her the details of my recurring dream. The tea smelled wonderful and was quite delicious.

As I told my dream story and sipped the tea, she listened intently for a few minutes and then rose, telling me to continue talking. She took two large herb bundles from the shelves on the wall. As I continued describing my dream, she walked around me slowly, hitting the herb bundles softly against me, swatting my shoulders and back, the top of my head and my arms. The powerful aroma of the herbs mixed with the *copál* and cedar in the air around me. She occasionally asked a detailed question, like, "how wide is the river," "what does the jungle smell like to you," and "what do the scales of the snake look like?" She asked questions about the woman's voice, the length of her hair, and the color of her eyes. As I replied to her questions, she hummed softly. So softly, that at first I wasn't sure if it was an actual hum or some faint guttural murmur emanating from deep in her chest. But it was musical and I found myself focusing on it, and on the aromas, and the rhythmic whacking of the herbs on my body. The mixed sensations gradually began to merge into a single state of consciousness, and the flickering of the candles created a mesmerizing play of light in the otherwise dark room. I found myself drifting deeper into my dream description than I had ever done with anyone else, describing in great detail the sound of the river, the trees, the complex smells of the tropical flowers and ripe jungle fruits, and what feelings I had as I tried to cross the river to get to the beguiling dark-skinned woman. Her questions drew me deeper and deeper into the dream as I slipped into a trancelike state. I felt I had actually re-entered the dream and *La Señora* was now with me, watching me at the river's bank, walking into the water with me, listening to the lilting cadence of the beautiful woman's voice on the other bank. The old woman's murmuring took on the rhythm of the river's sound, and my mind was filled with the smells of the jungle and its moist organic soil.

I opened my eyes, feeling they had been closed for a very long time. She was sitting on the chair across the table from me, unmoving. How long had my eyes had been closed? Ten minutes? Thirty minutes? She held the cards in her hands and said, softly, "Sueñas con serpientes." Smiling at me, she spread the cards across the tabletop. She pulled three of them out at random and moved the others aside. She lined the three up in the middle of the table, and said to me, "Now I will tell you what the cards have to say about your dream." I felt wholly connected to the woman.

When she turned the first card over it was a faded painting of a large yellow sea conch. Green seaweed adorned the background. She said, "You are a man of the sea." She turned the second card over and it was an image of a mermaid-like creature, only a beautiful, dark skinned, black-haired Latina version of a mermaid. The old woman made a small noise, a little gasp, and sat silent for a few seconds before looking up at me and softly murmuring the words, *La Sirena Negra*. When she spoke, the candles in the room flickered strongly and I suddenly felt a bit queasy. I saw that the cards were palimpsests, with various annotations and tiny handwritten symbols on them. As she moved toward the third card I felt a chill, as though a cold hand had been laid on my shoulder. When she turned it over, it was another painting of a woman, but not a mermaid. It was a young woman with short flaxen hair, wearing a sleeveless peasant dress. The dress was devilishly short, revealing her calves and most of her thighs. On her right thigh was a remarkable, blood-red birthmark that resembled a Catalonian rose. On its darker stem were two leaves and what appeared to be a half-dozen sharp thorns. The old woman flinched, dropped the card face up on the table, and pushed her chair back. The candles flickered again, strongly, and the table shook. I could feel the floor move beneath me. The woman stared into my eyes with great intent.

"*Señor*, you must be cautious. There are two women in your life who cannot be trusted. You are beginning a journey into unknown waters, and you will encounter difficult seas. The dream is a warning to you. You will be called upon to face great challenges. The crossing of the river is only the beginning. But, be cautious with these women."

Then she stood abruptly and walked through the door to the living room where Bob sat reading a newspaper he'd brought along. It took me a while to gather my wits. I rose from the table and walked out to them. I asked the *Señora* how much I could pay her for sharing with me her insight and interpretation, but she shook her head and said, "Nothing, *Señor. Vaya con dios.*"

As we walked silently from the house to the car, I noticed there were bright yellow marigolds growing under the cedar trees in the yard. Standing among them was a shiny black grackle. When we walked by the grackle, it hopped away. It had only one foot.

As I tumbled into the passenger's seat, I must have had a glazed look in my eyes. We sat there for a minute and Bob said, "Dude, what's up with you? You look like you're stoned."

I turned my head slowly to look at him. "Maybe I am. Wow, that was unusual."

As Bob fired up the car, he said, "Well, like, give me the details."

"I don't think I can. It was all rather surrealistic. I'm wondering if *La Señora* slipped me a Mickey."

Bob replied, "Shamans, healers, and priests should be presumed guilty until proven innocent. Hey, did you feel that little tremor while you were in there with the old gypsy queen? *Volcán Concepción* must be restless tonight."

"Oh, that actually happened? Hey, sorry I was in there for so long. Thanks for waiting."

"Odel, you were only in there for about a half-hour. No prob."

"A half-hour!" Damn, it felt like an hour. Really?"

"You *are* in a state of altered consciousness aren't you!"

As we drove home in near silence, I tried to process what had just happened. By the time we arrived back home, I'd decided to just let it go, chalk it up to an interesting experience that had little significance beyond entertainment value.

7

Bahía Montelimar, Nicaragua

November 1981

I awoke the next morning clearheaded and full of energy, though I had expected just the opposite. I walked into Beatriz's wonderful kitchen—Saltillo tile floor, white walls with colorful Talavera tile accents around a large picture window looking into the courtyard garden, the smell of refried black beans and plantains cooking on the stove, a basket of warm rolls fresh out of the oven. The combination of fragrances, Beatriz's happy smile and shinning eyes, her colorful T-shirt and luxuriant braless bosom, and my anticipation of a trip to the coast all combined like an elixir to put me in a good mood. Bob strode into the kitchen and asked me how I was feeling.

"*Fantástico, Roberto.* Never felt better!"

The smile broadened on Beatriz's girlish face, and she remarked, "Roberto told me you must have had some kind of transcendental experience last night!"

"Well, I wouldn't call it *transcendental*—more like just a trance! I think that tea she gave me must have had some mind-expanding qualities to it. But I guess I did go into an altered state of consciousness. Gads, I don't even remember the woman's name!"

They both laughed out loud, and Bob said, "Does it matter? Probably no one knows the old bat's name! She reminded me of my high-school algebra teacher."

Beatriz replied quickly, "Do not make light of *La Señora*, my friends. And her name is Circe. Neither should you discount whatever it was she said to you. As I mentioned yesterday, she has a good reputation. People trust her. There are many things we did not know about for a very long time. Things unseen by the naked eye nor even imagined, such as gravity, radioactivity, and germs. It is possible that the woman is simply gifted, that she can sense things that most of us cannot."

Bob and I were silent, both of us reflecting on Beatriz's words. Bob spoke first. "I suppose you can go wrong by being too skeptical just as easily as by being too trusting." Bob had a curious way of reverse engineering ideas. For twenty years he had been a committed yogi, and his views of the world were often colored by those deep commitments. He frequently taught yoga classes on the university campus in Managua.

Beatriz went on. "There are many examples of yet unexplained phenomena. People who wake up from comas and discover they are fluent in a foreign language they had never been able to speak before. Savants, or autistics who can rapidly read thousands of books and remember extreme details of each, or who can read books one page with their right eye and the other with their left. Some savants, blind from birth, and at the age of just 14 have played a Tchaikovsky Piano Concerto from beginning to end flawlessly, having heard it just once. Science has so far been unable to explain how some people can do these things, but we know they exist. One must presume these unusual attributes have a genetic basis, and if so perhaps they speak to a shared human subconsciousness or human potential that science simply does not yet understand. Perhaps, each in their own way, these people are mystics."

Bob asked me, "What exactly did Circe tell you about your dreams?"

"Hmm, I don't think I'm ready to talk about it, actually. Maybe later. For now, I just need some of Beatriz's fine coffee and cooking, then I have to hit the road for the coast."

"OK, old buddy," Bob said, "let's eat, and we can talk when you get back from your collecting trip. But remember— the size of someone's reputation can have little to do with their credibility!"

"Roger that," I said.

After a filling breakfast that included two big helpings of fried plantains, I threw the last of my stuff into the university van and headed off to the coast. The highway took me northwest from Managua past many small, rural *estancias* to the beautiful twin cities of León and colonial León Viejo, the latter founded in 1524 by Francisco Hernández de Córdoba— as Santiago de los Caballeros de León. I remembered that Anastasio Somoza García (the Somoza family patriarch) was gunned down in León in 1956. From there I wandered down a rough dirt road to the coast at Salinas Grandes, a slow and halting drive among bicyclists, motorbikes, salt trucks, donkeys, goats, cows, cowboys on horses, and endless potholes. As the name suggests, great expanses of salt flats fill the view as one approaches the shoreline. Salt mining is the principal economy here. But on the seaward side of the salt flats there is a long and magnificent white sand spit with a pristine beach facing the Pacific Ocean and running for many miles. In the early 1980s this gorgeous "barrier island" had few visitors. But I wasn't there for the beach. I checked into a small cottage just twenty yards from the shoreline, *Posada la Playa*, and sorted out my gear. By late afternoon I was snorkeling offshore in search of my specimens.

Over the years, I had developed an effective method of collecting small crustaceans on offshore sand bottoms.

Swimming slowly, either with scuba or by snorkeling, I stirred the sediment with one hand, forcing the sand crabs, amphipods, isopods, shrimp, and other critters up off the bottom a few inches and into the water. With my other hand, I quickly swept a plankton net through the water to capture my suspended quarry. After a couple hours of this, I would have a sizable sample of the benthic crustacean fauna. Back on the beach, I would transfer the sample to plastic jars, and later in my hotel room, I would pickle them in alcohol. In the case of rocky sea bottoms, the protocol was similar, only I would pick up the rocks and shake them under water to dislodge my samples. Along with the crustaceans would be numerous other benthic invertebrates—various worms, brittle stars, small sea cucumbers, molluscs, and such—that I passed along to my colleagues.

Before sunset that day, I had a nice collection representing the sandy bottom fauna of the Salinas Grandes open coast. I knew from years of experience that about a quarter of the species in my collection would be new to science—unnamed and undescribed species of invertebrates. This was typical for understudied areas such as tropical coastlines in developing nations. I would describe and name many of those new species in the years to come, and I would give the noncrustaceans in my samples to specialists on other groups, and they would describe the new species from among them. One of the great joys of taxonomic research is this endless discovery of new forms, puzzling out what the creatures are and where they fit into the great schema of life on Earth. Writing and publishing the descriptions can become a bit tedious, but coming up with new names for them was always fun.

Over the following days, I worked my way up and down the coast collecting samples. I was able to get as far south as the mouth of the *Río Tamarindo*, where the surf was too treacherous for sampling and the estuary uncrossable. Departing this pristine sandy coast, I drove back to the

Managua highway and headed south, toward a turnoff for the small coastal fishing village of El Tránsito. From El Tránsito, I could work my way north, back up to the southern side of *Río Tamarindo* estuary. At El Tránsito, massive serpentine boulders tumbled into the sea like a petrified river, revealing a geological story of ancient cascading lava flows from an explosive Miocene volcanic world. The coastline there had good rocky shore collecting, and I managed to fill many more jars with specimens. From El Tránsito, I again headed south on the Managua highway for the Montelimar turnoff. Due to the popularity of this beach "resort" the highway was one of the better roads, with alternating patches of asphalt and well-graded dirt.

But rather than driving straight to Montelimar, I first drove north to the remote San Luís area where I knew I could find some more good rocky outcrops along the coast, sea-battered cliffs and wave-carved sedimentary intertidal benches. I spent two days there, sleeping in the van because the area was so isolated there were no facilities. The only other car I saw on the coast the entire time I was there was one of the ubiquitous Mexico-produced Volkswagen Beetles, parked about a half-mile up the coast. The enormous VW assembly plant in the city of Puebla had been flooding Mexico and Central America with Beetles since the 60s. Thus, by the time I worked my way south to Montelimar, I was ready for a decent room, a hot shower, and real food. I already had a crate full of excellent samples, so I was in a celebratory mood.

Arriving just before sunset, I headed for the nicest place in town, which had been recommended by Bob and Beatriz, and checked in. The *Hotel Vista del Mar* was inexpensive by gringo standards. It had a nice restaurant and a terrific bar. Managuans who could afford to get away for a holiday at the beach frequented the hotel's *Bar Vista* for its fine ambience, regardless of where they stayed in Montelimar. Their specialty was, of course, rum drinks: *Ron con Coco*, *Ron y Pernod*, daiquiri, mai tai, hurricane, *Cuba Libre*, and so forth.

I was ravenous, so I cleaned up and headed straight for the restaurant. With a couple of ice-cold Toña beers, fresh fish, and *tostones*, I relaxed and congratulated myself on a so-far successful collecting trip.

After dinner, I walked straight to the bar and ordered a double shot of *Flor de Caña* over ice. It has long been my opinion that *Flor de Caña* is the best rum made—comparable to the finest Scotch or Bourbon whiskeys. It's a sipping rum, and I intended to sip some that night. I took one of the small round tables on the veranda, overlooking the shallow bay. The only competition for the silence of the night sky was the gentle sound of small waves lapping on the shore.

Coastlines can be perplexing. Some, like the *Río Tamarindo* estuary, seem to draw the waves and have rough water and beaches littered with flotsam and jetsam from distant lands. Others, like the small *ensenada* where Montelimar sat, are calm places where the waves are gentle and rhythmic, sailboats drop anchor, and beach bars spring up. Looking out over the peaceful water in front of me, it seemed like a million stars were reflected on the calm, silver-black surface of the bay. Tomorrow morning I would catch up with my field notes, in which I had taken special care to sketch the areas I'd sampled so far. I would also make careful sketches of the little bay of Montelimar.

There weren't many people in the bar, and the only other table on the patio with guests was occupied by a distinguished looking couple that, from the sound of their proper Spanish, might have been from Costa Rica, or perhaps Spain. The only lighting on the patio was from the small table lamps, and there was no moon in the sky. I could see lights on some of private boats bobbing gently in the bay. They were lined up more or less in two parallel rows, suggesting that the deepest channel into the bay ran between them. The shoreline was a long, graceful stretch of sand ending at a small rocky point in the south. It was that southernmost thrust of ancient bedrock granite that interrupted the force of the large Pacific swells coming in from the southwest and gave protection to Bahía Montelimar.

Just as I finished my second glass of *Flor de Caña,* a glimmer of movement behind me caught my attention. When I turned my head to look, I saw an arrestingly gorgeous woman entering the patio. She was thin and wore a white gown that undulated in the light breeze blowing off the sea. The fabric seemed as delicate as tissue paper. Her long black hair fell across her shoulders and hung to the middle of her back. She was slightly on the tall side, around five foot eight, and walked gracefully, like a dancer. She had a small purse slung over her shoulder and held a glass of rum in her hand. As she passed my table, she turned to look at me. *"¿Es un patio precioso, no?"*

When I looked into her eyes, they seemed hardwired into mine. Her irises were dark sepia flecked with gold, deep as wells, large and captivating, and they seemed to expand and contract as she spoke. Her hair glistened in the light from the table lamp. I found myself nearly tongue-tied, struggling to reply, *"Sí, es tan tranquilo, como el mar."*

She responded in English, "I can tell by your accent that you are an American. I don't see many Americans in Nicaragua these days."

Mustering my courage, I said, "Yes, I am a *Norteamericano.* Would you care to join me? I have the best table on the patio, and I would be happy to share it with you."

Her voice was like honey. *"Muchas gracias, Norte-americano,* I would be delighted. And with whom might I be sharing this perfect table?"

"My name is Odel, and I'm very pleased to meet you, Ms. . . . .?"

"I am Coquette. Like the bird."

I knew the bird. The Black-crested Coquette is a tiny, rare Central American hummingbird, just a couple of inches long, that few people have ever seen. It is striking in its coloration, having an emerald back, copper-spotted belly, and broad white band across its rump. But its most exotic feature is a cluster of long black plumes that rise from the top of its head to stream over the back of the bird like exquisite silk ribbons when it is in flight. *Like the silky flow of this woman's long black hair*, I thought. I'd searched for the bird several times but had not yet seen one. But I knew the other meaning of the name as well, and this beautiful woman seemed also to be *coqueteando*.

"Really? What an interesting name."

"Yes, so I've been told. But I suppose you would have to speak with my parents to get the details. What brings you to Nicaragua, Mr. Odel?"

"It's Bernini—Odel Bernini. Like the sculptor. I'm a marine biologist working on a project in several Central American countries. I also have friends in Managua. And I love the country and its people and its culture. And how about you, Coquette? Where are you from, and what brings you to this remote and beautiful place?"

"I, too, am fond of Nicaragua." She hiked her dress up just above her knees, revealing perfect bronze calves. "It is so warm tonight, isn't it? I am not here to work. Only to relax on vacation."

I forced myself not to stare at her legs, my eyes moving back up to her bewitching face, which was illuminated against the darkness by our lone table light. I realized she was somewhat dark-skinned, no doubt with some measure of African blood in her veins. Her beautiful and slightly oversized eyes danced above high cheekbones, and her face was perfectly symmetrical. She wore no makeup—and didn't need to. She seemed as succulent as a sea slug, *à natural*. My gaze fell to the outline of her breasts, visible through the voile of her dress, and then continued to her narrow waist, only to be ensnared again by her elegant calves, thin ankles, and sandals so delicate I thought for a second she was barefoot. Realizing how my mind—and gaze—had drifted, I quickly snapped my eyes back to hers.

She told me she was a freelance writer from the States, specializing in Latin America. We chatted about her writing, which she assured me I never would have seen because it was mostly boring little pieces for various government agencies. We talked about my own work. And we talked about Nicaragua, the revolution, the Somoza family, the Chamorro family, and the future of the country. We talked about how we both loved the tropics and gentle seas and good rum. And we drank many glasses of *Flor de Caña*. I sensed her elegant body was poised for escape from the simple cotton dress that covered it . . . but perhaps it was just the rum sloshing around in my head. However, by eleven o'clock I was tired and torn between having another drink with the beautiful and charming Coquette, or excusing myself to hit the sack. She sensed my fatigue and said, "I can tell you have had a long day, Odel. You must be tired. Forgive me for talking your ear off." She stood politely and bent over to retrieve her handbag from the floor. As she did, one of the straps of her dress fell from her shoulder and the bodice buckled just enough to reveal her stunning breasts, slightly pendulous, hanging sweetly, satiny bronze like her calves, and with very dark and tantalizingly erect nipples.

Coquette stood up, held my eyes for an instant, and then spoke in an easy melodious tone. "I hope we have a chance to see more of one another. You are an interesting man, and I find your work fascinating. I don't mean to sound bold. I am simply the kind of woman who speaks her mind."

I wasn't sure my own mind was even working at that point. I literally heard myself thinking, *this is the most attractive and seductive woman I have ever met*, so clearly, I was afraid I might be speaking out loud. But she stood patiently waiting. She could have easily charmed the pants off me with a few more flutters of her eyelashes. It wasn't just her peerless physical assets. She was also bright and had a soulful way about her. I detected depth in her personality. And her lyrical lilting voice was utterly intoxicating—like nothing else I'd ever heard. And she certainly wasn't lacking in temerity. I instantly wanted to trust her, yet I sensed something was hidden in her. But I felt certain I wanted to explore the hidden side of this beautiful, irresistible woman with the unusual name.

"Tomorrow I need to work—mostly snorkeling and collecting specimens from the bay. But perhaps we could meet here for dinner, say eight o'clock?"

"That would be lovely, Odel. I look forward to seeing you tomorrow then." As I watched her walk purposefully away from me, I knew I wasn't thinking straight. My thoughts shifted to Penelope; I'd never been unfaithful to her—but I decided to tuck that notion away and deal with it later. Right now, I thought, I would go to bed and sleep like the dead, and as I fell asleep, I would imagine Coquette undressing in front of me—which would, I realized, amount to no more than kicking off her sandals and letting her dress fall to the floor.

As I drifted into sleep with Coquette radiant in my mind, I had the feeling there was something deeply familiar about her.

8

Coquette

I woke just before sunrise, collected my gear, ate two granola bars, and walked straight to the beach. I had a lot to accomplish, but I was sure I could survey the bay in five or six hours. I didn't expect much in the way of benthic life because this area had been so disturbed for many decades. Besides the sewage and other waste flowing into the bay from the shore establishments, both sport and commercial fishing pressure was high, and locals had probably used the bay for hundreds, perhaps even thousands of years for subsistence fishing. The bay is heavily harvested for shellfish, and thousands of clams from Montelimar end up in Managua restaurants every year. Boat traffic pollutes the water with fuel and junk tossed overboard. Though I didn't expect to collect many crustaceans, I wanted to swim a few transects across the bay to render a rough sketch of its bottom contours in my field notebook. The bay is so small it hardly shows up on maps; it wasn't even labeled on the U.S. government hydrographic charts I'd examined in Seattle, even though those are the main maps used by mariners and by the U.S. Navy.

I stood on the sand as the morning sunlight turned the sky from purple to red and small waves lapped at my feet. I'd worked for so many years on these New World tropical shores that the moment had a familiar and comfortable feel to it. Pacific beaches have a magical sultry glow in the morning, when the relative humidity hasn't yet risen to an uncomfortable level. The deeply familiar smell of seaweeds, especially *Sargassum*, fills the air with a seductive sweetness as pungent as a lusty woman's armpits. I could feel the coral sand between my toes, tactile evidence of an offshore coral reef not far away—though not, I was certain, in this particular bay. The water was so calm that the boats anchored offshore barely moved. I was exhilarated for several reasons.

I strapped the depth gauge onto my wrist and adjusted my mask and snorkel for a good fit. My plan was to swim parallel to shore, back and forth across the bay three or four times until I'd gotten about half a mile from the beach. I expected the deepest channel to run right down the center of the bay between the two roughly aligned rows of small private sailboats and local fishing skiffs. This would give me enough information to accurately sketch the bay and also to decide if it had enough biological diversity to return the next day for a more serious sampling effort. But, most importantly, as my priorities had shifted, it should get me back to my hotel room in time to write up my notes, shower, and meet Coquette for dinner.

As I began swimming, thoughts of Penelope swept over me. Could I be unfaithful to her? If so, would I tell her? And if I did tell her, how much detail would I provide? How much detail would she want to hear? We had never really discussed the issue of fidelity. But I wasn't willing to put our relationship at risk for a fling with a stranger in Nicaragua. But god, how I was drawn to Coquette! Something about the woman struck a deep chord in me. Her intoxicating voice and exquisite body; her self-confidence and poise. And when I looked into her eyes, it was electrifying.

I swam slowly but deliberately, pacing myself. My body felt good, strong—as if I could swim all day. The bay was shallow and lacked the larger fishes such as groupers and snappers that frequent steeper beach slopes. I saw no rocky outcrops or coral anywhere. There were the ubiquitous schools of small surface-feeding fishes, needlefish and halfbeaks, and a few small barracuda.

I dived to the bottom to grab a handful of sand. Just a few inches beneath the surface, the sediment was black. Iron sulfide. It appeared the bay might be anoxic beneath the surface, depleted of oxygen, eliminating all but a few of the most specialized invertebrates and almost all the crustaceans. Black sediments like these are typical of eutrophic environments, places that receive too many nutrients, typically from anthropogenic sources. In the case of Bahía Montelimar, these nutrients entered the bay from sewage and other human activities. The nutrients cause excessive growth of plants, seaweeds, and phytoplankton, which, upon death, create enormous amounts of decaying organic matter on the bottom sediment. The large populations of bacteria and other microorganisms that consume this mass of decaying material suck all the oxygen from the water, rendering it nearly uninhabitable. Eventually there is no longer enough oxygen left even for the regular bacteria to survive—a kind of ecological mass suicide takes place—and then the whole food chain switches over from species that use oxygen-based metabolism to bizarre species that rely on sulfur-based metabolism. Sulfur-consuming bacteria produce iron sulfides as a byproduct. It is this ferric sulfide that coats the sand grains with black. Black sediments are a sure sign of greatly reduced biological diversity because few species can survive without abundant oxygen. If I found this condition throughout the bay, there would be little point in making a concerted sampling effort.

As I swam transects parallel to the beach, I recorded notes on a dive slate—distance from shore, depth, condition of the seafloor, and so on. I found what I expected. The bay was shallow, no more than 10 to 15 feet throughout. But running perpendicular to the shore between the two lines of small boats was a channel 20 to 30 feet deep. The locals and other mariners knew of the channel or deduced it in the same way I had, and they sailed or motored their vessels into the bay by way of this deeper rift. The channel was caused by seaward flow of a bottom current, returning water brought to the shore by waves and tides. It was standard stuff—Oceanography 101.

By early afternoon I had all the data I needed. Back on shore, tired but still feeling invigorated, I returned to my room at the *Hotel Vista del Mar*. I showered, had a snack in the restaurant, and sat down to compile the data I'd collected into a set of detailed notes and an accurate sketch of the bay's topography. It took about an hour. I had time for a short nap and decided to go for it. As I drifted off to sleep, visions of Coquette played in my mind. I'd learned quite a bit about her likes and dislikes, her broad enthusiasm for life and for Latin America, and that she seemed to be a free spirit. But I still didn't know much about her personal life. Was she married? Where did she live in the States? I realized none of that was important to me at that moment. Her alluring personality, dark-honey body, lustrous voice, and dramatic, penetrating eyes had me in a spell. Was she a woman, or a sylph? She seemed both. I just wanted to be with her. In every way imaginable.

I put on the last clean clothes I had in my duffel bag and walked to the *Bar Vista*. She was already there, sitting at a small private table in a corner, looking out the window over the dark calm bay, a glass of rum in her hand. She seemed like a dream. Sensing my presence, she turned her head toward me. I could feel energy exchanging between us. She stood as I approached. Again she wore only sandals and a thin cotton dress, pale blue this time, but the light of the setting sun gave it a glow like polished jade. As she stood, the dress fell over her like a diaphanous emerald shadow. I could see every curve of her torso. Her hair was up, exposing her slender neck, the course of tendons and veins visible beneath her amber flesh. The thinnest of shoulder straps revealed the supple muscles of her shoulders and her delicate collarbones. The extraordinary gold flecks sprinkled through her eyes seemed to dance, as her smile summoned me. I gave her a peck on each cheek, appropriate by Nicaraguan standards, drank in the exquisite bouquet of her hair and flesh with a trace of floral cologne, and sat down across the table from her. The bartender appeared with a glass of *Flor de Caña* on ice for me, clearly the consequence of an earlier conversation between he and Coquette.

As we chatted, I was compelled to let her know that I was married. I didn't elaborate. She didn't reciprocate, so I didn't ask. Instead, she said, "Odel, I believe that the more one loves, the more capable one becomes at love. I also believe that a grounded and self-confident person is rarely capable of jealousy. Such people have no need for jealousy. Furthermore, I believe the only sins we commit are hurting other people unnecessarily. All other 'sins' are just human inventions, mostly of churches and frauds." She never took her eyes off mine as she spoke.

Having put that rather comprehensive bit of personal philosophy on the table seemed to me an open invitation to join her in Valhalla. At least for the evening. I met her elegance with a lame reply: "*La vida es corta. Tome grandes bocados.*" She responded with the sweetest of smiles.

I suggested we order dinner, suddenly thinking to myself that I didn't want to sit in the restaurant all night. I ordered the "daily catch," *pescado al mojo de ajo*, and Coquette ordered *pulpo marinaro*. After dinner we returned to the bar for a bit more rum. She asked me many questions about my excursion that day. But after about forty-five minutes she said, "Odel, would you like to walk with me? The *cabaña* I am staying in is just down the beach."

"That would be delightful, Coquette. Lead the way." I felt my heart begin to race.

As we strolled down the *playa*, beneath a cloudless sky bursting with a glittering starscape, she took my hand and squeezed it. I could feel the strength in her forearm. Coquette may have been slim, but she was strong—workout strong. Halfway to her bungalow, she stopped and looked at me, inviting a kiss. When I slipped my arm around her, I could feel the ridges of her shoulder blades and the muscles of her back. For a split second I imagined her lifting weights, perspiring. We kissed only briefly, brushing our lips and tongues lightly. It was electric, and it sent waves of pleasure through my brain. Her scent had traces of plumeria, and the mix of aromas wafting up from her now slightly-sweaty body was galvanizing. I could not resist this woman, no matter what.

Her *cabaña* was right on the beach, parked behind it was a faded blue Volkswagen Beetle. As I watched her step up on the small veranda, I saw her calf muscles tighten, and I ached to run my hands along her strong, shapely legs. Again I felt as if I were in a dream, disconnected from reality, not sure what reality even was at the moment. I followed her as she stepped through the door and into her cottage. The beach house was simple, with a double bed under a slowly rotating fan, two comfortable looking rattan chairs, and a small table. I paused in the doorway, holding on to it and feeling like the ground was shifting beneath me. Coquette walked to the other side of the bed and stood, looking at me. She undid something in her hair, and it fell down her back and over one shoulder in big, flowing waves like a silk waterfall. Behind her the screened window was open, and through it I could see and smell the green of the coastal jungle foliage. She was captivating, and at that moment I would have followed her anywhere. From across the bed she stared at me in the doorway, and her eyes locked onto mine. Raising one arm toward me, her slender fingers unfurling one at a time, she said, "Odel, come to me."

Her gesture, and the sound of her voice saying those words, hit me like a steamroller. I felt like my brain was suddenly being rewired. Instantly I was back in my recurring dream. Behind Coquette was the tropical forest, and in front of her the bed had become a rushing stream. My feet were in the stream, sluggish. The distance between us suddenly seemed a labyrinth, a tangled web of uncertainty and confusion. My knees grew weak, and I felt like I might collapse.

For a few minutes there was only silence. Finally her gold-flecked eyes fluttered, bringing me back to the moment, and I said, "Coquette, I'm sorry, but I think I must return to my room. I'm feeling . . . odd."

"Oh, I'm sorry. I know you've had a long day, and perhaps the drinks are making you drowsy? But, Odel, I am leaving for Managua in the morning. I hate the thought of not seeing you again."

So many conflicting feelings were cascading through me, I couldn't embrace any particular one. Coquette walked to the table, reached into her purse, and pulled out a card. She glided toward me like *Sargassum* floating on a gentle ocean swell, handed me the card, and said, "You look terribly tired, dear friend. Why don't you go back to your room and get a good night's sleep? Here is my phone number in the States. When you are back home, please consider giving me a call. Perhaps we could see each other again."

I didn't look at the card. All I could do was stare into her eyes; the sweet scents rising from her moist body were intoxicating. I ached to take her in my arms, throw her on the bed, ravish her. At the same time, some core fiber in my consciousness was telling me to get away from this woman, fast.

"Yes, I'm . . . sorry. I'll call you. I must—I want to see you again. Things just aren't right at the moment."

She spoke softly, and her voice was alluring music. *"Siento en mi alma que debo verte de nuevo. Y sé que te sientes de la misma."*

I stumbled down the steps to the beach and walked back to my hotel, my mind swirling. Falling into a chair in my room, I thought, *what just happened there?* I was still holding the card she had given me in my hand. I looked at it. It was a simple white card with nothing but her name and a phone number on it.

9

Return to Seattle

November 1981

The next morning, I arose tired and disoriented. Although I'd not had the dream, my sleep had been fitful. I showered, threw on some clothes, and went to the restaurant for coffee. After the third cup, I made up my mind. I had to see Coquette again. I left some cash on the table and ran out of the café. Walking quickly down the beach toward her *cabaña*, I could see from a distance that she'd already checked out. The door stood open and a cleaning woman's paraphernalia sat on the deck. As I walked back to the hotel, my thoughts swirled. I realized that all I had was a name and phone number on a business card. Coquette Pallas, at a 213 area code—Los Angeles. I had work to do and knew I had to press on. I didn't feel especially clear-headed about it all, but I tucked her card safely away in my wallet.

Driving away from Montelimar, I couldn't shake Coquette from my mind. I knew I would look her up once I was back in the States. Staring at the road map, I made a decision to cut my work short by five or six days. I would drive down to the Rivas coast and collect in the Playa Gavilán and Playa Maderas areas, and then I would head back to Managua. I'd forgo the long drive south all the way to the Escameca–La

Flor region near the border with Costa Rica. I remembered the Rivas Highway being spectacular, threading along the narrow isthmus that separates Lake Nicaragua from the Pacific Ocean. The great volcanoes of *Concepción* and *Maderas* rise side by side to the east above the lake, and the far sweep of the Pacific stretches to the horizon in the west. I looked forward to the Rivas drive, thinking it would give me some peaceful time in a beautiful landscape and help clear my head after the whirlwind of the past forty-eight hours. I recalled that Violeta Barrios Torres, destined to marry Joaquín Chamorro and rise to international prominence, was born and raised in the cattle country of the Rivas Department.

I performed my collecting work expeditiously, and as the days went by my unease began to lift—though not entirely. I wondered if I should visit the *curandera* again. But what would I ask her? Was I beginning to take her seriously? *Damn, get it together, Odel,* I thought. *Just some unusual coincidences and a beautiful but somewhat mysterious woman, that's all.*

I got back to Bob and Beatriz's house five days before they expected me, but it wasn't a problem. They are so good-natured that they take most everything in stride. And they had two big pieces of news for me. Penelope had called to let me know that my *Field Guide to the Marine Invertebrates of the Caribbean* had finally been published after nearly a year in press. By the time my PhD dissertation was completed, I'd realized that, with just a bit more effort, I could expand it into a field guide. My field notebooks tended to be detailed, including lists and comments on all the spineless creatures I found while collecting crustaceans for my research. At the end of my third year at the museum, I'd submitted a manuscript to the publishing house at the American Museum of Natural History, and it had been accepted. Writing had always come naturally to me, and I thought such a guidebook might be popular with the vacationing tourists and divers that flocked to the Caribbean.

The second bit of news was quite different. Penelope had told them that the executive director of the Seattle Museum of Natural History, and the museum's chief financial officer, had both been fired—for embezzlement! The two had apparently cooked up a clever scheme to skim much of the overhead off government grants coming to the museum, moving it into their own discretionary accounts and spending it on personal expenses. They'd gotten away with it for nearly four years. The museum's board of trustees was in a tizzy and a full accounting had yet to be made. The scam was discovered by a new accounting firm the trustees had hired to handle the annual tax audit. Penelope thought that the director of human resources, Audrey Arente, would be appointed acting executive director while the search for a new permanent director was launched.

Those jerks, I thought. But I was happy to hear that the trustees might turn things over to Audrey. She was smart, level-headed, and as honest as the day is long—the kind of person my dad would have called a "real steady Eddie." Audrey was about twenty years older than me, bright, attractive, and in good physical shape. We had struck up an early friendship when I joined the museum's research staff. We thought alike, had good chemistry, and were attracted to one another. We had lunch together every couple weeks, and after a year or two she opened up about her marriage a bit. It didn't sound good, and I had a suspicion that her husband might be psychologically abusive toward her, although I never brought it up in our conversations. Mostly she just wanted someone to talk to and to give her a bit of emotional support and positive reinforcement.

That night, Bob and Beatriz and I celebrated my successful, if somewhat abbreviated, collecting trip, and my first book hitting bookstore shelves. Because I was still trying to process everything that had happened in Montelimar, I decided not to mention meeting Coquette.

Bob and Beatriz were excited about what was happening in Managua. "The new Sandinista junta is expanding education and health care so rapidly in the country—every day there's news of a new program or a new clinic opening in the rural areas," Bob said. "It's really heartening. The university's budget has even been increased, and there's talk of opening one or two branch campuses. And in a few years we'll have the first-ever free and open elections in Nicaragua."

Turning to look at me, Beatriz replied, "And meanwhile, your new president, Mr. Hollywood Cowboy, continues to resist our freedom movement and demonize Daniel Ortega, calling him a *comunista*. And I read an editorial by Violeta Chamorro in *La Prensa* yesterday that claimed Reagan is secretly planning another invasion of our country!"

I knew that Violeta Chamorro was a national hero and a force in Nicaragua. She had taken over the Chamorro family newspaper, *La Prensa*, when her husband Pedro Joaquín Chamorro was assassinated in 1978, continuing his policy of criticizing the Somoza regime. Violeta was by Daniel Ortega's side when the Sandinistas marched into Managua in July 1979. She became a member of the coalition Junta of National Reconstruction that replaced Somoza, along with Ortega and three others representing various national parties. However, not long after establishment of the junta, the Sandinista faction, with its Cuban-Marxist roots, began taking over television and radio stations and censoring newspapers. Although the junta announced a nonalignment policy and continued discussions on diplomatic, economic, and military relationships with the United States, they also developed strong ties with Cuba and the Soviets.

I asked Bob and Beatriz if there was truth to the rumor that the Sandinistas had signed formal accords with the Soviets.

Beatriz replied, "Yes, it is true. They are based on a belief in socialism and sharing the wealth of our nation with the people—an idea the oligarchs despise."

Bob dryly added, "The deal with the Soviets is mainly about a need for financial aid and petroleum."

Beatriz said, "We have read many articles in *La Prensa* about Reagan giving the CIA a go-ahead to start meddling in our homeland again. Out of one side of his mouth he boasts of defending democracy around the world, and out of the other side he works to undermine democracy and support dictatorships."

I replied, "I've heard that it was the partnership between the Sandinistas and the Soviets that led to Violeta Chamorro's resignation from the ruling junta last April. And that her exit has prompted other members of the junta also to resign."

"That's correct," said Bob. "Chamorro's returned to her role as editor of *La Prensa*. I have a feeling the newspaper will soon become quite critical of Daniel Ortega."

"She must be a powerful person in Nicaragua," I said.

"She's an educated, strong, intelligent woman who's become a symbol of free speech and women's rights," Bob continued, "not just here but throughout Latin America. She was born with a fire in her belly, to seek truth and what's best for her country. Even though she was raised in an upper-class family, she's become a hero to the poor and middle class of Nicaragua. And she isn't afraid of anyone. The killing of her husband by the Somoza regime in 1978 was one of the big events that pushed the Sandinista Revolution forward."

Beatriz said, "The Chamorro family has always been influential in Nicaragua. Many of the family members have been involved in public life in one way or another, but most of them have been on the conservative side of things. The Sandinista Revolution truly divided the family loyalties. But now I don't think Violeta trusts the Sandinistas *or* the Nicaraguan oligarchy."

"Nor does she trust the Americans," Bob added. "But, the whole world is watching Nicaragua closely now. There's no way Reagan will be able to cause us much trouble and get away with it."

"Roberto," Beatriz replied, "for over a hundred years the United States has forced Nicaragua into an unwanted, illegitimate, intimate relationship—what has amounted to political rape. The United States has done this throughout Latin America, though nowhere has the rape lasted so long as in Nicaragua. Your home country is a pathological serial rapist!" Turning to look at me, she finished her thought, "Do you really think they will not continue to try to do so?"

"I don't know, Beatriz, but I tend to agree with Bob. There are so many eyes on Nicaragua these days; I think it would be hard for Reagan to get away with anything. And your country has so much momentum now. Everywhere I traveled on the coast, people are excited and optimistic about the 'new Nicaragua' that's being built."

"Yes, just as it was when the great socialist, Salvador Allende, was elected president in Chile a decade ago. He only lasted three years before the U.S. government and CIA staged a coup d'état that put Augusto Pinochet into office—a ruthless dictator who tortures and murders Chilean civilians the same way Somoza did here in Nicaragua. The U.S. cannot be trusted."

Bob mumbled, "Just as it always was, and will be forever-more."

Beatriz and I looked at him curiously, but he maintained his deadpan face.

"Odel," she replied, "you are sweet, but I think you may be a bit naive. Before you think you can understand Nicaragua, you need to have a better understanding of the history of your own imperialist country."

Of course, Beatriz was right about the U.S. government's long-standing abuse of power in Latin America. I loved the woman's intellect and passion, and I valued her straight-talking, clearheaded analysis of things.

"History is simply a version of the past that a bunch of people have agreed on," Bob said, "in that sense, it differs little from legend."

Beatriz replied, "But there *is* a true history, Roberto, and it behooves us to seek that out, and to understand it. I am simply appealing to Odel's scientific nature."

Bob responded, "Remember the words of William Faulkner—the past is never dead; it's not even past."

And so our conversation went, until late into the evening, none of us realizing that the decades-long U.S. oppression of Nicaragua would end up extending well into the twenty-first century.

I spent the next day transferring my specimens from jars to plastic Whirl-Pak bags. Because the samples were saturated with alcohol, I could drain all the liquid from the bags and the specimens would stay preserved for several months. Doing so reduced the volume and weight substantially. I closed each Whirl-Pak tightly, sealing it with electrical tape for extra assurance. Using this procedure, I managed to get the material down to a fairly small volume. This I would pack into two shipping boxes, and Bob would have the university send them to me at my museum in Seattle. There, the specimens would go back into jars with fresh alcohol and proper labels, and the jars placed on sorting shelves. Over the coming months, my trained students from Northwestern Washington University would go through each jar, sorting the specimens under stereo-microscopes, which would result in many smaller jars and vials filled with the various groups—crabs, shrimps, isopods, and so on. These I would examine one by one, putting identifications on the known species, and preparing manuscripts that would name and describe the species that were new to science. I expected many new species, and this was part of the thrill of the work. I had already decided to name a couple of the colorful new shrimp species after Bob and Beatriz. The name Beatriz means, "one who brings joy to others"—perfectly appropriate for her personality. I would find a suitable Latin suffix to attach to her given name to honor her.

I cleaned up my field notebook, double-checking everything I'd entered about Montelimar to be sure it was correct. If the CIA did want to see these rather paltry notes, I at least wanted them to be accurate and presentable. But the CIA nonsense was the last thing on my mind. My thoughts continued to drift back to Coquette. Who *was* this woman, and why did I find her so irresistible? My thoughts also drifted to Penelope.

I'd been able to change my flight to the following day. That night would be a quiet dinner with Bob and Beatriz, early to bed, and off in the morning for Seattle. I didn't bother calling Penelope, thinking it would be fun to surprise her. My flight from Dallas–Fort Worth to Seattle's Sea-Tac Airport was scheduled to arrive at nine that night, so by the time I got home, she would likely be having an after-supper whiskey and watching television or grading papers. I missed her. It would be a great homecoming.

My last night in Managua was pleasant, with more rum and talk about biology and the state of things at the National University. Bob and Beatriz asked me a lot of questions about the Seattle Museum of Natural History. I told them that, like most natural history museums, it always seemed to be in a precarious financial position, and that in recent years it had come to rely more and more on the overhead from government grants, and from contributions by our major donors. The budget was around $10 million annually, but only half of that came from the city and county; the rest we had to raise somehow. We had a small endowment, about $5 million, but that generated an average of only a couple hundred thousand dollars annually—enough to cover only a few salaries. If there had truly been embezzlement of funds, it could have seriously been hurting our operations without any of the staff even being aware of it yet. Sweet Bob and Beatriz both encouraged me to consider a job at their university if things all went to hell at the museum. They assured me that, with my scientific reputation, my new book being published, and their influence, they could almost guarantee me a professorship. I thanked them profusely. "You two are very kind, and I would love to live in Managua and work with you at the university. But it's unlikely to come to that."

"Well," Bob replied, "things look different depending on where you're standing. See what you think after you've been back in Seattle for six months or a year."

One of the things I loved about these two was that they were straight shooters. I think they felt that way about me too. If they said they could get me a professorship at their university, they meant it, and they probably could. Beatriz asked me a lot of questions about my book and my flair for writing. For her, writing was the most difficult aspect of being a scientist. For me, writing was relaxing, almost therapeutic.

"What will the next book be on, Odel?" she asked.

"I have no idea, Beatriz. But I do know that one day I'd like to try my hand at writing something other than biology. Stretch myself intellectually, or at least creatively, just to see what happens."

"Oh, you should, you should. You have traveled so much and have had so many adventures, you should write about your own life. You have already visited so much of the world, and you are still so young! Write about some of those crazy scuba diving stories you've told us, on the Great Barrier Reef and other places. Write something about Central America. Maybe a naive gringo who loses his way in Nicaragua!"

"Thanks, Beatriz, but I doubt anyone else would find my life interesting." However, the idea lingered with me.

"Odel," Bob said, "why don't you give a seminar at our university here? You already know a lot of our biology profs, but it wouldn't be a bad idea to get you in front of some key administrators. Dazzle them, schmooze a little bit with our department chair and dean."

"Sure," I replied. "Any time."

The next morning went smoothly. Bob took me to the airport in the university van and then drove on to work. The Aeronica flight took me direct to Mexico City, with a quick transfer to the Dallas–Fort Worth flight and another quick transfer to my Seattle flight on Pan Am. My bags arrived safely at Sea-Tac, and I walked straight to the taxi stand. I expected to be home and in Penelope's arms no later than ten.

When the taxi dropped me off with my luggage I didn't see Penelope's car, and most of the lights were out in the house. The porch light, however, was on. *Maybe the car's in the garage and she went to bed early,* I thought. When I got to the front door, I saw a piece of folded lined notebook paper stuck to the wood with a thumbtack. I pulled the paper down and looked at it. The writing was in pencil—a scrawl, written quickly. It read,

I told you that if you ever saw M again it would be over for us. So now it is. S—

I read the note several times, trying to make sense of it. That queer feeling of my brain being rewired came back to me, and again I felt the ground was somehow shifting under me.

I took my suitcases into the house and sat them on the living room floor. Penelope wasn't home, and there were no signs that she had cooked dinner. I folded the note and put it in my shirt pocket, poured myself a triple shot of rum, and sat down at the dining room table to think. But . . . think about what? The note made no sense to me.

PART II. CROSSING THE RIVER

Everything comes to us that belongs to us
if we create the capacity to receive it.

Rabindranath Tagore, *Sadhana* (1916)

10

An Offer from the CIA

Winter 1981–Spring 1982

I heard Penelope's car pull into the driveway about 10:30.
She sat in the car for an unusually long time. It occurred to
me that she might be wondering if there was a prowler in the
house, since the lights were on and she wasn't expecting me
home for another five or six days. I opened the front door and
stepped out, waving at her. She jumped out of her car and
looked at me with a mix of joy and surprise. Running up the
steps, she leaped into my arms, squeezing me tightly. And
when she planted her big super-Penelope kiss on me, I melted,
and the rest of the world went away. I told her that my work
had gone smoothly, I'd finished early, and saw no point in
hanging out in Managua when my beautiful wife was in
Seattle. She explained that she'd been out to dinner and
drinks with her friend Marjorie. As we walked into the house,
I noticed the dark pinhole in the door where the tack holding
the cryptic message had been stuck.

Penelope said she needed a few minutes "in the powder
room," so I sat back down and sipped my rum. When she

reappeared, after more than a few minutes, she was wearing one of her long, flowing black nightgowns that had slits up both sides to her hips. She was such a beauty and knew just how to drive me wild. She smelled of fresh rose talc—a scent we both loved. I could also smell the familiar scent of her lust; the herbal aroma that floated like the breath of freshly-cut flowers from her body when she was aroused. She poured herself a Jack Daniels, and as her bare foot moved up and down on my leg we chatted quietly. Her toenails were perfectly painted with the bright red color I found so appealing. We didn't chat for long, and soon rushed off to the bedroom. Penelope was supercharged. So was I. And when she reached her apogee, I wouldn't let her go, holding her there for O after O, moan after moan, swoons, laughs, grins, and sighs. I held her there until she begged me to stop so she could catch her breath, and her final crescendo reaffirmed the vision of Saint Teresa's Ecstasy. Eventually we collapsed together as one and loving, naughty words were mumbled between us as we drifted into deep and peaceful sleep.

I'd forgotten all about the strange note on the door until I picked my shirt up off the floor in the morning to put it in the laundry hamper. I felt the paper in my shirt pocket, remembered what it was, and pulled it out to reread it. Something vague in my mind—perhaps a premonition—said it would be best to hold off bringing it up with Penelope right away. I refolded the note and tucked it into my wallet. When I did so, I noticed the business card from Coquette. I realized it was the first time in nearly three weeks that I'd not been thinking about her practically every minute. After a leisurely breakfast, Penelope left for the university and I headed to the museum, anxious to get the latest news and the backstory on the firings.

At the museum, I walked straight to the HR office to find out from Audrey Arente what the latest on the situation was.

Audrey, who Penelope had thought would be made acting director, informed me that the board of trustees had discovered a deeper extent to the theft and realized the museum was in an unstable financial position. Apparently William Harris and our CFO also had figured out a way to embezzle, month by month, a good deal of our endowment funds. Audrey was a good friend, and I trusted what she told me.

"So, they decided to appoint someone from the board of trustees as acting CEO until they can sort out the whole dirty mess," Audrey said.

"Well, I suppose that's not such a bad idea. Except that most of the people on the board are there because they're big donors or have political influence, not because they know anything about running a museum. Who did they select?"

"You're not going to be happy, Odel. They selected Bligh—Bill Bligh."

"Oh no! He's the guy who owns a temp agency downtown, right? He doesn't know anything about science, and he's a big bully. I've heard that, for Bligh, people are just pawns, not human beings. He's a misanthrope; maybe even a sociopath. No one on staff is going to be happy to hear he's the trustees' choice for acting CEO."

"You're right about that," Audrey replied. "But apparently no one else on the board was willing or able to devote the time needed for the task. Bligh's already called an all staff meeting for next week."

As I settled into my office, I took Coquette's card from my wallet and laid it on my desk. It had a naggingly familiar look to it, but I couldn't think what it was. I pulled down my Rolodex and thumbed quickly through the business cards I had stored in it. When I got to Antin Morales, I stopped. Extracting his card, I compared it to Coquette's. It was exactly the same design and appearance. I looked at the font characters under my dissecting microscope. The font was exactly the same style and size. I stared at the two cards in front of me for a long time. It could be coincidence, of course—but what if it wasn't? The ramifications were too complicated for my brain to process, but I felt like my reality was once again shifting in some unclear way.

I called Morales's office to inform him I was back in Seattle, and I asked his secretary to let him know I was available for a meeting if he was interested. Within an hour I heard back from him. We arranged to meet at his office the next morning.

Driving through the rows of look-alike gray office buildings on the outskirts of Seattle, I began thinking that perhaps this wasn't such a good idea. I wasn't likely to get any funding from the CIA; John Thornton had made that clear. And did I really want to get involved with these people? I was already feeling a bit in over my head, though I couldn't put my finger on exactly where that feeling came from. Although what they'd asked me to do was simple, painless, and seemingly innocuous, I vowed to reconsider any further involvement with the Agency.

"Dr. Bernini, pleasure to see you again. I hope your fieldwork was successful." Morales seemed unusually affable.

"It all went fine, thanks. I brought in my field notebook." As I handed it to him, I said, "The flagged pages cover the Montelimar area."

Without opening it, he buzzed someone to come in to retrieve the notebook. "I presume you don't mind if we make a photocopy of those pages?"

"No, not at all," I replied, a bit surprised by the abruptness of it all.

"Tell me, what is your impression of things in Nicaragua these days?"

"What exactly do you mean? Impressions of what?"

"Well, how are people feeling about Mr. Ortega and how he's running the country?"

"That's quite a broad question, and I'm not sure my impressions are particularly representative of the entire country. As I mentioned earlier, most of my friends are academics, and that's a small segment of Nicaragua's populace."

"Of course, I understand that. Nevertheless, what is the impression you've gotten from the folks you know there?"

I told Morales that everyone I talked with was behind the overthrow of the Somoza regime, and many were fully behind Daniel Ortega and the Sandinistas. However, I also told him that some of my acquaintances were beginning to feel betrayed by Ortega's move toward strong Cuban Marxism, his interference with free speech and the press, and his protracted steps toward free elections. And as part of me mused, *This might be the last time I am ever in these offices*, I said, "You know, I have to tell you that, regardless of where one is on the political spectrum in Nicaragua, I don't believe anyone there, nor in most of the Western world, would accept U.S. interference in the country again. No matter what the reasons given or the outcome."

Morales ignored my comment, asked a few more questions, and then the aide walked back into the room with my notebook. Again, no one opened it in front of me and Morales simply handed it back to me. "Thank you very much Dr. Bernini. Now, if you'll excuse me, I have another appointment coming up. It's a busy day for me."

I mumbled something feeble like, "Always happy to help," and showed myself out of the building. As I walked through the parking lot, I noticed how warm the notebook felt. Sitting in my truck, I opened it and flipped through the pages, realizing all of them were quite warm. They had clearly photocopied the entire thing—not just the pages on Montelimar. *Of course*, I thought. *Why wouldn't they?*

Two days later, I got a call from John Thornton. He asked if we could meet for lunch one day the following week. "Sure thing," I said, thinking I might never have anything more to do with the CIA, so why not ask Thornton a few pointed questions? *It's probably the last time I'll ever see him too*, I thought. He suggested we meet at one of his favorite spots not too far from the museum—Gabriela's Pupusería.

Thornton was his usual happy self. He was wearing a white Guayabera shirt and blue jeans. We talked about baseball and the growing traffic problems in Seattle, and drank Toña beers. I realized Gabriela's must be a favorite of Thornton's. Everyone there, including Gabriela herself, seemed to know him; it was obvious he ate there frequently. This was definitely a content guy sliding into retirement. Gabriela was a middle-aged woman, short in stature but trim and fit, quite attractive, and obviously well educated. She wore her long black hair tied high on her head, but parts of it tumbled out here and there, hinting at what was probably a beautiful, shiny mane when unfurled. She also had the look of a woman who'd seen a lot, been through a lot. But she looked spirited and determined. I sensed she might be sweet on Thornton, and it prompted me to ask him if he was married.

"I was," he replied. "But my wife passed away a few years ago." It came out as "pathed away." "Our darling daughter Leilani and I have managed to work through the grieving process together. Leilani's my best friend."

I expressed my deep sympathy. The man was becoming a bit more human to me.

Thornton's expression changed, and he replied, "Thank you, Odel. It was rather tragic, actually. My wife's death was unexpected—cancer. And just six months later, Leilani's husband was killed in a terrible car accident. They'd only been married a short while . . . he was no ordinary man. The whole affair set her back on her heels. But this past year she's been doing much better. She seems to be embracing life again."

He had said so much, in so few words, I knew it would take me a while to process it all. "My god, that's terrible,

110

John. You and your daughter must be so close. It's good you have each other for support."

"Yes, we are close. But we're both doing OK these days. Leilani's very bright and clearheaded, and when she puts her mind to something, there's no stopping her. She's quite a force actually. Although she lives in Los Angeles, we manage to see each other every few months."

"Well, that's good. She sounds like a wonderful person, and you sound like a great dad."

He asked me about my life, and we chatted a while about Penelope and her job and the situation at the museum. "Yes, I saw a small piece in the paper a while back about the director and CFO being under investigation. What a shame. It's so sad when people screw around with a good thing like your museum. By the way, did Morales give his 'patriot' pitch?"

I was growing to like John Thornton. And as our conversation continued I found myself viewing him more and more as a totally normal and very nice man who was looking forward to retirement.

"I guess so. The first time we met, he asked if I was a patriot. I wasn't sure what to say. That's just not a word that's bantered about in the academic world."

Thornton chuckled. Then, completely out of the blue, he said, "Odel, I believe I mentioned to you that the CIA has no grant-giving programs. However, we do work with a few nonprofits that provide grants to scientists and other scholars. One in particular funds professionals who work in Latin America. He opened his old battered leather briefcase and pulled out a manila envelope. As he slid it across the table to me, he said, "Here's the background information on the organization and the papers you'll need to apply for a grant from them. If you're still interested, I'd be happy to put in a good word for you."

I'm sure I looked a bit stunned, but he went right on. "I would suggest keeping your application narrative brief. Just tell them what you do and why you need to collect your specimens on the coasts of Nicaragua and other Central American countries. Be sure to send along a detailed résumé and a list of your professional publications. You might want to be a bit on the vague side about planned locations for your future visits to the region. And, of course, the Agency's hope is that you will be willing to continue to share your observations with us. But I want to be clear that that is not a prerequisite for funding from this foundation."

I was at a loss for words. In my mind I'd already halfway decided to dump this "relationship" with the CIA. But now, over beers and *pupusas* with a man I was growing to like, the landscape and the parameters had suddenly changed.

"How much does this nonprofit give grants for, and for how many years?" I asked him.

"I don't really know, but ask for what you need. My guess is it would be a year-to-year arrangement. If this helps you with your research, and you'd be willing to share your impressions of things you see with us, it could be a mutually beneficial arrangement. Naturally, either party could term-inate the arrangement at any time. This wouldn't be anything formal or contractual. Simply voluntary cooperation."

"I need to think about this a bit, John. And I want to talk with Penelope about it. But thanks very much."

"Of course, of course—don't rush into anything. And do have a good long discussion with your wife about it. She's a smart woman." The way he said it, it almost sounded as if he knew Penelope; but I had just given him a pretty broad background on her, so I thought it made sense.

As I drove away from the café, the still-unopened manila envelope on the passenger's seat next to me, my mind was swirling. I really liked this man Thornton and felt like I could trust him. And for some reason, I felt he liked me too. And I was elated at the thought of multiyear funding for my research in Central America. The "exchange" seemed fair and easy enough. *What do I have to lose?* I thought.

Through the winter of 1981 Daniel Ortega gradually became more and more strident in his Cuban-Marxist approach, and the Sandinistas began taking over television and radio stations around the country. And then, in early in 1982, *La Prensa* fell under strict censorship of the Sandinistas. With that move, the remaining non-Marxist members of the junta resigned in protest, leaving Ortega in effect a dictator, although he maintained his promise that free elections would be scheduled soon. To the extent that she could, Violeta Chamorro continued to use the newspaper as both an advocate of free speech and for opposition opinions against Ortega. But the Sandinistas kept tighter and tighter rein on her. It began to appear that she was leaning toward supporting the emerging Contra movement, though certainly not the idea of another U.S.-led intervention. And the more the opposition gained in strength and voice, the more Ortega cozied up to Cuba and Russia. The Sandinistas began buying military equipment of all kinds, including boats to build up its tiny naval fleets in Corinto and Puerto Sandino on the Pacific coast.

Inspired by the success of the Sandinista Revolution in Nicaragua, in October 1979 progressive Salvadoran military officers and civilians had overthrown the authoritarian regime of President Carlos Humberto Romero and fired nearly a hundred corrupt senior military personnel. That coup d'état was the beginning of El Salvador's twelve-year civil war. As Romero fled in exile to Guatemala, the new government stabilized around a coalition of military and civilian moderates, and it quickly began national reforms. As in post-Somoza Nicaragua, the people of El Salvador were taking back their country. In 1980 José Napoleón Duarte was appointed head of El Salvador's new junta. Duarte was a right-leaning moderate and former mayor of the capital city, San Salvador. But the wealthy elite of El Salvador were angry because, with the new moderate coalition government, they felt they were losing control of the country and watching their estate values diminish. However, the center-coalition

113

government also failed to satisfy the far left, the communists and Marxists who were hoping to follow in the footsteps of the Sandinistas. As a result, Duarte and the new ruling junta had to battle both the far right and the far left. Thus the guerrilla movement in El Salvador continued, and Ortega was said to be supplying them with Soviet arms he acquired by way of Cuba. The U.S. sent massive arms support to the Duarte government, and the CIA became deeply involved in suppression of the leftist movement in El Salvador.

11

The *Pupusa Chingón* and a *Big* Surprise
Spring 1982

The new year opened full steam ahead. I had a great many specimens to sort and identify. I would send the noncrustacean material (the worms, molluscs, echinoderms, and so on) from my Nicaraguan samples to other specialists around the world. And once I had all my crustacean data collated, there would be analyses to run. That would be the least fun step in the project; keypunching hundreds of cards with data and running them through the IBM System/360 mainframe in the museum's basement. It was a slow machine, dating back to the late '70s, but it was all we had, and it was the only way to analyze the large amount of information I accumulated for evolutionary and biogeographic patterns. IBM had just released the first of its new "desktop personal computers," but the museum had decided to wait a year or two before investing in the new technology. And, of course, the Internet and email were still a decade away. Life moved in the slow lane, though we didn't think so at the time.

Acting Director Bligh and the museum's board of trustees had made it clear that there might be some significant cutbacks in the budget before summer. Although they didn't mention layoffs, people were nervous.

The tight financial situation at the museum made the grant idea that John Thornton had suggested seem even more attractive. Penelope urged me to go for it, reminding me that she'd *told me so*. The nonprofit was called The Cleia Foundation. I'd never heard of it, but the name somehow had a familiar ring to it. When I read their trifold color brochure, it looked pretty good. The guidelines appeared to be structured after those of the National Geographic Society, from which I had obtained grants in years past. If a grant was approved, a check was sent directly to the principal investigator, not to his or her institution. This precluded the museum from taking its usual fifteen to thirty percent overhead. Although there was no required end-of-year accounting that had to be submitted, the foundation did encourage recipients to maintain a dedicated bank account for the project, in case of any future IRS issues. The annual reporting was to be kept to no more than two pages of text, plus copies of any scholarly publications that had resulted from the grant. In early February, I submitted my grant application. Penelope seemed certain it would be funded.

A few weeks later, I received a call from my old friend and colleague Simon Jolly, inviting me to spend three weeks on a ship out of Scripps Institution of Oceanography, diving and searching for natural products on the Pacific coast of Colombia, including the remote Gorgona Island. The trip was scheduled for April. The Scripps ship would sail from San Diego to Panama City, and the science crew would meet up with it there. I was immediately enthusiastic. Gorgona Island is separated from the mainland of South America by a thousand-foot-deep seafloor basin, and it was well known for its coral reefs and high number of endemic species. The main thing the Colombians used it for was an ultra-high-security prison, but there was a movement afoot to designate it a national park (and close the prison). In the seventeenth century the island was a haven for pirates working the Pacific coast of Central and South America. Gorgona Island had both a biological and a romantic lure.

In late February John Thornton called, suggesting we have lunch at Gabriela's Pupusería again. He offered to pick me up the next day in front of the museum. As we drove to Gabriela's, he told me he was very excited about something and was looking forward to sharing it with me. I couldn't help but think he was going to give me some news on my grant proposal. Or maybe he was going to reveal some secret CIA plan to me? Or introduce me to some new Agency person, perhaps a sultry redhead with a sexy foreign accent? He slipped his old Ford Fairlane into a curbside spot right in front of the café. We walked in and took the same table we'd taken at our last lunch. Thornton took the same seat, with his back against the wall. Gabriela was there and walked over to hand us menus. She had a big smile on her face.

"Just open the menu, Juanito," she said to Thornton, almost making it sound like a command. My menu lay on the tabletop as I watched Thornton open his. His face broke into a huge grin. He stood up and gave Gabriela a hug.

"Check it out, Odel," Thornton said, pointing at the menu in front of me. I opened mine, and there it was. A bold red piece of paper clipped at the top of the inside page read, "New! *Juan's Gran Pupusa Chingón.* Filled with three cheeses, ground pork, and fresh cabbage. Topped with pickled red onions and chopped poblano chile."

"It's my own brainchild, man. You've got to try it!"

"Jesus! I will, John, I will. No wonder you were so excited! How many people get a *pupusa* named after them!"

"It's not just any *pupusa*—it's my and Leilani's creation. And it's a killer! Hence the name."

We each ordered a *pupusa chingón* and a Toña. Thornton told me that when his daughter's husband had died, she'd moved in with him for a while, and they'd spent time cooking together. It was then that they invented the *pupusa chingón*. I could see his mind drifting to those times, and his incongruous smile turned to laughter. "It was one hell of a time, but we both got through it. Leilani took six months off work, and Gabriela here helped us along—she even delivered meals to us occasionally. And now look what she's done. Put our little creation on her menu!" I noticed that when he was excited, his lisp got worse. It made him even more charming.

Oddly, I thought it might be one of the proudest moments of John Thornton's life. *What a guy*, I thought to myself. *He's nothing like I imagined a career CIA agent to be like.*

When we had finished our *pupusas*, Thornton asked for the bill.

Gabriela popped two more beers and brought them to the table. She said, "Today is your birthday, Juanito. *No hay ningún cargo por su almuerzo hoy.*" She bent down and gave Thornton a big smooch on the lips—nothing sexual but definitely intimate and sincere.

As she walked away, I saw his face redden. "She's a sweetheart," he said. It struck me at that moment how handsome Thornton was. Clearly Gabriela felt the same way.

"Well, she's certainly fond of you!" I noted.

Thornton looked me in the eyes, and said, "Her husband, Francisco López, was murdered in San Salvador about eight years ago. By a death squad working for one of the rich sons of bitches that control most of the banking interests in the country. Francisco worked for the local paper, *El Diario*, and he'd written a series of investigative pieces about corruption in the banking business. The police who examined his body reported that all of his fingers and both knees had been broken before he was killed. The whole thing was devastating, and the family continued to get threats. I was able to help Gabriela and her two girls, Corazón and Alma, immigrate to the States and start this little business. Gabriela was a high school teacher in San Salvador; she's a very smart woman. But she always loved cooking, and things have worked out here for her and the girls. I'm fond of her. So is Leilani."

As spring progressed, the Contras began making serious raids across the border into Nicaragua. They were mainly stationed to the north, in Honduras, but they also had a "secret" facility on Nicaragua's southern border, in northwestern Costa Rica at a large ranch owned by a wealthy American on the Santa Elena cape.

About this time Omar Cabezas published his book *Fire from the Mountain: The Making of a Sandinista*, with a foreword by Carlos Fuentes, one of the most admired writers in the Spanish-speaking world. In Guatemala, General Anibal Guevara was "elected" president, but he displeased the military, and just two weeks later an army coup put General Efraín Ríos Montt in office. Ríos Montt had a reputation as a brutal and corrupt career military man; the citizens of the country were worried, especially the indigenous Maya.

In March I heard my grant proposal to The Cleia Foundation had been approved. I could expect a check in the mail within a few weeks. It was for thirty thousand dollars—easily enough for several field trips over the coming twelve months. Most important—there was no time limit on expenditures; I could spend the grant funds as needed, and any remaining year-end balance simply rolled over from one year to the next. I was elated. I busied myself preparing for the expedition to Colombia with Simon Jolly, digging up references and poring over maps for what I hoped would be productive dive sites. The science crew would meet the ship in Panama City, and steam from there to Gorgona Island to begin the work. I had not yet tried to get in touch with Coquette, but the notion of traveling to Panama prompted me to pull out her card. I laid it on top of my desk at the museum and stared at it for several days, trying to decide what to do. It had been three months since I'd seen her, but my memories from Montelimar remained incandescent. It occurred to me that I had not experienced the recurring dream since I'd met Coquette.

When I called the number on her card, a woman with a bland voice answered the phone. I told her I was calling for Ms. Pallas. She took my name and told me she'd give Ms. Pallas the message. Five minutes later, Coquette called me back. Even on the phone her voice was mesmerizing. It was, in every way, the same Coquette I remembered. In my mind's eye I could see her standing in front of me on that deserted beach in Nicaragua, her long dress and hair blowing gently in the breeze, her perfect almond skin glowing under the starlight.

"Coquette, it's so good to hear your voice. How are you? I hope you're well."

"And it is so good to hear your voice, Odel. I worried that perhaps I might not hear from you."

"Well, I've been very busy since my return to Seattle. But you've been on my mind. I feel badly about the way I walked out on you that night in Montelimar. I'm terribly sorry. I don't really know how to explain it to you. But perhaps if we could see one another again, I might try."

"Oh, Odel, you never need to feel bad about your feelings or your needs. You have a complicated life, I know, and perhaps the timing simply wasn't right for us. But I would love to see you again. In fact, I would go to considerable lengths to see you."

The way she said that melted me. It was one hundred percent sincere. It had to be. I could feel it in my bones. My desire meter was peaking.

"I'll be departing from Panama City on a ship in April. We'll be at sea for a few weeks, then returning to Panama. Perhaps I could stop in Los Angeles on my way to or from Panama and meet up with you. You do live in L.A., don't you?"

"Yes, I do. But in April I have plans to be back in Nicaragua. If it were possible for you to stop over in Managua on your way to Panama, we could meet up there. Or, Copa has inexpensive daily flights from Managua to Panama City, and I could meet you there instead."

My mind kicked into high gear. Managua or Panama—both good options. With little hesitation, I asked her if she'd been to the San Blas Islands on the Caribbean coast of Panama.

"No, I haven't. But I've heard they are interesting and beautiful. Those are the Kuna Indian islands, aren't they?"

"Yes, they are. The Kuna have autonomous control over the entire archipelago, nearly four hundred islands. There are virtually no tourists or facilities. But I do know one small accommodation on one of the islands. It's just a few bungalows, literally on the beach, with sand floors and scuttling hermit crabs. The bungalows are just a few feet above the high-tide line. But they're clean and agreeable, and the locals prepare three meals daily for the guests—when there are guests. Which I suspect is rarely. Would you be interested in visiting the islands for a few days with me?"

"Odel, that sounds absolutely heavenly."

We discussed the details of how it would all work. There was only one, rather unreliable, puddle-jumper flight daily from Panama City across the Darién jungle to the Caribbean coast. It stopped in El Porvenir on the mainland, and then went on to the only island in the San Blas Archipelago with an airstrip. Even on this, the largest island, the runway had to be constructed by extending it off the island on both ends, using rocks and cement brought out from Porvenir. The wheels of the twin-engine prop plane had to touch down on one edge of the runway and stop just short of falling off the other end into the sea. We set our plans to meet in Panama City at the downtown Hilton Hotel five days before I was to meet the Scripps ship and Simon Jolly's crew of chemists. We would meet in the morning, take a taxi to the national airport, and catch the midday flight to the islands. There was no way to make reservations but, as almost no one even knew of the "beach hotel," I was confident we would have no problems.

The rest of the day I ruminated on the plans I had just made. I had never cheated on Penelope. Could I go through with this? Coquette was irresistible. She drew me to her like no woman ever had. My mind raced with ideas, and by the end of the day I was beginning to agonize over it all. *How can this be?*, I thought to myself. *I don't even know who this woman is. And I'm a happily married man! What the hell am I doing?*

By the time I got home, I had decided to ask Penelope about the note I'd found tacked on our front door the night I got back from my last trip to Nicaragua. I knew I should have brought it up earlier, but it was one of those things I needed to mull over for a while. Or maybe I thought it was really nothing . . . Or maybe I thought otherwise but didn't want to deal with it. In any event, I couldn't wait any longer. At least, maybe, I could resolve one of the several issues eating away at me. After a delicious dinner of red pozole that I'd picked up at our favorite Mexican place on the way home, Penelope poured me some rum on the rocks and poured herself a Jack Daniels. During a brief lull in the conversation as we shared our respective day's events, I pulled out my wallet and extracted the handwritten note. I handed it to her, explaining how I'd found it.

"I'm sorry for not showing this to you sooner. I don't know if it was meant for you or not, but I was just so puzzled by it . . . Well, I guess I was just trying to process what it might mean. But I haven't done so well with that."

Penelope stared at the note for a long time, appearing to read it over and over.

"Odel, you always do this. Why must you wait so long to bring difficult things up with me?"

"I don't really know. I guess I just need to think about stuff before talking about it—or at least to get to a point where

I feel I understand the weight of a thing. So what's the note about?"

"I think it must be from Sonia. She hasn't spoken to me in months. She won't return my phone calls, and I even sent her a couple of nice letters. But not a word back."

I was puzzled. "But, Penelope, what is she talking about in this note to you?"

Another long pause. "Odel, you know I love you very, very much. But I am also very fond of Marjorie. Unfortunately, Sonia became terribly jealous of that. She demanded I stop seeing Marjorie. You know Sonia's a bit crazy." Penelope looked me straight in the eyes and took my hand in hers.

Now it was my turn to be silent. I was trying to understand what Penelope was saying. But the only conclusion I could get to was a disturbing one. "What, exactly, do you mean by you are 'very fond' of Marjorie?"

"Just that, Odel. But, baby, Marjorie's no threat to you or to our marriage."

"Penelope, have you and Marjorie been having sex?"

Pause . . . "Yes."

The pauses were becoming more protracted.

"I see. And for how long?"

"I don't know. A year or so, maybe."

I was taken aback. "Jesus—a year or so! Why haven't you said anything about it? What does this mean, exactly? Are you gay?" As soon as I said it, I realized it was a dumb question.

Penelope's posture changed. She let go of my hand and became stiff, speaking carefully in her reply. I could see the wheels spinning in her hyperactive brain. "Odel, I've always enjoyed sex with women. As much as with men. It's just the way I'm wired. When you and I fell in love and began having our spectacular sex, I guessed I might never again seek other lovers. But we never talked about this sort of thing, you know. And we've always respected one another's privacy. I

123

guess the simple fact is I am as drawn to women, at least to Marjorie, as I am to men, to *you*—sexually speaking. You know Marjorie, Odel; she's a sweet woman. She and I have often talked about a threesome with you." Another pause. "Maybe I was just laying the groundwork for that. I don't know, but the important thing is, I love you and it is no threat to our marriage."

I couldn't deal with it then and there. I stood up and told Penelope that I needed to go for a long walk to soak in this tidal wave of a revelation.

"Of course, honey. And when you're ready, we can talk more."

Her words had an unfamiliar, icy tone. I walked all around our suburban neighborhood, seeing nothing, my mind focused intently on the pieces of an ever-growing jigsaw puzzle that seemed to be tumbling out of the sky onto me. I noticed that the guilt over my emerging feelings for Coquette had suddenly vanished, or at least been laid aside for a while. It also dawned on me that Penelope's invitation to join her in the ladies' room at the Miami Beach Sheraton early in our relationship had much broader implications than I'd realized. After forty-five minutes or so I returned home with a head full of questions.

Penelope had been drinking quite a bit. She gave me a big kiss when I walked into the house. I responded at roughly twenty percent enthusiasm.

"So . . . I need to get this clear in my head," I said to her. "Have you always enjoyed sex with women—since you were, what, a teenager? Or is it something you discovered as an adult?"

Penelope sat down with body language that told me she was ready to tell all.

"Always. Since I was fourteen or fifteen."

"Fourteen or fifteen! How many women do you think you've had sex with?"

"Oh my goodness, Odel, I have no idea. How many women have you had sex with?"

"If I thought about it for a while, I could probably name them all. A couple dozen maybe."

Silence from Penelope.

"And have you been having sex with women the whole time we've been married? I mean, I presume you also slept with Sonia. Are she and Marjorie the only women since we've been married?"

"No, there were a few others."

"How many others?"

"I don't know, Odel. It doesn't matter—one or one hundred—it just doesn't matter. The sex you and I have is the best I've ever known. And I'm a thousand percent happy being married—and being married to you."

"Why is that hard for me to believe, Penelope?"

"I don't know. Because you're man?" The comment had an edge to it. She sounded a bit angry, which, given the situation, seemed pretty odd to me.

"Are you going to tell Marjorie about this conversation?"

"Yes, of course."

"And what do you think her reaction will be?"

"I'm sure she'll be concerned, worried about us—you and me, I mean. She's truly fond of you, Odel, fond of us both. Maybe we should try to spend more time together—the three of us. She's really a wonderful person, you know."

"Holy smokes, Penelope, I really do need some time to process all this."

"I understand—take all the time you need." She said it a bit too curtly, and I didn't like the way it sounded. I had noticed that recently, when Penelope had too much to drink, her personality would shift a bit. She would get harder, more irritable. It was a new thing in our relationship.

But then she rose from her chair, walked over to me, and plunked herself into my lap. I always loved it when she did that, the feeling of her svelte little body squirming on my thighs and crotch, her beautiful blue eyes staring into mine, the aroma of her hair and her breath in my nostrils. We stayed like that for quite a while. She knew she had me wrapped around her little finger. Finally she said, "Time for bed honey. Put this away for the night and come lie with me—be my friend and my husband."

We didn't talk about it for nearly a week, and then one night I told her I would like to just think about things for a while. Maybe we could revisit it all after I returned from my Colombia expedition. She said that was a fine idea. But she also suggested that the three of us—me, her, and Marjorie—go to dinner one night soon. She thought spending some relaxed time together would be healthy for us, calm the situation a bit. The three of us were, after all, good friends. I did like Marjorie; she had always seemed like a good person to me. I agreed.

Penelope and I didn't have sex for ten days or so, which was highly unusual. We normally had sex, in one fashion or another, almost daily. It wasn't that we didn't both want it; I was just not ready, being in a state of semi-shock. I'd been thinking about all the implications of the situation. Being a liberal open-minded intellectual, I searched for a possible positive side to it all. I truly did like Marjorie. She was bright, energetic, pleasant to be around, and certainly attractive. Would I be comfortable if she occasionally spent nights in bed with Penelope and me? Objectively speaking, maybe so. But, on the other hand, could I be comfortable knowing that she and Penelope were having sex privately, who knows how often? Could I eventually grow comfortable knowing that my wife had a habit of affairs with other women? At least it was with women, and not men! Does it really matter if Penelope occasionally had sex with women if she loved me and wanted to be married to me, and our own sex continued to be great? But what if she had an affair with a man? Would she even tell me? There were too many questions. I wondered why we had never talked about fidelity before our marriage. I wondered how many women Penelope had slept with in her life. I wondered what other secrets my wife might be keeping from me.

Finally, one night after a light dinner I'd thrown together—Caesar salad and grilled asparagus, with a good bottle of Oregon Pinot Noir—Penelope told me she was so horny for me, she felt she would burst if we didn't make love. I told her I felt the same way. We left the dirty dishes on the table and went straight to the bedroom. Penelope was like a wildcat in heat and her fever was contagious. Our sex was an unrestrained fifty-minute romp through all of our favorite maneuvers; a mutual exercise in corporeal pleasure and self-satisfaction. But as I drifted into slumber, I found myself reflecting on the lack of emotion and sentiment in what had just taken place. Despite the physical intimacy, there had been very little emotional intimacy. And I also found myself wondering how, exactly, Penelope and Marjorie made love?

12

The Hotel San Blas, Panama
Spring 1982

The Colombia expedition was just three weeks away. My plans to meet Coquette in Panama were set. My mind was racing with everything I still had to do in preparation for the fieldwork. Penelope had a week-long meeting in Mexico City scheduled for the same time I would be in Colombia. She was to deliver the opening plenary talk based on a paper she had just published—something about the shifty ways in which banks in Latin America moved money around to skirt international banking laws. Her work was clearly becoming well known. It occurred to me to call Antin Morales at the Agency just to let him know my expedition plans. When I did, he asked if I might be able to stop in Managua on the way down to deliver something to a colleague. I said sure, so long as I didn't have to carry anything illegal on my flight. He didn't find my comment amusing. He said stiffly, "Of course not, Dr. Bernini. Actually, if you wouldn't mind just picking up some papers in Managua and driving them to San Juan del Sur, the Agency would be grateful."

I knew San Juan. It was practically on the border with Costa Rica, a couple hours' drive south from Managua. I could easily complete the task in a day. I could hardly say no at this point, with thirty grand from The Cleia Foundation now sitting in a new bank account I had opened a few months earlier. And I could cover my expenses in Nicaragua with the Cleia funds. Morales asked me when exactly I could be in Managua and said he'd call back the following day with details.

When he called, his instructions were simple. I was to meet someone in the bar of the downtown Hotel Intercontinental. I would be given a packet of papers and an address in San Juan del Sur. I wondered why they would need me to do such an ordinary task. I thought about asking Morales that question but didn't. However, I'd come to trust John Thornton, so as soon as I hung up, I called him.

"John—Odel here. How are you doing? I hoped you might be in town. I'm leaving for my Colombia expedition soon, and your colleague Antin Morales has asked me to stop over for a day in Managua to do something. I wondered if we could talk about it briefly."

"Not on the phone, Odel. But how about meeting up for a *pupusa* lunch tomorrow?"

"Sounds great—see you at Gabriela's place at noon tomorrow?"

"Deal. See you soon, *amigo*."

We met the following day, went through our pleasantries, and chatted a bit with Gabriela; then I told him what Morales had asked me to do.

"It's such a simple thing, John—of course I don't mind doing it, but I'm just curious why Morales would need me to deliver some papers. Surely there are Agency personnel in Managua, or other trusted U.S. government people there who could do that."

Thornton was quiet for a while, and then said, "Odel, I can't really talk about Morales's request, but there are a few things you should know. First, it's best never to ask 'why' when you're doing something for the Agency. There's always a reason, even though you might find it ridiculous if you knew what it was. Second, in this case, there are *not* that many U.S. State Department or Agency personnel left in Managua. And one can safely assume that the Sandinista government knows every one of them, and if one of them drove out of Managua heading for the Costa Rica border, it's a pretty sure bet they would be followed. Third, it's not Morales asking you to do anything. It's his boss, or his boss's boss. Morales is a desk jockey. He's not high on the totem pole. He might not even know what it's about. And lastly—don't mess with Morales. He's got a bad disposition."

"OK, got it. Thanks for the advice, John."

"You know, Odel, the Agency is just like any place else in terms of staffing. These folks are government employees, civil servants trying to do the best job they can. Some of them are smarter than others, some of them are flakes, some of them work hard while others just put in their forty hours a week. The people I work with are conservatives and liberals, uptight and easygoing, friendly and not so friendly. I'm on the liberal, easygoing side of the spectrum. Morales is at the other end of the scale. But I will tell you one thing—all of us sincerely want to do what's best for our country. The problem is, we sometimes don't agree on what that might be."

Our lunch was pleasant, as always. My affection for, and understanding of John Thornton continued to grow. He was an intriguing guy. I asked him how Leilani was doing. He said she was doing well.

"In fact, the past week she's practically been her old self again—almost festively upbeat and happy. And she's working more and more."

"I'm so happy to hear that, John. I hope I have an opportunity to meet her one day."

"Oh, I suspect you will, Odel. I suspect you will."

"How did you come up with the name Leilani?"

"She was conceived when Isabella and I were on vacation in Hawaii. It was just a name we both liked."

"And if you don't mind me asking, how did Leilani's husband die?"

As he considered my question, his eyes went distant, and the wrinkles on his forehead deepened. "It was stupid. He was killed in a car crash on the highway south of Managua. Had there been better communication infrastructure and emergency response, he likely would have survived. But it was nearly four hours before the ambulance and medics got to him. Leilani was twenty-nine years old. They had only been married a year. It was fucking horrible."

I saw it was time to change the conversation. Thornton's mind was adrift with his losses. I tried to ease him back to less morbid thoughts. "What kind of work did your wife do, John?"

"Isabella was a biologist, like you. She worked at the National University in Managua."

"Really? What did she work on?"

"She worked on hummingbirds mostly. The evolution and geography of Neotropical hummers. My work involved a great deal of travel, including some postings in South America, so she eventually took a leave of absence from the university so we could spend more time together."

"Those must have been exciting years. Good years."

"Yes, they were. We enjoyed four wonderful years in South America—it was some the best times we had. Isabella spent the time working on her hummers in Argentina and Brazil. Leilani was just a teenager. We spent time in all the great cities—Santiago, Cartagena, Rio, Buenos Aires. Isabella homeschooled Leilani."

I turned the conversation to my own travels in South America, especially exploring the Andes, and Thornton began to emerge from his sadness—at least superficially.

As we left the café, I noticed that Thornton gave Gabriela a kiss on the lips, and she responded enthusiastically. I was happy for them. I sensed they were right for one another, and perhaps even needed each other. I secretly hoped to see their relationship grow, and I wondered how soon Thornton would be retiring.

In 1982 the Hotel Intercontinental Managua was a huge, unattractive, concrete pyramid in what was once an upscale residential area of the city. It was supposed to resemble a Maya pyramid but it fell short in countless ways. As a result of the '72 earthquake and the civil war, much of the surrounding area was now badly damaged and deserted. Homeless families had begun moving into the abandoned and half-collapsed houses. Not many people were staying at the Intercontinental then—mainly foreign diplomats, especially those from Cuba, the States, Germany, and a few from Russia. I had stayed there a number of times. It had a creepy feel to it, but it was about the only place to get reliable service, including international phone service and laundry. And it was a third the price of an Intercontinental anywhere else in Latin America. My stopover in Managua was so brief, I didn't bother to tell Bob and Beatriz that I was passing through.

I checked into the hotel in the late afternoon after an uneventful flight from Houston on Copa Air. At eight that evening I was to go to the bar, order a drink, take a table near the south wall, and await my contact. I had no idea what to expect; the bar was inhabited by a dozen or so disquieting-looking foreigners. After about twenty minutes, one of them rose from his table and walked over to me.

"Excuse me, are you Dr. Bernini, the marine biologist?"

"Yes, I am."

"May I join you for a few minutes? I know of your work. My son is an aspiring marine biologist, and I wonder if you'd mind giving me some recommendations to pass along to him."

Good grief, I thought, *this is so hokey.*

"Sure, please join me." I felt like I was in a B-rated spy film.

He actually asked me a few appropriate questions about careers in biology. Then someone dropped a beer bottle on the other side of the room. It hit the tile floor and shattered, and the customer made a loud explicative. The subdued ambience of the bar was disrupted, and all eyes turned to see what had happened. With practiced timing, the stranger at my table reached into his inside coat pocket and pulled out a thick envelope. Sliding it quickly across the table to me, he said nothing, but stood up and walked directly out of the bar. I put the envelope into my own coat pocket, thankful that the entire thing had transpired so rapidly that everyone in the place was still looking at the customer cursing about breaking his bottle of beer. *OK, maybe not so hokey. It seemed to work just fine.*

Returning to my room, I opened the envelope. Inside was a smaller, but still quite thick envelope and a single piece of paper with a short note that simply said, "Deliver this envelope, unopened, to Señor Eupeithes, 2 p.m. tomorrow, Café Delgadillo, San Juan del Sur. Ask him if there is any place to get a good steak in town. He must reply, 'not since 1979.' If he does not, do not give him the envelope. Destroy these instructions." I hid the envelope under my mattress and thought, *Damn, that's probably the first place anyone would look.* But I wasn't planning to leave the room until morning, so it seemed safe enough. I burned the note in an ashtray and then blew the ashes out the window of my room.

The next morning I stuffed the envelope under my shirt, grabbed my backpack, and headed directly to my rental car. I would stop somewhere along the road for coffee. I just wanted to get this silly "assignment" over with quickly. As I drove south from Managua, I pondered what might be in the envelope. It could be cash, of course. I estimated that enough hundred-dollar bills could be in the thing to add up to a few tens of thousands of dollars. Maybe it was destined for the Contra camp just over the border on the Santa Elena cape in

Costa Rica. Maybe it was detailed plans of some kind for the Contras, or important dossiers. Maybe it was cash for CIA "cooperators" on the Nicaraguan side of the border. The more I reflected on it, the less I liked it. Any scenario I came up with was not something I wanted to be involved with. The Contras were scum as far as I was concerned. But maybe it had nothing to do with the Contras. I had no idea, and I'd likely never know what was in the envelope.

As I drove south from Managua, vowing to myself not to accept another request like this from the Agency, a car appeared in my rearview mirror. It was moving fast, and as it got closer, I recognized the make as a Lada. *Well, I guess I shouldn't be surprised,* I thought. *But, man, those are the worst cars ever made. They're so bad, they make Renaults and Fiats look good.* For many years, they had been the cheapest cars I could get from the rental agencies in Ecuador and Peru.

All of a sudden, the Lada sped up behind me, right on my bumper, and then quickly pulled to the left to pass. When it cut back in front of me, I knew it was going to clip me. I jerked my steering wheel hard to the right, but the Lada's rear quarter panel hit my left front fender hard. I slammed on my brakes, cursing the bad driver, but kept my car under control. The impact, however, caused his car to go into a sideways slide. I could tell the driver was inexperienced because instead of turning the steering wheel to the left to correct out of the slide, he turned it to right, and the Lada flipped over on its left side and skidded down the road. I brought my car to a stop and watched as it slid into tropical shrubbery alongside the roadway and came to halt. I was shocked. We weren't traveling fast, maybe forty miles per hour or so, and I thought if he had his seat belt on, he'd probably be fine.

I pulled over to the side of the road and got out of my car. I was about to jog to the Lada, when I saw the driver moving rapidly inside the car. As I watched, he pushed open the right front door, now facing skyward, and climbed out. I could see blood on his forehead but nothing that looked serious. When he stood and turned to look at me, I saw it wasn't a *he* at all. It was a woman. A large-bodied woman, and definitely *not* a Latina. She had a thick head of a rusty brown hair, eyebrows that met one another over the bridge of a fat nose, and an unpleasant look on her face. She turned and ran into the bushes, fast, not stopping to look back.

"What the hell . . . " I mumbled. I walked over to the Lada and looked inside. There was nothing in the car at all. I quickly examined the underside of the car, noticing that the right front tie rod had snapped in half. That could have caused the car to go out of control and tip over. Tie rods should not break in half—another indication of what an inferior car the Lada is.

As I stood on the roadside, possible scenarios raced through my mind; none of them suggesting I should stay there and wait for the police to show up. No matter what the woman's motive was for running away from the scene of the accident, I didn't want to get involved with the cops. Especially not with an envelope full of who-knew-what from the CIA in my pocket. I sprinted back to my own car and eyeballed the extent of the damage. It was not all that bad. I had bought insurance from the rental company, so I wasn't too worried.

I got out of there as fast as I could, noticing a giant strangler fig on my side of the highway as I sped off. The tree was massive, the trunk probably ten feet across and extending almost onto the pavement of the road itself; big enough to hold a stack of VWs, yet grown from a seed smaller than a pinhead. I knew it was multi-centurial, probably five hundred years old. If it'd been my car that ran off the road, I could have easily careened right into that enormous *Ficus* tree and been seriously injured, or even killed. And as I passed the tree, I saw a large scar on it, the bark completely missing and the wood healing over. I wondered if the scar was actually from an old car crash. It was a good ten minutes before I passed a car going in the direction of Managua as I beat a fast track to San Juan del Sur.

I got to San Juan around half past noon, ate a plate of excellent *gallo pinto* topped with a fried egg at a family restaurant in the center of town and asked directions to the Café Delgadillo. At 1:45 I left to meet the mystery person. The café was old, with a worn wood floor, the air inside as still and heavy as a stack of wet newspapers. The place looked like an old accident that never got cleaned up. It was empty, save one person who I guessed was both cook and waiter. He had a lost, wretched look and a weary gray shadow darkened his purplish face. Dark bags beneath his eyes seemed filled to bursting with unspent tears. He was a man in body only, just a shadow of his past self, now bent and hollow. I felt that he and his café were at a nadir of some inescapable sorrow—both to be forever turned inward. I sat down at one of the five small tables, and he just stared at me with his heavy unknown sadness. His silence was like a scream. I asked him for a beer. When he brought it to me, with hands as rough as the wooden floor, he said: "Do you have the envelope?"

"*¿Cómo se llama señor?*"

"Eupeithes."

"Is there any place to get a good steak in this town?"

"Not since 1979."

"Here is the envelope, *señor*," I replied, removing it from my coat pocket and handing it to him. I wanted to ask him so many questions. *Who are you? What's in this envelope? Is this even your restaurant? Why do you carry the sadness of ages upon your face?* I wanted to mention the incident with the Lada and the strange, large woman who was driving it. But I kept my mouth shut.

"Thank you. Beer's on me," said Eupeithes. And I thought, *This man has the saddest, emptiest look on his face that I have ever seen. And this place should be called Café Pathos.*

I finished the beer quickly and immediately got into my car to drive back to Managua. As I approached the scene of my accident, I watched for the Lada on the side of the road. When I saw the big fig tree with the massive scar, I knew it was the spot, but the Lada was gone. It had already been towed away. It had only been a few hours! In this part of the world, I expected an abandoned car to sit on a roadside for at least a couple days before the bureaucracy of highway maintenance got around to removing it. I drove the next twenty miles into the city with extra caution.

That night, at the Intercontinental, I kept thinking someone was going to approach me about the highway incident. I hung out in the bar until eleven. But nothing. *Tomorrow I'll turn in the rental car and take a taxi directly to the airport for my midday Copa connection to Panama. The next day I'll see Coquette.* My mind was electrified with anticipation. Penelope's recent confession that she was bisexual, and that she'd continued having sexual relationships with women even after we'd gotten married, had mitigated the lingering guilt I had about my desire for intimacy with Coquette.

When Coquette walked into the Panama City Hilton's lobby at 9 a.m. she looked so beautiful and so sweet, it melted my heart. I almost teared up as I watched her walk toward me, a sublime smile on her face. She was wearing a short skirt and a sleeveless blouse. Her slender arms and legs, a perfect tropical brown, made her a vision to behold. And when she spoke, her silky sensuous voice washed over me like a voluptuous flow of red-hot lava. *What an adorable temptress this woman is.* And yet, something in the back of my mind told me to be wary. *Is she just a dream, a wish, a desire? Or is she a real person. Am I seeing her clearly?*

With her radiant smile she said, "Odel, I'm thrilled to see you."

My brain was reeling. I wanted to say, *I feel the same way, Coquette*, but my heart was racing, and I was tongue-tied. After what seemed like an eternity, I recovered enough to move close to her.

We held each other in a very long embrace, only after which did we kiss, our mouths open, but both of us holding back because we were in a hotel lobby with a dozen people staring at us. I suggested we grab a cab and head straight to the national airport. I had never been so excited in my life. Nor, perhaps, so nervous.

The Air Panama service to the San Blas Islands was notoriously unreliable. There was no way to make a flight reservation. In fact, Air Panama's in-country desk rarely even answered their phone. There was an unorganized crowd of Kuna families pushing their way to the ticket counter trying to get on the one-flight-per-day service to the islands. I reckoned there were more people hoping to get on the flight than the plane could hold. Seats would go to the most assertive! The Kuna people are short in stature. Coquette and I towered over them, and they almost imperceptibly made way for us as we edged our way to the front. We got the last two seats on the eighteen-seat plane and walked directly to the "waiting room"—three long wooden benches on a concrete slab at the edge of the runway. Coquette looked dismayed.

"Getting there is kind of weird, but trust me—the islands are a real slice of heaven."

Her frown turned to a happy grin as she replied, "I completely trust you, Odel. And I know it will be heavenly because we'll be together for a couple days. All alone—right?"

"Oh yes, seriously alone!"

The flight departed ninety minutes late, which was typical. The old plane shook so much on the forty-minute flight over the Darién jungle that screws were vibrating out of the overhead ceiling panels and falling to the floor. I hoped the jarring wouldn't break the bottle of *Flor de Caña* I had stashed in my luggage. At one point, a downdraft caused the plane to lurch into a brief plunge, and when it did, the seat in front of me tore loose from the flooring and fell back into my lap. After I shoved the Kuna man and his seat back into an upright position, Coquette whispered in my ear, "I had hoped to be the first one to sit in your lap on this little adventure, and here some stranger has beat me to it!" We laughed all the way to the islands. The pilot flew low, just above the jungle canopy. The view was spectacular.

The island landing was perfect. The plane might have been second-rate, but the pilot was superb. He taxied right to the end of the runway, made a perfect turn, and motored back to the one small concrete building on the airstrip. We grabbed our luggage as the pilot pulled it out of the cargo bay and walked across the tarmac. As we walked, a teenage Kuna boy approached and asked us, in stumbling Spanish, where we were going. I replied in English, "To the beach hotel on Franklin Island. Do you know it?" His English was better than his Spanish.

"I know it. It is the Hotel San Blas. I can take you there in my dugout. It takes about thirty minutes."

"And how much will we owe you for this service?"

He considered it for a few seconds, scratching his bowl-cut hair, and came up with a reasonable figure of twenty-five balboas. The Panamanian currency notes called balboas are essentially dollars, and the two notes circulate side by side in the country. Penelope had taught me that the value of the balboa is locked to the dollar at one-to-one by law, and the only way Panama got away with it is because of its long history of being a client state of the U.S. The legislated equivalency made the Panamanian currency stable, and thus its banks were safe places for the international community to park and launder their money, commonly money from illegal enterprises.

Coquette and I headed to the dugout canoe, which had a vintage 1960s thirty-five horsepower Evinrude outboard motor on the stern. We took off our shoes to cross the beach to the dugout, and we didn't put them on again for two days.

Franklin Island is only about six acres in size—not much more than an emergent sandbar. It is protected from storm surge, like all the other islands in the archipelago, by offshore reefs. One side of the island had four huts on the beach, just as I remembered. The other side had two cinder block houses for the single family that inhabited Franklin Island. A palapa stood in the middle of the island, and that is where meals were served for "hotel" guests. Next to the palapa was a small garden with greens and yams, two large manioc bushes, and a few things I didn't recognize. Rainwater was captured from the roofs of the two block houses, stored in barrels, and used as drinking water and for the garden. The island was pristine and so romantic we were both awestruck as we walked on the pure-white coral sand from the dugout to the houses.

We were met by a smiling Kuna woman in traditional dress—a blouse made of two molas, one on the front and one on the back. I knew that she had made the molas by hand herself, as Kuna culture dictates, using an intricate reverse appliqué technique unique to this indigenous group. The two panels were perfectly identical. They depicted a jaguar walking in a jungle with two macaws flying overhead. All around the margins ran a complicated, mazelike geometric pattern. The whole thing was vibrant with colors of emerald green and scarlet red.

She spoke a little English and some Spanish. As we negotiated a bungalow, she and her daughter, who looked to be thirteen or fourteen, showed us the four cabin options they had. They were all exactly identical. They were fifteen dollars a night, including meals. I handed her thirty balboas and thanked her. She told us the hours for meals and said if we needed anything to just let her know. Coquette chatted with them a bit in superb Spanish. The Kuna woman and her daughter were the only other people we saw for the next two days, except for a fisherman who delivered fresh fish and shellfish about ten each morning. The island, and the hotel's four *cabañas*, seemed to be a two-woman operation. It was perfect.

There was so much I wanted to ask Coquette, but I didn't want to rush into it. We spent the first afternoon walking around the island a few times, playing on the beach, and in what I can only describe as the most protracted period of foreplay in history. We teased each other, talked and laughed, and time stood still for us. I couldn't remember ever being so caught up in such sheer joy. Suddenly it was five-thirty and we realized dinner would be available in a half hour. Coquette asked if I'd mind waiting on the beach while she changed in our cabin. After a few minutes she emerged wearing the same beautiful flowing white gown I'd seen her in that first night in Montelimar. It clung to her body like iridescent seaweed draped across a bronze tidal rock. She was a naiad, her long hair flowing like black silk across her copper torso. As she exited the cabin, she reached out with her slender mahogany arm and said, "Odel, come to me. Come and hold me for a few minutes before we go to dinner."

My mind was spinning—part of it began flashing back to my dreams, the other part was saying, *At this moment, there is nothing on the planet but this island and this woman.* But it did seem like a dream. *Maybe it is a dream, and at any moment I will wake up.*

We went back into the cabin, and I held her. We kissed— truly kissed—for the first time. It was like no kiss I'd ever known. I felt her entire body and her heart oozing into me through that kiss. It was at once gentle and ardent, loving and erotic. It was electrifying. It took me away from the world I knew to someplace I didn't know but longed to be. I don't know how long that kiss lasted, but eventually we both pulled back and just stared at each other. She had clearly felt it too. My fingers danced slowly over each vertebra of her spine as they slid to her buttocks, one hand perfectly cupping each bun—they were tight and muscular, yet soft and feminine at the same time. I pulled her hips tightly against me. Fire shot back and forth between us. I knew we weren't going to linger in the dining room.

"Coquette, I've never felt like this before. It's as if I've slipped into some other dimension."

"Oh god, I'm so glad I'm not in this alone, Odel. I feel the same way. I've wanted this for so long."

That phrase caught me. "For so long." *What does she mean by that exactly?*

"But, I hardly know you. How can this be?"

"Some things are just meant to be. Perhaps it's fate. Right now, I'm just counting my blessings."

"I have so many questions. I want to know who you are. And I want to share some things about myself with you."

"There is no rush, Odel. That will all come with time. For now, let's just embrace the moment. I already know everything I need to know about you. And I know myself. And I trust my feelings. And I'm hungry!"

Her happy grin was contagious. We chuckled and agreed to eat quickly.

Dinner was unusual but delicious—yams, coconut, and crabmeat stuffed inside the shell of the crab that had donated its meat, with some cooked greens on the side. Warm cans of coke were served with the meal, which we mixed with the rum we'd brought to the island. There was no electricity on Franklin Island, but oil lamps lit the palapa with a soft orange glow.

Strolling back to our cabin a full moon lit the way. Coquette walked to the beach and stood there, warm ripples lapping at her calves. The radiance of the moon set ablaze golden wisps of clouds high overhead in the night sky, and it ignited the foam of the little waves as if there was fire in the sand below. The moonlight shined through her gown, making her appear naked but not naked. Tangible but intangible. Like a dream, a dream I had known all too well. I could see the outline of her light umber body beneath the fabric—her narrow waist, sculpted hips, slender thighs. Her moon-shadow stretched up the beach just to where I stood.

When we made love that night, it was something far beyond sex. It was excruciatingly emotional—every touch charged, every climax intoxicating. I'd never experienced such intimate connectedness. The fervent physical pleasures were there, but they were textured with something new to me, something profoundly heartfelt and sincere. At one point during the night, the full moon shone through our window like a spotlight. It was a passion moon; amorous, yellow-orange, overflowing with desire. Coquette was lying on her back, illuminated, almost on fire. I stared into her dark eyes; her coal-black pupils surrounded by golden-flecked ebony had a delicate, lacy appearance. Her face had a childlike quality to it, and at the same time her high cheekbones evoked thoughts of a Maya goddess. At that moment I was one hundred percent connected to this mysterious woman. I realized that, despite all the questions I had, being with her was the easiest, most natural thing on Earth for me.

"Coquette, in the morning I must tell you about a recurring dream of mine. I want to know what you think about it."

"That sounds interesting; please do. But don't get confused about things, my love. This is not your dream—it is our reality."

We didn't sleep much that night. A few thirty minute catnaps. We spent a lot of time just gazing into one another's eyes or examining each other's bodies in intricate detail with our eyes, hands, lips. Her skin had the feel of fresh rose petals. Her aromas were magical; a delightfully sweet herbal bouquet, at once familiar and exotic. Coquette's voice continued to hypnotize me, and when she murmured, it was like ethereal music, soothing and powerfully compelling at the same time. When we did sleep, she slept with her lissome body on top of me, her hair covering me like a sable cloak.

We spent most of the next day lying on the bed in our beach cabin, exploring one another in various ways, whispering sweet nothings to one another, talking about our feelings and our views on life in general terms, avoiding specifics but sharing enough to know we were on the same wavelength in terms of our values and sensibilities. We also laughed a lot—at the "hotel" we were staying in, at the funny hermit crabs scuttling about on the sand "floor" of our cabin, at the ironies of life. Coquette had a wonderful sense of humor, and I loved that about her too. We skipped breakfast, and sometime in the midmorning I told her about my recurring dream. I told her that I thought the woman in my dream must be her. The physical similarity was so striking, as was the similarity in gestures and voice. I didn't understand the colorful snake or the river or why I couldn't get across it to her, but I told her that I had not experienced the dream since she and I first met in Nicaragua. I wanted to tell her about the *curandera* in Managua but felt it would be . . . too much, or somehow risky to our relationship.

Coquette listened intently, intrigued by my story. She felt that the dream must have been prescient. "Odel, the reason you stopped having the dream is because you finally crossed the river. You came to me. And now, here we are in the San Blas Islands together. In your waking life, you have completed your dream-life. At least, the beginning of your dream-life. I guess now the question is, what's next? Maybe you need a new dream to help guide us? I know your scientist's brain must have trouble embracing the idea of dreams foretelling the future—but maybe it's not as paranormal as it seems. Maybe there are clues, or cues, in your life that you don't notice on a conscious level. Your dreams may assemble them into a rational story or a logical direction for you. Perhaps I've been there for a long time, buried in your subconscious. Perhaps you knew who I was

144

before we ever met. Or perhaps you knew of me from another, but you don't recall the moment. Your dream may have simply been your subliminal way of visualizing a desire, or your future."

Her comment about "what's next" made me think of Penelope for the first time in several days. "You do remember that I am married, right?" I said.

"Of course I remember. But I am not part of that life. You and I will have what we will have. The fate of you and Penelope is not for me to speculate on or interfere with."

Over lunch that day, I asked her where her skin color came from. She said, "My mother was Nicaraguan but of mixed blood, mostly Miskito Indian. She was much darker skinned than me and very beautiful. My father is of European descent, although he is an American." The way she phrased it caught my attention.

"Are your parents still alive?"

"My dad is. My mother's gone." She paused and tiny tears appeared in the corners of her eyes.

"I'm so sorry, Coquette. I didn't mean to pry. Please forgive me."

"No, it's OK. It was a highly aggressive cancer called liposarcoma. By the time it was diagnosed, the beast had invaded her entire body. There was nothing we could do. The doctors told us that the Miskito people are especially susceptible to that particular form of cancer, but I don't believe it. You probably know the Miskito are a mixed race, with Afro-Caribbean, Native American, and European ancestry. It seems to me that mixed blood should promote a stronger immune system, not the other way around. But I'm not a biologist, so who knows . . . and how about you, Odel? Tell me about your parents."

Seeing she wanted to change the subject, I went along with her wishes. "They are both first-generation Italian. They were good parents, but I don't see much of them these days. I'm just so caught up with my work, I guess."

"And Penelope's parents?"

"Quite different from mine. My dad is a butcher, about to retire . . . I hope. He never finished high school. He's 'old school.' Never allowed my mom to work. He believed she should cook, take care of the house, and raise me and my brother Lorenzo—and that's it. I think he felt if she took a job, it would diminish his manhood or something. She wanted to work and was terribly bored being at home all day long. In fact, she was so bored and frustrated that she started drinking. She became an alcoholic—a sweet, docile alcoholic. A pleasant-enough, but doddering woman growing old before her time and with nothing to say. Since I graduated from high school and left home, I've only seen my parents once a year or so."

"And Penelope's parents?"

"Oh, yes, sorry. Her dad works for the State Department, and her mom is some kind of contract employee with State also. I think. I was never too clear on what she did. Her dad has been a cultural attaché for most of his career, posted all over the world. He and Penelope are very close. They talk on the phone once or twice a week."

Coquette closed her eyes. She didn't pursue more about Penelope, and I didn't really want to talk about her either. Or her parents. So it was my turn to change the subject. "Tell me more about your work. What kind of stories do you write, and for whom?"

"I write short stories, but I haven't gotten any published yet. I make a living writing hugely boring reports, mostly for government agencies. I get an assignment, do the research, and write informational pieces. Anyone with half a brain and proper grammar could do it. But I do hope to one day get some of my creative work published. I love writing. I think you do too—judging from all you've published."

I wondered briefly how she knew about my writing but decided to save that question for another time. "I, too, write nonfiction for a living," I said, "but I also would love to write something purely fictional. Or, at least, not science."

"Oh, you should, Odel! You should write a story using all the wonderful experiences you've had in your life. You probably have enough details in your field notebooks to do that!"

Had I told her about my field notebooks? I couldn't remember.

Lunch that day was fresh-caught red snapper, fileted and swimming in olive oil and garlic. Manioc and black beans on the side. It again was delicious. I briefly wondered if the Kuna woman knew how to prepare manioc properly; the skin of the uncooked plant is loaded with cyanide. But given that this tuber is a major staple in the tropics, I figured the Kunas had long known how to prepare it.

Around midday, we began sipping from the bottle of *Flor de Caña* I'd brought along. There was no ice on the island, but we enjoyed it neat. We spent the afternoon chatting in thirty-minute breaks between making love. Not wild sex, but slow, purring, sweet, intimate love. Coquette continued to explore every square inch of my body, as I did hers. She avoided getting into details about her own life. She asked me more questions about my work, my love of the sea, my childhood, and surprisingly, she returned for a while to questions about Penelope and her dad. I told her stories of my diving trips all over the world with Simon Jolly, and my many years of work in the Caribbean and Gulf of Mexico. I learned that she lived in a nice townhouse in Santa Monica, just a block from the beach. She worked out in the gym three days a week and ran three days a week. She was disciplined about her fitness and health—far more so than me. She ran on the beach, and her legs were strong.

We talked and touched, drifting from thought to thought. I told her the story of the hermit crabs on Franklin Island; that they were "land crabs" evolved from fully marine ancestors adapted for living in the terrestrial world by the development

147

of a primitive lung. I told her about the largest land crustacean on Earth, a West Pacific land hermit crab known as the coconut crab, which reached weights of nearly ten pounds. But the ancestral link that land hermits have with the ocean has not yet been fully severed, and they all must return to the seashore to release their eggs, which undergo early-life development floating among the plankton. Like mariners, they always return to the sea.

Toward the end of the day, as we both realized we would fly back to Panama City the next day, we simply held each other a lot. I felt safe and happy and closer than I'd ever felt to anyone. At one point Coquette said, "You know, Odel, I've loved you for a very long time." It was a puzzling comment, but I liked it.

We'd had just two days to learn about one another and to make love on a firm foam-rubber mattress, on a sturdy hardwood bed frame, on the sand of the beach on Franklin Island. The only sounds we heard were the lapping of waves ten feet from our *cabaña*, the breeze in the palm trees, and the occasional click of a hermit crab shell bouncing off a leg of our bed—and our own moans, sighs, coos, and laughter.

In the middle of that second night we crept out of our *cabaña* on the beach to slip naked into the warm tropical water of the San Blas Archipelago. As we approached the sea, I saw a green glow in the wavelets lapping the sand. A dinoflagellate bloom had set in, probably *Gonyaulax*, which is common in the Caribbean. *Gonyaulax* are microscopic protozoans, most of which react to agitation in the water by emitting a beautiful blue-green luminescence. I'd often seen the phenomenon at sea, where their eerie glow lights the wake of a moving ship or outlines the shapes of dolphins riding the bow waves. I didn't know if Coquette knew about this natural wonder, so I held back and watched her slip into the water. She saw it immediately and was filled with wonder, as every move of her arms and legs lit up the sea like a blue-green cloak around her slender body. She stepped out of the water and back onto the beach, and as I watched, she stood naked under the full moon, each rivulet of seawater running down her exquisite body glowing like green fire and then extinguishing itself as it hit the sand by her feet. She was a mahogany goddess covered with glittering stars.

The next morning over coffee, while awaiting our dugout taxi to "Airport Island," I pulled the card she had given me in Montelimar out of my wallet. "Coquette, where do you get your business cards made?"

"Oh, I do so much work for the government, they offered to have some printed for me. I wanted to keep it simple, and they didn't want to put any particular office or agency name on it, since I am not a regular federal employee. Why do you ask?"

She'd turned the tables on me. I couldn't tell her why I was asking or that I had another card that looked just like hers, and it was from someone who worked for the Central Intelligence Agency.

"It's just an unusual card with nothing but a name and phone number." I thought, *If she's not being one hundred percent forthright with me, I can hardly complain because I am not being one hundred percent forthright with her.* And for the first time I realized the secrecy and implications of my CIA connection were beginning to mess with my personal life. With my potential relationship with a woman I was clearly falling in love with.

I pressed on with one more question. "Who was the woman who answered the phone when I called you? Do you have an assistant?"

"I wish! No, it's just a pool of people whose job it is to forward calls to government contract employees. She called me at home and told me you'd called. I'll give you my home number."

She wrote a new number on the card beneath the printed one. I decided her explanations made sense, so I let it go.

We held hands the whole way on the flight back to Panama City as the emerald canopy of the Darién jungle floated beneath us. This rainforest is so dense, so impenetrable, that it is the only stretch of the Americas where the Pan-American Highway has not been completed. One can drive from Prudhoe Bay, Alaska, to Ushuaia, Tierra del Fuego, in an automobile, except for the impassible Darién Gap; there, one must take a car ferry (or fly) from Panama to Colombia. At one point an enormous flock of blue-and-yellow parrots emerged from the canopy and flew along below us for a few minutes. It was magical. We spoke little but communicated intimately with nonverbal messages. After we landed back in Panama City, we caught a taxi to the small hotel she'd been using, the plan being to drop her off there and I would continue in the taxi to the port, where I would track down the Scripps ship and join Jolly and his crew. As we said our goodbyes in front of her hotel, she wished me success on the Colombia expedition.

"Odel, I don't know what to say—other than to tell you that these were the most wonderful two days of my life."

"I feel the same way, Coquette. And you will be on my mind every second of every day now. Once my expedition is over and I've returned to Seattle, I'll get in touch. It will be a bit complicated, but I'll be in touch."

As I climbed back into the taxi, she ran over to give me one last kiss. Pulling her head out of the taxi and grabbing the door to close it for me, she said, "I understand your life is complicated, and I've no doubt made it even more so—but, please don't feel guilty or anxious about any of this, or about you and Penny. It will be what it will be. Trust your feelings."

She closed the door and walked to her hotel, not looking back. She had used a name for Penelope that my wife hadn't used since high school. As the taxi sped off toward the port facilities, I thought, *No one calls her Penny anymore, except occasionally her parents.*

13

Saint Michael, the Archangel

Summer 1982

The Colombia expedition went smoothly. I'd picked good dive sites, Marie Mare joined our adventure to help with the diving operations and to identify the seaweeds we collected, and I had no problems working up the invertebrates, which were mostly the same as in the Galápagos Islands, a fauna I already knew quite well. The chemists seemed satisfied with our findings. Simon Jolly's radical diving style didn't kill him or anyone else. We were so busy that I had little time to think about Coquette or Penelope's recent revelations, except in bed at night, when I was falling asleep, exhausted. But when I did think of them, my mind was awash in conflicting emotions: love and resentment, joy and fear, trust and suspicion. The days were long, and the work was hard—two or three dives daily and a great deal of lab work to sort and identify the colorful creatures the dive teams brought up from the seafloor. And I collected and preserved a great many rare crustaceans to be shipped back to the Seattle Museum of Natural History for my own research.

Steaming back to Panama City, we encountered a storm off the Darién coast. The night the rain finally stopped, the sea was still rough and the black sky was exploding with dry lightning and thunder. The chemists were huddled together in the ship's library, but I wanted to enjoy the warm tropical air and stunning electrical display. As I walked out onto the deck, I saw something I'd never seen before; the tops of our two tall masts were alive with bright blue-violet flames shooting skyward—St. Elmo's fire! I was experiencing a privileged moment, a rarely seen but well documented phenomenon that occurs at sea. The "fire" is glowing atomic plasma, created when a strong electrical field causes electrons in nitrogen and oxygen atoms to spin out of their normal orbits. The freed electrons, or plasma, erupt as a glowing discharge from the tops of tall masts on ships.

Named after Saint Elmo, the patron saint of sailors, these rare ship-mast coronas have historically been viewed by seamen in a near-religious context. It is usually considered a good omen—the presence of their patron saint guiding them to their destination. References to St. Elmo's fire are found in the works of Julius Caesar and Pliny the Elder, and it plays an important role in Shakespeare's *The Tempest*. Charles Darwin witnessed it while voyaging aboard the *Beagle*. It was startlingly beautiful and drew my thoughts back to the night of bioluminescence on a beach with Coquette in the San Blas Islands.

As I watched the two mast-top dances of freed plasma, they suddenly expanded greatly in size, twisting, and swirling skyward a hundred feet or more like great blue snakes, their glow intensifying. I could feel the stray electrons crawling over my skin and penetrating into my brain. Every hair on my body stood erect, and I felt charged with a wild energy. Suddenly, one of the plasma snakes curled downward, enveloping and igniting me with dancing charged particles, filling my mind with free ions. The cold blue fire held me for a split second then vanished, leaving me vibrating on some crazy cosmic echelon. My awareness was heightened to an extraordinary level, and I could feel and hear and see a hundredfold more acutely. The waves lapping on the side of the ship became a symphony orchestra, the deck a multitextured carpet of three-dimensional steel, even the bolts and rivets of the ship's superstructure stood out like giant jigsaw pieces to my eyes. I could hear every stroke of the pistons in each of the ship's twin diesel engines.

I sensed a presence behind me and turned to see Coquette floating in the air just above the side railing of the ship, the gray sky and black sea behind her. Slowly curling about her was the snake from my dream, its scales pulsing green and blue, brilliant red feathers streaming from its neck. I could make out every detail of their bodies with extreme precision; Coquette's large, ebony, gold-flecked eyes, the smooth flesh that covered her high cheekbones, the tiniest wrinkles on her forehead. She had a forlorn look, a single tear running down each cheek. She spoke my name in a sweet sad way, and then she began to fade away toward the distant horizon. And when she disappeared all that was left was a tiny dark spot, and as I stared at the spot it became the pinhole on the door of the house where Penelope and I lived.

The feathered snake watched this passively, and then moved in to me, wrapping itself around my body with a single coil, and then lifted upward, giving me a deep caress as it moved skyward and disappeared into the dreary mist.

And then the mast-top displays disappeared, as if someone had thrown a switch and simply turned them off. My body trembled, my hairs relaxed, and I had a deep, peaceful feeling, as if I'd just finished ninety minutes of yoga with Bob. St. Elmo's skyward spiraling serpents had given me an offering. I didn't understand it exactly, but I knew it was a gift.

As we approached Panama City the next day, I made the decision to stop over in Managua on the way home. I wanted to see Bob and Beatriz, and I also was thinking about visiting the *curandera* again. As soon as the ship docked and the phone line was hooked up, I called Bob at the university.

"*Amigo Roberto, es Odel aquí* . . . Guess what? I'm in Panama City, but in two days I'd like to take a Copa flight to Managua and see you two for a few days. Are you around?"

"Hey, Odel! Good to hear from you. Sure—we're here, and the guest room is available. Beatriz will be delighted. Say, if you don't mind, could you bring some light bulbs— high wattage—and maybe some decent toilet paper? All we can get these days are forty-watt bulbs and third-rate Russian toilet paper."

"Of course, no problem."

I spent the next two days helping Jolly's crew secure gear and pack specimens for the ship's journey back to the States. Simon and his colleagues were excited about our finds. About a quarter of the sponges, tunicates, and seaweeds we collected showed preliminary antitumor activity. In the lab, extractions from the specimens killed both liver- and skin-cancer cell cultures, and spectrographic analyses of the extractions showed the likelihood of several discrete and potentially identifiable compounds in almost all of them. However, I knew that it was a long and tedious road from these preliminary findings to identifying the actual cancer-lethal compounds in the animals and algae, and then trying to synthesize those compounds. Not to mention the lengthy series of trials, beginning with tumor-cell lines in petri dishes, then on to white rats, then to pigs, and finally to human trials. By the time you get to the rat testing, you discover that most of the active chemicals not only kill tumor cells but also have serious side effects for vertebrates, ruling out the possibility of them ever becoming useful drugs for cancer treatment. The entire process can take ten years or more before it gets to the stage of human trials, and ninety-nine percent of the original target compounds never get that far. It's an incredibly expensive business and most of it is underwritten by the drug companies themselves. This is one of the rationales used by big pharma to defend the high prices of their drugs.

With the ship returning to Scripps, in San Diego, we would not have to hire a customs agent in Panama to handle shipping of equipment and specimens but could wait and simply offload everything stateside. This would include many crates of "specimens of interest," all preserved in alcohol for later laboratory analysis. Everyone enjoyed celebratory dinner parties, Marie and I took a tour of the Panama Canal's west locks, and my mind turned seriously to Penelope and Coquette.

It was, as always, good to be greeted at the Managua airport by my old friends Bob and Beatriz. But things were starting to get a bit uncertain in Nicaragua. Contra activity was picking up, though Daniel Ortega's military was keeping them at bay, using more and more Soviet weapons sent by way of Cuba. But as government censorship continued to expand, an increasing number of people were becoming disenchanted with Ortega and the new Sandinista regime. Violeta Chamorro, the inspirational leader of both the poor and the business class, had become an outspoken critic of the new government. Over dinner, Bob and Beatriz and I had a lengthy conversation about the situation. It was complicated.

"You see, Odel," Beatriz explained, "the businessmen of the country are cautious about moving toward socialism. Even the small businesses, the shop owners and restaurants, are uncertain about what it could mean for them. But they are not organized, and they do not have a strong voice speaking for them in the government. And the new government does not trust big business because they have spent so many decades in bed with the Somoza family and the U.S., and because many of them had associations with military and paramilitary groups. But many people, like Violeta Chamorro, are beginning to feel that the only support for free enterprise

155

may lie with the Contras, who are increasingly representing the country's business interests. But the Contras themselves are mostly terrible people who are threatening to reignite a civil war—and they are also in bed with the imperialist politicians in your country. And yet, Ortega and his cronies are beginning to look more fascist every day. It is a real dilemma."

"The Contras are vampires," Bob chimed in.

To which Beatriz added, "*Y dicen que los vampiros no tienen almas.* All the people want is good government, why does that seem so difficult?"

Bob mumbled, "Good government is an oxymoron; there's probably never been such a thing on this planet. And human nature seems immutable."

I looked at the two of them and asked, "So how can the Nicaraguan people come out ahead in this situation? It appears the game is rigged on both sides. If there are only these two possible paths the country can take, it almost seems futile."

Bob replied, "Of course the game is rigged. What game isn't? Everywhere, all the time. But if we don't have a stake in the game, we surely can't possibly change things."

I asked, "Ortega has promised free and democratic elections soon, do you believe him?"

"Perhaps," Bob replied. But promises are cheap, and Ortega is full of them. And I've noticed that people who constantly make promises in public usually have other bad habits as well."

"And I hear Ortega has now censored *La Prensa*, right?"

"Yes. And we are only as free as our press," Bob said.

I admired Bob's reflective way of expressing things.

As the night grew late, I told them I was thinking of visiting the *curandera* again. I asked Beatriz if her friend Dolores might be willing to talk with *La Señora* to set up a time for us to meet. Beatriz said she would call Dolores first thing in the morning. Bob made no comment, but he stared at me with a look that seemed both baffled and inquiring.

The next day, Bob and I hung out on campus, visiting friends and colleagues. I gave an impromptu talk to his lab group about the work Simon Jolly was doing and how it afforded zoologists an opportunity to partner with chemists in ways that were mutually beneficial. Around two that afternoon, Beatriz called Bob's office to let us know that Dolores had arranged for a meeting with *La Señora* that night at nine.

Bob couldn't keep quiet any longer. "Odel," he said, "as one scientist to another, I have to ask; why do you want to see that woman again?"

"Well, I never did tell you and Beatriz much about that visit we made to her place last year. But she did interpret that recurring dream I'd been having, and she made a prediction of sorts—and it all made sense; it still makes sense. I'm not sure where the line between science and nonscience is here, but I'm intrigued enough to see her again. Maybe her visions are no more than hypotheses that I am left to test on my own."

"If it can't be empirically measured, it isn't science!" Bob replied.

"Perhaps," I said. "But would you mind driving me over there again tonight?"

"Sure—no problem. But just remember: one man's belief system can be another man's belly laugh, so you might not want to tell too many of your colleagues about this newfound advisor of yours." He grinned broadly.

The three of us had a relaxed dinner at home. Bob grilled steaks from local range-fed beef, and Beatriz made her special *gallo pinto* with a light sauce of browned butter and tomatillos. As we finished up dinner and some *Flor de Caña*, I said to Bob, "It's time to visit my new friend over in Barrio Nueva Esperanza."

"Roger that, Odel," Bob replied. Beatriz again opted to stay home.

When we arrived at *La Señora's* home, I noticed the marigolds were still blooming, and as we walked to her door the one-legged grackle cawed at us from one of the cedar trees. When she opened the door for us, we walked into her living room and were struck by a new décor. The old treadle loom still stood in the corner, but she had acquired a new sofa—a bright orange velveteen job that was covered with a thick plastic protector. *Nice,* I thought. *The plastic will likely never come off that sofa.* And hanging on each of the two walls adjacent to the sofa wall were new pictures. On one was a painting of Our Lady of Guadalupe, while directly across from it was an excellent modern representation of Saint Michael the Archangel.

I was well aware of the hold the Virgin of Guadalupe has on the people of Latin America—it is legendary. She has also been known as the Dark Virgin, the Virgin of Tepeyac, and *La Criolla.* The unwavering devotion to this manifestation of the Virgin Mary is based on the story of her appearance in 1531 to a newly converted Aztec, or Nahua Indian, Juan Diego Cuauhtlatoatzin, in the village of Tepeyac (today, a suburb of Mexico City). Not only did the Virgin appear, but she also left an image of herself on Juan Diego's cloak, and placed in the cloak freshly cut red Catalonian roses, unknown in the New World at that time. Juan Diego, duly impressed, carried the cloak and roses to Bishop Zumárraga, with a request from the Virgin that a new church be built at the site of her appearance. Zumárraga was a compassionate man who built the first hospital, library, and university in the Americas. He was also the "protector of the Indians," entrusted by Holy Roman Emperor Charles V to enforce his decree of 1530 that Indians could not be made slaves.

Shortly after the miracle, an adobe structure was built atop the Hill of Tepeyac in honor of the Blessed Mother, Our Lady of Guadalupe. It was dedicated on December 26, 1531. This, just ten years after the Aztec capital of Tenochtitlán had fallen to the conquistador Hernán Cortés, and seventy-six years before the first permanent English colony would be established in the New World at Jamestown. Eventually, a larger church was built nearby and dedicated in 1622. A much grander baroque church was consecrated at the base of the Hill of Tepeyac in 1709 and dedicated as a basilica in 1904. A modern new basilica, *El Nuevo Basílica de Nuestra Señora de Guadalupe*, was opened 1976 next to the old one, and today Juan Diego's cloak is still on exhibit there.

The first published account of the apparition came more than a hundred years after the actual event, written by the Oratorian priest Miguel Sánchez in 1648. Sánchez's account was responsible for the popularization and spread of the devotion among the *criollos* of Mexico—that is, among those people of European stock who had been born in the New World. Though the only difference between *criollos* and Spaniards from Europe was their place of birth, the *criollos* were marginalized. Excluded from the topmost positions of government and suppressed by their second-class citizenship, they reacted by developing a strong sense of community and regional identity. Thus, Sanchez's book was not only a devotional treatise but a complex celebration of *criollismo* that used the vision of the Virgin of Guadalupe as proof of special divine favor toward the *criollos*: the Virgin Mary had revealed herself to the *criollos*, he argued, even if through the agency of a lowly Nahua Indian. And of course, the image on Juan Diego's cloak was of a dark-skinned virgin, so the Native Americans (and those of mixed blood, the mestizos) also viewed the apparition as meant for them. Thus a new bond began to form between the *criollos*, mestizos, and Native Americans.

The first political use of the Virgin of Guadalupe as a national symbol was during the Mexican War of Independence in 1810, when the Virgin appeared on the banners of the military general Miguel Hidalgo, while his troops proclaimed long life to her and death to the Spaniards. Thus, the long-standing rivalry between the Virgin of Guadalupe (*La Criolla*) and the Virgin of los Remedios (*La Conquistadora*) became clearly marked along nationalistic and political lines. It is not surprising then, that after Mexico's independence was attained the Virgin of Guadalupe emerged as the preeminent national religious symbol of Mexico and quickly spread throughout Latin America. So revered is the "Empress of the Americas" today, that both girls and boys are named after her. And, millions of pilgrims visit her each year at the *Basílica de Nuestra Señora de Guadalupe*, some crawling the last few miles on their hands and knees. As the acclaimed writer-philosopher Octavio Paz once observed, the Mexican people, after more than two centuries of experiments and defeats, have faith in only two things: the Virgin of Guadalupe and the National Lottery. Although the feast day of Our Lady of Guadalupe is December 12, the feast day for Juan Diego, who was to be declared a saint in 2002 by Pope John Paul II, is December 9 (the day of the first apparition).

The depiction of the Dark Virgin on *La Señora's* wall was not the typical one seen throughout Latin America. In this portrayal, the virgin floats in space with a background of mysterious celestial objects. She is wearing a lavender robe embossed with fanciful vegetation, and a lime-green cloak splashed with stars. The Catalonian red roses that often sit as a bouquet near Juan Diego's figure beneath the virgin are instead floating freely in space, accented by beautiful pink carnation-like flowers and wispy clouds. It seemed an enigmatic painting, secretive and mysterious

Saint Michael, of course, is a whole different story. He is a powerful archangel in Christianity, Judaism, and Islam. Traditionally depicted standing on a slain dragon, carrying a banner and sword, Michael is the guardian of the Catholic Church and Vatican City, and also of mariners, the military, and firefighters. Archangels are the penultimate superheroes of the angelic world, being at the eighth level of the ninefold celestial hierarchy. Only three archangels are widely recognized: Michael, Gabriel and Raphael. Saint Gabriel's calling is to be God's personal messenger, and in the Gospel of Luke he appears to Zechariah and the Virgin Mary, foretelling the births of John the Baptist and Jesus, respectively. In the Islam faith, it was Gabriel who took God's revelations to Muhammad, resulting in Muhammad achieving the status of prophet. Saint Mike is so powerful that, despite the rabbinical prohibition against appealing to angels as intermediaries between God and his people, he still came to occupy a place in the Jewish liturgy. In the New Testament's Book of Revelation, Michael leads God's armies against Satan's forces (and, fortunately, kicked their butts).

The painting of Saint Michael in *La Señora's* house was an unconventional, but gorgeous watercolor. He had wings like those of a white dove and wore a pastel blue tunic with gold-and-green trim. A coffee-brown cape flowed from his shoulders, with one wing in front of the cloak, the other behind. The thongs on his feet had blue leather straps—the same hue as his tunic—and the strappings crossed stylishly up his muscled calf nearly to his knees. His long, wavy brown hair flowed like a river over his shoulders. Breaking with tradition, this Michael was not standing on a dragon or stomping on Satan. He was standing on fluffy white clouds as he floated through the sky, stars and planets whirling behind him; he appeared as a cosmic traveler. And instead of the usual warrior's helmet, he had a crown of what looked to be soft coral polyps, flowing and waving against the spinning cosmos behind him. Floating in space about Saint Michael were four red Catalonian roses, each with long stems bearing two leaves. Clearly, this Saint Michael was more of a cosmological prophet than a warrior. And he had surely been painted by a heart overflowing with faith and devotion.

161

The woman studied me carefully. I wondered if she could read my mind and see the sense of irony in my assessment of her new couch. "That's a beautiful painting of Saint Michael," I told her. I meant it. As we stared at each other, I realized for the first time how attractive her long hair was. A perfect blend of black and white; lustrous to the point of almost glowing. It wasn't in elf-locks, but was neatly wrapped behind her head, though large locks hung loosely to tumble halfway down her back. *La Señora* was slender, handsome, carried herself well, and obviously had confidence and conviction.

She didn't respond to my comment about the Saint Michael painting but said simply, "I understand you wish to talk with me." She glanced at Bob gesturing him to the new sofa with a quick movement of her head and eyes. Bob promptly obeyed.

"Yes. I found your interpretation of my recurring dream to have great validity. But my life seems to be getting increasingly complicated, and I returned with the hope you could once again give me some advice."

"I cannot see the future nor give you advice. All I am able to do is call upon our shared pneuma, *nuestro aliento de vida*, to help you understand your situation. If you wish, we can see what the cards have to say. Perhaps they will offer some insight for you—or, perhaps not."

"*Muchas gracias Señora*, that is all I can ask."

I glanced at Bob, who was listening with interest. "Go for it, Odel. I'm happy to sit here and contemplate Saint Mike while you're away . . . wherever that might be."

I followed her into the same room I'd been in the past November. Here, there had been no changes—a cedar table in the middle of the room with a burning candle and a vermilion tea cup, two chairs, a dozen candles burning along a narrow wall shelf, bundles of herbs hanging from the ledge. And on the smaller table in one corner, a pot of warm tea and burning incense. She poured me a cup of her irresistibly delicious special brew and told me to sip it while I tell her the purpose for my visit.

I began my story. "I have identified the dark Siren in your cards. She is a real person. I've become quite fond of her, but I don't know if I should trust her or not. I want to believe that she is a good and sincere person, but the last time I saw you, you warned me that she might not be a good person. So I am confused about what to do."

She replied, "When you last visited me, the cards told us that two women in your life could not be trusted. But they did not indicate either was good or bad. That is something only you can be the judge of. I also warned you that you were beginning a journey into unknown waters. Has your journey begun?"

"I believe it has begun, yes. But, *Señora*, how can someone not be trusted yet at the same time be a good person?

She rose and turned to gather some bundles of herbs. As she did so, she said, "*Señor*, you have a richness of mind and you know many things, but you are a naive young man."

As she continued talking, she began gently slapping the herbs on my shoulders and neck. She spoke in soft, muted tones, with a slightly singsong voice. "Drink the tea and breathe deeply of these herbs and the incense. They will open your mind. There are many reasons why people hold back the truth. Not all of them make one a 'bad person.' Sometimes a lie can be kinder than the truth. I'm sure you have withheld the truth from others many times. In fact, I think that recently you have done so with those who you care most about. The dark-skinned woman you have met is like an exotic flower high in the carao tree. She seems close to you because you desire her to be so. You breathe in her fragrant scents, but yet she remains just out of reach. Her scent is musky, irresistible, even from a distance. Her voice is beguiling and she seems an exotic creature. And her eyes look into your soul. Your time with her seems a phantasmagoria. She evokes a goddess in your mind. But none of this assures that she will not lie to

163

you. Perhaps she lies to protect you. Perhaps she lies to protect herself, or someone else. You cannot know until you bring the flower down from the carao tree, bring the fragrant blossom close to you. To know this woman, you must occupy your dream señor. Because your dreams are *sueños lúcidos*, lucid dreams, you have the power to move into them, to control them."

The old woman went on like this for some time, as the tea and the incense and the complex smells of the herbs carried me into her voice. My eyes closed, and her words washed over me and through me. I felt her voice inside my head, inside my brain, and her words gradually became my unspoken thoughts. Or perhaps my thoughts were becoming her words?

"The snake you see in your dream is *Quetzalcoatl*, the Feathered Serpent of the Maya and the Aztec. In your dream he lies upon the ground, among mortals, observing. But *Quetzalcoatl* is also of the heavens and the underworld; he is a powerful and magical being, capable of traveling through space and time, heaven and hell. He can enlighten those who listen. But he also represents death and resurrection, and human sacrifice can be the price he demands for sharing his knowledge. It is a high price to pay *Señor*."

And then there was only silence.

"But let me turn the cards and see what they say." I opened my eyes and saw that she had sat down across from me. I wasn't sure how long my eyes had been closed. She spread the cards on the table, mixed them up thoroughly, and restacked them in front of herself. She picked the top card up and turned it over. It was the *Sirena Negra*. She laid the card down in front of me. She whispered, "The dark Siren has moved to the first position in your life."

She picked up the second card and turned it. It was a handsome man wearing a flowered shirt and a white sport coat. He also wore an exceptionally fine Panama hat. She laid it down about an inch from the first card and studied it for a long time. Then she turned the third card, and when she let go of it, it hung in the air for a split second, unmoving, before it floated to the table, landing about an inch on the other side of male figure. It was the girl with the straw colored hair wearing a sleeveless peasant dress. The short dress revealed the dark, blood-red birthmark on her right thigh that resembled a rose, with its stem, two leaves, and thorns. I heard the grackle scream loudly outside the house.

"This one! This is the woman you must be wary of. Be watchful of this woman with the flaxen hair."

"But who is the man? I don't recognize him."

"You will soon know who this man is. But notice his heart, *señor*."

Over the place on his chest where his heart might be was a vaguely familiar symbol—a simple black circle surrounding a black dot.

"These are both virtuous times and dangerous times for you, *Señor*. The river in your dreams is a river that flows through the lives of everyone; each of us must find our own way to cross it. You have crossed the river and your life path is changing, although you might not yet have noticed. But as you learn to shift your perception, you will realize there is evidence of things unseen all around you. The man in the middle—he is connected to both the woman on his left and the woman on his right, though you can see that he has a heart of gold."

When I looked from her eyes back down to the table, the two outer cards were right next to the middle card—the one with the handsome man—touching it on either side. Had she moved them together and I hadn't noticed? It was odd.

"Yes," I said, "I see that the gentleman is connected to the two women."

She stood and said, "That is all the cards are telling us." And she walked out of the room. I rose slowly and followed her. She was staring out of the window at the grackle hopping among the marigolds.

Even though my mind was only half here and half somewhere that I didn't recognize, I was compelled to say something to the woman. "Why does the one-legged grackle stay here in your yard, *Señora*?" I asked.

"Because I feed him, of course!" Her tone hinted at impatience.

"Oh, yes, I see," I replied. "And how do you know what the cards mean, *Señora*?"

She stared at me for a while and then said, "My mother had the gift, and her mother before her. It was passed on to me. My sisters did not have the gift, but I did. The cards I use are the same ones my mother used. I cannot help everyone. They must be willing to relax, drink the tea, open their mind, listen, trust. That is all. I can only turn the cards. It is the cards that inform. But without trust and an open mind, there is nothing."

I glanced at the treadle loom in the corner, with its worn cedar foot pedals, beams, shuttles and shafts. I saw the pile of fabric folded upon itself on the floor behind the loom; fabric that La Señora had made, but still attached to the ancient wooden device. The long warp threads emerged out of the fabric and stretched through the apparatus to appear in the front, by the stool where she sat and worked. Running across the warp were the weft threads, the horizontal fibers she slowly added, one at a time, painstakingly. Each weft that gently wove itself through the warp, thread by thread, established a moment in time, a minute in her life. Suddenly I realized that the old loom, the threads of the warp and weft, were as her life. The finished cloth piled on the floor behind the loom was her past, but the long threads of the warp in that fabric continued on, forever, into an unknown future. She could continue those threads for as long as she wished. Or some unforeseen circumstance could cause them to simply end. Each weft thread was an instant in her life when she connected her past to the present. Each fiber of weft was a living experience in her life, now fixed forever in the tapestry of her being, connecting past to present, laying out a direction for the future. The warp was time, the weft the days of her life; and the fabric was who she was and an inkling of what she might become.

As we walked the short path from the house through the marigolds to Bob's car, I saw a small bench under one of the large cedar trees that I hadn't noticed before. The flat top was a single slab of raw stone; the sitting surface looked as if it had been worn smooth by running water, polished over millennia in a mountain river, or perhaps by years of crashing waves on a lonely sea beach somewhere. The uprights holding the bench on either end were very old carved stone squares, and, though they had weathered over time, I saw that they were identical to one another and carved with the image of the Feathered Serpent—the most important deity of pre-Hispanic Mesoamerican cultures. Usually known as *Quetzalcoatl*, it is one of the oldest gods in the pantheon of Mesoamerica, dating at least to the Olmec civilization of 1400 BC. In the sacred *Popol Vuh*, the written history of the highland Maya people, the Feathered Serpent was depicted as the creator of the cosmos. The supernatural qualities of this deity are symbolized by the feathers of the Resplendent Quetzal that adorn its body, giving it a divine nature and ability to fly over the Earth and into the heavens, while its serpent nature represents its ability to also crawl on the ground among the other beasts of the Earth. The carved stones looked to be authentic Maya. I knew it was as the old woman had told me; the colorful snake in my recurring dream was this same beast—watching the dark Siren and me, simply observing. For now.

Driving back to Bob and Beatriz's house, Bob wanted details. He said I was only in the room for thirty minutes, and all he could hear was mumbling. He said that the aromas when we exited the room were intoxicating and that I looked stoned.

"Jesus, I thought we were in there for an hour, at least. The old woman sort of puts me into a trance, I guess. She does some card tricks and interprets the cards she turns over on a table in front of me. I don't have any idea what's going on. In November she basically told me that my recurring dream was portending the future. And it seems to have happened. At least part of it. The beautiful mulatto woman on the other side of the river, the girl in my dream that I told you about—well, I've met her, and I'm very attracted to her. But she seems dangerous somehow. And there is another woman in the cards, but I'm not sure who she is. And a man—I don't know who he is either. But the cards are connecting them all somehow. And that connection is something I need to understand. The connection between the three is important, a key that I need to figure out."

Bob just stared at me. "Ohhhhh-kay," he intoned. We drove home mostly in silence.

That night the three of us were especially close. We talked more about politics and the recent disturbing news that had come out in *La Prensa* that day. An investigative study had revealed that, in the 1940s, the United States had designed and funded, with cooperation from the Guatemalan government, illegal research on venereal disease in Guatemala. The research involved infecting as many as three thousand people with syphilis, gonorrhea, or chancroid without consent and without even telling them what they were being infected with. Those infected included Maya peasants, soldiers, orphan children, mental patients, and prisoners. The ostensible purpose was to test the efficacy of penicillin in treating the diseases.

"Just one more sad example of how the U.S. has abused Latin America," Beatriz moaned.

Bob asked, "How are you and Penelope doing these days, Odel? You haven't mentioned her once since you got here."

The question hung in the air for a while before I responded. "Oh, we're fine. I guess. I don't know—we both have our own things going on, you know?" I didn't know what to say.

Bob and Beatriz just stared at me. Then Beatriz, wise beautiful Beatriz, said, "Odel, what do you see when you look into Penelope's eyes?"

"What do you mean, Beatriz?"

"Do you see love? Or do you merely see a reflection of your own passion and desires?"

The question stopped me. "I'm not sure," I said. "If you'd asked me that a year ago, I would have told you I saw love *and* desire. But over the past six months, so many things have happened, a lot of changes . . . I seem to be reflecting more on life than I used to. I honestly can't answer your question right now. But I'll see her tomorrow, and I can tell you that the first thing we're going to do is jump in the sack and screw for two hours."

Beatriz replied, "Sex first, love later. That's our Odel!"

"Well, maybe I'm just realizing that life is more complicated than I thought. But I promise you this, Beatriz—I will look into Penelope's eyes after we've romped and report back to you what I see."

"Odel, sex is all around us," Beatriz said. "It is easy to find. Do not use it as your primary barometer of a healthy marriage. There are better measures—such as the simple joy of being with a person. Love—true love—ranges far beyond sex. Don't get me wrong, sex is a wonderful and pleasing thing and I am one of its biggest fans; just ask Roberto. But you can have sex without love, and vice-versa. But should they find one another and merge, then we truly rejoice in a relationship. Love is when two hearts are in perfect balance; when souls and spirits connect in such a flawless way that they are animated and enlarged by one another."

I noticed Bob listening intently.

"True love is a gift of the gods, bestowed rarely, sometimes never upon us. It calls forth fathomless trust, and deep and lasting friendship. It even makes us better people. It

169

is an unconscious seeking of a truth beyond your own. Love is when you know that the best times of your life are with your partner, and you would rather be with them than anyone else in the world. You know it is true love when your emotions and your feelings are incomplete until you have shared those pleasures or pains with your lover. It is the contentedness of just being in the same space together, and the excitement of knowing you have years in front of you to create your future shoulder to shoulder and continue building your bonds. As people grow together through the years, abiding love puts a beautiful patina on their relationship."

"I know that all makes sense, Beatriz, of course. But, to be honest, Penelope and I don't talk as much as we used to. She seems to have little interest in my work these days. And we never take fun weekends away or even go out for romantic dinners anymore."

"Those are just symptoms, not causes. You have always been a passionate man Odel, but let me ask you, how is the trust between you two these days?"

"What exactly do you mean by 'trust,' Beatriz?"

"I mean *trust*—in every way. Do you trust Penelope to be honest with you and not purposely hurt you? And does she trust you so much that she can turn herself, including her heart and her body, over to you fully? Do you trust one another that you both care about each other's joys in life and that you are mindful of each other's needs and desires? Or is it possible that your trust in Penelope is misplaced? Are you trying to trust your own image of her, or who you want her to be, rather than who she actually is? Penelope might not be exactly the person you thought she was, or the person you wish she were, although that does not necessarily make her untrustworthy. You must come to know who she is, and then seek trust in *that* person. And you may or may not find it."

"I'll have to think about all that. Right now, it just seems a bit heavy in my mind."

Being the nonpareil kibitzer he was, Bob chimed in, trying to lighten the mood: "Beatriz, that is all rather complicated— sometimes the easiest way to deal with a man is to never tell him too much about things he doesn't really need to know."

I could tell she didn't appreciate his sideways humor.

The flight home was uneventful. It gave me time to reflect on my marriage and my feelings for Coquette, and I decided I must tell Penelope about her—even though memories of Coquette and my visit to the *curandera* filled my mind with questions. Penelope was planning to pick me up at SeaTac, and I was looking forward to seeing her.

Penelope's car waited curbside outside the airport. She stepped out wearing a colorful, sleeveless linen dress that fell to the middle of her calves. I could tell from the straps on her shoulders that beneath it was a full black lace slip. I loved her in those, and she knew it. She was wearing my favorite cologne, *Roses de Provence*. She was bright and bubbly and full of enthusiasm. When we hugged, I could tell she was supercharged with sexual energy. And then she whispered in my ear, "Oh baby, you've been gone so long. I'm so hungry for you, I could burst."

I suddenly wanted only one thing: to peel off her dress and look at her exquisite body—that body I knew so well—in that sexy black slip.

When we got home and walked through the front door, I noticed the tiny hole that remained in the wood from the note Sonia had left for Penelope. It seemed a physical reminder of a turn, a new direction in my life, a road sign the size of a pinhead, a minute portal through which I seem to have passed.

We headed straight to the bedroom. Penelope immediately undid my shirt buttons and began kissing my neck and chest as her hands fumbled with my belt buckle and pants. I pulled the straps of her dress from her shoulders and let it fall to the floor. God, she was beautiful—and hot. I realized, again, for the thousandth time, how strong my desire was for this woman. I stepped back to admire her in the black slip. It fell to her knees, but on the right side it was slit to the middle of her hip. My eyes rested on her small feet, with bright red toenail polish, and moved slowly up her perfect calves. But then I noticed something odd, revealed through the open slit of the slip. Just above her knee was a dark brown line on her skin. I slowly pulled her slip open a bit more. There, on her thigh, was a tattoo of a long-stemmed Catalonian red rose with two green leaves and small thorns along the stem.

14

Cídabenque 2

June 1984

I was on the verge of passing out in the bed of the rusty old truck, in the sweltering heat under the dusty, bloodstained canvas tarp. I'd been perspiring profusely for forty minutes. I felt my brain going numb, my limbs tingling, and my heart racing. My back hurt and a headache was creeping up on me. The sounds of what I knew to be Guatemalan army regulars were close. And then I heard a strong, commanding voice above the others. There weren't any shots being fired now. My bladder gave out, and pungent concentrated urine spilled into my pants—not much, as I'd already lost most of my body water in sweat. My thoughts raced, *This was the only vehicle around; when they get to this truck, the first thing they'll do is throw off the canvas.* I knew I had no choice but to get out of my hiding place and try to sneak away.

I slowly lifted the back of the tarp to peek out. The rain that had fallen was now lifting like steamy clouds, a fog of moisture evaporating off the hot tropical ground. My view was limited, but I could see soldiers walking through the streets, fifty yards away. They were looking for something—people I presumed—and they were distracted enough that I thought if I moved quickly and quietly, I could slip out of the truck and move in the opposite direction, staying ahead of them. The edge of the village was nearby, just three or four blocks away. There, I could disappear into the impenetrable jungle foliage, slip in a couple hundred yards and just hunker down until this operation, whatever it was, was over.

I steeled my nerves and made my move. My legs were weak, but they responded. I realized at that instant that I must transmogrify my fear into purpose, strength, and action. I had the sense it was a defining moment, a turning point. This was part of my journey that the *curandera* in Managua, and others, had foretold long ago. Cautiously, I slipped out of the back of the truck and crept toward the front of the vehicle. I saw no one in that direction. Crouching, I moved swiftly down the street, planning to turn around the first corner, just past the church 20 feet ahead. I made the corner safely and turned sharply to the right, when in front of me stood a monstrously large man in an army officer's uniform. He towered over me and must have been six-foot-seven and three hundred pounds. He had the face of a decaying gargoyle, sweaty, puffy and pock-marked, with a damaged nose that gave him a pig-like appearance. His ears were huge and puffy, like punching bags. A black eye patch covered his left eye; a thick ridge of purple scar tissue exited the patch to streak down his cheek. His hair was greasy and combed straight back, and his uniform was sweat drenched. His odor was horrifying; rancid, reeking of aggression in a twisted sort of way.

I stopped in my tracks. He stared at me, half in disbelief and half in anger. His handgun was already pointed at my stomach. The name on his uniform was Lieutenant Enrique Polyphemus. When I read the name, a chill ran down my spine.

"¿Quien eres?" he asked calmly. "¿Qué estás haciendo aquí?"

I didn't know what to say. I stumbled with my words but knew I had to stick to the plan. I told him, in purposely-poor Spanish, that I was an American, looking for a town called Flores because I wanted to visit Tikal. I told him I was a marine biologist, visiting from a research ship in Belize City, just traveling for a couple days to see the famous ancient Maya city.

He sneered and asked to see my papers. I pulled my passport out of my pants pocket; it was wet with my sweat and urine. While he examined it, with the appropriate border stamps, he asked what I was doing in Cidabenque. I told him I had gotten off the bus thinking I was at Flores. I could tell he didn't buy it. He handed me back the passport and the corner of his upper lip curled, revealing broken and stained teeth. He looked like a hideous monster.

Behind him I could see the regulars approaching. He moved his face so close to mine I could feel the breath from his crooked nostrils, emanating in deep whistling sounds. As he slowly lifted the gun and pointed it at my forehead, I was overcome with the animal odor of his rising aggression; I sensed a red-hot pool of lava, an unstoppable force on the verge of exploding. "*¿Porqué está aquí, gringo?* And don't bullshit me, motherfucker!" His English was perfect. When the soldiers closest to us saw what was happening, they raised their M16s and began walking quickly toward us.

Shit, I thought, *this is it.* I tried to think of something to say, something to do. And just then a blinding flash of light and an ear-shattering sound filled the air. For a split second before I blacked out, I felt the sharp percussion of the blast hit my chest like a sledgehammer.

I was on my back next to a waterfall, heavy drops of water striking my face. My eyes were closed against the deluge from the sky. My ears were ringing with the sound of a cathedral bell—not clanging, but prolonged and continuous, like a siren, painfully loud. My skin was tingling and an oddly familiar metallic scent filled the air. Forcing my eyes open, I saw above me a dark leaden afternoon sky. Gradually, I realized it was raindrops hitting my face. My ears were reverberating as if I'd just walked out of a three-hour rock concert. The air was filled with smoke, and debris was everywhere. The gigantic, one-eyed, pig-faced, officer lay ten feet away from me. *He's dead*, I thought. A dozen soldiers lay farther away. My mind grappled with what I saw. *They're all dead, but I'm alive! Holy shit, we've been bombed!*

Then my thoughts turned to my body. *Is everything there? Am I missing any limbs? Can I move?* I moved my right hand and fingers, then the left. Everything worked. I wriggled my feet . . . They were both intact. My eyes were filled with dirt, and I could barely keep them open. I tried moving my left arm to push myself up onto my elbow. It hurt, but it wasn't broken. I struggled to my feet. No one else was moving. *What the hell do I do now?* I thought. And then the one-eyed monster groaned and twitched. *Damn, I've got to get out of here.* I grabbed the fiend's pistol from the ground and moved as quickly as I could in the direction I thought was toward the edge of town. To the jungle. I had to get to the jungle.

I reached the dense foliage quickly, glanced over my shoulder and saw nothing, then dived into the spiny vegetation. Huddling behind an umbrella bush, I didn't move. I strained to hear sounds of other people. I realized I'd left my backpack (and water) in the street when I ran out of the village. I stood and looked back at the carnage. To my shock, the soldiers were moving, starting to stand. Lieutenant Polyphemus was standing up, looking intensely through the smoke-filled air in my direction. It looked like a scene from Dante's inferno. *Fuck! They've come back to life! It's an army of the living dead, set free from hell.*

I began crawling on my hands and knees as fast and as quietly as I could. The soil was muddy slush, hanging vines oozed thick white burning sap onto my face, the spines of acacia and pejibaye tore at my flesh and my clothing. Squadrons of mosquitos emerged like clouds from the cached water in giant bromeliads and heliconia as I brushed against them. I don't know how long I crawled through the recumbent vegetation, and I wasn't even sure I was going in a straight line, but finally I had to stop. I was exhausted and thirsty. The skin on my arms was shredded, and blood joined raindrops running in pink rivulets across my flesh. My shirt and pants had tears everywhere. But I had my passport and a Nicaraguan Army–issue handgun. I looked at it for the first time. It was a Browning Hi Power, 9 mm, single-action semiautomatic; one of the most widely used military pistols in history, in use by the armed forces of at least four-dozen countries. I had no doubts that this one had come from the United States as part of some military aid package. Everybody wins. Except the peasants.

I caught my breath and tried to clear my head to think about what had just happened. And then I heard the monster's loud voice in the distance, again in perfect English. "Hey, gringo! Do yourself a favor and let me talk to you now. It would be better for your health than if you made me track you down. *¡Sé que tiene mi pistola, cabrón!* Talk to me now, or I shall put a mighty curse on your soul."

I forced myself to shrink between the expanded buttress roots of a giant ceiba tree. I rolled my body into such a tight ball, I felt I was swallowing myself; I focused on breathing slowly and quietly, trying to be invisible. I knew that if I were still, it would be hard to see me through the thick jungle understory, and I suspected the soldiers would soon give up slogging through the mud and fighting the thorny vines by hand—none of them carried a machete. One part of my brain tracked my senses second-by-second, especially what my ears were picking up. The other part of my mind began thinking about the political situation. *What would this giant one-eyed madman do with me if he found me?* Although the sociopathic

177

General Ríos Montt had been ousted from the presidency a year ago, I knew that some of his worst protégés in the army, like Polyphemus, had gone rogue and were still patrolling the countryside as bands of renegades. They continued to terrorize the Maya peasants, especially in remote villages like Cidabenque. Hundreds of small Indian villages like this one had been totally destroyed, and thousands of Maya killed. Captured Maya were often hacked to death with their own machetes, and unspeakable stories of mutilation had circulated for years—Maya men having their penis cut off and shoved down their throat so they would choke or be asphyxiated by their own organ. Paramilitary goon squads also roamed the countryside, and they, too, had no bounds. Decapitations were commonplace.

The rain came down harder, masking the sounds of the soldiers.

15

Odel's Ménage à Trois
Fall 1982

I stared at the tattoo, my eyes wide and my mouth hanging open.

"Surprise!" she said. "Do you like it?"

"How . . . how long have you had that tattoo?"

"I got it the week you left for Panama. You were gone nearly a month you know. It's all healed now, though still a bit tender. And guess what? Marjorie got one too—the same tattoo, in the same place." Penelope giggled and whispered, "We want to take you to bed together, so you can enjoy two roses making love to your strong, beautiful body, baby!" She smiled seductively at me.

I was speechless. My mind was swirling with disconnected thoughts.

"You and Marjorie . . . " I mumbled. "Were you sleeping with her while I was gone?"

"A month is a long time, honey. I missed you terribly, and I got lonely. Marjorie and I talked about all sorts of fun things we could do with you once you got home."

I was having trouble processing it all, my mind running in ten directions at once. *Penelope and Marjorie making love to me at the same time! My god, that sounds fabulous! But, what does it mean that they have the same tattoo? And did they have sex every night while I was gone? Were they having sex in our house—in our bed! Did Marjorie simply move in while I was out of town? Am I becoming the secondary lover in Penelope's life? How could it be that they have* that *tattoo? Is Penelope the flaxen-haired girl on the curandera's cards? She must be! That would mean she's the one I must be wary of. This is crazy! The curandera told me she cannot see the future. But the cards—the cards do the talking. Do her cards see the future? What does all this mean? And who is the man in the Panama hat, and how is he connected to Penelope and to Coquette?* I once again had a feeling that my brain was being rewired.

I heard Penelope's voice in a fog. " . . . What do you mean, 'the man in the Panama hat,' Odel?"

"What?"

"What do you mean, 'Who is the man in the Panama hat?'"

"What are you talking about?"

"Odel, you just asked me who the man in the Panama hat is. I have no idea what you're talking about."

"No, I didn't!"

"Honey, yes, you did. You said, 'Who is the man in the Panama hat?'"

How could she know about that? I thought. *No one knows about that card but me, and La Señora. Not even Bob and Beatriz know about the man in the Panama hat. And if Penelope does know who he is, why isn't she telling me? La Señora was right—I can't trust this woman!*

I looked into Penelope's bright blue eyes. Beatriz's question about what I saw when I looked into them tugged at me. I didn't think I saw love there at that moment. I certainly didn't see what I saw in Coquette's eyes. I did see passion, but I couldn't tell if it was Penelope's or just a reflection of my own desires. I stared hard into her eyes, searching for answers. Searching for anything to guide me through this jungle I suddenly found myself in. I began to feel pejibaye thorns snagging my shirtsleeves, slicing through my skin, blood running down my arm. I could see a river in front of me, maybe 30 feet ahead. Coquette was on the other side. Next to her was the vigilant serpent, its scales blue and raised, pulsing, wanting to become feathers. Behind her was a man in a white sport coat and a Panama hat. He was approaching her. I had to get to her. *Was the man threatening?* Then Penelope appeared, behind the man. I saw Coquette turn to look. "Penny!" she said, and when she spoke, the man disappeared.

"Odel, what's wrong. And why did you just call me Penny?

"What . . . ?"

"Baby, you've never called me by that name. No one has since high school, except my parents. What's going on in your sweet little head, honey?"

Her voice snapped me back to the bedroom, to our house, to this reality. There was Penelope, in front of me, her pale lean body in a silky black slip. The rose on her thigh.

"I . . . I don't know."

I stumbled out of the bedroom and into the kitchen. I sat down at the table and tried to clear my head. *Jesus, am I losing my mind!* Penelope got me a glass of rum, put it down in front of me, and sat next to me. She put her arm around me and leaned her head on my shoulder. She said nothing for a long time.

My brain was spinning like a whirling Sufi. I couldn't think straight. She brought me a second glass of rum and slowly sipped on a Jack Daniels as she watched me. Finally she said, "Odel, let's just go to bed, honey. We can talk in the morning. Turn off your mind, baby, because it's not working right just now. Let's snuggle and try to sleep, and tomorrow morning we can start over. OK?"

181

That night I slept fitfully, waking up in cold sweats but forcing my mind to be quiet. I knew I needed to get some sleep. One of the museum's curators had called and left a message with Penelope that we had a meeting at the museum at ten in the morning, and it was an important one. I would need a clear head. But I knew my head was *not* going to be clear, and I'd best say as little as possible in that meeting.

In the morning Penelope tried her best to take care of me. Strong coffee, poached eggs on toast, and three aspirin. I got to the museum just in time for the meeting. I was able to force the previous night out of my thoughts temporarily, and I did my best to adjust to the setting. I gave passing courtesies to my friends and colleagues as I walked the long hallways in the massive four-story building, but all of it seemed oddly unimportant to me.

As Chief Curator, I had made the decision long ago that our meetings would be open and democratic. Thus, the curators rotated among themselves for who would lead each meeting. If someone had a pressing issue, he or she could call a meeting and even lead the meeting. I made sure that I led our monthly meetings three or four times a year. Our curator of birds, Frank Aquila, had called this meeting.

As the meeting began, I listened to the words, nodding my head appropriately but contributing little. I struggled to stay focused on what was being said. But in time, I realized I had no interest whatsoever in the discussion. It all seemed like another world. It was as if I had a realization that the museum, my role in it, my colleagues at the table, all of the issues they were complaining about—all of it was an alternate reality, a parallel universe. My "real" reality, or my "new" reality was somewhere else. On an island off the Caribbean coast of Panama. In a *copál* smoke-filled room in Managua. In a jungle on the Miskito Coast of Central America. Was this meeting no more than a reminder or an instant in time from a lingering past that was still clinging to me like a grass burr in my sock?

Suddenly I found myself speaking. "Wait, what did you just say, Arthur?"

"I said, the rumor is that layoffs will begin soon. And Audrey told me in confidence that acting director Bligh has already suggested they should begin with the science staff because they are the 'least important' component of the museum. Can you believe that! We're the 'least important'!"

"How soon?" I asked.

"Probably by October."

The meeting ended in general pandemonium, and I promised to speak with Director Bligh and HR as soon as possible and to get back to everyone with an update.

Waiting for me in my office were a pile of phone messages, a stack of mail, and a half-dozen packages to wade through. I wasn't in the mood. I called Bligh's secretary and scheduled a meeting with him the next morning. I realized I'd best call Morales to let him know that things had gone smoothly in Managua and that the delivery had been made.

When Morales answered the phone he already knew, of course, that the drop-off had been made successfully. He thanked me and said, "Dr. Bernini, I'm sorry about the Russian thing. That was completely unexpected. But you apparently handled it well, and there were no problems. We will need to be a bit more careful in the future."

Having no idea what he was talking about, I said nothing. Morales responded to my silence with, "Well, if there's nothing else then, thank you again," and hung up.

I immediately called John Thornton. The woman who answered the phone said he was out of the country but would call when he was back in town in a few days.

As I began wading through my mail, I came to an envelope with a return address that said simply, "Coquette." I quickly opened it and read the short message.

"My dearest Odel. Thank you for giving me one of the most memorable experiences of my life. You are the most amazing man I have ever known, and I'm crazy about you. I hope all is well with your life in Seattle. Looking forward to hearing from you soon. We have so much more to talk about. Love, Coquette. P.S. I just finished a large writing project that you might find interesting. I will send it along as soon as I get copies."

I reread her note several times, and then sat there staring into space, realizing that I was dying to see her again as soon as possible.

That evening, Penelope and I said little to one another. But she kept a close eye on me and pampered me with a dinner of ribeye steak paired with a fine bottle of Stag's Leap Cabernet Sauvignon from Napa Valley. She was probably worried I was losing my mind. I was a little worried myself.

The next morning I met with Acting Director Bill Bligh and Audrey Arente. It proved to be one of the more bizarre conversations I'd ever experienced. Bligh was clueless. He was also one of the most obnoxious men I'd ever known. He was easily fifty pounds overweight, acted like a bully, and had the intellect of slug. He knew nothing about the role of science at the museum, or of science in general. But at least he was direct and didn't mince words.

"Yes, Odel, the museum is indeed facing a serious financial crisis," he said, cutting right to the chase. "Audrey and I have been working hard to find where we can make cuts, but it isn't easy. We will probably need to trim nearly three hundred thousand dollars off the budget. The only way that will be possible will be by reducing our payroll burden. We will obviously cut staff where it will do the least harm to the institution. That means clerical help, technicians, perhaps some housekeeping staff, and some science staff. We must protect the public exhibits, our membership obligations, and our educational programs first and foremost. We have to keep the doors open, you see. Serve our constituents. But we probably aren't going to have the luxury of supporting the large science program that we currently maintain. Curator salaries are a major outlay. We have no choice but to reduce that expense."

Audrey was ashen, seemingly still in shock herself.

I replied, "Bill, you do realize that the museum's research curators are some of the best scientists in their respective fields in the world? Much of the museum's excellent reputation is based on the work these people do. And their only cost to the museum is their salaries; they all have research grants that cover their fieldwork and other expenses. It would be a terrible blow to the museum's stature if we lost any of them."

"I don't know how important they are to the museum's reputation, Odel. But I do know that we are first and foremost a public exhibit and education facility. We must be realistic here. Once we stabilize and get back on our financial footing, perhaps we can rebuild, hire new curators."

"How many curatorial positions are we talking about, Bill?"

"Not sure yet, but perhaps a half-dozen. We'll track the budget for six or nine months and then determine if any more cuts are needed."

I was shocked. Audrey just stared at her hands in her lap, unable to make eye contact with me. "A half a dozen! Jesus, Bill, that's a quarter of our research staff. It will cripple our science programs and make headlines in the museum world! And these folks have all been with the museum for many years—they've built their reputations here. They've built large and important research collections for the museum, especially in their areas of specialty."

"Sorry, Odel. That's just how it has to be. The board put me in charge to clean up the mess that William Harris left behind. That's what I must do. They'll have to find other jobs."

"Listen, specialists like these can't just 'find another job.' There are probably only four or five positions that exist in North America for each of these kinds of professionals. You're not talking about blue-collar workers here or temp employees—you're talking about people who spent years and years in school, and even more years becoming highly regarded experts in their fields. How many Miocene gastropod specialist positions do you think there are in the country today? They could be out of work for a year or more until something opened up somewhere, and even then they would be competing against a dozen other mostly younger people. You're talking about dealing a serious blow to some exceptionally good mid-career scientists."

"I don't know about any of that, and, frankly, it sounds like intellectual snobbery to me. But if all that's true, then perhaps they should think about making a career change— start teaching high school or something. There are plenty of jobs out there. I know the world of employment, Bernini. It's what I do."

My god, I thought, *this man can't see the difference between highly trained PhD scientists and the temporary employees he brokers through his agency.*

The conversation went on like this for about forty minutes. No matter what I said, Bligh could see things only through the eyes of a temp agency owner. He had no sense of what it means to devote twenty years of one's life to understanding the fishes of Puget Sound, or the lemurs of Madagascar, or the marine crustaceans of the Neotropics. As time passed, I realized he also had no understanding or appreciation for the museum's research collections. People were like chess pieces to him, and the collections just "took up valuable space."

Demanding she look at me, I asked Audrey how she and Bligh would decide which curators would be laid off. Audrey's lips were quivering she was so upset. Bligh said, "We don't know yet. But no one's exempt from consideration. That includes you, Odel. Maybe we'll just draw straws. Or I might need your help with making those decisions."

The thought of me being involved in deciding who to cut from the science staff made my gut wrench. "Draw straws! You're talking about people's careers here, Bill, and their livelihood. Most of these folks are in their fifties. You don't make career shifts at that age after devoting your entire professional life to one subject."

I could see he was getting annoyed. He looked irritated, and his voice took on a peeved tone. We ended the conversation and I returned to my own office. I asked our science-pool secretary to schedule a meeting of the curators for the next morning. That would prove to be a frustratingly difficult and sad meeting.

Five days later, I got a call from Thornton. We scheduled a lunch at Gabriela's place for the following day.

When I arrived at the *pupusería*, I was greeted at the door by Gabriela's older girl, Alma. She was even happier and more bubbly than usual. Thornton waved at me from his usual table, and I joined him. He was wearing a plain gray cardigan over a bright floral print Hawaiian shirt. He hadn't shaved in a few days. He looked like an aging Waikiki beach bum.

"Alma sure is in a good mood today," I said.

"Rumor is, she has a new boyfriend," he said with a big smile.

"Well, romance seems to be in the air these days," I replied.

"So I hear, so I hear," Thornton said, his smile growing even wider.

I wasn't sure what he meant by that, but when Gabriela appeared at our table, I thought he must have been referring to her and him. Gabriela was bubbly too, and the joy she carried made her even more beautiful than usual. She was, I realized, one of the most attractive mid-sixties women that I'd ever met.

And despite his past tragic losses, today I thought, *John Thornton is a lucky man.*

As we began enjoying our *pupusas chingónes*, with Gabriela and her girls out of earshot, his voice took on a more serious tone.

"Odel, I'm really sorry about that Russian thing. We were blindsided. But I understand you handled it remarkably well—very professionally."

I suddenly began putting the pieces together. It could only be one thing. It wasn't a freak accident or simply a reckless driver.

"John, could we talk about all this a bit? First, are you referring the car accident I had on the highway south of Managua?"

"Yes, of course."

"I thought that was a simple case of a lousy driver in a crappy automobile having some bad luck. Are you telling me it was something more?"

Thornton stared at me for a while and then said, "Odel, it's best if you try not to be too naive about these things. Not when you're doing something for the Agency. Did it not seem odd to you that the Russian woman would run away from the scene of the accident, abandon her car like that?"

"It did seem odd, but some people just want to avoid dealing with the law down there. But let me get this straight— she was Russian? She was following me?" I thought more about it. "If she was following me, then why was she trying to pass me?"

"Pass you? I doubt she was trying to pass you! I suspect she was trying to run you off the road. Probably to scare you. Probably to suggest to you that you're in the wrong line of work. Fortunately for you, she *was* a bad driver. And from what I've heard, you're a good driver and you handled yourself well. And you got out of there before anyone else showed up."

"Actually, I think the reason her car went out of control was because of a broken tie rod. It might have had nothing to do with her driving skills."

"How do you know this?"

"The car ended up on its side. After the woman ran off, I checked it out. It was plain as day. Ladas are probably the worst cars built on the planet—I'm not too surprised the tie rod snapped."

Thornton saw the look on my face. With a grin, he said, "Don't look so worried Odel; bad luck makes for good stories!"

I wasn't amused and continued, "So, point being, if not for that mechanical problem, this Russian woman, this seriously large and bitter-looking Russian woman, driving a shitty Russian sedan, might have run me off the road. This is not the kind of stuff I signed up for, John."

Thornton was silent. I went on, feeling my anger building.

"And I also didn't sign up as support staff for the Contras. I want to make it clear that I think they are a bunch of thugs. Our government may think they're important to support, but I don't really want to be part of that."

I stopped talking when I realized my voice was rising and I saw the look of confusion on Thornton's face.

"Odel, what are you talking about? No one's asked you to help the Contras. And, not that it matters, but you should know that most of the people I work with feel the same way as you do about them. They *are* a gang of thugs. But things aren't that simple. *Life* isn't that simple. You should be aware of that, given your education and your travel experience. Certainly given your years in Latin America. But—and I'm reducing it to the simplest of terms here—right now they're our only option to keep the Sandinistas from turning Nicaragua into another Cuba. Which seems to be exactly what Daniel Ortega aims to do. Do you want another Cuban Missile Crisis, only this time in Central America, on the mainland? And you know yourself that there are many Nicaraguans who don't want their country to go down the road of Marxist communism."

"Do you know what was in the envelope I carried to San Juan del Sur? Was it money for the Contras, or for Nica sympathizers of the Contras?"

"I can assure you it had nothing to do with the Contras." He paused and a sad look crept over his face before he went on. "Look, I'm stepping way out of bounds in mentioning this, and I don't think I need to tell you that it's something you should never repeat. Not to anyone. Not even to Penelope. Especially not to Penelope. It was cash you carried—you figured that out correctly. A lot of cash. But it was for a friend, a good man from Managua who is now living in the south. His wife and son were in the wrong place at the wrong time a while back. They were killed by stray mortar fire the week the Sandinistas took the capital. He's been struggling for years to put his life back together. It's taken forever—the wheels of government grind at a slow pace—but he had been a friend of the U.S. for a very long time. A lot of us wanted to help him out. The money was simply our way of saying how sorry we were for his losses, and to help him rebuild his life."

I stared at Thornton and saw in his eyes what I thought was a fatherly look. He seemed sincerely concerned about me, and about my take on things. He also suddenly looked exhausted. He went on.

"Listen, we may get caught up in some dastardly activities, but most of the time we're doing righteous work, Odel. Oh, we're not perfect. Sure, we make mistakes. But we're playing in a modern world, a world where every country is engaged in covert activities, and often things get a bit dirty. Like your Russian lady friend in the Lada. America has no choice but to try to hold its own in the game. But don't make the mistake of thinking it's me, or my boss, or his boss, or the CIA, or the National Security Council, or even the State Department that makes the decisions of who to support around the world. We aren't the ones who decide to keep some two-bit slimeball dictator in power, or when to move him out. That's the politicians—Congress and the White House. We're just the foot soldiers. We're given our marching orders, a toolbox, boundaries, and told to do our jobs. The Agency may have an unusually diverse toolbox and rather broad boundaries, but we're still just doing what the politicians order us to do. Even if we disagree with the politicians—which we often do—we must still follow orders."

I listened intently. It seemed there must be some truth to all this. But, of course, I had also heard that CIA director William Casey had far more influence over President Reagan's thinking on foreign policy than usual, even if it was Reagan who ultimately called the shots. I asked Thornton about this.

"The president's got the final word. On everything. And the Agency's job is largely helping him and the State Department stay out of trouble. And that requires diplomacy, which is all about control."

"The State Department is about control? I don't get it, John."

"It's all about how much control you have in a situation, or how much you can leverage. And the one thing that is most difficult of all to control or to manage is escalation. Almost anything anyone does elicits a corresponding response from others. This is obvious in situations such as an arms race, but it also plays out in other areas, and that's why we have the State Department and diplomats—and the CIA—to assure control and manage escalation."

Thornton continued, "But, look, we're also human beings with feelings, and we care about people. Most of us, anyway. And, by the way, that brings me to another thing I wanted to mention; you won't be dealing with Morales any longer. Your new contact person will be Nestor Papadakis. I think he will be more appreciative of your background and your obvious skills. He's smart and mature, and he's not the sourpuss Morales is. He's a happy Greek."

I needed some time to digest all this. I thanked Thornton for sharing the information about the envelope delivery with me, and I promised him my confidentiality. But I also wondered if he was being fully truthful. How would I ever know? Maybe it *was* cash for the Contras, and he was just covering it up. I wanted to trust John Thornton. I felt like I could. But these days, I wasn't sure who I could trust.

Then, looking at me as if he'd known me for thirty years, he said, "Life is like riding a bicycle, Odel. To keep your balance, you have to keep moving forward."

"Albert Einstein," I replied. He just smiled back at me.

"I think you can expect to hear from Nestor soon. But, Odel, I'd stay away from the Hotel Intercontinental for a while."

Fall weather began to settle into Seattle, and the sunny days of our brief summer were nudged aside for cloudy skies as the leaves on city streets turned from green to yellow to scarlet. The days grew chilly, with the nights slipping into the low forties. For reasons that were vague and shadowy, yet tangible in my mind, I still hadn't told Penelope about Coquette. I intended to, but something wary in my thoughts urged me to wait a bit longer. The *New York Times* and the *Washington Post*—the only reliable U.S. sources of news about events in Central America—reported occasional border skirmishes between the "counterrevolutionary forces known as Contras" and the Sandinista government in Nicaragua. Although everyone suspected the Contras were being supported by the CIA, President Reagan refused to admit it. More and more Cuban and Russian "advisors" poured into Nicaragua. The civil war in El Salvador grew more violent as the United States supplied the ruling party with increasing weaponry. In Guatemala the new president, Efraín Ríos

Montt, strongly supported by Reagan, was proving to be even more ruthless than his predecessors.

Penelope and I got along, but it was not the same as it had been. Sex had become perfunctory—physically but not emotionally satisfying. I was certain she was sleeping with Marjorie regularly and suspected she also might be having sex with other friends as well. But I didn't bring it up with her—what would be the value of talking about it anymore? In evenings when she drank too much, she often took on a strong, irritating tone. Sometimes she would tease me about something, but it wasn't light or fun; it had an undercurrent of disparagement in it, and it would go on far too long for my comfort. When she used to get tipsy around me she tended to slip into a romantic state of mind, but this new side of her was just the opposite, as if she were trying to pick an argument with me. It was discomforting.

In late October, Bill Bligh dropped the hammer at the museum. Six curators were laid off—a quarter of our science staff. There were also layoffs in housekeeping and various support staff positions. The local newspapers picked it up for a week or so but then quickly moved on to the next headline. The mood in the museum was somber.

One day, there was a package from Coquette in my museum mail. Inside the small box was a neatly wrapped book titled *Nicaragua. A Country Study, 2nd Edition.* No authorship appeared on the cover, but in the preface it was noted that the book had been "Edited by C. Pallas." The book was copyright by "Secretary, U.S. Army." When I opened the front cover, I found a short note from Coquette. It read, "Dearest Odel. This has been my biggest research/writing project to date, and coincidentally, one that I thought you might find interesting. I think of you daily and miss you terribly. Wishing you all the best. Love, C." I sensed a slight trace of Coquette's plumeria cologne on the note.

Nestor Papadakis called that same day to ask if I could stop by to meet him and chat. His voice lacked the dry, distant tenor of Morales; instead it was warm and upbeat, almost inviting. We arranged to meet in the same building where I had met Morales, the following morning.

That night Penelope reminded me that we were almost out of firewood and needed to order more to get us through the winter. I called a friend of ours who had a small family business salvaging wood from felled trees at development projects around the city, and he said he could deliver three cords of firewood the next afternoon at four. He didn't have time to stack it for us, but he and his son could dump it near where he knew we always stacked our winter supply. As we lay in bed that night—each of us reading our respective novels, Penelope sipping her Jack Daniels, me my rum—she suggested we ask Marjorie if she might be able to help us stack the wood and then stay for dinner. I said sure.

The next day I met with Nestor Papadakis in his "real" office—not in the interview room where I'd met with Morales. Nestor was older, a few years younger than Thornton, much warmer than Morales and with far more personality. His handshake was genuine and friendly. We made small talk for a while, and he asked me a lot of the same questions Morales had about my research travels and reasons for spending time in Central America. I could tell he was experienced and knew the region firsthand.

"Odel, it's obvious you're a bright chap and quick on your feet. You've been a big help to the Agency, and we appreciate it. I'd like to ask if you might be able to spend a few days on the coast in Corinto for us. Perhaps you could visit as a tourist—maybe it could be a sportfishing trip or something. Just hang out and be sociable with the locals. Get a feeling for things there. In particular, try to get a sense of how much shipping and naval activity is taking place in the port. How many boats, and what kind, are in the harbor." Papadakis was far more candid than Morales had ever been, and I appreciated it.

"Nestor, I haven't been to Corinto in a few years, but I know it's the country's main shipping port, so I'm sure there are plenty of ships coming and going. And I think Nicaragua's largest navy fleet is stationed there, though it's never been much to shout about. Mostly small craft, a few old patrol boats and such, I think. Unless things have changed recently, it shouldn't be hard to walk the port area for a day and make a brief assessment. But why are you interested in Corinto?"

As soon as I asked the question, John Thornton's words came back to me: *It's best never to ask "why" when you're doing something for the Agency. There's always a reason, even though if you knew what it was, you might find it ridiculous.*

I quickly tried to recover. "Oh, sorry, I'm sure you have your reasons. I didn't have to ask that question. After all, it *is* one of only two significant ports on the Pacific coast."

Papadakis chuckled. "No problem, Odel. I'd like to show you some of the information we have on Corinto and ask if you could commit it to memory. That way, when you return, you can comment on its accuracy—perhaps help us update things. We know there's been considerable activity there over the past twelve to fifteen months."

"That shouldn't be a problem," I replied.

"How soon would you be able to travel?"

"Good question. I'm dealing with some issues at my museum right now, but they seem to be in stasis for the moment. I'm dealing with some things at home too, but some time away might be just what I need. So, I guess I'm free any time."

"Could you get away within the next two or three weeks?"

"I think so. Let me look into it, and I'll give you a call tomorrow or the next day."

"Great. Do you have time to look some things over now? A couple of maps, mainly?"

"Sure, let's have a look."

Papadakis opened a drawer in his desk and pulled out a thin but oversized folder. On the outside was stamped CENTRAL INTELLIGENCE AGENCY. CONFIDENTIAL.

"By the way," he said. "You might already know that you've been given an interim security clearance. It's the lowest level but enough that we can talk about this material."

"Actually, no, I had no idea I had any kind of security clearance. In fact, I'm not really sure what that means."

"At the level of 'Confidential,' it doesn't mean much. But it helps us. And you."

Papadakis pulled the material out of the folder. It comprised a printed map and a satellite photo, both with the seal of the U.S. Department of State on them, and a crude hand-drawn sketch map of the port showing the commercial and military wharfs, what appeared to be fuel storage facilities, and a number of unmarked buildings on shore that were outlined in red.

"You won't be able to remember all the details here, but just look this over and absorb what you can. For all I know these maps are still accurate, but there might have been some expansion in facilities since these were made. They're about eighteen months old. Those round objects are fuel storage tanks. There are four of them on our maps. We'd really like to know if there are more now, and if so where they are located. The buildings marked in red are optional. You might not remember exactly where those are, and we can't let you take these maps with you, but you'll notice they are all within a block or two of the port. So if you walked those streets, you might just pay attention to what you see. I think it best if you don't take any written notes while you're there. That Russian thing has us all a bit nervous, and we don't know if you've actually been made or not."

"Who was she, Nestor?"

"I'm afraid I couldn't tell you that even if we knew. But we're not sure. There are now daily commercial flights from Havana, as well as several noncommercial flights. We just have no way to monitor passengers traveling from Russia to Havana to Managua. And our reconnaissance satellites don't yet have enough resolution to be much help. We don't even know how many Russian agents are in Managua these days, but it could be dozens, or even hundreds."

He paused and then went on. "My guess is the bar at the Intercontinental is watched rather closely, and someone simply saw the exchange between you and one of our people on the ground there. That prompted what happened the next morning. Shit happens."

Papadakis continued, "Do you have funds to cover your travel? If not, you might need to contact The Cleia Foundation and ask for a year-end supplement."

"That won't be necessary; I have the funds."

"And, Odel, please realize the sensitivity of this. You shouldn't tell anyone. Not even your wife. If you don't think a 'fishing trip' will wash, think up some other reason to visit Corinto. Maybe you could even do some work at the university, spend time with your friends there, and then take a few days off for a fishing trip at Corinto?"

When he said it, it struck me that of course the Agency knew about Bob and Beatriz, that they were good friends of mine. "Of course, I completely understand, Nestor. I'll let you know what I come up with."

What Papadakis didn't know was that I had an exceptionally good memory, especially for visuals and graphics. I remembered the port at Corinto quite well, and the maps and sketches jibed with my memory of the place. There were only two large wharfs, one for naval vessels and the other for commercial and private boats. Between them was a crude concrete stretch along the waterfront that boats could use for temporary mooring.

As I prepared to leave the his office, Papadakis said, "Oh, wait, one more thing. I don't know if this will be any help to you or not; I actually haven't even looked at it yet myself. Some copies just arrived." He handed me Coquette's new book on Nicaragua.

As I took the book from him, I looked him straight in the eyes and said, "You know, I'm actually a bit surprised to hear I've been given any kind of security clearance with the CIA. Given my political persuasions and my—how should I put it—youthful exuberance."

He laughed heartily, sounding a lot like John Thornton, and said, "Because you're a socially liberal Democrat who smoked pot when you were young? You're not so different from a lot of us who work here, Odel. Including me." He laughed again.

I smiled, no doubt appearing a bit relieved, and said, "So you do know about that. I was just wondering."

"Odel, don't go getting all naive on me. We would not have had the conversation we just had if I didn't know everything about you."

"Everything?" I actually was surprised at the way he said it.

"Just about. And from what I can tell, you're a good guy—young, smart, clever, and with a lot of experience. Besides, anyone John Thornton recommends, I trust." His smile turned into a grin as he patted me on the back. I liked Nestor Papadakis.

As he opened his door and walked me back to the entry foyer and elevators, he added, "You know Thornton's got your back." It was both a question and a statement. I didn't know how to respond—and I didn't know exactly what the implications of the statement were. I smiled, said "thanks," and left. As I walked past the lunch tables behind the building on my way to the parking lot, I noticed Antin Morales and another man at the far end. They seemed to be arguing, but were speaking in such low voices that I couldn't hear anything they were saying. Morales definitely gave off bad vibes.

I spent the afternoon in my office, thinking about this new ask from the Agency. Thinking about Nestor's comment that he knew "everything about me." And thinking about Coquette. Of course, my mind drifted to the thought of trying to see her again, meeting up with her in L.A. en route to Managua perhaps. At three o'clock Penelope called to remind me that the firewood was being delivered at four, and Marjorie was planning to meet us and help stack the wood "in exchange for dinner." With so much having happened that day, I had forgotten all about the firewood-dinner party. I jumped up and shot home to find Penelope putting the finishing touches on her famous cumin-braised beef stew, with the delicious smell of homemade bread wafting from the oven. Two bottles of Dry Creek Zinfandel were open and breathing on the kitchen counter.

Moving and stacking three cords of firewood is a fairly big job, and even with three of us, it took nearly an hour. We all worked up a good sweat. After the wood was neatly piled, we tromped back into the house and collapsed around the kitchen table. Penelope poured three strong *Cuba Libres* and we gulped them down, the still-untouched stew warming on the stove. I stared at the beads of perspiration on Marjorie's and Penelope's foreheads.

"Whew, it's hot in this house!" Marjorie exclaimed. We all agreed and stood to peel off our jackets and then our sweaters. As soon as we did so, the room filled with the sweet aroma of fresh sweat. My hypersensitive nose kicked into high gear. Years earlier, when I was in college and began having more frequent sex with women, I discovered to my delight that they each had their own distinct palette of odors. I'd never come across a feminine odor that I found distasteful. And the sweet-pungent scent of a woman's perspiration had always been a powerful aphrodisiac for me. As an adult, I had come to most appreciate aromas of things earthy or bodily.

Penelope's bouquet was instantly recognizable to me. Her fragrance had a crisp mineral and grapefruit tang to it, sweet and citrusy, like an aged white wine from Bordeaux. It made me think of southwestern France and it was highly erotic. But Marjorie's scent was new to me. She smelled of luxuriant moist vegetation, with sweet musty overtones. It reminded me of the smells of the jungle—rich damp earth, ferns, and mushrooms. It was exotic and intoxicating. Penelope noticed me noticing them, taking in their natural pheromones. She knew how it turned me on. She slowly unbuttoned her flannel shirt and let it drop to the floor, revealing a thin cotton cami with no bra underneath. The cami was damp with her sweat and clung to her every curve. She looked at Marjorie and nodded almost imperceptivity; Marjorie followed suit. She, too, was wearing a simple cami and no bra. Their odors swirled in my nose and stimulated that subconscious part of my brain where sex never sleeps. My limbic system went into overdrive, and testosterone began surging into my blood stream. They both saw it happening. Marjorie got up and walked over to me, threw one leg across me, and sat in my lap, staring at me. My eyes were inches from her breasts and I could see her nipples stiffening beneath the delicate cami.

She said, "Odel, I hope you don't hate me for being in love with Penelope. You must know she loves you and wants you, and that what we have is no threat to your marriage. I love you too Odel, and I only want the best for both of you. Please don't be angry at me or at Penelope." And then she leaned down and gave me a closed-mouth kiss, but wet with a combination of salty perspiration, sweet saliva, and *Cuba Libre*. It was a divine mixture of flavors that danced like three nubile nymphs just outside the window of my imagination. I could feel my heart rate increasing and my reliable old friend stirring. The way she said it was sincere, and the taste of her kiss was exhilarating.

Penelope rose from her chair and walked over to us. She leaned down and lightly licked my lips, picking up the flavors that Marjorie had just left there, and, loud enough for Marjorie to hear, whispered to me, "Let's go into the bedroom. Marjorie and I want to make love to you." She quickly unbuttoned her jeans, and when she pulled them off, the fragrance was like an erotic sensory steamroller crashing into me; a seductive, aromatic rush of wind wafting up my nose and into my brain, stimulating familiar nerve tracts. And then Marjorie dropped her jeans to the floor. For a few seconds, all I could do was stare at the two rose tattoos. I felt as if I were in a fantasy or a dream, but one with no clear ending and no obvious meaning. The two of them standing there seemed to me a dangerous sexual chimera, but one I could not resist.

Shaking off apprehensions, I said, "OK, I give." My whole body was screaming for it.

For the next two hours, the three of us explored every position we could think of. The girls did indeed work their magic on me, leaving no stone unturned. And watching the contortions of those four perfect white thighs with two identical rose tattoos moving above me, under me, and around me was mesmerizing. It was intensely exciting, and the physical manipulations they performed on me defied imagination. They were clearly enjoying taking me for a ride that danced the fine line between long, soaring flights of intense pleasure and the barely tolerable but erotic pain of excess. After they had exhausted me, they took to each other, giving me a glorious front-row show of lesbian love. They were tireless and thorough and continued to pleasure one another for another forty-five minutes or so. The bedroom steamed and roiled with a mix of delightful fluids, delicious aromas, and wild animal sounds.

As I watched them, my arousal overtook my exhaustion, and I was ready to join in again. But I began to notice how deeply Penelope was enjoying sex with Marjorie, and after a while I wasn't sure she even sensed my presence. I felt she was more intensely submerged with Marjorie, in a more abandoned way, than she ever had been with me. It was apparent they'd known one another intimately for a very long time. There was great sensitivity, tempo, and nuance in their lovemaking. And when Penelope paused to bring out some of her favorite toys, they both knew exactly what to do with them. Their timing was impeccable, their movements subtle, and the junctures of their orgasms carefully measured and quite spectacular. I'd never seen Penelope sustain such intensity, so charged with passion, or so insatiable. As terrific as sex had always been between Penelope and me, that day I came to believe she enjoyed coupling more with women, or at least with Marjorie. Of course, there were some things I could offer Penelope—any man could offer her—that Marjorie couldn't. But not much if you thought about it, given a little creativity.

We enjoyed a fashionably late dinner of hot beef stew and freshly baked bread smothered in butter. It paired beautifully with the big, fruity, Dry Creek Zin. We invited Marjorie to spend the night, but she said she had an important meeting at the university at eight in the morning and needed to get a good night's sleep—which she knew wouldn't happen if she stayed. But, she insisted on a rain check.

The next morning Penelope was running late and ran out of the house, forgetting her briefcase. I had volunteered to wash the dishes from the previous night's dinner, and to get the bedding into the washing machine. She called the house when she got to her office and asked if I could drop the briefcase off with her on my way to the museum. I was moving slowly, my head still swimming with all the events of the previous day and evening. I sensed the trajectory of my life changing course, though it was not at all clear what the new course was. About forty-five minutes later I put everything in my pickup truck, tossing Penelope's briefcase on the passenger's seat. It hit the edge of the seat and tipped upside-down on the floor. It wasn't closed tightly, and some of her papers spilled partly out. *Damn*, I thought, walking around to the passenger's side of the truck. I opened the door and quickly bent down to stuff the papers back into her briefcase when something caught my eye. It was an envelope that had been neatly sliced open with a letter opener. It looked familiar to me. It was addressed to Penelope at the University of Washington. The return was printed on the back flap. It was from The Cleia Foundation. I picked it up and, hesitating for only a moment, pulled out the contents. It was a one-page letter informing her that her thirty-thousand dollar grant had been renewed for another year. The rest of it was exactly the same as the letter I had received from the foundation in March, stating the reporting obligations, recommending a dedicated bank account, and so forth.

16

The Man in the Panama Hat
October–November 1982

I didn't mention The Cleia Foundation letter to Penelope. In my typical fashion, I needed to think about it for a while before saying anything to her. Some things I processed quickly, others I needed to chew on. It's just how I am. In the meantime I called Coquette in Los Angeles. I got through immediately, told her I would be visiting friends in Managua in a few weeks and asked if there might be a way we could see each another. She was thrilled, but she said she would be attending a workshop of some kind in Mexico City around then. Without hesitation I said, "Perfect, let's meet there for a few days." We worked through the dates, concluding that I could stop over in Mexico City on my way back to Seattle, just after her meeting had ended. I suggested we get a quiet B&B in Barrio Coyoacán, where we would have privacy and be close to good restaurants and museums, including the fabulous Frida Kahlo Museum, known locally as the *Casa Azul*. When I asked her if she'd seen *Casa Azul*, she said no but that she'd always wanted to—it was the house Frida grew up in and where she and Diego Rivera had lived for many years. I told her I knew a couple of swell places to stay in the Coyoacán district and would give them calls over the coming week.

The days flew by as I wrapped up odds and ends at the museum. It had become a gloomy place, and I no longer enjoyed going into my office. Penelope was her usual upbeat self and mentioned she had a five-day conference on international banking to attend in San José, Costa Rica, during the same time I would be in Nicaragua. With travel days, she'd be gone a week, returning around the tenth of December. I suddenly began wondering just what her Central American "conferences" really were. I had been more or less honest with her about everything I was doing since establishing a CIA connection, although I glossed over the details of my mystery envelope delivery, and I would not mention any details to her about my Corinto plans. I knew that the secrecy between us was growing larger, looming over our relationship—or what was left of it. But somehow her secrets seemed so much more! She knew I was receiving funds from Cleia, so why hadn't she told me she was as well? I realized I had no idea how long she'd been getting grants from the foundation. I was beginning to resent the extent of her secrecy, the ongoing sexual affairs with women, and whatever it was she was doing for Cleia, or the State Department, or the CIA—I had no idea. The Cleia Foundation seemed legitimate; perhaps her grants had nothing to do with the CIA. And how much transparency could I reasonably expect from her, given my own growing list of secrets? But I knew this all was chipping away at our trust, and at our wobbly marriage.

I also thought deeply about Penelope's sexuality and about sex within the context of our marriage. As exciting as the threesome with Marjorie had been, I knew that, for me, it was more a fulfillment of curiosity and raw sexual enthusiasm than anything else. Perhaps it was no more than what Beatriz had called "a reflection of my own desires." It seemed almost like self-gratification. But then, *what was wrong with that?* And yet, I wasn't sure I wanted to rush into it again. And the idea of Marjorie being in our bed on a regular basis was somehow disquieting to me.

These thoughts were beginning to change my views on our marriage in ways I didn't yet fully understand. And, perhaps not surprisingly, it made me miss Coquette all the more. I was longing to see her, to hear her mesmerizing voice, to gaze into her deep, dark eyes, to feel her enveloping presence, to breathe in her exquisite fragrances, to experience the unique sweet, soulful sex we had—a kind of emotional intimacy that I had never before experienced. I yearned to be alone with her, completely alone, wrapped up entirely in one another. My entire sexual history with other women, including Penelope, was emerging in my mind as having less depth than I had imagined. Not that I saw it in any negative way—just in a different way. Making love with Coquette had a profound wholeness to it. It seemed almost spiritual.

A week later I called Coquette again.

"I found us a great place to stay in Coyoacán. It's on Calle Ignacio Allende, close to the Frida Kahlo Museum, just north of Plaza Hidalgo. They have plenty of rooms and said we could just show up whenever."

"Oh, Odel, I can't wait. I miss you so." The way she said it melted my heart.

"Me too, Coquette. How about we meet at the rooftop bar of the old Hotel Majestic on the main *Zócalo* in Mexico City on December fifth. I can catch a flight from Managua that arrives at one that afternoon; I should get to the Majestic by two or so. We can have a drink overlooking the Metropolitan Cathedral and the *Zócalo*, then taxi to Coyoacán."

"Deal," she said.

And the secrets grow, I thought to myself.

I called Bob in Managua and told him I'd like to take him up on his offer to give a seminar at the university. I wanted a solid excuse to visit Managua. It was easy for him to arrange, and three days later he called me back to confirm. I could give a seminar on campus in late November. I would spend a few days with him and Beatriz, deliver a seminar on campus, head to Corinto for my "fishing trip," and then fly to Mexico City. I would be home just a few days after Penelope got home from her Costa Rica trip.

I called Nestor Papadakis to fill him in on my plans, and he thanked me. I called John Thornton to see if we could connect before I left for Managua, and we arranged to meet at Gabriela's for lunch a few days later. Over *pupusas* and beers, I filled him in. He asked me how I was getting on with Nestor and I told him I liked the guy. He again reaffirmed that Nestor was 24-karat and that I could trust him. Thornton asked me how well I knew Corinto, and I told him I knew it fairly well. It wasn't a complicated town.

"Listen, Odel, from what I can tell, that Russian snafu was just a one-off. I think one of their people just happened to have seen the handoff in the bar and decided to mess with you. I doubt anyone there knows who you are. But, please, do be careful in Corinto. Honestly, I would feel terrible if anything happened to you."

His words gave me pause. *Shit,* I thought, *Is this silly exercise actually something I should be worried about?* "John, what exactly are you saying?"

"I'm just saying to be careful, that's all. Do *not* take any unnecessary risks. None whatsoever."

Papadakis's comment that Thornton "had my back" came to mind. I made a decision to dig a bit. "Are you always so concerned about cooperators? The Agency must have thousands of people like me."

"Not thousands, but we have a number, of course," he said. But then he went on. "*Amigo,* you are young, bright, quick on your feet, and quite talented. But you're new at this, and—please don't take offense—you're a bit naive."

I winced and rolled my head. "Damn, I'm getting tired of people telling me I'm naive. Listen, John, I can scope out Corinto in one day. It's not that complicated, and I remember it quite well."

"Just be mindful, Odel. That's all I'm saying."

The weeks slipped by, and the day of my departure for Managua approached. I realized I wasn't going to say anything to Penelope about my discovery of her Cleia connection until I returned from my trip. I didn't feel any sense of urgency about it. In fact, it might give me some time to snoop around a bit more before I confronted her. I updated an existing seminar talk I had from a year or so ago on the biogeographic origins of the Caribbean marine fauna and gave it as much of a Nicaraguan spin as I could. It's a very cool evolutionary and geographic story, with marine life accumulating from several different sources over millennia. Some of the Caribbean animal lineages are remnants of an early shallow sea that formed when the supercontinent Pangaea began fragmenting nearly two hundred million years ago, and the New World separated from the Old World to begin its slow westward drift to open the Atlantic Ocean. Other lineages are much younger, descended from an ancient seaway that once connected the Caribbean to the Pacific Ocean across what is now the Isthmus of Panama, probably around two and a half million years ago. Other species arrived from the south, sharing their genealogical relationships with various marine animals from the coast of tropical Brazil. I had plenty of carefully prepared maps and graphics, as well as photographic slides of beautiful marine creatures—flowery sea anemones, colorful undulating sea slugs, spectacular octopuses—all of which typically brought *oohs* and *ahs* from an audience.

The day before my flight I had to make a run to the airport to pick up a delivery of specimens that I'd been expecting from a colleague in Panama. The material was sitting in airfreight customs. I found myself driving in the vicinity of the building where I'd met with Antin Morales and Nestor Papadakis. For some reason, I felt an urge to drive by the place. As I approached the nondescript property, I thought I saw Penelope's car a block or so in front of me. I slowed but kept my eyes on the vehicle. The car turned into the parking lot behind the eight-story building that I knew. I was pretty certain it was her. I drove past the parking lot entrance and pulled over a half a block down the street. Jumping out of my truck, I walked quickly back to the lot. It was Penelope; I saw her walking across the asphalt toward the back of the building where the lunch tables were. I thought for a second that it would be foolish of me to follow her, but I couldn't resist. Staying behind the highest cars and vans in the lot and keeping a safe distance, I watched her approach the grassy patch were the tables were set up. And then I saw a man wearing a white sport coat and Panama hat sitting at one of the tables, his back toward me. Penelope walked straight to the man and said a few words to him; he gestured for her to sit across from him.

I got as close as I could without risking being seen. I could hear their voices but couldn't make out their words. What seemed to start out as a normal conversation quickly escalated, as both of their voices grew louder. At one point Penelope was almost shouting, but the man in the Panama hat, though clearly upset, kept his cool. I could only hear snatches of the conversation. The man said something to her about a "charade," and she replied, "You're a fine one to talk." They obviously knew each other well. The man held up a finger toward Penelope, picked up a walkie-talkie lying on the table, listened for a second, said a few words, and then laid the radio back down.

Penelope and he continued talking, and their voices quickly became elevated again. The argument reached a crescendo, and then they both fell silent. After a minute or two, they spoke softly to one another. The man reached over and took one of Penelope's hands, holding it and caressing it with his other hand. She shook her head back and forth, and I thought she might be crying. She stood, then he stood, and then they embraced. He held her tenderly. She rested her head on his shoulder. Finally she pulled back, and they looked into each other's eyes, holding outstretched hands, and she shook her head affirmatively.

As Penelope walked away back toward the parking lot, the man in the Panama hat turned to watch her. He was wearing a familiar Hawaiian shirt under his sport coat. It was John Thornton.

PART III. INTO THE MYSTIC

Hark, now hear the sailors cry
Smell the sea and feel the sky
Let your soul and spirit fly
into the mystic

Van Morrison, 1970

17

Destiny

November 1982

I didn't say much to Penelope the night before I left for Managua. But seeing her with Thornton that way seemed like another nail stuck into the doorway of my shifting reality. My mind was spinning with possibilities. The rug was being pulled out from under me. I tried to be objective about it all but felt anger flooding through me. My wife and a new "friend" of mine, someone I had been growing to trust, had both been dishonest with me. They clearly were, or had been lovers. I wondered for how long their relationship had existed. And what about Gabriela? *Shit*, I thought to myself, *What kind of people am I dealing with here?* I felt awash in a rising tide of uncertainty.

By the time I got to Managua, my anger had grown to the point that it was consuming me. I picked up my rental car and drove to Bob and Beatriz's house, steaming the whole way. They could tell I was upset. We stumbled through dinner, and I was drinking heavily. Finally Beatriz said, "Odel, you seem upset. Are you struggling with something? Do you want to talk about it?"

I did want to talk about it, but what could I say? I was sinking deeper and deeper into a vortex of secrets. I was certainly being dishonest with Penelope. And I hadn't been exactly transparent with Coquette either, and I was keeping more and more from my dear friends Bob and Beatriz, who, at that moment, seemed like the only friends I could still trust. I felt a need to get something off my chest. I wasn't sure what—but something!

I cautiously began to tell them about my discovery of Penelope's bisexuality. How I stumbled upon it, that she'd been bisexual her entire adult life, and that she'd been secretly having affairs with women, presumably ever since we'd gotten married.

Beatriz exclaimed, "*¿Jesucristo, mi amigo, este es un gran problema, no?* How do you know Penelope is only sleeping with women and not also with other men? She obviously has not been honest with you about all this."

"I *don't* know . . . I don't know anything. In fact, I do have reason to suspect she's having an affair with another man—an older man. Or perhaps the affair has recently ended. I'm not sure. Although he's older, he's quite handsome and interesting. Someone I thought was a friend, actually. I like him . . . or, *liked* him . . . but, it's all so complicated. I can't even begin to tell you how complicated. I also think she's in love with a woman she's been sleeping with for some time, the one I first mentioned to you. Her name is Marjorie, and she's actually very sweet. And, I must admit, very sexy. The two of them seduced me just before I left to come down here—it was really quite an experience. I think Penelope is working up to asking me if it would be OK if Marjorie moved in with us. It's all sort of mind boggling."

Bob's eyes widened and he straightened in his chair, but I went on. "You know, I'm a seriously liberal and open-minded person, but I'm not sure I'm comfortable thinking Penelope's sleeping with other women on a regular basis and I'd never really know about it. And there's more. She's also not told me about other things—things that I've stumbled upon accidently. It's not that she's outright lying to me; she just isn't fully forthcoming. She keeps things from me. I believe she thinks it's her right, her privilege, to have this separate, private side to her life. It's hard for me, intellectually, to argue against that. But there's something else that's even worse. Over the past year I've discovered another side to Penelope that she didn't show me before we were married. A dark side. It comes out when she's had too much to drink. It's unbecoming and unkind—and can be relentless, no matter how I try to tamp it down. She almost delights in demeaning me when this side of her comes out. I feel like she was dishonest with me during our courtship period, hiding that part of herself. Either that or she's changing, becoming a different person. Someone who is less loving and caring. And she's drinking more heavily—too much, really."

Bob, who had been silent, cut in and said, "Wait, back up a minute Odel—are you telling us you had a ménage à trois with these two beautiful women? And that Penelope is going to ask if you might be OK sleeping with the two of them every night? Jesus fucking Christ man!"

Beatriz glared at him.

"Yes, I guess that's it. And there's more. Do you remember those dreams I'd been having—the ones that seemed so lifelike? And do you remember what *La Señora* had to say about them? Well, she was right. About everything. She warned me about a beautiful blond woman in my life who could not be trusted, and the woman had a rose-shaped birthmark on her thigh. I saw it on the card that the old woman used to interpret my dreams. The last time I got home from traveling, Penelope had gotten a rose tattoo on her thigh exactly like the one on the woman's card. Not only that—her girlfriend, Marjorie, had gotten the exact same tattoo on her thigh."

214

I could see that Bob was fascinated. "Odel, my mind is reeling at the thought of you and these two extraordinary, rose-tattooed women rollicking in bed together. But, really, man, this is all pretty wild shit. I think I need more details about the ménage à trois."

Beatriz told him to clam up, whereupon Bob uttered, in a reflective fashion, "Ah yes, but perhaps they were no more than simple victims of the flesh."

And then Beatriz's Catholic upbringing got the best of her; she made the sign of the cross and said to me, "My dear friend, this is not funny, and it is not trivial. I think it would be wise if you did not see *La Señora* again. I'm sorry I even suggested that you see her to begin with."

Bob spoke up again, "Odel, this business with the *curandera* lacks even the slightest trace of scientific underpinning. How can you be so confident in this mysticism?"

But Beatriz quickly responded, "*Amigos*, as I have told you before, just because we do not understand the science behind something today does not mean there isn't a scientific explanation awaiting discovery. You are biologists—do you recall the scientific establishment's response when Fracastoro proposed his germ theory in the sixteenth century? He was ridiculed, and his idea was suppressed for three hundred years! He had even discovered syphilis and typhus, but the work was ignored because no one felt it had a 'trace of scientific underpinning.' And Fracastoro was Italian, Odel—like you!"

I ignored them both and went on. "And do you remember the girl in my dreams—the beautiful mulatto across the river, with the Siren's voice? *La Señora* knew about her too. Or I suppose I should say her cards informed us about her. I've met her. And I think I'm in love with her. And Penelope knows nothing about her. You see, I have not been forthcoming with Penelope either."

I stopped speaking abruptly, realizing what I'd just said. *Christ*, I thought, *this must all sound insane to Bob and Beatriz! I've said enough.*

"And there's more," I said. "But I think I've said enough for now."

Bob asked me how I felt about all this. I told him I was mostly just confused. And angry. He replied, "Well, as the Everly Brothers told us long ago, love is strange."

Beatriz frowned at him and said, "Our poor, dear friend, Odel. You are indeed confused. Penelope is not a 'different person' than the woman you married. She is the same person. You simply didn't know all the aspects of her personality; you did rush into the marriage, you know; and you were still in your twenties! Perhaps you should have lived together for a few years before you made the marriage commitment. Although I'm not sure what kind of 'commitment' you two actually have—you are both so independent. But, *mi quierdo amigo*, everyone has within themselves many sides; some are hidden, some can be dark—even in the best of us. Humans are complicated creatures, and most of us carry around both good and evil spirits inherited from our childhood or from our parents—perhaps even through our genes. We are all terribly imperfect Odel, which is why we must learn to forgive. And, honestly, we do have the right to keep some of these spirits and secrets to ourselves. Our thoughts are privileged places within us, and everyone has a right to their own private reflections. Even our fears and our dreams may be kept private should we so choose. Penelope might truly be bisexual, and that's simply how she is wired, and she is just being true to her inner nature. You must give her credit for that self-awareness and personal honesty. But that nature may be incompatible with your marriage, and it was something she should have explained to you before you took your vows."

"You make good points Beatriz, as always," I replied.

Bob shook his head back and forth and commented with a facetious seriousness, "Life can be perverse in its complexities, my friend."

Beatriz gave him a frustrated look and continued, "Our personal goal should be about making ourself the best possible person we can be, to 'strive for a higher level of consciousness,' as Roberto would say. But very few of us ever fully shake our demons. And demons have a way of escaping that box we try to keep them in, inside our mind. They escape in the dark of the night in our dreams, or in the light of day when we're stressed or perhaps have had too much to drink. That Penelope has a dark side does not surprise me, although I am sorry to hear she is thrusting it on you. What surprises me is, you seem more concerned about her occasional lapses than you are about the issue of trust in your marriage."

Beatriz could see Bob and I listening closely to her words.

"You may choose to call Penelope's lack of forthrightness a matter of choice or her right to privacy, but I do not—not in the context of a marriage. To me, they are simply lies. A healthy marriage cannot exist in such circumstances."

Bob suggested that perhaps Penelope's increased drinking and berating of me might be linked to some new stress or frustration in her life. "Maybe she's just unhappy with you or with your marriage at the moment. Maybe she's unhappy with herself. Maybe she wishes she were married to Marjorie—shit, man, maybe Marjorie's just better in the sack than you!"

"Enough, Roberto!" Beatriz exclaimed.

"Well, who's to say, who's to say . . . " Bob mused.

Turning to look at me, Beatriz said, "Perhaps it is simply that Penelope does not know how to love. It seems to me she has always had difficulty letting others in. And to love without knowing how to love can torment both people in a relationship."

It was all a lot to process and my mind was still catching up. "You know, it never occurred to me that Penelope's dark side could be something inherited from her father," I said. "But now that you mention it, I can see a strong similarity in her bad behavior to what I've seen in her dad."

"And what is your dark side, my friend?" Beatriz asked.

I thought about it for a few minutes and then had to admit that I didn't think I had a dark side. We all had a good laugh at that, and Beatriz said, "Well, just think about it for a while." I admired her relentless pursuit of the truth. Bob, on the other hand, opined, "Some are saved from sin by their simple ineptitude."

We talked long into the night, and having these friends to spill my guts to made me feel better. But in the morning, my anger was still there. Over strong coffee, I told Bob and Beatriz that my irritability was lingering, and I didn't know what to do about it. Beatriz said, "Do not let it eat you up. Anger can be like a cold wind in your mind, trying to blow out the flame of beauty."

Bob said, "Hang on to that anger for a while, *amigo*: it is not only natural, but it's an emotion that can be usefully employed when the right circumstance arises." Beatriz rolled her eyes.

I'd already decided to visit *La Señora* again. I didn't mention it to Beatriz. But I went to the university with Bob, and we called Dolores from his office. A few hours later it had been arranged. I would go to the old woman's home at nine that night. I spent the day finalizing my seminar, to be delivered the following day at ten, and checked out the room I'd be speaking in. The room was large, with around three hundred seats.

"Bob," I said, "this room is like a theater. It's far too big. I don't expect more than twenty-five or thirty people to show up for my talk. Your lab folks and a few others."

"You underestimate your fame at our university. I predict we'll fill the room to capacity. We have a strong connection to the sea in this country. Your Central American research and wonderful book on Caribbean sea life has made you famous in this neck of the woods."

We had an early dinner that night. Over our meal, I told them I was going to try to relax with a day of sport fishing out of Corinto. And then I told Beatriz that I was going to see *La Señora* at nine. Her response surprised me.

"That woman knows too much, Odel. She has gotten into your head, and I don't think it is a good thing. Please do not visit her again." Beatriz was emphatic.

"I must see her again," I replied. "Don't you see? She's the only person who might know what's happening to me."

"She has only given you bad news, told you sad things, and injected confusion into your life. If you stop seeing her, perhaps you will stop experiencing these unfortunate things. I think she might be a witch who is casting an evil spell on you."

"Well, just one more time. I'll see what she has to say."

I figured I could find the woman's house on my own now, so at eight thirty I climbed into my rental car and headed to Barrio Nueva Esperanza. I got turned around a few times but managed to pull up to *La Señora's* house just at nine. It was an unusually cold night. The one-legged grackle was nowhere to be seen. A stiff breeze had picked up, and I felt a storm might be brewing. The marigolds in her yard were hanging their heads, looking cold and sad—like I was feeling. I knocked softly on the door, feeling a bit nervous because this time I was all alone. When the door opened, a strikingly attractive woman I judged to be a few years younger than me stood there. It was the last thing I expected. I just stared at her.

She stared back at me, saying nothing. Her skin was golden, a shade lighter than *La Señora's*. It had a polished glow, like freshly browned butter. She was around five-foot-seven and light in build. Her hair hung nearly to her waist, looking as if it had just been carefully brushed. It glistened like black velvet except for an inch-wide Mallen streak, a startling burst of pure white hair, as if a meteor were on her head with the long tail slashing dramatically toward the ground. Her eyes were also astonishing—large, like *La Señora's*, and brilliant, one golden-brown, but the other emerald-green. The green eye had oddly familiar flecks of the same gold-brown; as if a painter had dabbed a brush into her golden eye, then sprinkled glitter from it across her emerald eye. I felt she was taking me in, assessing me, probing my mind with her eyes. Without words, she invited me in. Gesturing to the plastic-covered couch, she walked out of the living room without speaking. A few minutes later *La Señora* entered the room. But instead of inviting me into her "card room," she sat on one of the wooden chairs and spoke.

"*Señor*, what brings you to this house again? I see tension and distress in your face and demeanor."

It seemed odd, not what I'd expected, but I plunged ahead. "*Señora*, everything you have told me has come true. I am astonished at the accuracy of your . . . what your cards have told me. But now I am unclear what to do. I no longer know who I can trust. I need your advice."

"The cards do not lie. But I thought I had made it clear, *señor*—I cannot offer advice, nor can I see the future. All I can do is turn the cards. For some, this is insufficient, or inadvisable. Perhaps you should not have visited me to begin with. It is clear that you are on a new and challenging path, but I cannot help you navigate it. I think the cards have spoken all they are able to speak for you."

I didn't know what to say. Suddenly I felt desperate. Was she saying our visits were over? I stared at her in silence.

"*Señor*, you are young, strong, and intelligent, and the great cycle of your journey has already begun. All men are sailors though many, like yourself, choose to travel their own seas. You are still on your path to wisdom. You will need courage for your voyage, and you seem to have that. But it is the journey itself that will give you the wisdom you need. You will suffer losses, and through those you will gain knowledge and sagacity. But suffering can bring wisdom only if you do not cling too long to your sorrow. You must let go of the life you had planned, so as to accept the one that is waiting for you. Your destination, you see, is not a place, but a new way of looking at things."

"I understand, *Señora*." It seemed like a feeble thing to say, and I actually didn't understand at all. At that moment, I felt totally adrift.

After a long pause, neither of us moving or speaking, she said, "It is possible that you need to speak to someone else. Someone with a different gift. Perhaps it is time you meet Destiny. This is not a coincidence. In this house, there are no coincidences."

I felt goosebumps on my flesh. *Tonight? I am to meet my destiny tonight? Here, in this house, in this run-down barrio? All alone?*

She went on. "I cannot promise you anything. But she sees things I cannot see."

Huh? Who sees things? I thought. *Well, what do I have to lose at this point?* But it seemed like a sweeping and decisive statement!

"I am ready to meet my destiny, *Señora*, if you would be so kind as to direct me to it."

She looked at me curiously, shook her head as if to say "this stupid gringo," and then rose and walked out of the living room. I sat on the plastic-covered velveteen couch for what seemed like an eternity. I stared at the beautiful painting of Saint Michael and the deeply moving painting of Our Lady of Guadalupe, which I sensed had universal qualities to it, even for me, an atheist. I wondered what my destiny was to be and in what way I might be shown my future. I could hear voices, a muted conversation in the adjacent room. Finally the door swung open, and the attractive young woman who had greeted me when I first arrived walked in. I stood. She reached out with her small hand and said, "*Señor*, my name is Destiny. My mother has told me of your plight." Her English was perfect. I noticed she was wearing the faintest hint of lipstick, and it made her lips appear moist and inviting. I also noticed her very pleasant and somehow familiar body aroma.

I might have smiled uncontrollably, but I tried to suppress it. Destiny was, I realized, a singularly attractive young woman—slender and with gorgeous hair, like her mother. And she did *not* look like a *bruja*, although her hair and eyes were certainly exotic. But then, outside these thoughts, I suddenly felt embarrassed. How much did this lovely young woman know about me, and did I really want to talk with her about the very personal situation I was in?

La Señora walked out with two cups of herbal tea. She didn't look at us but walked straight into the room where we had twice met before and sat them on the cedar table. Her daughter followed her into the room. I followed Destiny.

We sat across from one another and said nothing as her mother lit the candles and a *copál* burner in the corner before leaving the room. Destiny stared at me intensely, her large bicolored eyes catching the flickering candlelight in the dark of the room. We sipped our tea in silence for a few minutes, and then she spoke.

"It seems that you have begun a journey, and there remain many passages before you. It is not to be a peregrination, but a voyage to an entirely new place for you. This much my mother knows. Please take another sip of tea, and then hold my hands." She stretched her willowy, golden arms across the table to me. I followed her instructions.

She closed her eyes and held my hands gently. I sensed I should also close my eyes, so I did. The strong herbal fragrances of the tea and unusual *copál* wafted into my nostrils, and I began feeling vaguely light-headed. She turned my hands palms up and rested two fingers of each of her hands on them. Her fingers made light circles over my palms. They felt charged. She began a soft humming melody—was it the same melody her mother had used? I began to feel disengaged from the room, and soon all I could feel was her electricity in the palms of my hands. This continued for some time, and eventually I opened my eyes and saw that she was staring at me with a keen intensity. Her eyes had changed; they were wide open and on fire. Both had become a brilliant, electric emerald color. They shimmered with strength and mystery. Her head didn't move, and she didn't blink. It seemed as if she were not breathing, in a trance. I stared into her remarkable eyes, transfixed, and felt them boring into me, through my own eyes, through my skull, into my brain, exploring, attaching to neurons and coursing through my thoughts. I was frozen in time and place. I knew that Destiny was inside me.

After some time, she closed her eyes again, and then reopened them. She gripped my hands once again, gently. Her eyes were their normal-though-paranormal doppelgänger moons. She said, "*Señor*, what you are seeking is not out there; it is already within you. Your journey will require physical strength, but it will require far greater inner strength. Strength of spirit and dedication to your kismet. I have seen you in the jungle, alone and frightened. But you are not alone. When you confront the greatest challenges, you will find your power deep within yourself. You will discover that the way down may also be the way up. This will be the opportunity you must seize."

"I can also feel your anger—a great deal of it. Do not squander it, but harness it to help navigate your passages. Do not let your anger tear you down, for it can be even more destructive than the betrayals that you sense. Doors are closing behind you, but new ones are already opening ahead of you. Do not dwell on the closed doors, but look to the new portals before you. Through those, you will be able to soar above the fray and have extraordinary vision. And do not be quick to judge others whom you encounter; you have many friends, and they are there to help you on your travels. The universe is shifting for you, repositioning your forward path, offering you guidance along the way. What you might think are coincidences are actually the crossings of your life's threads on your journey from the past to the future—they are connections between the warp and weft in the growing tapestry of your being. Nor are the people you will meet coincidental; they are other pilgrims who are there to help you on your voyage. This is how providence can assist you, but only if your heart and mind are open to it. Be courageous, but do not be foolish. Your journey has already begun."

I wanted to absorb every word she said, but I could barely keep up with her thoughts. She went on.

"Every day, the world around you tries to make you into someone you are not, someone like everyone else, trapped in amber. The great challenge to your spirit is to find yourself and to be true to your nature, to your innermost yearnings. That will require embracing your difficulties and your sufferings; but such hard things can be worthy of your labors. And this cannot be achieved without solitude, which you need not seek as it will find you."

Her eyes and words seemed to me almost as a poem.

She stopped talking and stared at me in silence. But her eyes spoke to me, and they said, unequivocally, *You can trust me.* And then, ever so gradually, a faint smile appeared on her face. I interpreted it as one of happiness, or even felicity. And she said, "Dreams are the raw stuff of imagination, the place where mind and heart meet and, brick by brick, lay the foundation for a new path in one's life. I can see that you are a man of passion. Sometimes it is better to see with your heart than with your eyes."

And then she seemed to breathe the words, "Perhaps we will meet again, farther along in your pilgrimage."

Destiny stood, her smile remaining, and she looked at me in what I felt was a caring, almost loving way. She caressed my cheek slowly and softly with her warm hand and her scent went deep into my brain—it was as exotic as her eyes, yet strangely familiar. I lost myself for a moment; and then realized that Destiny had turned and was walking out of the room. I felt it was the one and only time I would ever see her, although in some little corner of my mind I had filed away a clear image of this beguiling woman with the electric touch and extraordinary eyes. And her parting words were burned into my memory.

When I walked back out to the living room, *La Señora* was standing by the front door. She opened it for me and said, "We are done here, Señor. We have nothing more to offer you." Her words were like a heavy weight laid upon me; a weight I didn't fully understand. And as I moved toward the door, I could feel the eyes of the Dark Virgin following me.

When I left the house, a cold wind blew through me like ice: I shivered and held my light jacket tight to my chest. Stumbling into the rental car, my mind was reeling. I was trying to remember all the things that the two women had said to me. I wished I had had a tape recorder in my pocket. But the older woman's powerful parting words were lodged in my brain—"we are done here, Señor." I drove back to Bob and Beatriz's house, my thoughts spinning. The weather was getting worse. I knew a storm was headed my way.

I got back to the house around ten thirty. Bob and Beatriz were waiting up for me, a bottle of *Flor de Caña* on the kitchen table. Over *ron en rocas*, we chatted. I told them about my final experience in Barrio Nueva Esperanza. When I mentioned Destiny, Beatriz started. "The daughter! I thought she was still in the hospital?"

"You know about the daughter?" Bob asked.

"Only stories I have heard from Dolores and some others," Beatriz replied. "It was a difficult childbirth. *La Señora* nearly died. They had to do a cesarean section, and when they opened her up they discovered that she was all messed up inside. It was as if the baby had tied her insides into knots.

They fixed her up and managed to save the infant, but it was the only child she could ever have. No one knows who the father was. It is also said that *La Señora* had two sisters, but they were estranged and never visited her. The child—I did not know her name until now—was unusual in many ways. Perhaps autistic—I don't know. Her eyes were said to be of two different colors, and she had a witch's streak in her hair. She had many problems in school, and by the time she dropped out of high school she had become an outcast, taunted by the other children for her odd ways and strange appearance. She lived with her mother and never married or even had boyfriends. She rarely left the house. No one knew her well, but it was said she had special powers, that she was a seer. When people encountered her on the street, they would avoid her and would never look her in the eyes, which were said to have magical powers, or perhaps they could cast spells on a person. The rumor is that some years ago she had been committed to an institution for the mentally incurable. Apparently she had quit eating and would no longer speak to anyone, not even to her mother; she had entered some kind of state, or perhaps she was possessed by the devil. I don't know how much of this is true. It is just what I have heard."

I replied, "Well, I can tell you that she didn't look crazy to me at all. In fact, I found her quite sane and very attractive."

Beatriz replied, "Odel, when will you start thinking with your brains instead of your testosterone?"

I ignored the comment and continued. "She did go into some kind of trancelike state when she was with me." I told them about the fiery green glow that came to her eyes and the electricity I felt running back and forth between her hands and mine. And I told them that *La Señora* had made it clear our visits were done and over with.

"*¡Gracias a Dios!*" Beatriz said.

"Criswell Predicts," mumbled Bob.

"I'm going to bed," I said. "Tomorrow's a big day for me; my seminar, and then packing for the drive to Corinto.

Although, the way the weather's shaping up, a day trip on a sportfishing boat might not be possible."

Things went smoothly the next morning. The university had a slide projector all set up and, thank goodness, a spare bulb on hand just in case. As the hour of my talk approached, students began to trickle into the large room. I was concerned that the room would only be a quarter full, with everyone sitting near the back, and it might be an embarrassment for me. But by ten forty—twenty minutes before my talk was scheduled to begin—the room was nearly filled. And by ten fifty every seat had been taken, and people were beginning to line up in the aisles. I expressed my astonishment to Bob, who was planning to introduce me.

"Odel, I told you—your name is famous here. Your many scholarly works and your Caribbean book and all the help you've given our students over the years have earned you a place of honor at this university. Most of our biology faculty are here, and I see several deans and at least one of the vice-presidents. I'm sure you will have to stay and sign copies of your new book after you've finished speaking."

And that's just what happened. The crowd seemed to love my talk, they asked endless, and excellent, questions, and then Bob invited those who wished to come to the front of the room to meet me and get my autograph. The book signing went on for another hour, and many of the younger students wanted their friends to take photographs of them with me. I was patient with each person who came to me, asking them questions about their own interests, making sure I spelled their name correctly as I signed their book, thanking them for their interest and trying to encourage them. I'd never felt like such a celebrity. The VP for research, a formal and distinguished-looking gentleman, was effusive in his gratitude and suggested I consider some kind of honorary appointment with the university. For a few hours, my anger and confusion disappeared, and I was happy.

Bob and I went to lunch off campus so as to avoid encountering any further "fans." He knew a great little steak place by the lake, with excellent aged beef from young range fed cattle in the Chinandega region to the north. The winter storm lingered off to the west, still over the Pacific, but winds had already kicked up the waves on Lago de Managua, and the little fishing boats were bouncing around like corks. We drank rum and Cokes, ate delicious beef with rice and plantains, and Bob told me once again that if I was ever interested, he could almost guarantee me a professorship at the university. I whined about how the Seattle Museum of Natural History seemed to be collapsing, how my wife had proven to be less than honest with me, that a new "friend" had turned out to be part of her dishonesty, and that I was even uncertain about the new dark-skinned girl I was falling in love with.

"I've never been a great admirer of the human race," Bob said. "In fact, if there were any other race I could join, I would, but so far I haven't had that option. But you've got to make the best of your life, man. Take control and make it what you want. Tell me more about this new woman in your life—the girl from your dream."

I appreciated Bob's existentialist approach to things.

"She's the most beautiful, soulful, genuine person I have ever met. I ache to be with her. But it's complicated. There are other things going on, things I can't talk about. But I think I trust her. Actually, at this moment in time, the only people I really trust, beyond my brother and cousin Marco, are you and Beatriz . . . and Coquette."

"Coquette! Her name is Coquette?" Bob smiled.

"Yes. But she's named after a hummingbird called the Black-Crested Coquette. It's small and beautiful, like her. Her mother was an ornithologist who studied hummingbirds."

"Odel, I do believe you are love-struck. I've never seen you like this. So what are you going to do?"

"I don't really know. But I know that I must confront Penelope and get things out in the open."

I didn't mention to Bob that I would be seeing Coquette in Mexico City on my way back to Seattle. And I told him very little about her. Part of me wanted to tell him everything, but I knew I couldn't. If Bob and Beatriz ever found out I was doing anything for the CIA in their beloved country, it would likely destroy our friendship forever. I would be a quisling in their eyes. All of a sudden I again felt that I must stop this foolishness of working with the Agency. There were too many secrets everywhere. I was getting way outside my comfort zone.

Beatriz cooked a fabulous dinner for the three of us that night, and she served it up with her beautiful brown eyes and beckoning bosom. She had been in the audience for my talk, of course, and told me it was best seminar she had ever heard. She said that all over campus there was excitement about my talk and me. Students were proudly showing off their autographed copies of my book.

As I headed off to bed, Beatriz warned me to be careful in Corinto. "It is like all port towns—rough and dangerous. Stay away from the bars along the waterfront; they are the worst places, where bad things tend to happen." But, of course, that's exactly where I intended to spend much of my time while there.

18

Odel Becomes a Hero

Late November 1982

In 1982 Corinto was a small port town, with a population still under ten-thousand. It sits at the entrance to an immense, mazelike mangrove estuary that penetrates deep into the northern countryside of Pacific Nicaragua. Half a dozen rivers empty into the mangrove-lined bay, the largest being the *Río Posoltega* with its headwaters on the western slopes of the massive *Volcán San Cristóbal*—the highest volcano in Nicaragua and one of the most active, with frequent eruptions that rattle the landscape of León Department.

The drive from Managua is easy. North on the Pan-American Highway to the old capital city of León, then through the town of Chichigalpa (home of *Flor de Caña* rum, with its sugarcane fields lying in the shadow of *Volcán San Cristóbal*), and on to the town of Chinandega. From there, it is a quick shot straight to the coast and out the peninsula that embraces Corinto at its tip. This is a key truck route that moves goods between Corinto's port and Managua, and the highway is well maintained. I was glad the road was good, because ten miles out of Managua the rain came.

My memory of the port was that there existed only three minimal facilities for larger boats or ships, one at either end of the buttressed seaward shore of town; in between them a single broad expanse of concrete to which larger vessels could tether. Nothing fancy. The innermost wharf was the small navy dock. Landward from the navy dock were several large fuel storage tanks. The whole waterfront didn't comprise more than a dozen blocks. Behind the long concrete wharf, along *Avenida Central*, were businesses and bars, while residences were further inland from there. Nestled among the mangroves, artisanal fishermen had established "fish camps" at various locations inside the bay, which meant small fishing skiffs mingled dangerously with the larger commercial and navy boats and ships that moved about in the bay and deeper estuary channels.

I got to Corinto quickly. The rain let up, but it was cold and wet. The town was dirty, damp and sad looking; few people were on the streets. As I checked into the only decent-looking hotel on *Avenida Central*, I had a conversation with the manager about my desire to do some deepsea fishing the next day. He told me, of course, that due to the storm it was unlikely I'd find anyone willing to take me out of the bay and into the open sea for a fishing trip. He recommended a guy who had a larger boat and suggested I check with him. I stowed my bag in my room and hit the streets.

Pesca Deportiva Chuy was a colorfully painted shack that stank of old fish near the big central wharf. Chuy was in, listening to loud music on his radio and reading the newspaper. He told me the same thing: that no one would be fishing for a few days, until the storm blew over. Wanting to firmly establish my excuse for being in Corinto, I told him I might look around to see if I could find someone else willing to take me out. From there, I began my walking tour of the small port.

It didn't look much different than I remembered it, except for the waterfront itself. The old seaward dock was unchanged, but the long concrete buttress area had been greatly improved, and it now had a large new electric crane for moving cargo to and from ships. A ship from Havana was being unloaded as I watched. Strolling along the waterfront, I eventually came to the fenced boundary of the inner dock and the navy base. Inside I could see a construction crane and the tops of far more vessels than I would have imagined—at least fifteen or more. I thought, *The entire Nicaraguan Navy probably didn't have that many ships twenty years ago.* Being unable to see the ships' hulls from outside the fencing, I didn't know if they were Nicaraguan or ships from other nations. But the most striking thing was the increase in fuel storage tanks. I counted eight that I could see, and it looked like several more were under construction. I fixed their locations in my mind. My stroll back into town was along the east side of *Avenida Central*, where I casually checked out each establishment I passed. Nothing seemed unusual to me. I stopped at a few places—a boat mechanic's shop and a few *tiendas*—and drank beer in a couple of the bars. About a block from my hotel, I turned and walked across the street to stroll back down the west side of *Central*. Again, nothing seemed suspicious to me. Just a lot of down-and-out flophouses, bars, *comida corrida* joints, and tiny *tiendas*.

As dinnertime approached, I returned to my hotel and asked for a recommendation. The fellow working the desk suggested *El Pescador* on First Avenue, a block away. It turned out to be fantastic—flounder so fresh it had to have been swimming in the bay just a few hours before it hit the frying pan, chopped garlic (surely from a local garden), whole butter from the dairy farms around Léon, rice, and refried black beans. I chatted up the waiters, told them I'd been rained out of a fishing trip, generally trying to look like a gringo fisherman out for an adventure.

As night fell, I began hitting the bars along *Avenida Central*. There were six or seven of them, so I just slowly sipped a half-a-beer in each, pacing myself, chatting with the locals in my second-rate but understandable Spanish. Most of the people I talked to thought I was from *Inglaterra* or *Canadá*. They probably couldn't imagine an American being in Corinto these days.

I was growing weary from the long day, the hours of walking, and one beer after another. Everyone I talked to held the same opinion—they were happy to see business flourishing in the port because it brought jobs and money. They didn't care where it came from, and if the Cubans or the Russians wanted to invest in their country, so be it. I thought I'd try one last bar and then call it a day. The last place was a real dive. Dirty, reeking of stale beer, a few rough looking characters. As I walked in, I noticed an attractive young lady sitting with a fearfully drunk man at one of the tables. They were arguing about something. My first thought was, *What's a nice girl like you doing in a dump like this?* But, my bladder was full, so I headed straight to the men's room. I could barely endure the reek of old urine accumulated on the floor and the other unmentionable sensory assaults. The men's room hadn't been cleaned in weeks at best. As I stood at the urinal, an annoying cloud of mosquitos buzzed around my face and made forays to my cheeks and forehead to take their blood meals. I could hear the argument in the bar growing louder and more heated. The man was yelling rudely at the girl. It sounded ugly. Then I heard a crash. I thought I'd call it a night and skip the drama at this place. But when I walked out of the bathroom I saw the girl on the floor, her mouth bleeding, two chairs on their side, and the man standing over her. He was large, red-faced, and dead drunk. He reached for a beer bottle on the table, swung it hard against the edge, and held on to the neck of the jagged glass weapon. He was out of control. The few customers in the place had left, and the bartender was yelling at the man.

Suddenly, all the anger that had been building in me over the past week hit a crescendo. Even the filthy men's room became part of my rage. I could feel the blood rushing into my head and my mouth going dry. Every muscle in my body tensed. I was about three large steps away from the man. I reached him just as his hand raised the broken bottle into the air. He was so concentrated on the woman, yelling at her, she screaming back at him, that he never saw me coming from behind. I kicked the back of his left knee as hard as I could, and he immediately went down. I told the girl to get out of the place, now! Her eyes were as big as saucers and as dark as roasted almonds. The man was cursing me and clearly in pain. But he was also full of adrenalin. And he still clutched the broken beer bottle. He put his free hand on the floor to push himself up. I knew he was in a state of rage and could do some real damage, both to me and the girl. My brain raced. What to do? My dad's words came back to me: *There's no such thing as a fair fight.* I stomped hard on his hand on the floor. I felt, even through my shoe, bones breaking. He screamed and rolled onto his back, cursing me in a string of undecipherable Spanish epithets. The girl, who couldn't have been more than twenty or twenty-one, just stared at me, open-jawed. *"Sal de aquí. ¡Ahorita!"* I told her loudly.

She jumped up and ran out of the place. I followed quickly. She ran north, up the street. I began walking south, briskly, back toward my hotel. I got there in just six or seven minutes, went straight to my room, grabbed my things and headed out the back door off the lobby to the small dirt parking lot. I don't think the night clerk even saw me, though I wasn't sure. I certainly wasn't in the mood to be hauled down to some miserable police station in the middle of the night in Corinto. I jogged to my car, jumped in, and got the hell out of town. I made it to Bob and Beatriz's house in just over three hours.

Bob came to the door, sleepy eyed. Staring at me, he said, "Whatever your situation is my friend, it is the fruit of your own doing. You've no one to blame but yourself."

"Thank you, as always, for your shared wisdom, Roberto, but all I really want is a drink and a bed for the night. I'll tell you about it in the morning." He pulled out a bottle of *Flor de Caña*, handed it to me, and went back to bed.

As I sipped the rum, I contemplated what to do. The hotel proprietor was the only person who knew my name in Corinto—I had shown him my passport. Would the police end up talking to the bartender? Would they obtain my name. And would they somehow track me down here in Managua? It seemed unlikely. How could they possibly know where to look for me? The drunk asshole probably went to the hospital. The bartender may or may not have called the *pinche yuta*. If Corinto was like everyplace else in Latin America, folks avoided the cops if they could—simply because they were so corrupt, so inept, and such a hassle. If the police did get involved, would the bartender tell them I saved that young woman from a bloody catastrophe? How soon might this all come down on me? I decided the best thing to do was head for Mexico City first thing in the morning. My scheduled Copa flight was not for three more days. Copa's offices would open at seven. I'd call in the morning and try to bump my flight up to tomorrow afternoon.

I slept like the dead. My alarm went off at six forty-five, and I fell out of bed, half awake. Thank god Beatriz was already up, and the smell of strong Nicaraguan mountain coffee filled the kitchen. I poured myself a cup, and the only things I said to her were "Sorry for getting in so late" and "Thank you for the coffee, Beatriz—you are a beautiful heaven-sent angel."

Just after seven, I dialed up Copa and, amazingly, got right through. They had a flight to Mexico City at one in the afternoon, and I was able to get on it. I hit the shower, packed my stuff, and walked back to the kitchen. Bob and Beatriz sat at the table staring at me.

"Well, Helen Keller once said, 'Life is either a daring adventure or nothing,'" Bob mumbled. Beatriz just smiled her beautiful smile and gave me a sweet look of sympathy. She really was a gorgeous woman. I knew that aging would suit her well, improve her the way time improves a good Burgundy wine. I sat down with them and provided an abstract of the events in Corinto the night before.

"Odel, you never fail to amaze me," Bob said. "You did the right thing jamming back here. Getting involved with the police in a small port town like that in this country would only be problematic."

Beatriz said she would call a friend in Corinto and ask her if she had heard anything about the bar incident. When she walked away to the phone, Bob said, "Are you fucking nuts, dude? You could have gotten yourself killed or maimed or, worse yet, ended up in some shithole jail cell in Corinto!"

"Man, I just exploded. I think it was all the pent-up anger in me. Besides, that guy was a real jerk, and the girl was just a kid."

A few minutes later Beatriz walked back into the kitchen. "Well, Odel, it seems you've done it again."

Oh damn, I thought. *Now I'm in trouble.*

Beatriz went on. "It seems you are a hero in Corinto this morning. Everyone is talking about it, and there is even a short piece in the local morning newspaper. The guy you put in the hospital is well known around town as a drunk and a woman beater. He's been arrested numerous times. But this time he's really in trouble because the girl he attacked is a niece of Violeta Chamorro. The girl was in Corinto on assignment for *La Prensa*. I'm sure the family will press charges. You are now '*el pescador gringo misterioso quien rescató a la Señorita Chamorro en el bar frente al mar.*' A hero at the National University and a hero in Corinto! I'll bet someone from *La Prensa* tracks you down before this day is over."

"Well, if anyone from the press, or even the cops, show up here or at the university, just tell them the truth. I went to Corinto for a day of sportfishing, looked all over town for someone who would take me out, but because of the storm, no one was willing to do so. I had a few drinks around town that night, rescued a fair maiden in a bar, and returned to Managua. Hopefully I'll be winging my way to Mexico City before anyone shows up."

"You're going to Mexico City before you head home?" Bob asked.

Damn, I thought. *I let that one slip. I'd better not tell them it's just a plane change because they will likely call me at home or in my office tomorrow with an update on things here, and I won't be there to answer the phone.* "Yes, I'm going to visit a colleague at the National University, UNAM, for a few days before heading on to Seattle. I'll give you a call tomorrow from Mexico City to see if there's any news on this."

I finished up some things around the house and headed for the airport, giving myself plenty of time to turn in the rental car and get to my gate. I wanted to be the first person boarding that Mexico-bound flight!

19

The Pyramid of the Sun and a Confession in Coyoacán

December 1982

I arrived in Mexico City around three thirty, caught a cab for Coyoacán borough, and found the hotel I'd arranged for Coquette and me. I hadn't been to Coyoacán for a few years, and it was soothing to my frayed nerves to be there—a green and peaceful colonial neighborhood in the massive sprawl of frenzied Mexico City. Tiny Christmas lights had already been strung in many of the trees that lined the narrow cobblestone streets, and some of the government buildings were installing elaborate, indigenous-influenced manger scenes. *Mexico City is one of the greatest metropolises on Earth* I thought, as the taxi approached the hotel. *I could easily live here for the rest of my life.* It was a feeling I'd had numerous times in the past.

Our hotel was in a late eighteenth-century Spanish colonial building that covered two-thirds of a block. The exterior was constructed from huge hand-cut limestone blocks, many with bas-reliefs of carved animals—jaguars, monkeys, and Resplendent Quetzals. The animal images were worn and smoothed from two hundred years of weathering; the monkey faces looked blurred and grotesque, and the long, streaming tails of the quetzals, the most magnificent of all the trogons, were eroded to near invisibility. The building's design and construction were exquisite, with roots deep in Moorish architecture. Over the years, two more, less ornate stories had been added above the ground floor. The hotel was too old to retrofit for elevators, but it now showcased a beautiful, early twentieth-century, fossil-filled, Italian marble stairway. There were several rooms available, so I picked one on the ground floor adjacent to the green inner courtyard and garden where bougainvillea and hibiscus flowered in profusion. In the center of the courtyard was a charming three-tiered fountain cut from dark volcanic rock, circled by four ornate bronze benches.

The name Coyoacán comes from the Nahuatl word for "place of coyotes"; it was the name given to the original village by native people long before any Europeans had set foot in the New World. In 1521, when Hernán Cortés arrived in the place now called Mexico City, the great Valley of Mexico was a cluster of lakes; indigenous people lived on islands and along the shorelines. Coyoacán was on the southern shore of Lake Texcoco. Its inhabitants, the Tepanec People, were dominated by the powerful Aztecs who controlled the entire region. Thus, the Tepanec welcomed Cortés, who used the area as headquarters during his conquest of the Aztec Empire. So it came to be that Coyoacán was, for a short time, the first de facto capital of New Spain—from 1521 to 1523. Fiercely maintaining its individuality, it wasn't until 1857 that the municipality was absorbed into the expanding Federal District of Mexico City. But in 1928 it regained its political standing when population pressure forced the bloated Federal District to be divided into sixteen distinct boroughs, one of which was Coyoacán. Many of the original plazas and streets in this neighborhood remain little changed since the sixteenth century. Our hotel was near two large plazas, each filled with ancient and enormous Indian laurel trees.

Coyoacán, like Oaxaca and Guanajuato, is a musical destination, and artists come from all over the country to perform in these venues. Wandering the streets or the plazas at night is to immerse oneself in the joy of music, from big bands that play in closed-off streets, to soloists that play in coffee shops or the gazebos of the numerous plazas. I also knew that I was walking the same timeless stone paths that the Spanish conqueror Hernán Cortés walked upon 430 years earlier. Barrio Coyoacán is also home to the great National University of Mexico (UNAM), the first university built in the New World, giving the borough a perpetually youthful and intellectual flavor. And it is also the barrio that Frida Kahlo grew up in, and her house is now a museum, the *Casa Azul*. The Kahlo house was a genuine bijou, but for me the crown jewel of Coyoacán had always been the church of San Juan Bautista, or Saint John the Baptist.

The building of *Iglesia de San Juan Bautista* was commissioned by Cortés himself, and it is one of the oldest churches in the New World. It was built on the site of a *calmecac*, a school for the sons of Aztec nobility, the ruins of which still exist beneath the cloister. Originally built by the Dominicans, it was eventually taken over by the intrepid and fearless Franciscans. The interior has seven chapels. The main altar and the Rosario Chapel are almost unchanged today from what they were in the 1500s, the latter flaunting an insanely ornate baroque altar. The massive hand-cut wood beams and decorative carvings were crafted by trained and talented indigenous neophytes and still astonish visitors. In Mexico, the feast day for Saint John the Baptist is June 24 and a special altar is installed in the church for that day's masses, the midday one of which has mariachi music and a meal for the citizens of the barrio. To linger in *Iglesia de San Juan Bautista* is to travel back in time hundreds of years. It is the only Catholic Church I'd ever been in that lacked the ubiquitous Stations of the Cross—perhaps symptomatic of its great age.

I settled into our room and immediately made a hand sketch of what I'd seen in Corinto—the expanded docks, enlarged navy base, numerous new fuel storage facilities, and so on. My memory was good, though not infallible. Then I took a stroll from the hotel along Calle Ignacio Allende to Plaza Hidalgo, Coyoacán's main plaza. *Iglesia de San Juan Bautista* sits on the south side of the giant square of grass and trees. In the center of the plaza, there is an early twentieth-century kiosk with a stained-glass cupola topped by a bronze eagle. The kiosk was donated to the then-village by Porfirio Díaz in 1910 for the upcoming centennial of Mexico's independence, during the last of his astonishing seven terms as President. The plaza is named after Father Miguel Hidalgo y Costilla, and a statue of the beloved priest, created by Luís Arias, graces the beautiful gardens. Plaza Hidalgo is a tranquil green respite in a peaceful barrio of the largest city in the New World.

As I approached *Iglesia San Juan Bautista*, I saw a flyer announcing a concert to be given in the church on December 9—the day after Coquette was to arrive. It would be a performance by members of the Coyoacán Chamber Orchestra; they were going to recreate Ignacio de Jerusalem's original *Matins for the Virgin of Guadalupe*. I didn't know the written music even still existed, but apparently it had been recently rediscovered somewhere in Europe. The group was going to play on instruments thought to be the same or similar to those of the time it was written.

In the eighteenth century, two hundred years after Juan Diego's vision of Our Lady of Guadalupe, the road to fame for aspiring composers in Italy was the writing of operas. But for their New World counterparts, the most prestigious genre was *maitines* (or *matins*), a Roman Catholic service traditionally performed in the early hours of the morning. The *matins* provided a range of opportunities to display compositional skill, as they juxtaposed a wide variety of textures and styles, commonly paralleling that of an Old World opera but with monophonic *psalms* in chant, intoned *lecciones* that could preach or weave a story, and sets of *responsorios* that elegantly combined voices with instruments. In 1742 the Italian composer Ignacio de Jerusalem was recruited from Europe to Mexico City to help strengthen the musical resources of New Spain's growing empire. In 1750 he was appointed to the top post of Chapel Master at Mexico City's main cathedral. In 1764, in Mexico City, he presented his masterpiece, *Matins for the Virgin of Guadalupe.* It captured the zeitgeist of New Spain at the time and catapulted him to fame, but the composition had since been lost to obscurity. This concert was a special opportunity that I hoped Coquette would enjoy.

I walked into the park and strolled its garden paths, glancing at sweethearts on benches, watching kids playing ocarinas and penny whistles, and had a delicious *pollo en mole* dinner with a few *copas de mezcal* at an open-air café. After dinner I picked up a bottle of *Flor de Caña* and returned to our room. It wasn't too late, so I used the phone at the hotel desk to give Bob and Beatriz a call. Sure enough, just as my plane was taking off from Managua, a reporter from *La Prensa* had shown up at their house. No police, though—thank goodness. They expected something to be in the next morning's edition of the newspaper.

The next day, I took an early bus to the famous Teotihuacan archaeological site, about an hour outside Mexico City. I hadn't seen the site in seven or eight years and thought wandering the expansive plazas and climbing a pyramid might help clear my head of the confusion with my marriage—and also help prepare me for a few days alone with Coquette. The ancient city of Teotihuacan and its suburbs are huge, covering about eight square miles at an elevation of 7,500 feet. As I walked from the bus stop to the site, the thin winter air was brisk and refreshing, the azure sky filled with massive white cumulous clouds. It was one of those perfect days, when it felt good to be alive. I already felt my head clearing, thoughts coming more clearly to me than they had in months. A flock of screeching green parrots flew past me, breaking the calm silence of the morning.

Approaching the entrance, I breathed deeply of the unusually clean air. It was still early in the day and there were few visitors. I knew I'd have Teotihuacan mostly to myself for a few hours. Near the entryway, a middle-aged woman was selling empanadas. They smelled delicious, and she said her mother had made them that morning. I asked for one, but before I had even finished saying the words the woman had already picked one out for me, using a piece of cut newspaper that she skillfully wrapped around the bottom half as she handed it to me. I bought my ticket and went into the site, eating the flavorful though unusual herb-filled pastry as I walked slowly across the massive grass field toward the Avenue of the Dead.

Teotihuacan is one of the great mysteries of Mesoamerican archaeology. Probably founded around 100 BC, the city evolved into one of central Mexico's largest pre-Columbian urban centers with sprawling suburban enclaves. Indigenous groups migrated here to live, temporarily or permanently, from all over what is now Mexico, bringing many languages and trades. It grew to become a major cultural, political, economic, and religious center with a diverse population estimated at one hundred to two hundred thousand people. A great fire around AD 550 marked Teotihuacan's downfall. Curiously, there is evidence that the burning was intentional. We know little about the people of Teotihuacan—the *Teotihuacanos*. To the Aztecs, who came to prominence almost nine hundred years after the fall of the city, it was considered the place where the gods had brought the world into existence. The Aztecs were the people who

243

gave the abandoned city its name, and they also named its two magnificent great pyramids—the Pyramid of the Sun and the Pyramid of the Moon.

Archaeologists believe the patron deity of Teotihuacan was the Storm God (who brought vital rains for crops), but the ultimate symbol of power in Teotihuacan was the Feathered Serpent God, *Quetzalcoatl*, who created both time and space. Carvings and paintings of the Feathered Serpent God depict a huge rattlesnake partly covered with the iridescent green, blue, and crimson feathers of the beautiful Resplendent Quetzal. The word *quetzal* in Nahuatl means "beautiful" or "resplendent"—thus, early on the bird came to bear this singular name. *Coatl* is serpent, hence *Quetzalcoatl*. And, of course, the shedding of a serpent's skin has long been a symbol of rebirth and renewal.

One of the most mysterious structures at Teotihuacan is the Temple of the Feathered Serpent itself, and all four of this pyramid's facades are decorated with dozens of exquisite stone carvings of the feathered creature. It sits on an immense plaza known as the Citadel, which the *Teotihuacanos* periodically flooded in rituals that turned it into a simulacrum of the primordial ocean of the Mesoamerican creation myth. When this happened, the pyramid symbolically became the sacred mountain that emerged from the sea at the dawn of time. It wouldn't be until early in the twenty-first century that archaeologists would discover the subterranean chambers and thousands of hidden treasures beneath the Temple of the Feathered Serpent.

As I walked down the wide, dusty *Avenida de los Muertos*, the enormous Pyramid of the Sun cast a pale silhouette over me. I marveled at the thing; at 200 feet tall, it is the third largest pyramid on Earth, after Cholula in Mexico and Cheops in Egypt. It was built in one single, massive effort around AD 200. No one knows exactly how long it took, or how many people were employed, or how they accomplished it without the help of wheels or draft animals. Was it built in one ruler's lifetime? Or was the idea so grandiose that it took several generations to complete the task? Either way, the concept far exceeds most other construction projects in the world at that time. The long north-south avenue ends at the Pyramid of the Moon, the first large pyramid the *Teotihuacanos* built, perhaps around AD 50–100. It started small, but over time it was repeatedly enlarged to finally reach a height of 140 feet. For archaeologists, each new layer hid a treasure trove of artifacts and new puzzles to solve.

Throughout the great city, scientists have found obsidian flakes. Like jade, obsidian was such a hard (and rare) stone that it held great importance for pre-Columbian people in the New World. In Mesoamerica it was carved into blades of all shapes and sizes, as well as into elaborate ritual figures. The *Teotihuacano* rulers took control of all the obsidian deposits in the region, organized excavation crews to acquire the raw material, and oversaw the artisans who carved it. They even carved thick disks of highly polished obsidian through which they could observe solar eclipses. Jade was also precious to Mesoamerican people, and its use was reserved for the elite classes. Nearly as beautiful, though not as hard, was the more common *tecali* stone, a greenish-white mineral also known as onyx or alabaster. Large quarries of *tecali* were mined in the area now known as Puebla and carried by hand to Teotihuacan for carving.

As I contemplated the great Pyramid of the Sun, I began to feel light-headed. Could I make the 200-foot climb in the thin air at this elevation? The "steps" were so high and steep that climbing it had to be done crouched over, using hands, feet, and sometimes knees. Walking around to the backside of the pyramid, where the brown grass met dusty brown bushes, I sat down to rest and shake off my dizziness. I had sat for only a minute or two, when a wrinkled and twisted old Indian woman appeared. She must have been in the bushes. She was tiny and wrapped in a gray rebozo, but the dirt and dust of ages that clung to the fabric had turned it a burnt-sienna color, like the winter vegetation around us. She wore tattered leather sandals; her feet twisted and dark, her toes crooked. She was so diminutive and blended in so well with the grass and shrubbery that, with a sideways glance, she could be mistaken for a leafless bush. She held out her hand. *A beggar*, I realized, *but how did she get in here? They don't allow panhandlers in these archaeological sites.* I stood up, a bit wobbly, dug my hand into my pants pocket, and pulled out what change I had. When I dropped the pesos into her skeletonized hand, her clawlike fingers curled up to touch my palm—and the strangest thing happened. It was as if our hands were magnets, and her fingers were stuck to me. With our hands in that position, she looked me in the eyes, holding my gaze, and then her eyes turned from dull deep brown to bright amber, and she spoke.

"You will soon be confronting new provocations, *señor*. You will need to find within yourself great strength. If you do, the gift of knowledge will be given to you. Fight ferociously, but embrace both courage and fear for they are the reciprocal faces of wisdom."

"What?" I said, astonished at the words this strange mendicant was saying to me.

She continued speaking. "The things you believe are coincidences are merely echoes of the past, colliding with your future. Love fully, for you are part of a greater story."

A guard spoke sharply from behind me, telling the woman to stop harassing the visitors. I turned to look at him, but when I turned back to the woman she was gone. She had faded back into the brush. I turned back to the guard, but he too had disappeared. I sat back down on the grass, still dizzy, as a large cloud shadow passed over me and darkened the steep side of the Pyramid of the Sun. *Had I imagined that, or did it actually happen?* I thought about what Destiny had said to me about coincidences; it was almost the same as this old woman's words. I looked up at the great pyramid and knew I must climb it.

Sitting on the floor of the carved stone temple atop the flat-topped Pyramid of the Sun, looking through the unusually clear morning air, I could see the suburbs of Mexico City in the distance. Flashes of sunlight glinted off planes that were lined up in the sky, preparing to touch down at *Aeropuerto Internacional*. As I caught my breath from the long climb, I thought about the bewildering construction of this massive monument, the expanse and history of the Teotihuacan culture, the subsequent rise and fall of the Aztecs and the Maya, and other great civilizations of Middle America. And the brutal 300-year subjugation by colonial Spain, the growth of modern Mexico City, and the long sweep of history throughout Latin America. Almost the entire Western Hemisphere had gone from formidable, often majestic, indigenous civilizations to a subjugated Hispanic world in the blink of an eye, and then the two profoundly different cultures merged, creating the mixed-blood culture of modern Mexico, Guatemala, Nicaragua, and the Andean nations of South America. The bloodlines of those who built the pyramids of these lands still flow in the *mestizos* of the Americas today.

It occurred to me that so much of humanity's beauty, and so much of what drives our restless pursuit of knowledge, stems from the invisible connections between the ages; connections carried through ideas woven into history by people of particular times and places. The minds and souls of every person in time carry forward the cultural memes that leave enduring etchings on the cave walls of humanity's legacy. Modern man's grandest architectural achievements are simply makeovers of the Pyramid of the Sun.

I began to see myself and my situation as small, even trivial in this larger scheme of things. I was just a blip, a pinpoint on the moving radar of civilization, but somehow still an integral part of it all. I was nothing, yet I was part of everything—part of a "greater story" as the old woman had said. Suddenly my internal struggles to deal with Penelope and our marriage seemed needlessly exaggerated in my mind, while my relationship with Coquette seemed to loom larger. Perhaps, as I'd been told, the way forward was not to dwell on the past but to courageously explore the "new portals opening before me." And to "love fully," as the dusty woman had enjoined me.

Many hours later, as I boarded a bus back to Mexico City, I saw the small bent old woman again. She was some distance away, but walking beside her was the younger woman who had sold me the empanada that morning. The younger woman had her arm through the old lady's arm, steadying her as they walked. Destiny's words came back to me: *The universe is shifting for you, repositioning your path, offering you guidance along the way . . . The people you will be meeting are not coincidental; they are other pilgrims who are there to help you on your voyage. Be courageous, but do not be foolish. Be aware that your journey has already begun.* As I settled in for the ride back to Mexico City, Destiny was on my mind.

That night, back in Coyoacán, I felt an odd sense of both exhaustion and exhilaration. I'd walked for miles at Teotihuacan and climbed one of the tallest pyramids in the world. My legs ached a bit, though the rum was easing that. But I also felt supercharged and mentally refreshed. I was boundlessly excited at the thought of seeing Coquette the next day.

I slept late the next morning, had a leisurely breakfast in the plaza, and then again called Bob and Beatriz from the hotel desk. The story of my escapade in Corinto had been on the front page of *La Prensa* that morning. Reporters from the paper figured out who I was, and they even knew about the talk I'd given at the university. I was a temporary hero in Nicaragua. It made me chuckle, and it made Bob and Beatriz laugh. I thanked them for helping me achieve my fifteen minutes of fame.

I caught a cab for the Hotel Majestic at one thirty. I had no way to contact Coquette and was nervous that she might not show up for one reason or another. I got to the hotel just at two o'clock. As I entered the lobby, my memory and spirit were refreshed by the spectacular neocolonial architecture in the wonderful turn-of-the-century building. Giant hardwood beams supported the thirty-foot-high ceiling, and the lobby desk and furniture were of aromatic, polished dark cedar from the sierras of Michoacán. The ceiling was made entirely of glass tiles, and above them was a gigantic atrium that welcomed sunlight into the lobby from seven stories above. The accents, including the wide spiraling stairwell, were covered with lavish Talavera tiles created by the celebrated Puebla ceramics work, *Uriarte*, which began producing authentic Spanish ceramics in 1824 and continues to this day using the same hand-painted designs and production methods brought to Spain by the conquering Moors in AD 711.

I was so excited about seeing Coquette that I almost raced up the stairs, but the rooftop bar was a few too many flights up. So I waited for the single ancient elevator, which was operated by a gracious gentleman in a black Western suit.

When I walked into the rooftop bar, Coquette was already there. She was sitting at a small private table next to the edge of the open-air seating area, her slender chestnut-colored arm resting on a low wall that separated her from the air and the sky and Mexico City's grand central *Zócalo* seven stories below. Her hair flowed in satiny charcoal waves over her shoulders and down her back. She sensed my presence and turned her head. When she saw me, her face lit up and the beam of her smile was as bright as a brittle star. It ignited every cell in my body. *My god*, I thought, *she is the most beautiful woman I have ever seen.* I felt my thoughts of Penelope melting away like candle wax dripping off a table.

Was it my imagination or just my own longings that made me see love spilling out of Coquette's dark moist eyes?

She stood as I neared the table, her soft ankle-length cotton dress following every curve of her perfect body. I walked up to her, and our hands involuntarily linked together. We stood there for a long time, hands clutching, our gazes streaming into one another, her incredible aromas filling my brain with fireworks, and my heart racing. *My world is here. Right here*, I thought, *with this woman who I feel must be my soulmate.* I'd never had such a thought before.

We kissed lightly, our lips barely touching, our hands and eyes still joined. We kissed lightly again, and this time her tongue dragged slowly across my lips, moistening them with her sweet elixir. She said softly, "Oh baby, I've missed you." My knees nearly buckled; I had to sit down. Looking at her across the table, I told her I was speechless. She said nature had invented kisses as a means of communication for when words failed. She suggested we just hold hands and give each other goo-goo eyes for a while—there was no need to talk. Her smile electrified me and I agreed.

Below, in Mexico City's enormous *Zócalo*, we watched strolling mariachi bands, break-dancers with boom boxes, a group of teacher protestors, and some nearly naked *Mexicas* chanting and dancing to what they claimed were 600 year old Aztec rhythms. We sipped *Cuba Libres* and slowly began to talk. She told me her conference had gone well, though she found it all a bit boring—probably because all she could think about was meeting up with me. I told her my talk at the university in Managua also went well, and I had been astonished at how many people showed up. She told me I was too modest and didn't realize how well known my work was. She asked me what else I did while in Nicaragua, and her eyes took on a devilish look. I said, "Coquette, I have so much to tell you. But now is not the time. How about we stroll through the *Zócalo*, check out the Metropolitan Cathedral, and then head to Coyoacán to settle into the hotel and have a nice dinner."

She agreed, and then she said, "Odel, there is so much I need to tell you too. I must tell you more about me, and I need you to tell me more about you."

"Agreed," I said. I told her about the concert the following day at *Iglesia de San Juan Bautista* and she was thrilled at the idea.

"I had no idea there was a musical composition written in honor of Our Lady of Guadalupe," she said, "How fortunate we are."

"Yes," I said, "In so many ways."

We strolled the *Zócalo* and the massive cathedral, holding hands the entire time. We laughed and joked and smiled and felt euphoric. As we walked, Coquette teased me wonderfully, whispering softly as she lightly bit my ear, pressing her thigh into my crotch when she looked over my shoulder, and at every turn brushing against me so that I could feel the stiffening excitement beneath the thin fabric of her dress. No one—not even Penelope—had ever excited me the way Coquette did.

After just forty minutes of walking, we were both so worked up that we agreed we had to catch a cab to the hotel. When we got to our room, I opened the bottle of *Flor de Caña*. Coquette suggested I pour just one glass that we could share. The rum disappeared quickly; Coquette slowly removed her shoes, and then turned and asked me to unzip her dress. I took my time, feasting on every inch of her milk chocolate skin as the dress slowly opened, the contours of her scapula, back muscles and ribs, the inward curve of the small of her back, two small dimples just above her buns. I let the dress fall to the floor, and I admired her perfect naked rump as I slipped my arms around her narrow waist. I was melting. She turned to face me, gave my lip a little bite, and began to slowly undress me.

And then we soared. We connected in flesh and spirit like I'd never connected with anyone else in my life. And I was sure she felt the same way. She was uninhibited and wild, sweet and exploring, and she remembered all the nuanced moves that we'd discovered the last time we were together, on a tiny island in the Caribbean Sea. And we found new moves. We spent two hours or so in bed—and on the floor and on the furniture—before we both admitted we were starving.

As we walked out of our room and into the interior garden of the hotel, Coquette stopped and turned to me. She said, "Odel, being with you like this is a dream come true for me. You have no idea."

I wasn't entirely sure what she meant by that—if it was just a figure of speech, or something metaphorical, or if there was more to our growing love affair than I realized. I replied, "Perhaps you will tell me more about that after dinner. Maybe on a park bench in Plaza Hidalgo."

We had a delicious meal at *El Restaurante Michoacáno*, enjoyed a flight of five local *mezcales* for dessert, and then strolled into the plaza. The fragrance of jasmine flowers mingled enticingly with the smell of Coquette's hair and body. The trees were filled with tiny white Christmas lights that twinkled like stars. Many of the benches were taken by smooching teenagers. Others were occupied by sweet elderly couples sitting contently with their shoulders and hips pressed together and gentle smiles on their faces that spoke of their years of intimacy.

Some of the benches were occupied by old men, friends of decades who sat quietly in the park on warm evenings. They had been friends for so long, they'd repeated every story they knew many times and now had little to speak of. Each had seen joyous times and each had survived tragedies. They'd laughed like clowns and wept like widows. All of their memories were tucked away, each in their own little gilded cedar chest, neatly stacked in tidy rows in the recesses of their minds. When the key to a particular chest was revealed—in a sight, a smell, a thought—the right box opened and memory was set free for a while, putting grins or frowns on the men's faces, or sad longing looks. Each had their own versions of shared memories, and over the years each had crafted their own nuanced stories to suit their needs. One of them would sometimes mention an incident from the past, speaking only a few words—"do you remember when the woman from Barcelona visited Coyoacán?"—and the story would reappear in their minds as they sat silently with it playing in their heads, smiling into the park's humid air. And if a youngster's stray ball rolled to their feet, they would pick it up, look about for the child, and roll it back to them with a gentle grin. They had the kind of tenderness of old men who had worked hard their entire lives but now had the time and inclination to pay attention to profitless things.

The plaza seemed filled with joy. And as we strolled, Coquette sung softly, in her magical musical voice, those simple lyrics from the old Donovan song:

Happiness runs in a circular motion
Thought is like a little boat upon the sea
Everybody is a part of everything anyway
You can have everything if you let yourself be.

We found an unoccupied bench and sat. Coquette positioned herself at one end, took off her sandals, and turned sideways to face me, putting her feet up on the seat and pressing them against my thigh. Her slit dress fell aside to reveal her exquisite legs, shapely and strong.

"Your body is in such perfect shape, Coquette. Is it just the gym and running that keeps you so fit?"

"Mostly, but I also practice karate two days a week."

"Karate?" I asked.

"Yes. Shotokan karate. It's a very active form of karate that gives me an intense ninety-minute workout. My father insisted I learn some kind of self-defense when I was a teenager. I tried several things but found Shotokan to my liking. It's a bit like yoga in that it keeps your limb joints

253

open and flexible, but it also teaches you defensive moves and postures. And it gives one self-confidence." Considerable time would pass before I was to learn that Shotokan karate is also one of the most deadly offensive combat skills that has ever been developed.

"And tell me, Odel, how do you stay in such great shape?"

"I don't really try. Just my Sicilian genes I guess. Although I'm sure swimming and diving help keep me fit."

I lifted her feet onto my lap. They were perfect. Everything about her was perfect. And then she said, "Odel, I love you. So I must tell you some things. But I'm afraid to, because I fear you may become upset or even get angry with me. But we cannot continue seeing each other if we aren't more open about our lives."

I was both surprised and perplexed. *There is nothing this woman can tell me that would make me upset or angry with her*, I thought.

"OK, who goes first—you or me?" I said, smiling.

"Me," she said. I was gently massaging her feet, and I wanted this moment to last forever. Until she began telling me her secrets.

Coquette looked cautiously around the plaza, eyeing the nearby benches in an odd way. And then she spoke. "Odel, our meeting in Montelimar was not a coincidence. I was there to keep an eye on you. To see if you were reliable and how you handled yourself. You see, while I do not technically work for the government, I often do contract assignments for them. Things other than the writing and research I've told you about. You had been assigned to me by the Central Intelligence Agency some time ago as a possible important cooperator. Someone who had a great deal to offer. And, of course, you've proven yourself to be wise, fast on your feet, and trustworthy. You know your way around Latin America, and you have legitimate reasons to travel there."

While I suspected there might be more to Coquette than met the eye, I didn't expect this. She saw the look on my face and quickly went on.

"But please, please understand that I did not expect to fall head over heels for you. That wasn't part of the plan, and not everyone at the Agency is happy about the fact that we are now lovers."

"Wait, Coquette—you're telling me you work for the CIA, and that people at the Agency know about us? That we're lovers?"

"A few do, of course. Two or three of them probably know everything. That's what they do for a living. But there's more—so much more, my love. Please be patient with me. And do not stop holding my feet because I so adore the feel of your strong hands." She continued. "Actually, Odel, I have known about you for a long time. Since you married Penelope. I'm sure you know she also does contract work for the Agency . . . "

"Whoa, stop right there," I interrupted her. "Now you're telling me that my wife works for the CIA? How can that possibly be? Do you know Penelope?"

"She doesn't 'work' for the Agency. She is just a personal contractor, like me. We both take on odd jobs, if you will. I'm sure you know about her work with them in matters of banking and finance. She's very talented and highly respected."

"No, Coquette, I do *not* know about that. Though, I did recently discover that she's getting funded by an organization called The Cleia Foundation. But she has always told me her travels were related to her academic research."

"Yes, the same foundation that is now funding you. The foundation her father started a dozen years ago."

I put my hand up, palm to her, and she stopped talking. "Coquette, you need to slow down here. First off, Penelope's father works for the State Department. He's spent his life in career posts as a cultural attaché in embassies around the world, especially in Central and South America. I've talked with him numerous times about his work."

"Oh, Odel, are you really that naive?" The word stung. Big time. "Do you not know that 'cultural attaché' is a common code title for an undercover CIA operative that works through an embassy? Surely Penelope has explained all that to you. Her dad is highly regarded in both the State Department and the Agency."

I suddenly felt a bit nauseated. "Jesus Christ—OK, I know I am a bit naive. In fact, I've heard that word a few too many times lately. But no, I did *not* know cultural attachés were commonly CIA operatives. And how long have you known Penelope? How well do you know her? And what the hell is going on here exactly?"

Coquette scooted her firm little derriere across the bench toward me and put her face in front of mine, the tips of our noses nearly touching. Her alluring scent washed over me, but I forced it out of my mind. She said softly, in her magical, melodic voice, "Baby, what's going on here, right here—right now—is that I love you and want to be honest with you and clear the air. But I didn't realize how many things needed to be cleared up. It's hard for me to believe that Penelope hasn't told you about all this."

Suddenly my anger at Penelope was back, growing into rage. "How long have you known my wife?" I asked flatly.

"Since before you met her. Once you and she started dating, I began paying attention to you. She was—*is*—a friend, though we don't really see one another anymore. In fact, I haven't seen her or talked with her since you two got married. We just drifted apart, went our separate ways. You know how that is. But I was curious about you. The more I learned about you, the more . . . " She paused, searching for the words. "The more special you seemed. I could see that Penelope had made a good catch. A great catch. A smart, handsome, interesting, adventurous, professional man." Her fingers brushed down my cheek; I forced myself to ignore the electricity. "So when the Agency asked me if I'd be willing to shadow you for a while, I jumped at the opportunity. I confess to you now Odel, I think I was already falling in love with you before we'd even met in Montelimar. The more I learned about you, the more I was drawn to you. Part of my mind, or something deep inside me was telling me we were meant to be together."

"What do you mean, 'learned about me'? Where, how, why?"

"Oh, baby, surely you must realize that the Agency knows all about you now. You can't get involved with them—let alone get an interim security clearance—without a pretty large dossier being compiled on you. I even know you like kids, dogs, music, good food and good wine, and ancient ruins."

I was silent, trying to process it all. "Are you still 'watching over me,' Coquette? Is this meeting—our dinner tonight, our private time—all part of your job?" I heard the sarcasm slipping into my voice.

"No, lover, I'm on my own time now. You've already proven yourself and become a valuable emerging asset to the Agency. You're no longer my case. And that had nothing to do with my feelings for you, or us being here now. I'm here with you now because I've fallen in love with you. And because I ache to be with you." Her voice was mesmerizing.

I realized that I had no choice but to believe her, no matter how crazy it all sounded. She was so sincere. But I was now driven to understand everything.

"Let's back up," I said. "First, how long have you been working for the CIA? And, second, how long have you known Penelope?"

"I want to tell you everything Odel, and I will tell you everything I can. But, unlike you, who are just a cooperator, I am a paid contractor with the Agency. There are some things I cannot tell you. It would put my security clearance at risk, my job at risk, and, more importantly, it could put other people at risk. I promise to tell you everything I can. But please understand—there are some things I simply cannot talk about."

I repeated my questions. "How long have you been working for the CIA, and how long have you known Penelope?"

"I've done contract work for the CIA for a long time, and I've known Penelope for a long time." Then she was silent, staring into my eyes. I could see her eyes moistening. Tears were close at hand.

But then she decided it was time to turn the tables. "And now, my love, it's your turn. Tell me about your involvement with the Agency. How long did you plan to keep that from me?"

Fair enough, I thought, I hadn't been forthright with her either. But we both knew it was different. I told her how I'd contacted the Agency as a random wild shot, and how things had progressed since then, and about the people I'd met at the office in Seattle.

And then she said, "You do realize that Penelope recruited you for them, don't you? She was the one who suggested you contact them and then that you push for The Cleia Foundation money."

Shit, I thought. *I am fucking naive!* "Actually, I'm just now putting that together," I said.

And then, as gently as a mother might be with a troubled child, she said, "Baby love, Penelope has not been entirely honest with you. There is no reason she needed to keep all this from you. I don't mean to judge her. Not at all. But between a married couple . . . " She let the thought hang in the air.

"That's not all she's kept from me," I replied.

"I think I know," Coquette said, and her eyes looked down.

"What do you mean, 'you know'?"

"I know of her sexuality. There have been rumors around the Agency."

Oh my god, I thought. The nausea came back, my stomach roiled, and my head began to throb. The rage was growing.

"Wh—what do you know of her sexuality?" I stammered.

"I know that she is a beautiful, sensual, sexually-driven woman. I know that men and women find her irresistibly attractive. I know that she has always been sexually active. With men *and* women. She is able to manipulate people so easily. Odel, I am not judging her. I like Penelope; I truly do. Even though we've gone our own ways, she is a longtime friend. She isn't a bad person—she's just who she is. And I've no doubt she loves you. I've never seen her devoted to anyone the way she is to you."

"Honestly, Coquette, right now I don't think I even know who my wife is. But all I care about is getting to the truth. Are you telling me that before Penelope and I met, she had a reputation at the Agency for her sexuality?"

Coquette looked at me for a long time. And then she said, softly, "I'm not sure how much has changed since you've gotten married. She's very discreet and prudent. But no matter how cautious one is, people talk."

Suddenly I felt like screaming profanities—but I didn't. "Do you know about her friend, Marjorie?" I asked.

"Only a bit; just that Penelope has a new and more serious lover by that name."

My head was swirling with so many questions; I could barely organize my thoughts to keep talking.

"Who assigned you to watch over me?"

"I can't tell you that, but, honestly, it's irrelevant. It's common practice at the Agency."

I asked her if she knew Antin Morales, and she replied, "I've met him once or twice; I don't care for him. I know he and Penelope are friends."

"And how about Nestor Papadakis?"

"I know Nestor. He's a truly good man."

"And John Thornton?"

She paused and then said, "He's a prince."

Some prince, I thought. *Banging my wife. Along with who knows how many other CIA boys and girls!*

The two of us sat there in silence, each of us lost in our thoughts. Then she leaned forward and kissed me, long and slow, on the mouth. And she said, "By the way, I'm very proud of you for your heroic moves in Corinto last week. I like the idea of my lover being a national hero!"

"How could you know about that? You've been here in Mexico City."

"I called . . . a friend at the Agency who I trust and told him I was meeting you. He told me they'd just heard about the article in *La Prensa*."

"So, what, I have no privacy left now?"

"The story was on the front page, Odel. Anyone reading the paper knows about you now. If you want privacy, don't become a public hero."

"Well, I didn't plan on it—believe me."

"You did the right thing," she said. "And I mean it when I say I'm proud of you. But you do realize it changes things in terms of what you can do for the Agency in Nicaragua now. Everyone knows who you are. My guess is they will back off on your work there for a while."

"I couldn't care less. I'm not sure I want anything more to do with the CIA."

"Understandable. It's usually like this when people first start learning more about the Agency. But I hope that doesn't mean you want to stop seeing me too. Baby, that would kill me."

I didn't give her an answer but instead suggested we set the discussion aside for the evening and resume the following morning. My brain was swirling, and I needed time to absorb everything I'd heard and to clear my head, organize my thoughts, and come up with a new slate of questions. And I seriously needed some rum.

As we rose from the park bench, she looked me straight in the eyes and said, "Odel, I may not always be able to answer all your questions. But I promise you this—I will never, ever lie to you. And I am not lying to you now, when I tell you that I am completely in love with you. And that I will always have your best interests at heart."

20

More Revelations and a Visit to
La Casa Azul

December 1982

The morning after our shared "confessional" in Plaza Hidalgo, I woke before Coquette. She lay in the bed next to me, her beautiful face looking peaceful on the pillow, her arms outstretched in front of her as if reaching out to me. I looked at her silently, absorbing the color of her cinnamon skin, perfect complexion, long eyelashes, and silky hair. My sleep had been fitful, and I woke often thinking about all the things she had told me the evening before. When I woke, she responded to my restlessness with her sweet words of assurance and promises of unconditional love. At one point, she even whispered in my ear that she would "always protect me." I thought, *That's an unusual thing for a woman to say to a man; but this is no 'usual' woman.* Several times through the night we consummated our passions, taking one another on sweet, erotic flights in our dark, quiet room in the ancient barrio of Coyoacán. I loved her, and I knew she loved me. In fact, we were euphoric in our adoration for one another. But I was conflicted. Could I trust her, or would she turn out to be another Penelope entering my life? Just how naive was I?

Our morning began with a long breakfast over which many subjects were discussed and many questions answered. Or dodged. At one point I said, "I just realized, Coquette, I don't know anything about your academic background. It seems obvious you must have college degrees."

She smiled and replied, "You know, Odel, one of the many things I love about you is that you are just now getting around to asking me that question. For most academic types I've known, the first thing they want to know is what degrees someone has, or what university they attended."

"Yes, I know. And that's one of many things I hate about academics. It's such a snob club and that attitude is such a bore. Honestly, I don't care whether you have degrees of any kind at all. That's not what attracts me to you. Besides, you are clearly smarter than any university professor I know!"

The comment made her giggle. "Ha! You're sweet. Well, I do have a PhD from Harvard in modern American literature, with an emphasis on political literature, and a minor in Spanish."

"Wow," I said. "You're something else. You're like . . . Superwoman!"

"Now you're really going to make me laugh! And you, Dr. Bernini, are my super-man."

"Why aren't you in some fancy university position? How did you end up doing what you're doing?"

"That's a long story."

"We've got all morning. And I'm dying to know everything. After all, you've already read everything about me in some bloody dossier, so you owe it to me to reciprocate!"

"I do, and I will. But baby, the most important things I know about you aren't in any dossier." She leaned over and gave me a soft, lingering luscious kiss.

I asked her again how long she'd known Penelope. And again, she responded vaguely. "I wish I could tell you everything about Penelope and me, but I can't. However, I can tell you that we became friends even before we both made the decision to do work for the government. Both of us had fathers in public service, and we grew up in rather similar ways. Oh, there were differences, of course. My family was more academic leaning and liberal; hers was more political and conservative leaning. My mother was a biologist, like you, and she and my dad loved hiking, bird watching, and exploring together. We were a close, loving family. Penny's parents were 'city folks,' both of them working for the government, and they never seemed as tight, in emotional ways, as our family was. They were intensely private people, and that's probably one of reasons Penelope and I eventually drifted apart. I felt like she could never fully let me in, if you know what I mean. It seemed as if Penelope was always 'acting' in ways she *thought* she should be, rather than just being herself. But I've always had the greatest respect for her and for her family."

I was listening intently, trying to fill in the missing pieces in my mind. The occasional use of "Penny" for Penelope told me the two might have known one another since at least early college days. And she clearly knew Penelope's family well, or at least she used to.

"You told me you don't care for Antin Morales. Neither do I. Why do you think it is that he and Penelope are friends?"

"I think it's just because they are similar in some fundamental ways; politically conservative, comfortable with secrecy, and so forth. As I said, it's just the way Penelope grew up. I know that Morales is especially fond of her, but I don't know how much of those feelings are shared. But, you know, Odel, we all have a right to our own friends; people we connect with in some essential way and that we're comfortable around."

"Of course, of course. And you have known of Penelope's . . . sexuality all along?" I asked.

"Since we first became friends. She's the most sensuous woman I've ever known. She seems to have been born with that architecture, though she certainly practiced and honed her skills to a fine art. I used to watch her interacting with men and women, turning on her charms, seeing how she captivated them. Honestly, I think I learned how to make myself attractive to men by watching Penelope." She giggled.

For Coquette, this seemed a trivial comment. But for me, it opened yet another layer of mystery. So I probed deeper. "Are you telling me that my wife taught you how to be the deeply seductive woman that you are? Does that mean you have had a life like Penelope's—of seducing men? And women?" As soon as I said it, I realized it was inappropriate.

Coquette just stared at me, and tiny tears formed in the corners her eyes. "Oh, you don't know me at all, do you? Penelope and I are profoundly different people, especially in that regard. I am not, by nature, a flirtatious woman. I said Penelope helped me learn to be more attractive; I didn't say she taught me how to flirt. Although I suppose there was some of that too. But she taught me how to dress, how to have self-confidence and poise, how to be more feminine. I was really a tomboy, like my mom, when we first became friends. And I have not had that many lovers in my life. My flirtations with you were unique; they were coming from the deepest place in my heart. They were loving flirtations because I wanted you so badly." And then the tears came. *Too many tears*, I thought, *there's more to this story—much more*.

I held her hands in mine and told her I was sorry for my question and that it had been improper. But I wasn't ready to let her off the hook quite yet. I had to know more.

"What did your dad do, or does he do—is he still working or retired?" I asked her.

"Oh, he's still working. I can't really tell you what he does exactly, other than he specializes in Latin America."

I wondered what that meant. *Did she mean she didn't know herself what he did exactly, or she knew but couldn't tell me exactly what he did?* But I moved on.

"Coquette, you are the most beautiful woman I've ever met. And you're smart, charming, and interesting. How is it that you don't have a husband?"

She could no longer hold back the tears. "I had a husband once," she said. "His name was Michael, and he was a saint. We were very happy. But he died in an accident about four years ago. You're the first man I've been with since . . . his death." She stood up. "Excuse me, I think I need to find the ladies' room. I'll be right back." The tears were streaming down her delicate cheeks like dew drops on a dark rose petal.

Holy shit, I thought to myself. *There is so much to this woman. I think it might take years to get to know her well. And now I've peeled away yet another layer, and I must be more careful. I don't want to hurt her, but I need to know these things. Don't I?*

When Coquette returned from the ladies' room, I felt it was time to stop probing and change the subject. I suggested we stroll the Coyoacán neighborhood and find our way to *Casa Azul*. We talked as we strolled, but in the back of my mind I continued to process all I'd learned. I congratulated her on her Nicaragua book and told her that Nestor Papadakis had also given me a copy. She was happy to hear that. "I've seen your book on Caribbean sea life," she said. "It's beautiful, and I'm sure so useful. You're a really good writer, Odel. I told you once that you should write a story about your life. People would find it interesting—thrilling, even."

"Thanks, Coquette. Maybe I'll do that one day. When I'm old and too tired to travel."

We strolled toward the Frida Kahlo Museum along ancient cobblestone streets and crumbling stone sidewalks, beneath towering *Ficus* trees and twenty-foot-tall purpled bougainvillea. The cerulean sky was pillowed with puffy white clouds, a gentle breeze blew across our skin, and exuberant children played everywhere. I again had the thought that I could easily live right here in Coyoacán for the rest of my life. Perhaps with Coquette.

A block away from *Casa Azul* we heard haunting music coming from behind a closed door in one of old colonial blocks. We stopped to listen and recognized it was a Spanish rendition of Van Morrison's evocative *Into the Mystic*. No doubt a small concert was going on in the interior courtyard— a band with one or two marimbas, a couple woodwinds, and a guitar accompanied by a soulful duet of male and female vocalists. I'd always felt that this song, with its simple lyrics but powerful melody was, like Paul McCartney's quintessential *Hey Jude*, akin to the most moving and enduring of the modern classics—Edvard Grieg's *Peer Gynt Suite No. 1*, Aaron Copeland's *Fanfare for the Common Man*, and Carl Orff's *Carmina Burana*. We stood still on the sidewalk under the shade of a giant laurel tree, and listened to it until the final words were sung, both of us feeling they were a message to us from the barrio, "*es demasiado tarde para parar ahora*/It's too late to stop now."

Echoes of the music still hung in our minds, imposing a kind of spell over us both, when the brilliant cobalt-blue walls of the Frida Kahlo house became visible a block away. It was the house where she was born in 1907 and in which she was raised. It is also the home that she and her husband, the great muralist Diego Rivera, lived in for some time and in which she would die in 1954. And it is the house in which political exile, and Frida and Diego's friend, Leon Trotsky lived with them after his escape from Joseph Stalin's Russia. It contains many of Frida and Diego's paintings, including pieces never seen in books or traveling shows of their work. And it includes their spectacular tropical garden and personal collection of pre-Hispanic artifacts, the urn containing Frida's ashes, and her wheelchair positioned in front of an unfinished picture of Stalin still on its easel—an easel given to her by Nelson Rockefeller when she and Diego lived briefly in New York City. Frida's trademark colorful Tehuana-style dresses are also on exhibit, as are many of the byzantine leg and back braces and special shoes she was forced to wear throughout her life. Kahlo was struck by polio in childhood, which would leave one leg significantly shorter than the other. And then, at the age of eighteen, the bus she was riding home from school in collided with a streetcar. She sustained multiple injuries in the accident, including a broken pelvis and broken spine. The doctors didn't expect her to live. One sees the pain and suffering of her life in her exquisite paintings. Like the Virgin of Guadalupe, Frida Kahlo is a powerful symbol in Mexico, representing hardship, suffering and femininity, and honoring Mexico's indigenous roots.

We enjoyed a late lunch and returned to our hotel to freshen up before the five o'clock concert at *Iglesia de San Juan Bautista*. Coquette decided she wanted to shower after our long morning of walking. Standing next to the bed, she kicked off her sandals and slipped out of her dress—the only pieces of clothing she wore. The sweet smell of her sweat filled my nostrils and lit me up like a Sicilian candle. Noticing my arousal, she lay down on the bed, spreading her bronze arms and legs wide, and said, "Why don't we have an afternoon delight, my love? And then we can wash one another in the shower before the concert."

We made love, slept our little death for twenty minutes, and then played as we bathed. As we walked to the church, another question entered my thoughts.

"If you know so much about Penelope and her sexual activities with others, am I to assume that she also knows about us?"

Her reply was thoughtful. "I don't think so. It's quite different you see—because of her reputation within the agency and her promiscuity. You are my first lover in many years. And I've been very careful. Honestly, I think only two or three people know about us. And I believe they're happy for me because they know it isn't frivolous. Though not all of them think it's a wise move on my part! But the people who know about us are people I trust."

I didn't respond right away, prompting her to continue. "Odel, you do see how different it is, don't you? Baby, I'm in love with you. This isn't some flighty thing. Not for me anyway." She looked concerned.

"Of course I see the difference, Coquette. And believe me, this is anything but frivolous for me."

When we got to *Iglesia de San Juan Bautista*, it was packed. We found space in a pew near the back and settled in. The smell of ancient cedar and wafting Catholic *copál* blended with hushed conversation in the high-ceilinged, 430-year-old church to create a dreamy atmosphere. The concert was mesmerizing. Neither of us had ever heard such music. The unusual compositions and harmonies carried us both to uniquely peaceful places in our minds. We were practically in a trance as we walked slowly out of the old church, holding hands but not speaking.

We enjoyed a romantic dinner on the patio of one of the many cafés surrounding Plaza Hidalgo. I opted for a *mole amarillo* dish, Coquette for epazote-spiced rice and *Huachinango Veracruzana*. I had a flight out of Mexico City the next morning; she was staying on for a few more days to do some work with colleagues at UNAM. I thanked her for opening up to me and told her I felt I had no choice but to confront Penelope with these revelations—though I would do so without mentioning Coquette's name. I told her I was still confused about how all these secrets could exist and how Penelope could be so devious. She said that when you grow up in a world of the State Department, NSA, and CIA, you learn to compartmentalize things in your life and in your mind. "It's a culture of secrecy, and it's the only way that Penelope knows. Her parents are the same way. I might have been that way, too, were it not for my more open-minded and progressive-thinking parents."

I slept much better that night, and we lay with our bodies entwined or with Coquette's lithe body atop mine—something she seemed to crave and I found thrilling. We made love only once, but it was long and tender and impassioned—a slow, delicious burn in the dark of a quiet Mexican night. I told her I'd never enjoyed sex so much in my life. She said, "But Penelope must be such an expert; I find that hard to believe." I replied that it was so different it couldn't be compared—ours was so emotionally fulfilling it felt transcendent, sublime. She sighed deeply and snuggled her body even closer to mine, and as we drifted asleep I felt our breathing come into perfect alignment.

21

Odel Confronts Penelope
Winter Solstice 1982

Coquette and I took separate cabs in the morning, promising
one another we'd be in touch soon, and I told her I'd let her
know how my "big discussion" with Penelope went.

When the cab from Sea-Tac Airport dropped me off at
home, Penelope was there. As always, she welcomed me with
open arms, smiles, and kisses. As I walked into our house, my
eye caught a tiny black speck on the door. Sonia's pinhole
was nearly gone now, the dry wood slowly healing itself,
though it was still a minute visible reminder of the beginning
of my journey. As soon as I dropped my suitcase inside the
house, Penelope wrapped her arms around my back and held
me tight, her mouth pressed against mine, moist and warm. It
was a cold winter in Seattle in 1982, but even through her
jeans and heavy sweater, I was reminded of what an exquisite
body she had. As her tongue began exploring my mouth, I
knew that I wouldn't be able to suppress the lustful desires she
brought out in me. It was nearly dinnertime and I could smell
a pot of her delicious green chile pork simmering on the stove.

When I pulled out the bottle of *Flor de Caña* that I'd purchased in Managua airport's duty free shop, she said, "Oh goody, let's celebrate. My handsome husband is home and it's the Christmas season."

Penelope joined me for rum on the rocks as we filled each other in on our respective trips. I told her of my successful seminar, how Bob and Beatriz were doing, and that I'd experienced a failed attempt at a fishing trip to the coast. When I told her about the incident in the bar in Corinto, she looked sincerely concerned. I tried to laugh it off, but she said, "Odel, you shouldn't have even been in some sleazy bar in a port town like Corinto—what were you thinking! You must be careful; I don't want my perfect hubby to get hurt in some stupid bar fight! Promise me you'll be more cautious. I need you in one piece, baby, not damaged."

That night Penelope did her best to make wild love to me. But I was unable to get Coquette out of my mind, and the revelations she'd told me about Penelope's long-standing promiscuity took the emotional closeness out of our intimacy. I realized that I was now leading two lives, or perhaps I was trapped in a "no man's land" *between* two lives, adrift in a sea of murkiness, and I wasn't comfortable with it. I couldn't stop wondering who Penelope might have been sleeping with while I was out of town. That night, Penelope's sexual talents and enthusiasm assured the physical satisfaction was there, but our psychological connection was faltering. Nevertheless, I told myself I'd give it a few days before opening up our "discussion."

My first day back at the museum was depressing. Some of the curators had started coming in only a couple of days a week, preferring to work from home. There was a dark cloud over the once-happy place, and everyone felt it—except, perhaps, Acting Director Bligh. Bligh ran things like a dictator. In my mail was a letter from The Cleia Foundation asking for a report on my first year's funding and inviting me to reapply for another year, which would begin in March

1983. I had only spent about half the funds from the first grant. If I asked for more funding, I would roll the remainder over and begin building a surplus in the dedicated bank account I had established. Suddenly I had the thought that Penelope might have been doing just that—for years.

I called Nestor Papadakis and told him I was back from Nicaragua with the information he wanted. We set up a meeting for the following week.

Penelope and I dragged the boxes of Christmas stuff out of the garage and decorated the house. We picked out an innocent tree and festooned it with baubles and lights. I collected my thoughts and prepared to confront her with what I had learned. She hadn't mentioned Marjorie at all.

Nestor was again in a jolly mood. We made small talk for a while, but eventually he got around to asking me about Sandinista versus Contra sentiments in Nicaragua. I told him that I thought the populace was divided. So deeply divided, in some cases, that it was prompting breakups among families and friends. Most of the people I talked with hated the Contras but wanted free enterprise; they wanted the new government to succeed but were frustrated by Daniel Ortega's growing censorship of the press and his embracing of Fidel Castro and the Russians. Everyone knew that Ortega was moving Russian arms from Cuba to the rebels in El Salvador. It was pretty much common knowledge in Nicaragua—socialists helping socialists, despite the fact that in the United States politicians played it up as if it were some big secret of the Sandinistas. It was a difficult and frustrating situation for the people of Nicaragua—who simply wanted peace, prosperity and democracy. I told Nestor that if the United States would have just propped up the post-Somoza regime properly, things might have gone differently.

"Everyone knows that, Odel. We're as frustrated as the Nicas are, but the White House policy has consistently been that a free and open democracy was necessary for our continued support. And things such as press censorship and supplying the Salvadorian rebels with arms are simply unacceptable. At least, that's the official line. Actually, it's a big goddamn mess—just like Panama and Honduras and Guatemala and a lot of other places in Latin America. It's a damn shame things in the world can't be just black or white."

Nestor was delighted with the revised map and new information I gave him on Corinto. But he made it clear that my role in Nicaragua would be forever altered since I'd been "outed" as a gringo hero. He asked if I'd be willing to gather some information for the Agency in Guatemala. I told him I'd have to think about it, "Some things are changing in my personal life, and I need time to sort them out."

"I completely understand, Odel. You need to do what's right for yourself, what's best for your life."

But I also knew I needed to do some collecting on the coast of Guatemala; it was a "black hole" for marine biology, with virtually nothing known about the region.

"Nestor, what is our government going to do about Nicaragua?" When I said it, I realized I was becoming more direct and comfortable with Agency people, at least with Papadakis. He seemed like a good man, and I liked him. I thought I was beginning to better understand how the CIA worked, how complicated the situation in Nicaragua was, and that most of the Agency people were probably just regular blokes trying to do their jobs. And I was also realizing that I had nothing to lose. Except Cleia funding.

"I'm not at a pay grade that allows me to know the answer to that question Odel, and even if I were, you know I couldn't tell you." He had one of those fatherly quasigrins on his face. But I couldn't help thinking, *Is he sincere, or is he manipulating me*?

When I got out of bed on December 22, the morning paper said it was the winter solstice—sixteen hours of darkness and only eight hours of daylight. I thought, with a sense of irony, *Now is probably the appropriate day to have my conversation with Penelope.* Over our morning coffee, I told her I wanted to talk about some things that night after dinner, and I wanted to be sure she had no other plans. She offered to bring home a pizza for dinner from our favorite Italian joint and said she'd also pick up a bottle of my favorite Nero d'Avola at our local wine store. The pizza would be Neapolitan style, and the Nero d'Avola would be Duca di Salaparuta, from the famed Sicilian winemaker Duca Enrico. Penelope knew how to play to my taste buds and my family roots.

At the museum that day, I got a sweet note in the mail from Coquette. She just wanted to be sure that I was OK. I hadn't written or called since my return to Seattle. She told me that she felt the stars were realigning in our lives and that we would be seeing each other again soon. I felt she might be right, but there were still too many uncertainties in my life to be sure of anything. I also received a short letter from Violeta Chamorro thanking me for rescuing her niece in Corinto and inviting me to visit her at the *La Prensa* offices if I was ever in Managua again.

That afternoon, Audrey came into my office and closed the door behind her. She told me, in confidence, that she was feeling so stressed that she'd begun looking for another job. She was fairly certain there would be more layoffs in the coming spring. She told me that several of the curators—the best ones actually—were also actively looking for new jobs and that Stanley Appleton, an internationally recognized paleontologist and one of our top scientists, had already gotten an excellent offer from the University of Amsterdam. I often ate lunch with Stanley, and occasionally he and his longtime partner, Benjamin, had dinner with Penelope and me. I knew him well enough to know he'd take the job; he'd always loved Europe, and the Dutch culture would suit his personality.

Stanley and Benjamin were openly gay and, although they loved Seattle, the liberal culture of Amsterdam probably sounded attractive to them.

As I drove home, I realized that the museum and my job there were becoming less and less relevant to me. The place was a mess, and I had so many other, more important things swirling in my mind these days. I had the sense that, as Destiny had told me, new doors were opening in front of me. Bob and Beatriz were trusted and stabilizing forces in my life, I could probably have a professorship at the National University in Managua any time I wanted it, I was a national hero in Nicaragua, and Violeta Chamorro was my "new friend." I also thought about how much I loved Mexico City, and I wondered if I could get a job at UNAM and live in the lovely barrio of Coyoacán. My desire to be with Coquette had only grown, as my happiness with Penelope had begun to wane. Maybe old Albert was right—life *is* like riding a bike, and if you stop moving forward, or keep looking back, you'll lose your balance and crash.

With the pizza gone and the bottle of Nero d'Avola nearly finished, I stumbled forward with Penelope, beginning with my discovery last summer that she was being funded by The Cleia Foundation.

"Odel, honey, why do you always brood on things for so long before bringing them up? Yes, I've gotten grants from Cleia. Why do you think I suggested the grant idea to you! It's a perfectly legitimate nonprofit foundation; they just happen to also have an arrangement with both the State Department and the CIA that is mutually beneficial for everyone."

"I don't brood, I ruminate. Is it legal?" I asked.

"Cleia? Of course it is. It wouldn't have been around all these years if it wasn't."

"Why didn't you tell me your father worked for the CIA and that he established The Cleia Foundation?"

Her voice took on a perturbed tone. "I don't know who you've been talking to, but that's not correct. Dad works for the State Department, as you know. Like a great many people in the Foreign Service, he also happens to help out the Agency on occasion. In fact, he helps out many government agencies—not just the CIA. Most State Department personnel do. And he didn't start The Cleia Foundation; he just came up with the idea. The State Department and some patriotic private funders developed the 501(c)(3). He's on the board of directors, but he's just one of a half-dozen or so people on the board. It's a perfectly legitimate nonprofit that supports important research in Latin America."

Penelope's comment about patriotism reminded me of Antin Morales. "Well, these nuances are interesting, but why didn't you just tell me all this a long time ago? Why all the mystery, and why keep so many secrets from me? After all, Penelope, I am your husband! And especially since you're drawing me into this maze, why wouldn't you be more forthcoming?"

Penelope looked down, and I could see sadness creeping across her face. She moved her head slowly back and forth, and her eyes grew moist. "I know I should have been more open with you. Others have told me the same thing. But please try to understand . . . it's just the way I was raised. My family has spent their entire lives working in situations that demanded great privacy. I grew up in a house full of classified documents and secrets and things that were simply never discussed—not even amongst ourselves, not even between my mom and dad. I grew up imbued with a 'need to know' mentality. I've never lied to you, Odel. But I realize now that I should have been more forthcoming about some things."

"Yes, you certainly should have been." I pressed on. "And how long have you been getting funding from Cleia?"

"For a few years. I don't know how many exactly—six or seven."

I decided to get straight to the point. "How much money have you accumulated in your dedicated Cleia research account?"

She stared at me with wide eyes. "I don't know. Maybe twenty or thirty thousand dollars?"

"Seven years, Penelope! Could there be sixty or seventy thousand dollars in that account—or more?"

I could see a change taking place in her demeanor, from mild guilt and sadness, to defensiveness. I sensed she was consciously repositioning her feelings.

"Odel, you are out of bounds now. I do have a right to some degree of privacy you know. Besides, why does it matter?"

Her comments seemed so ludicrous I didn't bother to respond. "And in addition to your Cleia grants, you also do contract work for the CIA, right? And do they pay you directly?"

"I used to do small jobs for them and also for the State Department. Mostly training and teaching gigs. You know that I've frequently led workshops for them on Latin American banking and finance; it's my area of specialty, Odel."

"My understanding's always been that you were participating in workshops and conferences as an academic, not that you were the lead on them, or that you were being paid by the government to do that work, or that the CIA was ever involved with them. When was the last time you were paid by the CIA to do something?"

"Odel, I can't answer that question." Silence.

"I see. Well, I think you just did answer it. And who do you report to at the CIA?"

Penelope's eyes got wide. "Have you heard of IIPA—the Intelligence Identities Protection Act? It was passed by Congress last June. It makes it a federal crime to reveal the identities of covert agents of the United States government.

Maybe you need to do some homework, now that you're cooperating with the CIA." She said it in a snide way.

I finished the wine in my glass and wondered where to go next. I had so many questions. Taking another big leap, I said, "Did you have sex with anyone while I was away?"

She stammered a bit and then said, "Yes."

"With Marjorie?"

"Yes. You surely aren't surprised, are you?"

"With anyone else?"

"No, absolutely not."

"Penelope, you once told me you hadn't had sex with anyone else since we'd gotten married. That was obviously a lie. Why should I believe anything you tell me now?"

Her face reddened and I could see the anger rise. "I *never* told you that. What I told you was I'd not had sex, nor had any desire to have sex, with another *man* since we've been married. And that is the truth!"

I had to think about that one. I wasn't sure, but knowing how cautious and calculating Penelope is, she was probably correct. "OK, I'll accept that for now. But tell me this, Penelope, why do you want to be married to me if you enjoy sex with other women so much? Particularly Marjorie."

Now she was clearly upset. "Odel, isn't it obvious! First off, I love you and *want* to be married to you. You're smart, handsome, successful, funny, caring . . . what else could a woman want in a husband? And you're the most exciting man I've ever been in bed with. Second, just because I enjoy sex with women doesn't mean I don't want a stable and conventional marriage. There are endless benefits to marriage that I desire and enjoy. And third, I'm beginning to feel like you're viewing me as some kind of deviant or freak or something, and I don't like it!"

It took me a minute to process what she'd said. *Endless benefits to a conventional marriage? Even though you want to spend your free time fucking women left and right? Sorry,*

Penelope, but I'm having trouble seeing the 'love, trust, and devotion' in all that. I switched gears again.

"Who encouraged you to recruit me to the CIA? Or was it all your idea?"

"Recruit you? No one asked me to 'recruit you,' for heaven's sake! You were out of grant funds and starting to feel a bit desperate. I simply saw an opening to suggest an opportunity for you, that's all. I had no idea if it would work out or not. I'm just happy it did, and I thought you were too. You haven't been complaining to me about it!"

I felt like my brain was trying to process things through a kaleidoscope. Coquette's take on them, Penelope's explanation of them, my own uncertainty about it all. I didn't know what to believe. If I took Penelope's words for what they were, completely literally, I could believe that she had never lied to me. But at the same time, she had not been open or transparent with me. At best, she had been disingenuous, and I didn't like it. But then, if she had grown up with that way of thinking, of behaving—should I cut her some slack? Her beautiful blue eyes were moist with tears and tracks of earlier tears streaked down her soft white cheeks. *I do believe she loves me, but we're just so different in some very fundamental ways. Do I really care if she has sex with a woman now and then?*

And then I blurted out, "Tell me about John Thornton."

She fell silent. It might have been the first time I'd ever seen Penelope at a loss for words. I could see her gathering her strength and poise, formulating her words. With teeth clenched, she said, "There is nothing *wrong* with me, Odel. I love you and want a conventional marriage. But I also want to enjoy relationships with my women friends. They are no threat to you or to our marriage, unless you choose to view them that way. And John Thornton is an old friend, nothing more. Why do you ask?"

My turn to be silent. A beat passed, and I said, "OK, Penelope, I respect your right to have your own feelings and views on things. I completely respect that. And I respect you. But I'm simply not sure your views are compatible with mine, especially when it comes to marriage. I think I need more openness and honesty, more forthrightness. You can shave these things thinner and thinner, twist them around to suit your needs, nuance them ad infinitum, but that's not what I need. I need simple, straightforward honesty—clarity and transparency. At least, some greater degree of transparency than I've gotten from you in the past. How long have you known Thornton?"

I could see her anger transitioning into something else, something I'd never seen in Penelope. *Was it frustration or fear or, God forbid, defeat?*

"Baby, I'm sorry I haven't been more open with you about things. But please believe me when I tell you that I love you with all my heart, and I want to be your wife, and I want to please you. I believe in marriage—and I believe in *our* marriage. This has been a good discussion. But please, Odel, can we let this go for now and talk more later on? I feel we should both just calm down and think about all this for a few days. Then we can talk some more."

"Sure. I agree, that's enough for tonight. Just one more thing though—how long have you known Thornton?"

"Since I was fourteen."

22

The Issue of Trust
Spring 1983

I lay awake most of the night trying to process everything. But I couldn't. There was too much, too many loose ends. It seemed as if everything in my life was in transition. I was realizing that Penelope and John Thornton and their pals at the Agency all lived in a twilight zone, in that place where the eyes play tricks and clarity is fraught with uncertainty. What I saw of them were only indistinct snapshots in place and time, half-truths, fragments of their real lives. There was no way to ever really know such individuals—I was just chasing shadows, and there seemed even to be shadows within those shadows. Was Coquette also caught up in that vortex? The only people I felt certain I could trust were Bob and Beatriz, my brother Lorenzo, and my cousin Marco. Although I desperately also wanted to trust Coquette. The museum was collapsing under the burden of its own debt and staff melancholy, and my colleagues were either getting fired or jumping ship. My marriage was headed for the rocks, and I realized that I didn't really know or understand my own wife.

And yet I loved Penelope, and I believed she loved me. And all the while, my thoughts kept drifting to Coquette. I felt ungrounded and directionless, as if I could no longer focus clearly on my life.

Penelope and I didn't talk about these things for a while. We both knew we needed time to calm down and to collect our thoughts. We spent a quiet Christmas alone and tried our best to have a pleasant time, to avoid difficult conversations, to just be friends. We had some decent evenings with good food and good wine. Marjorie didn't come up in any conversations. Penelope was especially attentive to me in the bedroom, using her finely honed sexual skills. God, she knew how to please a man (and apparently also a woman). But it somehow left me feeling hollow and unfulfilled.

As winter struggled to brighten into spring, things at the museum just got darker and darker. In February there was another round of layoffs and three more curators lost their jobs. All our remaining top scientists were now looking for positions elsewhere. Stanley Appleton resigned, and he and his partner began packing for their move to Amsterdam. The board of trustees was making no moves toward opening a search for a new permanent executive director. Audrey said they felt that finances needed to stabilize before they would be able to recruit a good person to the directorship. In early March, Audrey left for a new job at the Seattle Community Foundation. I hated to see her go, but I was happy for her. She had been a good museum friend for years. A few weeks later, our director of education left for a job at the University of Seattle—another huge loss for the museum.

I got letters from Coquette regularly, but she knew I was struggling with things and was careful not to push me in any way. She was supportive and loving and told me that she was there for me and would always be there for me. I wrote back but kept my letters short because I didn't want to dump my confusion and uncertainties on her. I had heard nothing from Nestor Papadakis since December, and I also heard nothing from John Thornton—until mid-March, when he called and suggested we meet for lunch at Gabriela's place. I agreed, thinking it was time to confront him with the fact that he had known my wife since she was a teenager and *why the hell hadn't he said anything to me about that!*

When I arrived at the *pupusería*, Thornton was already there in his usual seat. He could tell from the look on my face that something was on my mind. Or was it the other way around? Corazón greeted me with a hug and a peck on the cheek, and Gabriela waved to me from the kitchen. This was such a happy place. And I so wanted John Thornton to be part of it—to be a happy, honest friend. As I looked at him, I thought, *Why can't he just get on with his retirement plans, marry Gabriela, and lead a normal life?*

When I sat down across the table from him, he asked Corazón to bring us some rum on the rocks. Gabriela didn't have a hard liquor license, but I wasn't surprised to see that special customers could get a glass of rum. We didn't order anything to eat, and the ladies seemed to know to stay away from our table for a while. I was ready to launch right into it, but Thornton beat me to the punch.

"Odel, I can tell you've got a burr under your saddle, and I'm concerned there might be some misunderstanding between us. I want to be sure that isn't the case. I also need to warn you that sneaking around in the parking lot behind our federal building is not wise behavior. Surely you must know that there are video cameras all over the place, and armed guards as well. If I hadn't told them to let you be, you could have easily been arrested."

I felt stupid, but at the same time I didn't care. And I told him so. "Actually, John, I don't give a shit right now. I thought we were becoming friends. I trusted you. Why didn't you tell me you've known Penelope since she was a kid? And what kind of relationship do you have with her anyway?" I saw no point in mincing words. *What do I have to lose?*

"So, I see there *is* a misunderstanding. Listen to me, Odel, we *are* friends. In fact, I might be the best friend you've got right now."

I huffed at his comment.

"Penelope's parents and I have known each other for a very long time—since she was just a kid. We were all rather close for a while, though long ago. I've been something of a second dad, or at least a good friend to her since you two moved to Seattle. What you saw from your federally-videotaped hiding place in our parking lot was a 'father-daughter' kind of discussion, nothing more. In many ways, I love Penelope like I love my own daughter. And I think you probably know by now that she has done training sessions for the government that have included some of our people from the Agency. She's an extraordinarily bright woman and a fine instructor. So I've also had an off-and-on professional relationship with her. I have nothing but respect for Penelope, and for her parents as well."

"And why are you just now getting around to telling me that you've known my wife for years and that she's a contract worker for the CIA? A friend wouldn't try to hide that kind of information."

"You're right Odel, a friend wouldn't. Under normal circumstances. But I *wasn't* trying to hide it; there are some complicated and delicate matters at play here. First off, I've been practically begging Penelope to tell you about her work with the Agency since the day you two got married. I thought about telling you myself, of course, but honestly, I felt it was her responsibility, not mine . . . It's her business, her decision to make. She's your wife; if she wanted you to know, she should tell you."

I grunted and slugged down the rest my rum. Thornton did the same. *I suppose his point is valid*, I thought.

"And it's more complicated than that, my friend. It's one thing for *her* to tell you she does contract work for the CIA but quite another thing for me to tell you. There are a hundred federal laws that prevent me from saying too much to anyone about employees and contractors for the Central Intelligence Agency, ranging from the 1917 Espionage Act, to the National Security Act of 1947, to the 1982 Intelligence Identities Protection Act. And a slew of others. There are some things I simply cannot tell you, because I'd be breaking the law. Or worse, I'd be putting someone's safety in jeopardy."

OK, I thought, *that makes sense, too, I suppose. And it corroborates things I'd heard from both Coquette and Penelope.* I wanted to ask him if he knew about Penelope's sexual affairs with women in the Agency, but the words didn't come out of my mouth. I probably didn't want to hear his answer.

"Do you know Coquette Pallas?"

"Yes, I do."

"How long have you known her?" I asked.

Thornton smiled that fatherly smile he sometimes got and said, "Oh, for quite some time."

"Do you know that she and I have been seeing one another?"

"Yes, I do know that. But, again, it's really none of my business."

"Who else knows about Coquette and me?"

"As far as I'm aware, only two or three others. And I've made it clear to them that it's not something to be shared."

"Does Morales know about us?"

"No, to the best of my knowledge he does not. And frankly, I've gone out of my way to be certain he doesn't."

"And do you know that Coquette does contract work for the Agency also?"

"Yes, of course I know."

Thornton looked toward the kitchen and gestured to Corazón to bring two more rums. *How much of this can I believe?* I wondered. *And how much is he not telling me?*

As if reading my mind, he said, "You can believe me, Odel. Every word I've told you is the truth. Look, I know it's sort of weird when you first start understanding the need for some measure of secrecy in this business. But surely you can understand it. And you do get used to it. You learn who you can trust, and that's the main thing."

Damn it, this guy sounds so convincing.

"OK, John, let's let this lie for now." We both took a long sip of our rum. John waved to Corazón again, turned to me and said, "The usual?" I shook my head, and he said to her, "Bring us two *pupusas chingónes* darlin'."

Thornton said, "Can we talk about work matters a bit?"

"I suppose so," I said.

"The information you gave Nestor was good. Excellent, actually. It's precisely what we needed—thank you very much."

"It was no big deal, John. Any bozo could have done it."

"But not just anyone could have done so and at the same time made themselves a national hero in Nicaragua. Not to mention endearing himself to Violeta Chamorro!" He laughed out loud.

"So you heard about that, eh? Well, it certainly wasn't in the plan!"

"No, it wasn't. But it all ended just fine. Although it does change things a bit. By the way, have you heard from her?"

"Coquette?"

Thornton laughed again. "I can see who's on your mind! No, Ms. Chamorro. Have you heard anything directly from her?"

I couldn't help smiling. "Yes, she sent me a very gracious thank you note. She told me to drop by her office next time I'm in Managua."

"Great. Perfect. You're remarkable, Odel. We couldn't have planned a better strategy! Are you just lucky, or is your life charmed these days? Either way, you now have perfect cover in Managua."

"Whoa, not so fast *amigo*. I don't even know if I want to keep doing this stuff for you guys."

"I understand completely. You need to take some time. But I think it might be wise to keep you out of Nicaragua for a little while. We don't want your visit to Corinto be linked to anything going on there for a few months."

I didn't really understand Thornton's comment, and he quickly continued. "How familiar are you with Guatemala?"

"Pretty familiar. You probably know that one of my hobbies is Mesoamerican anthropology, particularly the Maya culture. I've visited many of the highland villages and some of the eastern lowland villages. I've been to Tikal a number of times."

"When you're ready, let me know if you'd be willing to do us another favor. In Guatemala. And, in the meantime, I think you need to renew your Cleia grant, don't you?"

Damn, I thought. *For a guy who's on the cusp of retirement, he sure still knows a lot about what the hell's going on.*

"I probably will, John. Just give me time to sort some things out. There's a lot coming at me right now."

"I know, Odel. No rush. Think things through."

I thanked him for his candor regarding Penelope and other things, but in the back of my mind I wondered how much truth there was to his words. *Was he like Penelope—not literally lying but holding back critical information that would give crucial context to what he was telling me? Things that I needed to know. Or did I? But who has a right to decide what I need to know and don't need to know? And could it be that Penelope and Thornton, and even Coquette were all being "truthful" with me, each in their own ways and in their own minds, and yet their versions of the story differed.*

Ten days after my conversation with John Thornton, I got a call from my brother Lorenzo. Our mother had died in a tragic hospital accident.

Mom had suffered from congenital arthritis since she was in her twenties. By the time she was fifty, the vertebrae in her spinal column had grown so many spines and spurs that they were abrading the nerves branching off to her arms and legs. When she had flare-ups, the only way the doctors could treat her was with a cocktail injection rich with corticosteroids, carefully sliding a long steel needle between the vertebrae to load up the nerve roots with the drug. In the early 1980s those injections were still a fairly new treatment, and they were done without the aid of real-time X-rays; in other words, the doctor doing the injection was navigating the spinal column by dead reckoning. A young doctor who had not done many of the tricky procedures screwed up and slid the needle right into her spinal cord, injecting forty milligrams of the chemical cocktail directly into her central nervous system. She died six and a half minutes later.

Penelope and I got a flight to Los Angeles as soon as we could. My father was beside himself, immobilized, unable to act. His younger siblings, my Uncle Sandro and Aunt Adriana, were handling things with the mortuary and our parents' long-time parish church, St. Vincent de Paul. Little by little, the whole extended Bernini family showed up. I hardly recognized the majority of them and had never even met most of my cousins' kids. Dad was distraught and after the wake, a typically pagan Catholic service, and the ritualistic Catholic burial, he fell into a deep depression. No one offered to throw a party in celebration of our mother's life, something that could be uplifting and honor her. My Catholic-Sicilian family was too traditional for such things. I knew how close my parents were, married in every sense of the word—the trope "joined at the hip" hardly sufficed to describe their bond. I knew Dad would have trouble moving on, let alone trying to "celebrate" Mom's life. As the days went by, he spoke little, ate practically nothing, and had a blank and distant look in his eyes. He frequently wept uncontrollably. Penelope was heroic in every way—dealing with the entourage of my aunts, uncles, and cousins, helping with the logistics of everything, trying her best to console people, including Dad. I couldn't have asked for more from her.

My brother and I were surprisingly unmoved by our mother's death. In thinking about our feelings, or lack thereof, we concluded it was because we simply were not close to her. Her alcoholism had long ago driven us both away from her— away from the house altogether. Even when she had been with us in conversation, she wasn't really "with" us. She was shallow in thought and not clearheaded. One could not have a meaningful conversation with her. Oh, we tried, but two sentences into a discussion, she'd drift off or bottom out, and, for Lorenzo and me, that meant the conversation was over. In a sense, we grew up without a mother. My dad, on the other hand, was so busy making a living for the family that we rarely had time with him at all. But when we did, it was always high-quality time. When Dad was with us, he was one hundred percent with us. Explaining things to us, teaching us important facets of life (such as how to eject a drunk from his shop or how to bluff in a hand of seven-card stud). It was a curious thing about our family, that my brother and I felt closest to the parent we saw the least of.

My brother and Penelope both had to get back to work, but I decided to stay on for a while to keep tabs on Dad. Little by little, the Bernini family dispersed back to where they lived and resumed their lives. My cousin Marco and I hung out; he was the only member of my extended family I ever felt really close to, despite his mafia connections. Eventually, I also had to get back to work. I thought about trying to see Coquette since I was in L.A., but my heart was so heavy I didn't think it was good timing. The great sadness that fell upon my father was like a thick fog. He just sat. And he wept. And the weight of the thing made him stoop and sway in an uncharacteristic manner. It wasn't normal grieving; it was an inability to accept that Mom had left him. He could take no comforting from me, regardless of how I approached him. He went deep inside himself and was alone in his sorrow. I don't think I'd ever seen such sadness in a person. After my return to Seattle, I called him daily, but he would only pick up the phone every third or fourth day.

I arrived back in Seattle with mixed feelings. My anger at Penelope had changed, morphed into my own incarnation of sadness—sorrow for my father, melancholy for my marriage, despondency over the museum's situation. I admired Penelope and, I thought, loved her for many reasons. Part of me truly wanted our marriage to work. She had been so kind since my last return from Nicaragua, not drinking too much, being mindful of what she said to me. But part of me knew it was unlikely I could reconcile her behavior, her way of being, with my own need for trust in our marriage. My sadness grew as a summation of the loss of my mother, my father's deepening depression, the demise of a once-great research museum, and incipient grieving over the likely loss of my marriage. *Shit,* I thought, *am I just feeling sorry for myself? Sinking into the quicksand of my own self-pity? Or am I approaching some kind of fundamental juncture in my life?*

I began to turn the idea of "trust" around in my mind. *What is it anyway? Is it simply belief in someone, or in the reliability of someone? Or is it more than that?* I thought about Coquette, and how I so wanted to have the kind of trust in her that was unshakable, a trust so complete that I would never question her sincerity or authenticity. I felt this might be possible with Coquette, but I was beginning to realize I could never have it with Penelope. I definitely felt I had it with Bob and Beatriz, and Lorenzo and Marco. But I wasn't certain that I had it with anyone else. I had the kind of confidence in Bob and Beatriz that assured me they would never hide something vital from me, that they were genuine people, and that they had my best interests at heart. To have complete trust in someone, they must be so transparent that they always were what they appeared to be. But maybe I was kidding myself; maybe no one is that transparent. And should Bob and Beatriz have that kind of trust in me, given the secrets I was now keeping from them? In the context of our friendship, they seemed wholly trustworthy, yet I was not. But of course they, too, must have their own secrets. What would those be? And can people be trustworthy with some, but not with others? What would that mean? Maybe trustworthiness is a trait of relationships, not of individuals—a mutualistic kind of symbiosis. Or perhaps trust is situational, coming and going depending on circumstances. Maybe trust is something unique only to specific relationships, a manifestation of human interactions rather than a general quality of individuals. Perhaps John Thornton is honest with me and Gabriela and his daughter, but not with most other people he knows. After all, he had cautioned me to "learn who I could trust." Perhaps trust is a temporary quality of a relationship, with a finite lifetime, such that it can be there for a while but then dissipate or change. Or maybe it's the other way around, and trust is a kind of faith, built only over years of experience. They say trust must be earned, and there seems little doubt of that.

And how can there *ever* be trust between two people when a relationship is clouded in fog, awash with arguable nuances, a dance in the gray zone of uncertainty, forever trapped in the ambiguity of individual interpretation? Yet, that's what my marriage seemed to have become. Had it been like this all along, and I'd simply not noticed? Is all of life a "gray zone," and at some point in our maturation as an adult we simply come to realize that? Is life never black and white, but always something in-between? Are our seemingly definitive, black-and-white memories just illusions? How can trust ever not be fleeting in such a world? And what is the relationship between trust and caring for another. Can you trust someone who you feel isn't mindful of your feelings, of your love for them? Or is that simply a matter of individual sensitivity, ar.. perhaps has nothing to do with trust?

The issue of trust is further clouded by expectations. In fact, many people use their own expectations as a measure of another's trustworthiness. But what if one's expectations are inappropriate, or too high, or too low. And is it even fair to measure another by your own expectations? And what of those who, for one reason or another, simply cannot trust? I have known women who are unable to trust a man, any man, no matter the circumstances. And vice versa.

And then I had the thought that even what a person sincerely believes to be true must be shaped and configured by the geography of their own mind, their particular view of the world. But we all see the world slightly differently, colored by our past, our emotions, our subconscious biases. Penelope and John Thornton may not be lying to me; they may simply be articulating the truth as their mind sees it.

In the end, I could only conclude that trust is a very complicated human emotion.

I decided to go ahead and submit a proposal for a second year of Cleia funding. I did need to sample the coast of Guatemala for my work, whether or not I did anything for the Agency. And with so many things around me seemingly falling apart— or, at best, lost in a mist of uncertainty—perhaps a good collecting trip to a tropical shore would regenerate me. If there was one certainty in my life, it was love of research, discovery, and fieldwork.

In late April I heard back from Cleia that my grant renewal would be funded, and two weeks later the thirty-thousand-dollar check came in the mail. With the unspent residue from the first Cleia grant, I now had fifty thousand dollars in my dedicated Cleia account. I deliberated calling John Thornton, and eventually I did.

"John, I'm thinking about a collecting trip in Guatemala soon. Probably this summer."

"Thanks for the head's up, *amigo*. If you'd like to come in and talk with Nestor, he can tell you about a little recon work you could help us with. What do you think?"

"I suppose there's no harm in chatting with him. Let's see what he has to say."

"Great. He'll be in touch then. But listen, Odel, Guatemala's not like Nicaragua. It's the Wild West. Things can get a little rough in the highlands. It might be good if Nestor gave you a bit of a background briefing on some stuff."

"Whatever." I thought, *Maybe I can learn something interesting about the mountain Maya from the Agency. Although, my guess is I'm more familiar with those villages and roads than Nestor is.*

Three days later Nestor called. "Dr. Bernini, I'm happy to hear you might be able to do us one more favor. And John Thornton tells me you're ready for some background briefings—that's excellent. When can you set aside three days to spend with us?"

"Three days? Well, I might not need all that much time, Nestor. I've been traveling in Guatemala for a dozen or so years, and Maya culture is a special interest of mine. I know my way around the country."

"Right, I'm sure you do. But let's plan on a few days anyway, and just see how it goes. How about next week? I think I can arrange things quickly."

"Sure, that's fine with me. I'm available Wednesday, Thursday, or Friday next week."

"That would be great, thank you. See you in my office next Wednesday morning at eight."

"OK, see you then." I thought, *I'll move things along quickly with these guys, and we should be able to cover everything in a few hours. We definitely won't need three days, or even two.*

I decided to call Coquette. She was home and thrilled to hear my voice. And hearing her voice nearly knocked me over. The sweet melodious lilt to her speech gave me butterflies in my stomach. Listening to her transported me to a beach in Montelimar, to our sand-floor "hotel" in the San Blas Islands, and to Barrio Coyoacán in Mexico City. It was almost as if her voice had a tangible fragrance to it, and in my mind the smells of her hair and her flesh danced in my memory. I filled her in on things and she listened intently, asking many questions. And she told me what she'd been up to. We confessed how much we missed each other, and we agreed to meet somewhere, somehow, during my upcoming Guatemala trip. Just before we hung up, she asked me if the Agency was going to brief me on anything before the trip.

"Yes, next week in fact. They want to talk with me for three days, but I doubt that much time will be needed."

"My love, if they want to brief you for three days, I think it means they are going to ask you to go someplace risky. Into the mountain villages of the north, perhaps. I don't know much about Guatemala, but I do know the northern sierras are dangerous these days. This new president, Ríos Montt, has apparently let loose the army and the death squads in the high country and Maya villagers are being killed left and right. And the insurgency is also growing stronger. Did you hear about the peasants from Quiché Department taking over the Spanish Embassy a couple years ago? I really think it was a turning point in the civil war. The Guatemalan army laid siege to the building against the express wishes of the Spanish government. They burned much of the embassy building, killing dozens of people inside. Spain terminated diplomatic relations with them. Since then, and since Ríos Montt took control, the war has escalated greatly. Honestly, I don't think you should do this."

I explained that I would be collecting on the Pacific coast for most of the time, with only a few days—maybe a week at most—checking some places out for the Agency, though I didn't know exactly where yet, but that I would be very cautious. But I could hear the genuine concern in her voice.

23

Odel's Big Briefing

June 1983

I met Nestor Papadakis at 8:00 a.m. sharp; I was skeptical. In his office, he asked if I knew much about the political situation in Guatemala. I assumed, at this point, that he knew who my wife was and that Penelope knew a great deal about the banking and finances of Guatemala, as well as the culture of the capital, Guatemala City. She did not, however, know much about the Maya or the rural peasant culture of the country. I told him I knew a fair bit about the political and social history of Guatemala, and that I thought it was mostly just sad.

"In my opinion, Nestor, Guatemala has never escaped the shackles of its Spanish colonial roots—rule by the wealthy elite and military, and the persecution of the native Maya population. Personally, I'm fascinated by the Maya culture, and you probably already know that anthropology is a particular interest of mine. The Maya are unique in the region because, like the Inca of South America, they're an indigenous civilization that has lived in the same place, in the same way, speaking the same language for thousands of years. Their time on Earth began two thousand years before Christianity; they survived in their lands as the Roman Empire rose and fell, as the great Chinese dynasties came and went (and the Great Wall of Chia was built), throughout the Dark Ages and the Renaissance, and even through the European conquest of America. They are, literally, the living history and memory of pre-Hispanic Mesoamerica. And I'm sure you also know that Europeans and their descendants have been systematically slaughtering the Maya since the sixteenth century. And from what I can tell, presidents in Guatemala are virtually always military men, put in office through fraudulent elections or military coups. I believe the army is thoroughly corrupt yet basically runs the country."

"Right on all counts, Odel. The army creates presidents, and the army destroys them. And corruption is an intrinsic part of the culture. Guatemala is generally viewed as a pariah by its neighbors, and it's one of the poorest nations in the Western Hemisphere. So, why, exactly, do you enjoy traveling there?"

"Well, if you've been there and gotten outside Guatemala City, you know that it's a spectacular landscape, with a magnificent indigenous culture. Driving in the highlands is to be in an endless green terrain; a thousand different shades of green, punctuated by explosively colorful Maya villages. Those high mountains are the southernmost extension of the Sierra Madre range of Mexico—for a biologist, that mountain region is extraordinary. A rugged landscape of pine and fir forests and canyons filled with exotic endemic species of plants and animals. And the gradual fall of the sierras to the east is breathtaking as it drops into the massive lowland jungle of the Petén and on to the coasts of the Caribbean and the Yucatán Peninsula. Most of the Petén is still virgin, extraordinarily rich in biodiversity. There are dozens of species of hummingbirds in Guatemala, and nearly as many trogons and motmots; not to mention the giant anteaters, tapirs, three species of monkeys, five species of big cats, and on and on. For a naturalist, it hardly gets any better. And the Maya, living everywhere, eking out a living from the soil and native plants in the same ways they have for thousands of years—it's an anthropologist's paradise. I'm simply fascinated by it all. Guatemala City may be mostly *ladino chapín*, but once you leave the capital, the landscape is *puro Maya*."

"Yes," Papadakis replied. "It is beautiful. However, the Maya might have the numbers, but the white oligarchy and the military have the power. We've been working to reign in the abuses, but we haven't been particularly successful. Maybe you heard about Pope John Paul's visit a few months ago?"

"I did. It was last March, I think? The pope pleaded with President Ríos Montt to spare the lives of six Maya boys who'd been convicted on bogus charges by a secret military court. But just a few days before John Paul's arrival, they were executed by firing squad. An awful tragedy."

We chatted for an hour or so in Nestor's office. We talked about the different lifestyles of the mountain Maya and the lowland Maya. Although in both regions the people live in small villages and rely on subsistence agriculture, they lead different lives. The two groups rarely emigrated from one area to the other, unless forced to do so by government harassment and the need to save themselves and their families from slaughter. They raise their own food, forage for their water and fuel wood, don't have bank accounts, and get no help from the government. They're OK with that—they just want to be left alone to live in their traditional ways.

Papadakis went on.

"As you probably know, Odel, the people of Guatemala began actively resisting military rule and government lawlessness a long time ago, in the 1960s actually. The Maya, in particular, were under constant attacks and harassment from the army. Several organized resistance groups appeared during that early period, as Guatemala's civil war began to emerge. In response to growing resistance from the native population and the public sector—which, by the way, included the Catholic Church and many university students and professors—the government encouraged paramilitary organizations to expand. Those new right-wing gangs of thugs, such as MANO (Organized National Anti-Communist Movement), ESA (Secret Anti-Communist Army), *Ojo por Ojo* (Eye for an Eye), and the infamous "Death Squadron" are ruthless and cruel. They operate outside the government and the army but have tacit approval from both."

I said I'd heard of them, but the stories were so outrageous that I wasn't sure if they were true or not. Papadakis replied simply, "They're true." He went on.

"These bands of barbarians and sadistic misanthropes are perverted in ways that defy imagination. They're the dregs of society, the mentally ill, and the sadists in Guatemala's society. They use torture, rape, assassination, and 'disappearing' to subjugate the Maya people and the unempowered *mestizos*. Even people merely "suspected" of sympathizing with the resistance are targeted and then maimed or murdered. But over time, the more atrocities the army and the paramilitary groups perpetrate, the more the people's resistance grows, and the cycle of civil war escalates."

"And how has the CIA been involved in all this?" I asked flatly.

"It's no secret that, beginning in the '50s, the Agency's had a close relationship with the Guatemalan military. It wasn't until the late '70s, when President Carter acknowledged the brutality of their military dictatorships, including forced conscription of Maya children as young as eleven and twelve years old into the army, that the U.S. pulled back military aid to the country and the Agency was told to downsize in the country. But then Reagan was elected, and he reestablished everything. In March last year, a group of young army officers staged a successful coup d'état that ousted General Anibal Guevara, who had served as president for only two months. They installed General Efraín Ríos Montt as the new president. I don't know how much you know about Ríos Montt, but he's an animal."

I waded in again. "I know a bit about him. Was the Agency involved in that coup?"

Papadakis gave me a faint smile but didn't respond to my question. He went on. "Ríos Montt wasn't even in the country at the time; he was in California, active in the evangelical movement. He returned to Guatemala as the new president, and Reagan felt he had a reliable Central American ally in the battle against Nicaragua's Sandinista government. U.S. aid began flowing to Ríos Montt's government, and Reagan referred to him as 'a man of great personal integrity and commitment.' I'm just giving you the facts here, Odel; I'm not judging or evaluating anything. The U.S. has been supplying the Guatemalan army with massive armaments and also negotiated with the Israelis to install a countrywide phone-tapping system that Guatemala's security forces could use."

I knew that one of Ríos Montt's first acts as president was to fire every elected mayor in the country—all 324 of them. It was an astonishing move. In their place, he put his handpicked cronies. He also shut down the legislature and rescinded the country's constitution, replacing it with a decree giving him complete autonomy and authority.

Nestor continued: "Under Ríos Montt, government terrorism of the Maya—and anyone else who opposes him—has escalated beyond anyone's wildest imagination. Reagan knows this; we all know it. Ríos Montt has been sacking, burning, and bombing whole villages. Captured Maya are brutally murdered and torture has become commonplace—basically institutionalized—and unspeakable stories of mutilation are now circulating. Ríos Montt's goon squads have been unleashed with no constraints. Decapitation in the streets is becoming routine. We don't have good numbers, but we know that thousands of Maya have been killed, and hundreds of thousands forced to flee their homes and villages."

"Is the resistance gaining traction anywhere in the country?" I asked.

"Not really. Ríos Montt's response to opposition from the Catholic Church has been to confiscate churches and murder the clergy. In Quiché Department churches in many villages have been converted into military barracks. Even in Guatemala City, Ríos Montt's forces are identifying labor and student leaders as enemies of the state and snatching them off the street to be killed or disappeared. And when international organizations present evidence of massacres to Reagan, he sides with the Guatemalan military, who blames the guerrillas for the killings. However, the evidence, public opinion, and reports by the Organization of American States and the United Nations have become so damning that the U.S. State Department was recently forced to admit that the army has been behind the massacres. Yet Reagan is still not willing to cut off funds for the Ríos Montt government."

"Speaking of Quiché," I interjected, "I've heard things are especially bad in the Ixil valley."

I knew that beautiful valley fairly well; in fact, it used to be one of my favorite places to visit. As you drive up the steep mountain highway into the Quiché region, you float up through the clouds, in rarified air, over the ridge of the Sierra de los Cuchumatanes and into the surreal landscape of Ixil Valley. Surrounded by mountains and volcanoes, this lush, isolated basin gets rain year-round. Sometimes the sun forces the heavy afternoon clouds to lift, revealing a scene so majestic that it conjures up visions of Shangri-La. The entire valley is luminescent with bright emerald and floral colors year-round. As you drive the narrow dirt roads in the sierras off the main highways, Maya women sit along the roadside in small groups with the *copál* and firewood and mushrooms they've collected, chatting and waiting for a pickup truck to come along and give them a ride to their village. The locals here speak a Mayan dialect found nowhere else in Mesoamerica. The indigenous Ixil people enjoyed a simple lifestyle of subsistence agriculture for more than 1,400 years before the arrival of Spanish conquistadors. I had already heard that Ríos Montt was targeting this idyllic landscape.

"Yes," Papadakis replied. "He's unleashed the army to undertake what amounts to systematic massacres in the valley. They've declared all of Ixil to be guerrilla supporters."

What neither Papadakis nor I yet knew was that in the coming August Ríos Montt would be overthrown by his own defense minister, Óscar Humberto Mejía Víctores, in another coup d'état. We also didn't know the full extent of Ríos Montt's savage killing spree. During the seventeen months of Ríos Montt's rule, his scorched-earth policy in Ixil alone would result in the torture and murder of over twenty thousand Maya peasants. Fifteen years later, the United Nations Truth Commission would examine Ríos Montt's time in office, detailing the complete annihilation of almost six hundred Maya villages across the sierras in Guatemala. The Inter-American Commission on Human Rights would report that army patrols had gone from village to village, spreading death and destruction on a scale that could only be interpreted as genocide. Whole villages, hundreds of people in each, were slaughtered. The villagers that escaped these death squads took to the most remote mountain regions where they suffered from hunger, cold, and disease. Or they managed to cross the border into Mexico's state of Chiapas. Even the beautiful historic town of Chichicastenango would not been spared. The UN investigation would document that the town of Nentón, in Huehuetenango Department, had gone from a population of 15,000 to 125, as people fled the death squads and brutal attacks from Ríos Montt's Army. Children were knifed and macheted to death, and women were raped and killed in front of their families. But in June 1983, I was unaware of the scale of this genocide.

I thought Papadakis could see that I had a fairly good grounding in Guatemalan sociopolitics. Next, he systematically walked me through some key players, especially among the higher-ranking army officers.

"Do you know about these rogue army lieutenants?" he asked, "The ones who control their own little armies in the highlands?"

"Not really," I replied. "They seem to know better than to harass tourists, and I've never run into anything horrible myself. But, really, these guys don't seem much different from the army or any of the paramilitary squads—unscrupulous, nearly impossible to control."

"Philosophically, they are the same. But these rogue units are basically bands of renegades from the army who subsist by extorting peasants for money and food. They're miscreants who take pleasure in raping and killing. Ríos Montt claims he's tried to put a lid on them but with little success. They're problematic because they're well-armed, and their uniforms give them an air of legitimacy that terrifies the people they want to intimidate—mainly the Maya villagers. There are three or four of these renegade military bands floating around the country, mostly in the highlands, but some of it is also going on in the Petén. One of the worst, the most ruthless, is a Lieutenant Enrique Polyphemus. He has a small band of thieves under him—maybe forty former soldiers—and they're constantly on the move. We've had trouble keeping track of his whereabouts."

"Nestor, this doesn't sound like the kind of thing I want to get mixed up in. I'm a marine biologist, not a damn commando!"

"No, no, of course not. But it's important you have this background clear in your mind. It's just context, Odel, that's all. All we would want you to do is visit a few of the smaller villages in the far north of the country, as a tourist, of course. In the Huehuetenango and Quiché Departments. Just go to the weekly markets and buy a few trinkets. I'm sure you know that every village has its own market day, so you could just follow those markets around like the other tourists do. Just keep your eyes and ears open. You seem to be good at that."

"There aren't many gringo tourists in that part of Guatemala. They hang out on the 'tourist circuit'—Guatemala City, Antigua, Panajachel. There are German tourists everywhere, of course, but I don't speak any German, so I couldn't fake that."

"Well, there are a *few* Americans everywhere. And some Brits and Australians travel to those mountain villages for their market days. They call it 'adventure travel.' And you don't have to talk much, except in Spanish. Few people in those villages speak English anyway. In fact, most of them don't even speak Spanish."

"That's true. So, all you want me to do is travel to the villages on their market days and hang out?" I thought of Antin Morales. "By the way, maybe Mr. Morales should be involved in this discussion—I have a suspicion he might have family in Guatemala."

Papadakis's face took on a slightly annoyed look. "Morales relies on his ancestry the way a drunk relies on a lamppost—for support, not illumination. We don't need his input on this. But thanks for the suggestion."

OK, I thought, *Score two points for Nestor.*

"All we need you to do is just look around, pay attention, see what's going on. Especially keep your ears open for anything that suggests one of the rogue army groups has been around the villages, or if there are rumors that they might be headed in a particular direction. The 'human telegraph' among those communities is excellent. They know far more than the Guatemalan police or secret service know—not that the Guatemalan authorities are worth a shit anyway. We can't trust the information we get from Defense Minister Mejía's people. There's growing pressure from Congress and from the international community to stamp out these gangs of thugs. If the Agency can help that cause, be better at informing our

State Department folks at the embassy about things going on there, maybe we can encourage the Ríos Montt government to take stronger steps to stop these goons."

It was lunchtime, and Papadakis suggested we take a break and reconvene in a couple hours. I grabbed a bite at a nearby dive I'd noticed. I had to admit, the conversation was interesting. And Nestor seemed pretty up-front about things, although a little voice in the back of my head kept saying, *Don't trust this guy. Don't trust anyone working for the CIA. Don't even trust John Thornton.*

When I returned to Papadakis's office, he said he'd like to hand me off to Manny Eumaeus for a few hours for some basic arms pointers.

"Arms? As in guns?" I asked.

"Yes. Nothing complicated or formal, just a bit of awareness coaching on what kinds of arms are floating around Guatemala these days. Good to have a basic grounding in this stuff. They're mostly U.S. and Israeli weapons; nothing exotic. Are you comfortable around guns, Odel?"

"Well, I'm not *un*comfortable, but it all depends on the circumstances. I'm uncomfortable around them when they're pointed at me. But I did grow up in a hunting family; we had plenty of handguns and rifles and shotguns and such. But they were all hunting guns."

"Same difference. It's just useful to us if you can distinguish an M16 from a Galil, or an Uzi, or a Kalashnikov AK-47. Or a Browning from a Colt, or a Walther, or a Beretta. It's unlikely you'll actually see many weapons, but should you stumble upon a firearm here or there, it would be especially helpful if we knew what it was and where you saw it. If you're looking, you'll certainly see plenty of M16s; they're standard issue for Guatemalan army regulars. But the Maya resistance often carries Uzis or AK-47s. We'd like to know what firearm a person is holding and what the person looks like—white or brown, mestizo or Indian, in a uniform or not, alone or in a group of men—that sort of thing. That kind of information from these remote areas can help us build and recognize patterns of armed groups in the highlands. You'd be surprised how useful such simple data points can be for our intelligence analysts working at the embassy down there."

As Papadakis talked, I felt the landscape of my mind expanding. I guess I shouldn't be surprised at all this. But how deep do I really want to dive into this business?

Papadakis escorted me to an elevator on a different side of the building from the others. We took it to a basement floor that hadn't been indicated on the sign by the elevators in the public lobby. There, he introduced me to Manuel Eumaeus, a bright young man likely of Mexican ancestry. For the next three hours I learned what kinds of rifles and handguns are used by the military, paramilitary, and resistance fighters in Guatemala. There was also a small firing range in the basement, and I learned how to fire each weapon, just in case I ever had the need. Eumaeus had me listen carefully to the sound of each as I fired it. The M16, Galil, Uzi, and AK-47 each had a slightly different and distinctive sound. I felt their fired rounds also had distinctly different smells but wasn't sure that would be useful in any way. Then he went to the far end of the shooting platform and fired each of them himself, asking me to describe the sounds. Doing so, he said, would help me recognize them in the field, should I ever again hear them. I doubted that. In fact, I doubted I'd ever even hear the sound of guns while traveling in Guatemala. But it was an interesting exercise. And in any event, I had to agree with Papadakis—guns aren't rocket science. All rifles are pretty much the same, as are all handguns. In one sense, the whole exercise was actually rather fun.

That night I told Penelope that I was planning a collecting trip to the Pacific coast of Guatemala for July. I didn't elaborate. She didn't like the idea.

"I know you like traveling in that country, Odel, but I don't like the idea. Especially not now, with this new guy

Ríos Montt in charge. He sounds like a sociopath to me. Violence has escalated so much since he took office."

"I know, but I'll keep it short, be very efficient. I just need a couple weeks, four or five key coastal sites, and I'll be able to get what I need. I'll be supercareful."

"Honey, did they ask you to do anything for them?"

"Not much. Just nose around, keep my eyes peeled. I'm not going to take any risks. I'll just be the typical gringo tourist, that's all." I didn't mention the firearms lesson.

Penelope looked worried and said, "I don't like it. It doesn't smell good to me."

Day two of the briefing was fascinating. First thing in the morning, Eumaeus walked me through the rifles and handguns again. He was surprised that I remembered everything. "I've got a pretty good memory," I told him. Then he moved on to some of the more nuanced ways in which I might recognize the handguns from the grip alone, should they be holstered. After that morning refresher, he walked me down a long corridor to the other end of the basement, knocked twice on a door, and walked in without waiting for a response. It was a conference room, with a large polished oak table surrounded by two-dozen comfortable looking but empty chairs. At one end sat a nice looking, clean-shaven, well-dressed young man with spectacles, a jersey sweater, and slacks. He was small in proportions, slight, bony as a boy, and his ears were too big for the rest of him. But he carried a long, unruly head of shiny blond hair that framed his face like the sun. His sweater was baggy on his rangy body and loosely hung frame. He reminded me of one of my young college professors from years past. Behind him was a chalkboard. On the table were a telephone, a large rolled-up document, and a box of white chalk.

"Helios, this is Dr. Odel Bernini. Dr. Bernini, meet Dr. Helios Demopoulos. He's just back from a twelve-month tour of duty at our embassy in Guatemala City. I'll leave you two to discuss the ins and outs of regional politics and such." *Another Greek*, I thought.

Eumaeus left the conference room as Demopoulos walked over to shake my hand. His hands were like those of a young girl, his grip was delicate and gangly. He spoke quickly but precisely, as he explained that we were going to spend a few hours talking about the current political situation in Guatemala. "And I'd also like to be sure you're aware of the new Intelligence Identities Protection Act just passed by Congress," he said.

"I've heard it mentioned, but frankly I know nothing about it."

"You need to know now that you've got a temporary security clearance—even if it's only low level. Someone should have briefed you on it already. Your security clearance makes you doubly liable to the federal government to respect the letter of the law. Do you know who Philip Agee is?" He talked rapidly, as if he wanted to get through this first part of the briefing straightaway and on to the rest.

"Only vaguely," I admitted. "I think he was that CIA agent who quit his job and blew the whistle on a lot of the Agency's operations in Latin America."

Demopoulos then proceeded to give me the background. "None of this is any big secret," he assured me, "but most people simply don't know about it. The Intelligence Identities Protection Act, or IIPA, was approved by Congress and signed by President Reagan last June. It was, in large part, a response to Philip Agee's exposure of Agency activities and, importantly, the names of numerous undercover agents, first in his 1975 book, and then later in some magazines he published. One of his magazines included articles by well-known critics of U.S. foreign policy, people such as Noam Chomsky and Michael Parenti—those names are probably familiar to you. We succeeded in finally stopping the publication of Agee's first magazine, with the reckless title *CounterSpy*. However, he replaced it with a new magazine that he calls *CovertAction Quarterly*. He's still publishing it. Do you know of it?"

"No, I've never heard of it. I'm a biologist, not a politician or a spy. However, my wife is a political scientist, and I think she's used some of Parenti's essays and books in her classes—*Democracy for the Few*, in particular. And, of course, I've read some of Noam Chomsky's popular articles."

Demopoulos continued. "During the '60s, Agee became uncomfortable with his work and with the activities of the Agency in Latin America, especially its support of authoritarian governments. But most governments in Latin America were authoritarian then, as they still are today, so the only way the U.S. could have any influence in the region was to work with them on some level. We can't cut political ties with our neighbors just because we don't like their leadership philosophy. Sometimes it may appear that our own policies don't always align with our values, but it's often the only way we can get our foot in the door to try to move repressive regimes in better directions. This is especially true with regards to issues of human rights."

"That's understandable," I said. I had the feeling I was sitting in a college classroom again, and Demopoulos was my voluble instructor. "It's too bad everyone doesn't play by the rules."

Demopoulos made a sardonic chuckle, more like the sound a pig makes than a human laugh, and said, "Dr. Bernini, everyone *does* play by the rules. That's the point. But they play by different rules, by their own rules. So sometimes we have to bend ours to stay on top of the game." His face seemed hard, thin skin over bone. "But, back to the point, Agee's 1975 book, called *Inside the Company*, identified over two hundred CIA officers and agents. It was devastating for the Agency. And his current magazine has the express goal of promoting the destabilization of the CIA through exposure of its operations and personnel. His activities have been seditious at best, and treasonous in the minds of many." I could see that Demopoulos was becoming agitated; he seemed a loose construct of flesh and cartilage and energy. "Some time after his resignation from the CIA, Agee began cooperating with both the Russian and Cuban governments. In 1979 the U.S. revoked his passport, and he went on the lam. He sued in federal court, and the case eventually reached the Supreme Court, which ruled against him just a couple years ago. Maurice Bishop's government in Grenada gave him citizenship and he took up residence on the island for a while, but that ended with the collapse of the Grenada Revolution. Now the Sandinista government has given him a Nicaraguan passport. He seems to be bouncing around between there and Cuba and Russia."

"This is all very interesting, Helios, but what's the point?" In my mind, Demopoulos's ungainly animation conjured an image of the Washington Irving character, Ichabod Crane, from *The Legend of Sleepy Hollow*.

"Point is, you should not talk to anyone about the people you meet in this building or the conversations you have here. And should you ever encounter one of our people or a State Department or military person who you think could be undercover, absolutely do not ever mention that person's name to anyone. Or you may end up in jail. Or on the lam in Cuba."

He said it all matter-of-factly, *Very professor-like*, I thought.

Unrolling a large map of Guatemala, Demopoulos said, "Now let's talk a bit about the road conditions and villages in the Huehuetenango and Quiché Departments."

For the rest of the morning, Demopoulos gave me detailed descriptions of the main highways and village side roads in the northern part of the Guatemala's high country. He showed me where the army posts were and told me approximately how many soldiers he thought were stationed at each. As he spoke, his delicate hands roved over the map, and even through his sweater I could see his sharp elbows sticking out like those of a katydid. His long thin fingers danced in the air between us in Saint Vitus movements. I agreed with him that so long as I stayed on the main highways I was unlikely to encounter any military checkpoints. But once I strayed off the main roads, I would almost certainly run into stops. Most stops would be legitimate, and it was mainly a way of turning around naive tourists to keep them away from trouble spots, which were usually military activities in and around the villages. I told him I'd run into these checkpoints in the past, and so long as I politely complied with their requests there was never a problem.

"Things have changed a bit since Ríos Montt became president. Not all the checkpoints are legitimate anymore. And the army is not as friendly as it used to be. However, all the players know that tourists, especially U.S. tourists, are off limits. And we've heard of no incidents with American tourists."

He went on to describe where I should and shouldn't drive, what I should look for at a checkpoint if I encountered one, what I should do if it looked to be a rogue group or fake military setup. He told me to notice how many "soldiers" were at each checkpoint or blockade, what kinds of weapons they had, if they had vehicles, and where, exactly, the stop was. I was to keep notes, but as brief as possible—just a code of my own creation, with numbers and letters that encoded the information in a way that only I would understand. He also told me about some of the rogue army brass, and what areas they might be operating in. We took a lunch break, and then continued on until nearly four that afternoon, and I thought, *I guess I needed this briefing after all!*

Demopoulos eventually picked up the phone and called Papadakis, who came to the basement to retrieve me. Back in his office, Papadakis said, "Well, Odel, I hope you feel a bit more confident now that you've had an initial briefing. Tomorrow I'd like to walk you through a few of the hotspots, especially in the Quiché Department, so you have a sense of what to keep your eyes open for."

"I guess I'm a bit ambivalent about it all, Nestor. Knowledge is power, as they say, but at the same time I'm somewhat nervous to hear how things have deteriorated since my last visit to Guatemala just eighteen months or so ago. Also, I'm not sure how much territory in those two departments I can cover—it's a vast area, and those roads are in bad shape, making for slow driving."

"If you need to prioritize, I might suggest Quiché would be most interesting for us. But we don't want you to do anything you're uncomfortable with. It's not like we're paying you; we just appreciate your cooperation. If you decide to do nothing but collect your bugs on the coast, no one's going to hold it against you."

I couldn't help but think how his comment that, "we're not paying you" seemed to carry an official quality of denial to it. It seemed to be a reminder that I do *not* work for the CIA. No employment, no contract, nothing in writing—no relationship other than me volunteering to "keep my eyes open" for them. A citizen volunteer on vacation in the high-lands of Guatemala. However, there was the Cleia funding. But, of course, that was a perfectly legitimate private foundation, and the paper trail there simply implies that the foundation is supporting my research. And there were no written reports of any kind that documented exactly how I spent the money. It would be easy, if need be, for the Agency to deny any kind of relationship with me. I was just some goofball biologist who voluntarily chatted with them now and then about the things I'd seen during my travels—even though I now had fifty thousand dollars in a private bank account. And there was also that unnecessarily long story Demopoulos told me about Philip Agee. It dawned on me that the CIA had just given me two thinly veiled threats. That they could, and no doubt would if necessary, deny any relationship with me in order to protect the Agency. And if I talked too much, they could throw me in jail or take away my citizenship.

My third day was to be, as Papadakis put it, a review of "recent and current events in the north." Helios Demopoulos again briefed me. He began by reviewing the coup d'état last March that ousted Fernando Romeo Lucas García and put Ríos Montt into the presidency. He noted that Lucas García actually had sufficient military power at the presidential palace to hold off the coup attempt, but Ríos Montt's supporters had held his family hostage and Lucas García surrendered when shown a photograph of his mother and sister on their knees, tears streaming down their faces and hands tied behind their backs, with the muzzles of two M16s pressed to their heads. "Such is how power is given and taken in Guatemala, Odel. You need to understand that."

Then Demopoulos hung a chart on the blackboard with a list of locations and dates, beginning with 1981. It was an inventory of towns and villages in Quiché Department that had been attacked by the army or by paramilitary groups, with estimates of how many civilians had been murdered. I was shocked by what I saw. In 1981, the capital of Quiché Department, Santa Cruz del Quiché, which was, in my memory, a beautiful and peaceful Maya mountain village, had been sacked twice; and in 1982 it had again been attacked two more times. Each time, a few dozen to over a hundred peasants were murdered in the streets, either by rifle fire or by being slashed to death with machetes. Dozens of other villages had also been routed, leaving dead Indians strewn through the streets of smaller settlements that I didn't know: Patzité, Lancetillo, and La Taña in the Uspantán municipality; Tzununul and Salinas Magdalena in Sacapulas; Rosario Monte María in Chicamán; and many others.

"Bear in mind," Demopoulos said, "this is just the Quiché Department. But this is going on all over the country. We have very little information on the extent of these activities. We don't have many staff in place outside Guatemala City or

314

Antigua. Our rough estimates suggest that about ten thousand civilians die annually in Guatemala due to government-sanctioned murders. Like Lucas García, Ríos Montt kills Maya people the way you swat flies in the kitchen. Human lives mean nothing to those kinds of men. In June of last year, Ríos Montt launched a new program called *Victoria 82* that he claimed 'will win the hearts and minds' of the peasant population. It's the same approach as always but combined with some token social programs and government assistance that he thinks will incentivize the village people to cooperate with the army. He's also creating something called 'civilian self-defense patrols' and conscripting the villagers into them. These are, of course, no more than lawless militias forcing these poor Indians to shoot one another. He's adding thousands of new conscripts every month, throughout the mountainous northwest of the country."

I was stunned by what I heard. "How on Earth can Ríos Montt recruit that many Maya *campesinos* when they must all loathe him and everything he stands for? And why isn't Reagan doing something to reign in the government?"

"The first question is easy—conscripts who resist or desert are marked for death or torture, as are their families. But the real effect is to recruit far more people to the rebel cause. In fact, Ríos Montt is creating a situation in which the entire Maya population is now ready to overthrow the government or die trying. However, they lack the organization, training, and arms to do so. As for President Reagan, you'd have to ask someone higher up than me what the hell is in his mind. Publicly, I'm sure you know, he's a great fan of Ríos Montt. I think he might be convinced that the peasant uprising is communist inspired. And there is some evidence of minor, though growing Cuban influence."

I felt that Demopoulos was trying to put logic, or perhaps a human face on an inhuman thing. Ten thousand Maya killed annually, village after village destroyed, families and lives shattered—for what?

The briefing continued until around noon, Demopoulos filling me on where the hot spots were, where to avoid venturing altogether, what areas the Agency was most in need of information on, what to expect at roadblocks that were legitimate army stops and those that weren't, and so on. He called Papadakis on the phone, and then the two of us had a bit of a wrap-up session in his office. Nestor asked me where I usually stayed when in Guatemala City, and I said "the old Pan-American Hotel downtown."

"Ah, yes, a lovely place. I've stayed there a few times myself. Good choice." And then he went on.

"I want to remind you again, Dr. Bernini, that while we appreciate your cooperation and sharing your observations with us, we are not asking you to do anything in particular. And, personally, I do not want you to do anything you feel might be too risky or that makes you uncomfortable while you're traveling in Guatemala. Should you decide to stay away from the countryside altogether, that is perfectly fine."

"I understand completely. And, in fact, if it weren't for my deep personal interests in the Maya, I probably would not venture into the mountains at all on my upcoming travels. But, as you know, I am anthropologically inclined. These 'village peasants,' as Helios referred to them, are the living descendants of one of the greatest civilizations in human history. But they've suffered religious and ethnic persecution for over four hundred years. It's a reflection of mankind's inability to recognize and value our own human history and the stories of native peoples. And it's a failure to understand that a culture far older than what the conquistadors brought with them to the New World is being destroyed. I've been to Guatemala more than a dozen times, and I've never failed to visit the Quiché region. It's unlikely that pattern will change any time soon. But we'll see—I can't make any promises."

As I drove away from the Agency building, I had the feeling I needed to talk to the old woman in Barrio Nueva

Esperanza again or to her mysterious daughter, though I knew
that probably wasn't possible.

24

Into the Sierras

Guatemala, July 1983

Plans for my July collecting trip to the Pacific coast of Guatemala moved along quickly. I had no close professional colleagues in Guatemala City, so I'd be entirely on my own. But I knew that finding a reliable rental car—one that could handle the rough roads to the coast—would not be a problem and there were a couple of agencies at the airport. The Pacific coast of Guatemala is poorly developed, and no highway runs along the seaboard through the thick coastal jungle. I would have to weave back and forth to the coast off the paved interior Highway 2. My first collecting location would be a straight shot from Guatemala City to Puerto San José and Iztapa. From there, I would return to the paved highway to drive north, then cut back to the coast to Tecojate. Then back to the main highway again, north to the Granada road, and back toward the coast to Champerico, essentially a coastal suburb of Granada. I figured three days at each of the three collecting sites would suffice; adding in driving time, it would be slightly less than two weeks. And then some "tourist sightseeing" in Quiché Department that would add another five or six days.

I called Coquette, and we agreed to meet in Antigua, an endearing and gracious colonial town about an hour west of Guatemala City. She would check into the old Casa Santo Domingo, a converted Spanish colonial convent, on the first of August. I would try to arrive the same day, or perhaps a day later, after my mountain travels were over. She pressed me for information on what the Agency wanted from me. I was completely honest with her, describing my three days of briefings and my plan to spend five or six days in Quiché Department. I wanted to be forthright with Coquette, and, in turn, hoped for complete honesty from her. It was critical if our relationship was to continue. I needed her to trust me— and vice versa. Her response surprised me.

"Damn that man. How can he ask you to do that? Odel, it's too dangerous. I don't want you to go into the Quiché region. I know you love that high country and the Maya villages, but it isn't like it used to be. I don't think it's safe for tourists these days."

"Oh, I don't think Nestor's such a bad guy. And he made it clear that he wasn't 'asking me' to do anything or go anywhere I didn't feel comfortable traveling. I know the area pretty well, although some of the villages off the beaten track are unfamiliar to me. I honestly don't think anyone is going to bother an American tourist."

"Not Nestor, Odel. He just does what he's told to do. And he *is* a nice guy, I agree. Anyway, I guess it's none of my business. But baby, there's something you might not know, and I'm breaking a dozen federal laws and risking my career telling you this, but you need to know. The Guatemalan army's officers working in the Quiché Department have been trained by the CIA and U.S. Special Forces to use Vietnam-era tactics, including the 'resettling' of displaced Maya into 'model villages' outside Nebaj and other places. They may be instructed to leave Americans alone, but they are not your typical Guatemalan soldiers. These guys are highly skilled and have carte blanche to do as they wish to the locals. It's just not like it was two or three years ago. So you'd better be damned careful. And you'd better be in one piece when I wrap my arms around you in Antigua. Odel, I couldn't stand to lose you right now. I need to have one hundred percent of you in Antigua. And I want to stay there with you for as long as possible."

Damn, I do love and desire this woman. Her words gave me joyful goosebumps and sent Morse code straight to my heart. But they also struck an icy tone in my core.

"Who does Nestor report to?"

"You know I can't tell you that. And it's beside the point. Just meet me at the Casa Santo Domingo and make love to me all night long. And at least promise me that you won't do anything foolish or risky. No more hero moves, OK?"

"I promise to do both, Coquette—I'll make love to you all night and all day, *and* I won't do anything foolish."

She let loose a soft and lyrical murmur, like a tropical bird, that I recognized. It was haunting, and it drew me to her like a magic spell.

"How long will you be able to stay in Antigua with me, my love?"

"I'm not sure, Coquette, but more than just a few days. I promise. I need quality time with you—unrushed, quiet, peaceful time."

She made the sound again. It was like a sorcerer's flute, tugging on my heart. "I can't wait to see you, Odel."

My relationship with Penelope had grown strained, and I felt we were losing our friendship. I longed for the loving intimacy I felt with Coquette; and I still hadn't told Penelope about her. Perhaps it was different for Penelope; it seemed like her heart was still in our marriage. She continued to whisper sweet nothings in my ear, told me she loved me, tried

320

to make me feel connected to her. But she wanted more from me than I was now able to give her. It wasn't that I didn't love her; I simply no longer trusted her. And without trust, something had changed in my ability to feel close to her. She rarely mentioned Marjorie and "went to dinner" with her only infrequently. I suspected they were hooking up during the day at Marjorie's house. I cared but also didn't care. The fact that she had a lesbian girlfriend was not the issue for me; it was the loss of trust and emotional intimacy that was eating away at our marriage.

Things at the museum continued to worsen. The mood of the place was sad. Beloved outreach programs were being cut, Acting Director Bligh raised the admission price, there was pressure on the gift shop to increase revenues—it was all about the bottom line. Even the docents were feeling it and grumbling.

My dad seemed stuck in his depression. He hadn't reopened his butcher shop since Mom had died. My brother and I were increasingly worried about him, though we knew there were plenty of our aunts and uncles around to check up on him regularly. And our cousin Marco frequently dropped by to see him. I planned my departure to Guatemala for the first week in July, feeling like it was time to "get out of Dodge" for a few weeks. Just before I left for Guatemala, Marco called to tell me he was worried about Dad. He had lost a lot of weight, was despondent, and never left the house. Marco and my Uncle Sandro had managed to sell most of the meat in Dad's shop to another butcher friend, and they'd put a sign up that read TEMPORARILY CLOSED. But Marco said, unless something changed, he didn't think my father would ever be able to go back to work. He offered to help Dad look into social security, his butcher's union pension benefits, and even the possibility of selling his store property. I thanked him and promised to go to L.A. to spend time with Dad as soon as I got back from my Central America trip. I trusted Marco like I trusted my brother.

The Pan Am flight out of Houston was on time. It was their three-times weekly flight to Panama City, with stopovers in Guatemala City and San José, Costa Rica. I was one of only a dozen *Norteamericanos* on the plane. My alarm had gone off at four that morning so I could catch the only direct Pan Am flight out of Sea-Tac for Houston, where I'd have a four-hour layover. I didn't want to risk missing a tight connection due to a delay with my first flight, and I didn't want to risk lost or delayed luggage by switching to a Central American carrier en route. I had all my snorkeling and collecting gear in a large duffel and paid the usual excess baggage fee. We arrived on time at La Aurora International Airport, and renting a car at the Avis office went smoothly. Then I braced myself for the drive downtown.

Guatemala City is among the worst in the world for driving—the streets are a shemozzle twenty-four hours a day. The rules of the road devolved into anarchy long ago, or perhaps it had always been that way. Most of the painted lines on the roads had worn away years ago, drivers paid little heed to stoplights, and the level of aggression was a cut above a professional hockey game. I hated driving in Guatemala City. If you weren't aggressive, it could take ten minutes to travel one block. It made driving in Mexico City seem like child's play.

It took me nearly an hour to get from the airport to the Pan-American Hotel in the center of town. The hotel was named after the Pan-American Highway, not the airline, though it had no formal relationship with either. It was a little known but fine old family-run hotel in the colonial center. Nearly the entire staff was Maya, thus the hospitality was gracious. The kitchen was superb, the Sunday buffet was a delicious smorgasbord of local cuisine, and the rooms were twenty-five dollars. I had stayed there so many times, the desk clerks and bellboys knew me. It was comfortable, almost homey. Normally, I stayed there only a few nights before and after my explorations of the countryside. There was no good reason to linger in Guatemala City. With a mostly mestizo population and a crumbling infrastructure, the city was noisy and dirty and had little to offer. Plus, the summers are hot and muggy, even though the city is at an elevation of 4,800 feet. I stayed just that night and then headed for San José and Iztapa the next morning.

The roads are bad everywhere in Guatemala, so driving any distance can be time consuming. However, I was able to get to all the coastal sites I'd planned to visit and acquire some decent collections. Twelve days later I was back at the Pan-American Hotel, packing my specimens up for shipment to the Seattle Museum of Natural History. I lingered a couple days, taking time to walk around the historic area, which I hadn't seen in a few years. Not far from the main *zócalo* was the century-old castle-like fort that was home base for the Guatemalan army. I wandered past the U.S. Embassy on Avenida Reforma, looking at it with fresh eyes, imagining Helios Demopoulos working on assignment there for a year.

That night, as I sipped my second glass of *Flor de Caña* after dinner, watching the Maya ladies dressed in their village huipils politely and quietly tending the tables, it occurred to me that I'd probably walked past both the large army base and the embassy a dozen times in the past but not really even noticed them. But today I had walked past them slowly, studying them, wondering what kinds of nefarious plans might be developing in the windowless strategy rooms behind the thick rock walls that surrounded them both. By my third glass of rum, I found myself thinking about what the *curandera* in Managua had told me, and what her daughter had told me, and what the beggar at Teotihuacan had said to me. They all told me I had begun a journey and that changes in my life were to be forthcoming. Would a divorce be part of that journey, part of the change? Was the mess at the museum part of the story? And what about the loss of my mom, and my decision to cooperate with the CIA? I hoped Coquette was to be an integral part of my future. But was I missing something? I sensed there was more, some notion clinging to the edge of my memory, but I couldn't put it into words.

By the time I'd started working on my fourth glass of *Flor de Caña*, I had begun wondering just how important this monograph of Central American Crustacea really was in the big scheme of things. Here I was, in the land of the ancient Maya, some of the most gentle and peaceful people on Earth, a timeless and continuous lineage of Native Americans descended from Siberian ancestors who migrated across the Bering Strait twenty thousand years ago, and who had preserved so much of their ancient heritage and lifestyle. And who were being slaughtered by the thousands every year by a wealthy oligarchy and a corrupt U.S.-supported government— empowered fair-skinned Guatemalans who didn't even admit to themselves that they had Maya blood in their veins as they carried out the largest genocide campaign in modern New World history.

And I thought about Coquette and what a stunningly beautiful woman she was, inside and out. How much I felt I loved her and wanted to be with her. She truly was my dark Siren. And I thought about Bob and Beatriz in Managua, and their aspirations for Daniel Ortega and his Sandinista followers freeing their country from decades of oppression under the dreaded Somoza regime, and how happy they were as a couple, and what a great life they seemed to have—so full of love and joy and hope.

In this larger context, the importance of my research project began to fade. There were so many human lives here, millions of people struggling so desperately to be free or to simply survive. There was so much goodness—and so much evil. There was the seemingly bottomless well of joy and optimism that imbues the Latino culture, jumbled up with the chaos of war and endless oppression. Did I somehow have a role to play in all this?

Guatemala's Quiché Department is the heartland of the Maya mountain people. The department capital, Santa Cruz del Quiché, was founded in the sixteenth century by the Spanish conquistador Pedro de Alvarado y Contreras, Hernán Cortés's second in command and governor of the Guatemala Territory. The town's Dominican church dates to that time. Pedro de Alvarado was known for his cruel treatment and mass murders of indigenous people. In Santa Cruz, he enslaved the local populace and used them to build the Spanish churches from stones harvested at the nearby prehistoric Maya site of *Q'umarkaj*. The Maya had developed an understanding of astronomy and the movements of celestial bodies that rivaled that of the Old World at the time. The larger Maya cities had astronomical observatories with openings in domes that aligned with known stars and other heavenly objects at certain times of the year. This knowledge gave them the ability to predict eclipses, understand solstices and equinoxes, and more. The great Temple of Kukulcán at Chichen Itza was constructed in such a way that, at the spring equinox, the fall of sunlight and shadow creates an image of a serpent descending the stairs; and at the summer solstice a shadow falls across the mighty structure in such a way as to divide it perfectly in half. At *Q'umarkaj*, Alvarado destroyed the most beautiful observatory in all the land of the Quiché to use its cut stones to construct his church in Santa Cruz.

Scholars believe it was at *Q'umarkaj* that a Quiché noble first transcribed the oral stories of the *Popol Vuh*, the sacred text of the Maya, in 1558. The survival of the *Popol Vuh* is credited to the Dominican Friar Francisco Ximénez, who in 1701 discovered the Maya version of the document hidden in the parish church of Santo Tomás in Chichicastenango and translated it into Spanish. Ximénez realized that it was a story codex, a history of the highland Maya People with tales of their great leaders over the millennia, interwoven with mystical cryptograms and heroic intrigue.

The Quiché region is also a land of extreme topography, with mountain peaks in the sierras approaching 11,000 feet in elevation and almost continuously shrouded in clouds, as well as steep river valleys that plummet to less than 500 feet elevation. With over 650,000 Maya, it is also one of the most populous departments in the country, although the people are scattered thinly over more than 3,000 square miles.

The region is named after the largest ethnic group, the K'iche' people, but another half-dozen Maya dialects are also spoken in this large area. Scattered throughout Quiché are long-abandoned Maya ruins—the former great cities of the K'iche' people's ancestors. Cities as large and well developed as London was when the Spanish conquistadors invaded the New World. Many of the ancient sites are still used secretly as ceremonial centers by modern Maya. The central highlands dominate the region, with the Sierra de los Cuchumatanes looming over the landscape and its villages, drawing the clouds and the freezing nighttime temperatures and nurturing the dark green conifer forests laden with mosses and lichens. At 6,800 feet, the ancient village of Chichicastenango is typically the only place in Quiché that adventurous tourists ever get to. The twice-weekly Chichi markets draw villagers with produce, chickens, pigs, and other home-raised edibles from many miles away. It was the villages that were even smaller than Chichi, far off the beaten track, that were now of interest to me.

The usual tourist loop for those few travelers who visit Guatemala is west from Guatemala City on Highway 1, the Pan-American Highway, to Panajachel, on the shore of Lake Atitlán, one of the most remote and beautiful high-mountain lakes in the world. The aquamarine lake is literally ringed by smoking volcanoes, and here the Earth often trembles beneath one's feet. Using Panajachel as "home base," day trips can be made by the more adventurous tourist to the nearby villages on their market days, the most spectacular (and usually the only one visited) being Chichicastenango. Traveling beyond

Chichi is rarely done. Even the truckers stay on the Pan-American Highway, bypassing Chichi and the more distant villages altogether as they make their way north to Mexico, where the last town of any size before crossing the border is Huehuetenango.

My first day's drive out of Guatemala City took me to Panajachel, where I encountered a regular army checkpoint. There is a sizeable base at the turnoff to Panajachel and I expected the stop. Long ago, someone constructed a thirty-foot-tall concrete army boot in front of the base; it looms queerly on the horizon as you drop down the road toward Lake Atitlán and its valley. This was more or less a permanent checkpoint and I'd gone through it many times on past trips. My American passport and visa were quickly examined, the usual inquiries were made—*¿Tiene armas señor?*—and then I was sent on my way. I was just another gringo tourist heading for Lake Atitlán to buy some cheap pot and chill out on the beaches in an exotic but relatively safe place.

The next morning I made the spectacular drive into the high country to Santa Cruz del Quiché by way of Chichicastenango. The approach to Chichi is so steep that the narrow road traverses a half-dozen or so 180-degree switchbacks, the cars creeping up a twenty percent grade in first or second gear. If two cars meet, one must back up the steep cliffside road and pull over to the side. The forest closes in on the highway with a fierce denseness of pines and, at higher elevations, forests of giant fir. The spectacular sacred fir, or *Oyamel*, takes over the forest above 8,000 feet. This magnificent tree is the queen of the cloud forest in the high sierras of Guatemala.

It happened to be Sunday, one of the two market days in Chichi, so I couldn't resist stopping for a few hours to wander the streets, packed with Maya from throughout the region. The Chichi market is one of the largest in the country. If you're familiar with the handwoven textiles of the Maya, you can recognize what village a woman is from by the patterns on her huipil. I recognized a dozen or so, but at the Chichi market there are locals from three-dozen nearby villages selling their goods. The streets are crowded with people, vegetables, stacks of firewood and *copál*, farm animals, machetes and knives, and handwoven fabrics that the women hope to sell to the few straggling tourists who find their way to the fabled Chichi marketplace. And everywhere women sit cross-legged on the ground, their backstrap looms tied to a tree or a post, weaving the fabrics of their traditional village design while they haggle with shoppers, the bright red and orange and yellow cotton and wool threads flying like hummingbirds across the gradually lengthening cloth.

Villagers walk for miles to get to the Chichi market. A few lucky ones pack themselves like sardines into the bed of a village pickup truck and ride to the market. It is a clash of colors and smells and sights like no other. It can actually be psychologically challenging until one gets used to the cacophony of powerful stimuli—the eyes, ears, and nose are taken on an electrified roller-coaster ride at the Chichi market. It was the avalanche of odors that took me the longest to adapt to—the farm animals, goats and chickens in particular, the intense ubiquitous acrid smell of chicken shit, and the many different floral aromas, especially the branches of wild sweet basil and *Targetes*, and the variety of *copales* burning everywhere. Around the church, the *copál* smoke can be so thick it is impossible to see more than a few feet in front of you—a literal fog of sweet *copál* vapor. And the scents of the people are strong, with their infrequent bathing opportunities and odd aromas of native plants with which they anoint their skin. All these scents and more are overlain by the ever-present, deeply resonating pine and fir smells wafting by on every gentle breeze. None of the aromas was distasteful to me, but all of them are exaggerated here beyond any place else

I've ever experienced. My hyperosmia always took me on a wild ride in Chichi.

On the steps of the Santo Tomás church, women sit in groups of three around small piles of burning *copál*, chatting softly, secretly. They are afraid to gather in groups of more than three, for fear a stray army regular might spot and harass them. Spread over the steps are designs made in flower petals, the meanings of which are indiscernible to outsiders. Inside the church, flower petals make similar designs on the stone floor, and everywhere is the thick smoke and scent of burning *copál*. Behind the church, men stand around in small groups, rolling cigarettes, talking, and drinking locally made liquor. It was their conversations I wanted to understand, but they were always in the K'iche' tongue. By the end of the day, many of the men would be passed out from the alcoholic beverage they drank but had no tolerance for. Sunday was the one day the women allowed their men to drink, and many of them did so with gusto. As the late afternoon clouds moved in to blanket the mountains, the role of the women and children was to pack up what was left of their market goods and figure out how to get the man of the house back home.

I left Chichicastenango for the drive north to Santa Cruz del Quiché, where I planned to spend the night. My friends at the Pan-American Hotel in Guatemala City had recommended some small tourist *cabinas* on the outskirts of the village, buried deep in the dark mist of the *Oyamel* forest. I planned to stay there and visit the town in the morning. About twenty minutes before reaching Santa Cruz, I encountered another army checkpoint. Helios Demopoulos had told me there was an army base somewhere in the area, recently grown sizeable, and to expect a checkpoint outside Santa Cruz. This one was probably also a legitimate stop. They appeared to be real soldiers, but there were only a half-dozen of them, and a jeep was parked on the side of the road. Each carried an M16, but one, apparently the highest ranking one of the group, also had a handgun holstered low on his hip. As the ranking man approached the car and I rolled down my window, I could see it was a Browning High Power—a popular semiautomatic pistol. The men surrounded my rental car, and one of them knocked on the passenger side window, indicating for me to roll it down as well. I showed my papers to the man with a handgun, spoke in my best "gringo tourist Spanglish," and asked politely why I was being stopped.

"*Hay guerrillas en la zona. No es seguro viajar por aquí.*" He asked if I'd seen any guerrillas on my drive and why I was going to Santa Cruz. I explained that I was a tourist looking to find authentic village weavings, and I'd been told some of the best could be found in Santa Cruz. He suggested I turn around and drive to Antigua, where I would find excellent fabrics from all over the country. I said I also wanted to take photographs of the weavers in Santa Cruz for my scrapbook.

"*Muéstrame tu cámara,*" he demanded. I pulled out my old point-and-shoot and showed it to him. Then he wanted to know where I would spend the night in Santa Cruz. "*No hay hoteles allí.*" I told him I'd be staying at the *Cabañas Turisticas*, on the edge of town. After conferring with one of his men for quite a while, he came back to the car and told me I could go forward, but that I should plan to spend only one night in Santa Cruz and then return to Guatemala City or Antigua because guerrilla activity had made things unsafe for tourists in the area.

I found *Cabañas Turisticas* easily enough. Nestled in the pine-fir forest, dark, damp, quiet, and shrouded in the mist, it was beautiful. And a bit eerie. In the morning I would spend four or five hours exploring Santa Cruz and then head out to the more remote settlements.

Two bad roads head east and northeast out of Santa Cruz del Quiché. The eastern route winds through a low valley to Chiché and then follows the river up into the high country to Chinique at about 7,600 feet. Then it drops down to another valley and to the village of Zacualpa, and finally it climbs steeply to the remote and cloud-shrouded settlement of

Joyabaj at nearly 10,000 feet. If I continued beyond that, I'd drop down into the low savannah vegetation and village of Pachalum, but I wasn't sure I wanted to get that far off the beaten path—Joyabaj might be my last stop on that road. The other, more northerly route ran for many miles to the village of Aldea Chujuyub and then much farther to San Andrés Sajcabajá. These were the most remote of the villages I wanted to visit. All of them would be new to me. I would not only be seeing new sights and increasingly rustic Maya lifestyles, but I also knew there were unexcavated Classic-era Maya ruins scattered throughout this region. I decided to explore the eastern route first, and my host at the *Cabañas Turisticas* gave me recommendations for lodging at Chinique and Zacualpa.

Demopoulos had told me that the army base outside Santa Cruz was a staging area for military control of lands to the north, and that they used this base as a launching point to control the Ixil Valley. He had also explained that Santa Cruz del Quiché was a core organizational center of the EGP (*Ejército Guerrillero de los Pobres*), one of the Maya people's most active resistance groups. Just a year earlier the EGP had managed to disable the state power facilities in Santa Cruz and blow up the El Tesoro bridge that the army relied on for troop movements. In January 1982 they blew up the power facilities at Santa Cruz a second time, as well as several other bridges that were giving the army access to many of the smaller villages they harassed. Ríos Montt had cracked down hard, repeatedly raiding Santa Cruz and leaving villagers dead in the streets. Innocent villagers had been forced to seek haven in the high mountain country and were labeled guerrillas by the army, even if they were simply peasants trying to mind their own business. The label gave the army permission to track them down and commit atrocities, including the murder of men, women, and children, although many of them died of starvation before the army ever found them.

Despite all this, Santa Cruz del Quiché seemed as charming as I remembered it. There were no overt signs of problems, though the streets were somewhat deserted. The beautiful old church stood tall and straight as ever, a testament to endurance, as were the Maya themselves. Although it was not a main market day, there were several small vegetable and wood markets around town, and I spent time in these, stopped for coffee several times, ate lunch, bought a gorgeous huipil for Coquette, and headed east for Chiché about one in the afternoon.

I got to Chiché in under an hour, with no problems and no military stops. I walked the streets, negotiated for a few huipils but didn't buy any, had coffee at a couple of little lunch stands, and heard nothing spoken but the local K'iche' dialect. There was only one small plaza, and it was largely deserted. Not much happening. I left after a couple of hours to drive on to Chinique.

Again, I encountered no stops as the road climbed steeply back into the *Oyamel* forest. However, as I approached Chinique, I heard the sound of distant gunfire in the forest to the north. I pulled over and turned off the engine to listen carefully. It sounded like M16 rifles, maybe 100 yards away. They were infrequent, and all emanating from the same place. *Probably just target practice*, I thought.

25

Odel's Temescal Experience
Joyabaj, Guatemala July 1983

Chinique was small in 1983—just a scattering of buildings around the main road through the village, a few small *tiendas* and home-front eateries. I found the tiny plaza, walked, sat on a bench, and had coffee. It was very quiet. I decided to press on to Zacualpa, a larger village where I hoped to spend the night. I had heard of an important colonial Dominican monastery and church in Zacualpa and looked forward to seeing them.

Manny Eumaeus also had told me that the Maya human-rights activist Rigoberta Menchú had once lived in Zacualpa. Rigoberta was one of the highest profile advocates of Maya rights. Just a year earlier she had narrated a book about her life, *Me llamo Rigoberta Menchú y así me nació la conciencia* ("My Name is Rigoberta Menchú and This is the Story of How my Conscience was Born") to the Venezuelan author and anthropologist Elisabeth Burgos-Debray. The book told her life story and revealed in great detail the suffering of the Maya people in Guatemala. It had just been released when I left for my trip, and I hadn't yet had time to obtain a copy. But the book would become an overnight success and eventually be translated into five languages. It would also catapult her to fame as an international icon during Guatemala's civil war.

About a half mile before reaching Zacualpa I encountered another checkpoint. There were only three men, and they were dressed in camo pants and old T-shirts. Two of them had M16s, but the third man carried an AK-47. The first thing I noticed was that there were no vehicles at the stop—just a couple of old orange road cones. *Definitely not a legitimate checkpoint*, I thought. I made sure my doors were locked and the windows were up as I drove up to the men. Leaving the car in gear but holding it still with my foot on the brake, I rolled the window down to talk to the man carrying the AK-47. He was mestizo and claimed to speak no English; even his Spanish was poor and I guessed he was illiterate. He didn't ask to see my papers but simply wanted to know what I was doing there and if I had any guns. I gave him my usual gringo tourist pitch. He told me they were part of a local "village protection force," and he asked if I had any money or food to donate to the people of the village. It was a straightforward extortion setup. I pulled out my wallet and showed him four twenty-quetzal bills in it—as always, I carried no credit cards or anything else in my wallet, except my driver's license. I offered him two of the twenty-quetzal bills along with some granola bars, and he took them. The three of them conferred heatedly on the situation, and after four or five minutes I had a sense things weren't going well—there was clearly not a consensus being reached. Following my instinct, I eased my foot off the brake and continued forward at a slow speed, waving and smiling as I passed them. ¡*Gracias, señores*! I yelled as I moved on. In the rear-view mirror I could see them waving and yelling at me to stop.

As I entered Zacualpa, the sun was slipping behind the high mountains. Wanting to find an accommodation before it got dark, I drove straight to the plaza and found the place that had been recommended to me by the manager at the Pan-

American Hotel. It was a decent enough looking hotel that had five rooms and off-street parking. The desk clerk, who was surprised to see a gringo wanting a room, assured me that the parking lot was patrolled by a guard all night, and no one who wasn't a guest of the hotel would be allowed in. Of course, I presumed that all it would take to get past the guard would be a five-quetzal note. He gave me a room with a window overlooking the parking lot, and I was apparently the only guest. Through the flawed glass of the old window my rental car became a wavy blur, as if it were moving. The room was nine quetzals (nine dollars U.S.). I freshened up and hit the streets to find a cold beer and some dinner.

As I began walking the plaza, I saw the seventeenth-century Dominican church set back from the square. It was massive, with three tiers of windows, three *campanarios* each with its own cross, and beautiful gigantic cedar doors that hung on three-hundred-year-old forged iron hinges. Behind it was the monastery. I was excited and couldn't wait to get a closer look in the morning light. The plaza was a pleasant place, and as it got darker, the kerosene lamps and gas lanterns of the street vendors came on, giving it a festive and peaceful appearance. I tried to chat with the locals as I strolled, drank a beer at the one place that sold beer, and ate a few small plates of black beans and plantains from the street vendors. I came across only three men who spoke any Spanish. All three wanted to know if I was a reporter looking to interview Rigoberta Menchú. It seemed most expedient to say I was and that I worked for the *Seattle Times*. Unfortunately, Rigoberta was in Mexico promoting her new book, they told me, which they regretted they would never read—because they could not read. I told all three of them that they should ask one of the local schoolteachers to do public readings from her book. One of them agreed; the other two said that couldn't be done because it would be too dangerous—the government would not allow it. When I asked if the government bothered their village much, all three clammed up and wouldn't talk about it.

335

My sleep was fitful, but I'd put a wedge under my door to prevent intruders and managed to get five or six solid hours. Around seven in the morning, I wandered back out onto the street to find some coffee and breakfast. I spent an hour or so in the church and wandering around the monastery grounds. A few more conversations were to be had, but I learned nothing new. After a light lunch, I decided to head on to the high village of Joyabaj. Although it wasn't far as the crow flies, the road had gotten bad, and I knew the climb up the mountains to this remote 10,000-foot-high community would be slow. Around one o'clock I drove slowly out of Zacualpa.

The road was filled with switchbacks and narrow cliffside passages. It was a bit nerve wracking and even slower going than I'd anticipated. About the time I felt I should be getting close to the village, I again heard gunfire in the distance; I was pretty certain it was M16s. I had a distinct feeling of remoteness, and this time I didn't like the sound of the rifles. And then a large explosion occurred, and my car veered onto the shoulder of the road. I slammed on the brakes and stayed still behind the wheel, not moving. The silence was so thick you could cut it with a machete. I was surrounded by a dark forest of *Oyamel* and other firs, so I knew I was at 8,000 feet or higher. The clouds were rolling in, beginning to shroud the forest in mist. As I sat there, the sounds of the forest gradually returned. I heard a loud *caw* overhead, climbed out of the car, and looked up to see a White-Breasted Hawk, a rare raptor that I'd only seen once before in my life. And then I looked down and saw my left front tire had blown, a one-inch tear in the sidewall. *Damn*, I thought, *Bad time for a blowout.* And just then something flitted into my peripheral vision—a Goldman's Warbler. Another rare bird of the Guatemalan highlands. *Well, maybe it will be an enjoyable tire change, with all the birdlife here.*

I opened the trunk, and my heart sank. The spare was flat! *Shit, what's wrong with me—I didn't think to check before I left the car rental. Fuck, and I'm in the middle of nowhere!* I had no choice but to walk on to Joyabaj to seek help. I felt it couldn't be more than a few miles farther up the road. But I didn't like that I'd heard rifle fire in the distance, and I liked it even less that the firing had now gone silent. *Had they heard the sound of my blowout? Were they coming to investigate what the noise had been? Were they military—or something worse?* I walked fast.

After just twenty minutes I began to get winded. *Maybe I'm closer to 10,000 feet*, I thought. *I'm definitely not used to exercise at these elevations.* As I rounded a turn, I saw a small group of Maya women sitting on the side of the road. They had stacks of firewood and *copál.* One of them, the oldest, had an apron full of wild herbs, twigs and mushrooms. They were as shocked to see me as I was to see them. I approached slowly, smiling and trying to appear nonthreatening. They didn't move, but their eyes didn't leave me for a second. When I got close enough that they could hear me, I asked if any of them spoke Spanish. None of them said a word. *Guess they don't.* I tried again in English, not really expecting them to respond. When they heard the English, they spoke softly among themselves, in K'iche'. Finally, the youngest among them spoke to me in Spanish. It was rough and hesitating, but I could understand it.

"I speak some Spanish. What are you doing here?"

I told her I was a gringo newspaper reporter from the *Seattle Times*, trying to get to Joyabaj. I wanted to see the village, maybe purchase some huipils, and hear about the lives of the high-mountain Maya people. But I had a flat tire a couple miles down the road, and I didn't have a spare. I needed help from someone in Joyabaj. She translated back to the others.

"It is too far for a gringo to walk to Joyabaj. If you wish, you can wait here with us. A bus should be along soon, and it will take you there."

"*Gracias señorita.* And please tell the other ladies I said thank you. I will wait for the bus." And then I congratulated her on her "excellent" Spanish. She said she'd lived with an aunt in Guatemala City for a year and learned some Spanish while there. She also said that almost no one in Joyabaj spoke Spanish, and no one spoke English, except perhaps one of the "professors" at the primary school.

I pulled some granola bars out of my backpack and gave them to her to share with the other women, and then I sat by the side of the road about twenty feet away from them. And, lo and behold, ten minutes later a dilapidated old school bus came chugging up the mountain road, swaying from side to side on exhausted springs and with its gears grinding like a stone agave mill. Black smoke bellowed out of its tailpipe. It slowed with an alarm of squeaking brakes that I knew meant metal-on-metal and stopped right in front of the women. On the side of the bus were the words, TOPEKA UNIFIED SCHOOL DISTRICT. The women all piled in, and I followed. The three front rows of seats had been pulled out to make room for the personal effects of the passengers, which included piles of firewood, a dozen live chickens with their legs tied together, bundles of herbs, two beat-up old suitcases, and one baby pig. The driver eyed me curiously. There were a half-dozen other passengers who also looked at me like I'd fallen out of the sky. The young girl said something to the driver in K'iche', and he shook his head affirmatively. She walked over to me and said he would drop me off at the *reparador de neumáticos*.

"*Gracias señorita, eres muy amable.*"

She replied that Joyabaj was not a safe town and that the only hotel had closed six months ago. She suggested the *reparador de neumáticos* might be willing to put me up in his house that night if need be. When I asked her why it wasn't safe in her village, she looked cautiously around at the other women. *Probably none of them speak any Spanish*, I thought. And she continued.

"The army is nearby. And others as well. When it is like this, bad things can happen. I do not know what they would do to a gringo, but it is not a good place to be now. You should fix your tire and go back to Guatemala City, where it is more safe."

We talked a bit more as the old school bus bumped and rattled along at ten miles per hour. I told her my name, and she said hers was *Rocío de la Mañana*, but that people just called her Rocío. I told her it was the most beautiful name I had ever heard. She giggled and thanked me. Rocío was surprisingly forthcoming. She said she had met some gringos in Guatemala City and liked them, but she did not like the Germans she encountered there. She said she hoped one day to go to university in the capital, to study to be a nurse. I asked her if she knew of Rigoberta Menchú.

She said, "Of course. Everyone knows *La Señora Menchú*. She is a very brave woman and a famous freedom fighter." *Rocío de la Mañana* seemed sweet as a sea anemone. I estimated she was eighteen or nineteen years old. As we chatted, I noticed the oldest woman of the group I'd met staring at us intently.

Rocío also told me that at the mid-August festival in Joyabaj, some specially trained men performed the *Danza de los Voladores* ceremony. I knew of the ritual and had seen it once in a Maya village in the Yucatán of Mexico. In the "Dance of the Flyers," four brightly costumed men climb a high pole, and when they reach the top, they tie cords to their ankles. Then they jump into the air, the cords catch them, and their bodies descend slowly to the ground, swinging around and around the pole. It's an ancient custom, performed rarely in a few places scattered through Mesoamerica, that might have originated with the pre-Colombian Nahua people of Mexico, as "bird people" appeasing some god.

When we got to the tire repair shop it was closed. Rocío volunteered to get out and nose around. She came back in a few minutes to say she'd talked with the neighbors, and they believed the repairman would be back in the morning. *"Necesitamos regresar por la mañana."*

I asked if she knew anyplace in town where I might be able to stay, which led to a rather lengthy conversation among the ladies I'd shared the roadside with. Eventually Rocío came back and made me an offer I couldn't refuse.

"My mother and grandmother said you are welcome to stay at our house tonight, but only if my father says it is OK. Our house is not much, but we have blankets, and you will be warm. You cannot sleep outside here; the night is too cold."

The bus dropped us at the small but pleasant central plaza, which was filled with fir trees and a small but attractive nineteenth-century church. I had a feeling Joyabaj could be the highlight of my excursion. Little did I know.

The walk to their home took half an hour. It was on the edge of town, twenty yards off a pothole-filled dirt track that lacked cars or streetlights. The nearest house was another fifty yards away. Both houses had small *milpas* in which they grew their vegetables. My hosts also had goats for milk, and countless freely ranging chickens from which they took eggs, and, on holidays, roasted one for dinner. Three men were home when we arrived. I waited outside, standing about thirty feet from the front door. The conversation began quietly, rose in tempo and volume, then gradually sunk back to something I could barely hear—not that it mattered, since it was all in K'iche'. After quite a while, Rocío and her father emerged from the house and walked to me. I had a small duffel bag and my backpack with me that the father looked at curiously.

"My father says you can sleep here tonight. You will have to sleep in the kitchen, but that is good because it will be warm from the dinner cooking." She tilted her head and gave me the slightest of crooked smiles when she stopped talking. It was subtle, but I almost felt it might be a Maya wink.

"Please tell your father I said thank you, and that I am honored and humbled to be a guest in his home."

"He also asks if you have any guns in your bags."

340

I immediately opened my backpack and duffel, so they could look at them if they wished, and said, "No, I have no guns or any weapons of any kind. I travel only with an open heart and an inquiring mind. Nothing more."

Rocío gave me another crooked-smile Maya wink and translated for her father, who nodded approvingly.

The afternoon was drawing late, the light and colors changing. As we walked into the house, I was happily surprised to find it had a concrete floor; judging from the outside, I'd expected it to be dirt. The walls were part cinderblock and part rough-hewn pine. The inside cinder block had once had a colorful paint job, but it had faded and peeled away. There were three uncomfortable looking wooden chairs and a stack of blankets in the corner. It was one large room in which the family lived and slept. The kitchen was separate, an add-on, with the connecting space protected by plastic tarps that had been neatly nailed down. The cooking area was large and quite nice. A big stack of firewood was in one corner. There was a well-constructed elevated rock fire pit, several pots and pans, and plenty of aging plastic dinnerware. Everything was spotlessly clean, and it smelled of mountain conifers and cedar. *This is going to be just fine*, I thought.

Rocío introduced me to her family but in the K'iche' tongue, and I couldn't pronounce their names even after hearing them several times through the evening. Her grandmother was simply, *Abuela*. Her two brothers were handsome and serious young men; the younger one looked about sixteen, the older one perhaps twenty-one or twenty-two.

Rocío's mother and *Abuela* were already at work in the kitchen. They were getting the wood fire started, slicing tiny sweet potatoes and onions, boiling water for rice, and chopping some kind of green from their garden. Rocío's father sat down on a chair and motioned for me to take one as well. He rolled a cigarette and offered it to me. I didn't smoke, but I knew refusing it would be inhospitable. Rocío appeared with a burning twig and lit my ciggy, while her dad rolled another for himself. She bent, and her pretty little face came close to mine, smiling as she held the burning stick for me. She lit her father's and then returned to the kitchen. The cigarette didn't taste like tobacco. It tasted herbal, and actually quite pleasant if I didn't inhale too much.

Dinner was delicious. Rocío and her dad and I sat on the three chairs; Rocío's mother and grandmother sat cross-legged on blankets on the floor in the posture they assume when working on their backstrap looms. The boys ate in a squatting position on the floor. The vegetables and rice were cooked perfectly, the black beans extraordinary, and the greens . . . unusual. Rocío also had made some small corn tortillas that were nothing like Mexican tortillas—about four inches across and quite thick. I suspected their garden must be luxuriant. I was aware of *Abuela* watching me closely throughout our dinner. With Rocío translating, I complimented the women on their cooking.

It was very quiet in the home, deep in the *Oyamel* forest, and the peacefulness of it all seemed to beckon me into the presence of things unseen. After the meal, Rocío and *Abuela* talked in whispers for a while. Then Rocío asked me if I'd like some of her grandmother's tea, to help me relax. I said, "Of course." When she gave it to me, I noticed that the only other person to take tea was *Abuela* herself. It was very herbal, and it had an oddly familiar odor and flavor, though I couldn't remember from where or when.

As I sipped the tea, Rocío talked softly with me. Her voice was sweet. She was sweet. I felt more and more relaxed. In the background I could hear the family chatting quietly in K'iche', but I was so focused on Rocío that they seemed a million miles away. Eventually, Rocío said, "*Abuela* has sensed that you are a voyager. She would like to go with you on your journey tonight. She is deeply experienced in these matters. I would also be with you, to translate."

I told her that I wasn't planning any travels tonight, but perhaps I'd misunderstood her. She replied, "I will let *Abuela* explain. I believe she has seen your thoughts."

Grandmother sat on the floor next to Rocío, and the two faced me. They spoke a few words to one another, and then Rocío turned to me and said, softly, reassuringly, "My grandmother senses that you are traveling on a new and uncertain path. That you have found yourself here is no accident. She has an awareness and wisdom, and she can help you. And perhaps you can help us. But only if you wish to travel with her."

I wasn't sure what the old woman was offering, but coming from lovely Rocío's lips, it sounded just fine to me. I was feeling quite content and relaxed.

"*¿A dónde Abuela quisiera que viaja?*"

"To a place that may not be familiar to you. But she knows it well, and she thinks you are in need of a spiritual journey." The more Rocío talked, the more drawn to her I was. I told her I trusted her, and therefore I trusted her grandmother. I turned my head to look at the old lady, and she immediately locked her eyes onto mine. Her gaze was so intense, I couldn't turn away. The wall behind her began slowly moving away as her eyes took on a yellow glow. I couldn't move. I couldn't even blink. Her eyes had phosphorescence, like the dinoflagellates in the water of the San Blas Islands. The wall behind her vanished, and there was nothing but darkness around us—only she and I and the yellow glow that ran like fire from her eyes to mine. She said something, and I sensed Rocío standing, reaching out to me with her hands. I took them, and she said softly, "*Ahora, venga a mi, señor Odel.*"

We walked through a door into the cool, dark air. There were a million stars overhead, brighter than I'd ever seen, and the smell of the fir was fiercely strong on the crisp night breeze. But as we walked the night grew darker and the stars began to sink deeper into the sky. At the back of the house there was a small, round-roofed thatched hut with an entryway no more than four feet tall. A faint glow emanated from the tiny entrance. There were old wool blankets spread over the pine needles on the ground in front of the hut. Rocío said, "You must remove all your clothing now; it will become very warm inside the hut." I didn't think twice about it. Off came my shoes and socks, my jeans, and my flannel shirt, and my underwear. I got down on my hands and knees to crawl inside. The old woman followed me. Rocío didn't come in, but she knelt at the entryway and said to me, "Trust *mi abuela*, *Señor* Odel. She is gifted." Somewhere nearby I could hear kindling wood being chopped with a machete.

It was indeed warm inside, with a small fire burning on the dirt floor and large round river stones spread about in it. A bucket of water sat next to the fire. An oil lamp flickered in the corner. A *copál* burner filled the air with a sweet scent and some deep memory in me said it was good and it was safe. Bundles of herbs were lined up along the floor. I sat cross-legged on a large blanket spread over the dirt, the old woman on her knees in front of me. She used her cupped hands to splash water over the hot rocks and red coals, filling the hut with steam. She began chanting in K'iche'. It was sing-song, melodic. I was already perspiring heavily. She picked up some herb bundles and began swatting me gently all over— my chest and stomach, my back, the top of my head, my legs, the bottoms of my feet. Her rhythmic chant grew a bit louder, and the herb slaps harder. More water and more steam. Louder chanting, harder beating with the herbs. I was in a heightened world of tactile-olfactory-auditory sensations. I was aware of nothing but the feeling of her beating on me, her rhythmic chanting, and the strong fragrances of the *copál* and herbs. Soon she was almost screaming, slapping me hard with the bundles of plants. I could no longer see her through the thick *copál* smoke and the steam. I closed my eyes for a few minutes, and when I opened them again, the curling smoke looked like snakes in the air, writhing and tying themselves into knots.

I was enveloped in an aromatic cloud, and I felt my body slowly lifting off the ground, floating up through the odors and the smoke, leaving the hut. The stars were brilliant laser points, and the smell of the pines and firs swept under me and elevated me as if I were on a soft coniferous carpet. I could see for miles through the darkness—the other barely-lit houses in the forest, even other villages in the distance. I saw the old woman's head floating in the blackness in front of me, but it was twice its normal size. When she spoke, Rocío's voice came out of her mouth. "*Señor* Odel, look north and then south, to your left and then to your right. Tell me what you see."

"I see the forest, and I see many campfires to the north. Soldiers with rifles. The soldiers have blackened their faces."

"How many soldiers do you see around the campfires?"

"Maybe three-dozen or so."

"What are they talking about?"

"They are on their way to Pachalum, where they wish to do bad things to the people there."

"Now turn around and face the other direction *señor*. Look far off into the distance, as far as you can see. What is there?"

"A great jungle and many poor people. And an ocean beyond."

"What are the people doing?"

"They are hiding."

"What are they hiding from?"

"From bad men with guns. The men want to kill them."

"*Señor*, do you see yourself there?"

"Yes. I am hiding too. I am in the jungle. It is very bad."

"Is anyone else in the jungle with you?"

"I see a young girl and an older man."

"Why are they there?"

"I don't know. They are talking. In English. They are gringos."

"They are there to protect you, *señor*. You must trust them."

And then, out of nowhere, a doleful pain swept through me, darkening my heart. A black curtain fell across my eyes and I could no longer see or hear anything. I felt a hard slap of herbs on my face. I opened my eyes, and the old woman was on her knees in front of me. She was chanting softly. Her eyes were closed. I lost consciousness.

I awoke fully clothed on the kitchen floor, covered with a heavy wool blanket. The wood fire was radiating heat, and delicious aromas filled the air—coffee, beans, cinnamon, and some kind of cornmeal. I felt wonderful and well rested. *Funny*, I thought. *I don't even remember going to bed.* I looked at my watch. It was almost 10 a.m. *Holy shit, how did I sleep so late? I've got to get that tire fixed on my rental car!* I jumped up, pulled on my shoes, and began folding the blankets.

Rocío walked in with a cheerful smile on her face. "*Buenos días, Señor Odel. ¿Cómo estás esta bonita mañana?*" Indeed, the morning seemed as bright and cheery as Rocío herself. Her black hair hung down to her waist, as is typical of Maya women, though they normally keep it wrapped on top of their head with bands of colorful handwoven fabrics.

"I feel wonderful, thank you. Forgive me for sleeping so late. I hope I have not inconvenienced your family in any way. I must find the tire repairman and get my rental car fixed. I'm afraid I will need a new tire, and I doubt I will find one in Joyabaj. And I'm worried about the car being vandalized on the roadside. By the way, Rocío, your hair is as beautiful as your name."

She smiled unabashedly and said, "Thank you, *Señor* Odel. In the mornings my mother and grandmother and I brush each other's hair. You might never see it down like this again." She giggled, and her smile was contagious. I realized she likely was not *puro Maya*. Her cheekbones were not as prominent or as high set as most Maya, and her nose had a more European shape to it. Her torso also lacked the square, boxy shape I'd come to recognize among the Maya. I wondered if the man she called father might not be her biological father. The ramifications of it were too complicated to grapple with at the moment, and it was an area of Maya sociology that I knew little about.

"Do not worry," Rocío said, "It is typical after such a journey for a person to sleep deeply and for a long time. It takes a great deal of energy to travel as you did. The tea and the *temescal* also help immerse oneself in sleep. *Abuela* says you are the finest *gringo* she has ever traveled with. But I think you are also the only *gringo* she has ever traveled with." Rocío giggled again. "You were very receptive and trusting, and your visions are extraordinarily clear. *Abuela* believes you are gifted. And there is no reason to worry about your car, as my father and brothers are taking care of that. And you can trust your car has not been harmed. This is the land of the Quiché Maya. Our people have great respect for the belongings of others. It is not like in Guatemala City, where the mestizos and *ladinos* steal everything they can get their hands on. May I get you some breakfast?"

Traveled with? What was she talking about? "Yes, some coffee would be great, thank you. And it is extremely kind of your father and brothers to help me with my car. Your family is generous, and I am most appreciative."

"It is what we do here. In these remote areas, we must all help one another."

After I'd eaten, I walked out into the yard and sat on a large log, sipping coffee and trying to remember the previous night. It was one of those rare mornings in the sierras that the land wasn't in clouds, and the bright sun in the thin air felt good on my skin. Little by little, the previous evening began to come back to me. The tea, the hut, the herbs. But I could remember very few details.

Rocío came out and sat on the log, as far away from me as she could. She asked me what I remembered from my travels, and I told her I didn't remember much. She smiled broadly and offered to tell me about it. *"Por favor, Rocío,"* I said.

She recounted the entire thing to me. I had been in the hut with her grandmother for nearly two hours. She said, I traveled "slowly but unerringly." After she had finished her story, and I'd thought about it for a few minutes, I said, "Rocío, I have some questions."

"¡Estoy seguro de que tienes muchas preguntas!"

"First off, how is your grandmother capable of taking people on such travels? And, secondly, how did I get my clothes back on?"

Now Rocío laughed loudly. "I do not know how *Abuela* does the things she does. She is truly skilled at her art, and I believe she is at her zenith. She sometimes says to me, *'tal vez también soy maldita.'* She is a midwife, a *curandera,* and a *yerberas.* She has a large and trustworthy reputation among the Quiché. As for your clothes, *Abuela* and I bathed you and dressed you, and we put you to bed in the kitchen. I took the liberty of removing your car keys from your pants pocket, so my father could help with your car today. You are not only a talented traveler; you are a very handsome man." She smiled sweetly. She wasn't embarrassed in the least. The notion of it all made me reel. But, when I thought about it, I realized she must have seen her father and brothers naked many times in their one-room house.

She went on. *"Señor Odel,* who was the beautiful girl you saw in the jungle?"

"I honestly don't know, Rocío."

She stared at me in a curious way, as if she didn't believe me. And then Rocío said, "Grandmother believes that you are

348

ready for the next step in your journey. Today, she wishes to take you to a sacred Quiché place. A great city where our ancestors once lived. We call this place, *Q'uabaj*. She says your ability to travel is extraordinary, and being in this sacred place should connect you to the spirits of our ancestors, allowing you even greater capacity."

As we talked, I gradually remembered more and more of my experience from the night before. What Rocío described was there in my memory. It was extraordinary, and I had no idea what to make of it.

"Please come into the house. *Abuela* wishes to speak with you. And don't worry, I will be with you the whole time, translating, and helping you should you need it." Another big, beautiful smile. Here is what Rocío's grandmother said to me.

"*Señor*, last night you saw things in your travels that help the people of our village and of other villages. Your vision has already been shared with our neighbors. They know how to prepare for *la violencia*, for those soldiers whose souls are fractured and who carry hatred in their hearts. But your vision of the lowlands, the green jungle of the Petén, is for you and you alone. There was a painful moment in your vision there, a dark moment that you could not see or understand."

Rocío looked hard into my eyes, and continued. "On today's voyage, you will see things that you have never imagined. They might not fit into your understanding of the world. You must be mindful not to fool yourself, for you are the easiest person for you to fool. The truth may not be what you'd like it to be, or what would seem best for you, or what your preconceived notions tell you it should be. So unless you recognize how easily you can fool yourself, you will."

I told her that I was excited to experience a journey to a new place and that I would do so with an open mind. I also told her that, although I was a gringo, I was somewhat knowledgeable about the history of the Maya people. And I had great admiration for them.

"Let us go then. The *sendero* is not difficult. It is less than an hour's walk to the west, through the *bosque nublado*."

26

Odel's Journey within a Journey
Joyabaj, Guatemala July 1983

We left Rocio's house following a footpath that led past the family's abundant garden to an indistinct trail. It was easy walking, lush and damp; Spanish moss hanging from the limbs of the trees brushed our heads as we negotiated our way. We strolled on a thick carpet of pine and fir needles, the air cool and invigorating, the aromas of tree sap and wild mountain herbs invigorating. The birds were noisy and plentiful. A pair of Resplendent Quetzals even flew along with us for a while— the sacred bird of the ancient Maya people and the largest and most extraordinary species in the trogon family, with an emerald-green body, brilliant red chest, and tail feathers more than two feet long. The entire bird is iridescent, and as it flies through the sunlight-dappled forest its colors change in kaleidoscopic fashion. Only the highest-ranking nobles that ruled ancient Maya cities were allowed to use their plumes as adornments. The Feathered Serpent god of both the Aztec and Maya civilization was a giant rattlesnake adorned with feathers of the Resplendent Quetzal.

Abuela led the way, slow but sure. She had good stamina for an old woman and showed no signs of getting winded as we hiked in the thin mountain air. But, of course, she had grown up and lived her entire life nearly two miles high in the sierras, so her body was well adapted. Rocío, who carried a fabric bag, followed her, and I walked behind Rocío. I couldn't help but notice her shapely calves and the sway of her hips, neither of which were typical among Maya women. And then the clouds rolled back in, visibility fell to just a few feet, and the tiniest of water droplets formed on the hairs of my arms. As we walked in the soft heavy mist of the cloud forest, I could no longer recognize the trail. It looked more like a simple game trail than *un sendero para la gente*. I could barely see Rocío in front of me, and I didn't know north from south, or east from west. Without Rocío and *Abuela*, I would be completely lost.

We topped a high crest and stopped, looking downslope in front of us. The clouds passed, and sunlight spilled into a small moist valley. At first I saw nothing but the green blanket of forest below. Then, as my focus gradually adjusted, I saw it: the top-most portion of a temple, darkened by wet moss and lichen, protruding a few feet above the canopy. Then, vaguely recognizable through the trees below it, I could see glimpses of the angled sides of a pyramid, hidden in the dense foliage of the high-mountain woodland. The temple itself was rectangular, with two openings on one of its long sides. The walls were intricately carved, though from where we were I couldn't make out the details. I estimated the whole pyramid was at least 80 feet tall. As we quietly approached, clouds wafted in and out, and visibility fluctuated from nothing to a hundred feet or so. Most of the pyramid was covered with earth or overgrown with vegetation. Roots as thick as Rocío's waist snaked over the carved stone blocks. Were it not for the temple peeking out above the canopy, it would be unnoticeable.

We walked to the base of the pyramid where a massive stone stela lay on the ground, also overgrown, but with the carved Mayan glyphs still clearly in place. And then I saw another and another—at least a dozen stelae. Most were still erect, though they listed like ancient gravestones. A few steps of the massive pyramid were exposed 20 yards from us, and they were heavily carved with hieroglyphics—a sign of Classic Maya architecture. *My god,* I thought, *this place is a treasure, an unknown Maya city, probably from the Classic Period, buried in the 10,000 foot-high Sierra de Chuacús just a couple miles from Joyabaj.* And then a large Horned Guan flew down from a tree; it landed and stood on the forest floor, staring at us. I'd never seen one before. Turkey-sized, with glossy black plumage set off by a brilliant white band across its rump and a bizarre fleshy orange "horn" on the top of its head, it's one of the strangest and rarest birds in the world. *Abuela* stared at the guan and said, "The clown of the forest greets us. This is a good sign."

As we walked around the base of the pyramid, I was struck by the quality of its workmanship. I was well aware that the rockwork and stone carvings of the Maya were comparable to the finest work in Europe at the time, only it had been accomplished without the aid of metals, draft animals, or the wheel. Maya pyramids also far exceeded those of Egypt in craftsmanship. We came upon a second structure, also made of carved stone blocks. This one was a single story, just a row of rooms—perhaps a dozen. It was partly buried and almost entirely covered with foliage. The entrance to one of the rooms had been cleared of vegetation. As we approached it, I could see that the facade around the entryway was carved in an intricate pattern that included some of the Maya gods I was familiar with: *Chaac,* the rain god; *Bahlam,* the jaguar god of the underworld; and *Jacawitz,* the mountain god of the Quiché Maya. The ancient Maya had dozens of gods. They even had one called *Chin,* god of homosexual relationships and patron of homosexual prostitutes.

When the women arrived at the doorway, they wrapped their skirts tightly around their legs and stooped to enter the small stone room. Inside were a couple of blankets and some candles, a small *copál* burner, and a colorful folded fabric. I knew this was *el lugar de la abuela*. We sat on the blankets in the dark room, and I could smell the damp limestone blocks that surrounded us. Rocío lit the candles and *copál*, an unusual one that I'd never smelled before—highly aromatic but mild and producing almost no smoke. Although the candlelight was dim, I could see that all around the walls ran a beautiful and intricate ribbon of colorful design, about ten inches wide, with red, yellow, green, blue, and black. The colors were still vivid, the paint barely faded. *Incredible—I've never seen such brilliant colors remaining on a Maya structure*. Here, in the ruins of this uncharted Maya city, the abiding splendor of an ancient civilization survives, faithfully resisting the modern world's insanity. As my eyes became accustomed to the low light and I could make out the details of the colorful band, I followed it around the walls to the end, and there was the head—*Quetzalcoatl*, the Feathered Serpent! At the other end of the long panel was the rattlesnake tail of the chimera.

The earliest known depictions of *Quetzalcoatl* are from the enigmatic pre-Aztec city of Teotihuacan, near Mexico City, around the first century BC. But by AD 600 the Feathered Serpent god had spread throughout most of Mesoamerica and become one of the most powerful symbols of the land. For the Aztecs, *Quetzalcoatl* was the god of wind, air, and learning. In the ancient Maya world, the Feathered Serpent was the embodiment of the sky itself, as well as a "vision serpent" that could travel through space and time to reveal to mortals the hidden worlds of the gods. The sacred Maya text, *Popol Vuh*, refers to the Feathered Serpent as "the Wind Guide." I would soon come to understand the significance of that epithet.

Grandma unfolded the colorful, backstrap-loomed fabric that was in the room. Inside it were dried herbs, roots, small cactus buds, and mushrooms. There was also a small heart-shaped object, made of amber. *Abuela's* wrinkled hands quickly sorted the stuff into little piles. Rocío pulled a jar out of the bag she'd been carrying and told me it was drinking water. The old lady set aside one of the mushrooms, refolded the cloth, and put it back in a corner of the room; she retained the amber amulet in her left hand, stroking it gently with her thumb. She and Rocío chatted softly in K'iche'. Rocío turned to me and said, "*Abuela* would like you to eat this small mushroom. We call this *teonanácatl*. I have this water for you as the mushroom is quite dry. This will help you travel with her. I am not sure where your voyage will take you, but she may already know. I will be right here by your side, *señor*, so do not worry. *Abuela* has brought many people to this sacred place to help them travel. And she has powerful apotropaic energy." She reached over and held my hand lightly for a few seconds, gazing into my eyes with a look on her face that gave me complete confidence.

I ate the dry, bitter mushroom, washed it down with water, and waited. Grandma closed her eyes and seemed to slip into a trance, the amulet clutched in her hand. Rocío and I chatted softly. I asked her where she had grown up.

She said, "I am from Santa Cruz del Quiché. I never knew my biological parents. The soldiers came to our town one day and killed many of the men and raped some of the women. My mother became pregnant from that, but she died in childbirth—thus I was born an orphan. The family you now know took me in and raised me from infancy. They have been wonderful. My mother and father are wise, *mi abuela* is gifted, *y mis hermanos son chispudo, chambeador y bien chilero*—my brothers have always protected me." She said all this in a matter-of-fact way, without obvious emotion. I knew this was a sad but common narrative among the Guatemalan Maya.

I told Rocío that her family garden was beautiful and appeared bountiful. She replied that her family devotes a great deal of love and attention to the garden. "To spend one's days tending a garden, feeding your family, what could be better or more important? The food we put in our bodies is the most intimate thing in our lives. More intimate even than when mamá and papá have their loving moments together in the dark of the night. Our garden and our food is what our bodies become." Her simple statement bent my mind in an entirely new direction.

As she told me stories of her childhood growing up in Joyabaj, I found myself focusing intently on her words, the movements of her lips, on her attractive face and lustrous hair. I had almost forgotten where we were when *Abuela* said something. Rocío didn't even turn to her but continued looking at me and said, "*Abuela* asked if you have noticed the painting along the wall."

"Yes, of course I did—it's *Quetzalcoatl*, the Feathered Serpent."

Abuela spoke again, and Rocío translated. "*Quetzalcoatl* is the Nahuatl word. The Maya people usually call this creature *Kukulkan*, although in the K'iche' tongue it is sometimes called *Tohil*. The serpent will help you travel and see all that is below you in the land of the Maya. Look closely at the serpent's body and see what you will see."

I stared at the long, colorful snake. It was intricately patterned. Each scale on its skin had been carefully depicted but differed from place to place. In some places the scales were rectangular and one solid color, deep cobalt blue, forest green, or an intense scarlet. Other scales were like jigsaw puzzle pieces, multicolored and complex. The places where the jigsaw pieces interlocked seemed to glow and vibrate, making the snake's skin crawl and come alive. Along the top and bottom of the snake, the scales were also moving; they glowed an emerald green and pulsed, expanding and contracting rhythmically. As my eyes traveled along its length, the uppermost and bottommost rows of scales slowly increased in size, elongating, growing, taking the shape of feathers. When I got to the end of the painting, the head of the serpent radiated an emerald green, and its eyes were ablaze with red-orange lava. Around the neck, the feathers had grown very large and thick, with the dense green-and-blue plumage of the Resplendent Quetzal. The entire body of the snake began to undulate. The eyes were molten, bubbling, boiling—they appeared as volcanic craters on the verge of erupting. The painting of *Kukulkan* was demanding its right to be reborn again.

The snake heaved and rippled, and its feathered body rose off the wall and into the air. I saw it undulating over the conifers and other tall trees of the cloud forest, rising into a blue-black sky. I felt myself inside the snake, above the sierras, looking through its fiery eyes and seeing what it saw. In the distance I could hear Rocío's sweet and dependable voice, though I didn't know what she was saying. And as the serpent moved higher, I realized I wasn't *in* the snake—I *was* the snake; seeing the world through its eyes, hearing through its ears, smelling the land and the people through its nostrils. Together, we had become an incarnation. I could feel the sinuous movements of my long body as I moved above the forest canopy, the rush of air over my scales and feathers. I spread my arms to swoop low over the treetops and my arms were the wings of the Resplendent Quetzal.

Below me I saw the temple we were in, but in the distant past—in the center of the living Maya city of *Q'uabaj*. Brightly dressed royalty strolled around the great hand-cut stone pyramid, and farther away villagers worked the land. There were patchworks of cornfields that seemed to stretch on forever. The feathered snake picked up speed and moved away from *Q'uabaj*. We sped westward over the forest canopy, and there were more villages, more pyramids, more temples, and people everywhere. Thousands, tens of thousands of Maya. We came to a very large city called *Q'umarkaj*, capital of the K'iche' Kingdom and home to fifteen thousand people. There were many pyramids and other buildings and a massive ball court 130 feet in length.

Atop the largest pyramid was a great temple dedicated to *Bahlam*, the jaguar god and patron of the city. Beyond the Jaguar Pyramid was a strange circular temple, honoring *Kukulkan*, and more temples devoted to other Maya gods. Stretching out from one of the smaller pyramids was a line of five unusual structures, each with an alternating pattern—a circular platform, then a square platform, followed by another circular platform and so forth. Nobles wandered the inner city, merchants and artisans lived and sold their goods around the periphery of the central complex, and farther out were the farms. In one area, slaves from captured armies cut the rocks that engineers would use to construct the buildings of *Q'umarkaj*.

The massive Jaguar Pyramid overlooked the ball court and was adorned with bas-reliefs and colorful paintings of the sacred cat. Captured leaders from other warring villages were often thrown from the temple atop this pyramid, killed as they tumbled down the long steep angled stones, their decapitated heads to be placed on a skull rack. But at this moment, a half-dozen people in colorful regalia were in the temple, standing in a circle around a young woman. She was captured family royalty from a city in the north and she lay across a massive raised round stone, naked and on her back, her arms and feet stretched apart and outward, tied down with cords made of agave fibers. She was a virgin, barely through puberty, with soft almond-colored unblemished skin; her long black hair cascaded down from the round stone platform she lay across. Her face bore a look of terror. The man who would remove her heart wore a cloak of the rare black jaguar—*la pantera negra*. He moved around her slowly, chanting, holding an eight-inch obsidian knife in the air. The handle of the knife was decorated with inlays of jade and turquoise. The jade was excavated from the nearby mines that *Q'umarkaj* and allied cities controlled in the Motagua River Valley. The source of the turquoise was a closely guarded secret. Feathers of the Resplendent Quetzal hung from the knife's handle.

The priest quickly and efficiently sliced open the girl's chest, reached in, and pulled out her beating heart. The obsidian blade of his knife was sharper than today's surgical scalpels, and it easily sliced the large arteries, veins, and tendons that still tied the pulsing organ in his hand to the girl's body. The priest held the girl's heart high as rivulets of thick red blood ran down his arm and he intoned to the gods that the virginal sacrifice to *Bahlam* had been made. He next made a perfect incision between two vertebrae in her neck, expertly decapitating her. Two other priests using sharp flensing blades cut away the skin and muscle of her small head reducing it to a bloody skull. The raised stone platform and temple blocks ran red with rivers of blood. The young virgin's headless body was thrown down the steep steps of the Jaguar Pyramid, tumbling like a rag doll, the bones in her delicate arms and legs snapping like twigs and leaving a crimson trail down the stairway of the monolith. The small lifeless mass of flesh would be burned in a fire so hot it would leave nothing but ashes. The great Jaguar God would be appeased. Small holes would be drilled through the sides of her skull, so that it could slide onto a pole and rest beside those of other sacrificed virgins—each with the petrified look of death forever fixed on their bony faces. In a few weeks, the birds and insects of the forest would pick the remaining flesh from the bones and her ivory skull would shine bright like the others on the rack.

And then I saw the *Q'umarkaj* lords inviting the Spanish conquistador Pedro de Alvarado to come to their city to talk. Alvarado had just conquered the Maya of the Quetzaltenango Valley, in the north. But when his army arrived at *Q'umarkaj*, it captured the king and the priests and then ravaged and burned the city, leaving many Maya dead and others fleeing into the cloud forest. The Maya's spears and obsidian knives were no match for the Spaniard's modern technology of horses, protective leggings, and long steel blades. Even *Bahlam*, the great jaguar god, could not protect them from this new tribe from across the sea. Many of the young Maya women would be raped and made captives of Alvarado's army, their offspring being founders of a new mixed race of people—the Mestizo.

I saw the forest reclaim the land after the people of *Q'umarkaj* disappeared and the Spaniards left the area. Soon all that could be seen were the temple tops of the highest pyramids; all else lay beneath the accumulating soil and vegetation. More than a century later, I saw the great explorers John Lloyd Stephens and Frederick Catherwood discover the ruins of *Q'umarkaj* as part of their remarkable journey through Middle America. Speculation about ancient hidden cities in the forests and jungles of Mesoamerica had circulated for decades, some of the myths even claiming that Egyptians or Arabs had constructed them. But few speculated that it might have been the ancestors of the quiet, dark-skinned indigenous people that lived in modern Guatemala and southern Mexico today who had created one of the greatest civilizations in the history of mankind.

More time passed, and I saw the banana plantations of United Fruit Company growing like a cancer on the eastern seaboard of the great Petén jungle. The plantations spread up the Motagua River, which flows east from Chichicastenango for 300 miles to the Gulf of Honduras. The Americans used native labor to grow fruits and coffee, floating the produce down the *Río Motagua* to the coast. The enslaved Maya natives were maltreated and beaten, and the women were frequently raped by the Americans and *ladinos*.

And then more time passed, and I saw the armies of President Ríos Montt savagely roaming the land of the Maya, torturing the people and burning their villages to the ground.

His army denounced the Maya as vermin and animals. The heritage of the conquistadores lived on in the black hearts of the fair-skinned mestizos, and the suffering of the Maya continued. I heard Rocío's voice from somewhere: "For nearly five hundred years, the *ladinos* have tried to steal our language and our beliefs from us, but we did not let them. We will not be erased!"

And then I saw into the future, when the great Russian linguist Yuri Knorozov arrived in Guatemala. He was the first person to crack the Mayan language code, giving modern people a way to understand the glyphs, or writings, of the ancient Maya—he'd found the "Rosetta Stone" of the Mayan language, one of only three places in the world where complex writing had independently evolved. It was through his work that we learned the Maya had the most highly developed system of writing in pre-Columbian America. Due to Perestroika, Knorozov was finally allowed to leave his native Russia in 1990 and actually visit Guatemala for the first time. But soon after his arrival in Guatemala City, he got a phone call with a threat; if he didn't leave the country within seventy-two hours, he would be killed. Death squads had tracked down the great scholar whose research had proven that the brown-skinned indigenous people that the ruling class had worked so hard to vilify had a literary culture older than that of the Spanish.

These things I saw in my travels were disturbing, but Rocío's reassuring voice in my mind kept me steady. And then I heard her voice direct me to the Caribbean lowlands, to the wet jungles of the Petén. She asked me to go back to the place I had seen in my travels the day before, when I was in the *temescal*.

I felt my feathered body turn and fly rapidly, down the eastern slopes of the sierras, across a small tropical savannah, and into the thick wet emerald Petén. I saw myself in the jungle again, and I saw soldiers searching for me. I was crouched between two large buttress roots of a giant ceiba tree, half asleep and half awake. My clothes and skin were soaked with rainwater and sweat, and coagulating blood covered my arms. It was pitch dark and chillingly quiet, but from my place in the sky, looking down, I could see faint images of the man and woman I'd seen with *Abuela* the day before. They were walking with flashlights through the jungle, about fifty feet apart, swinging the lights back and forth as they moved. I saw myself frightened as a viper crawled across my legs. I didn't move, tried to breathe slowly, and raised the pistol clutched in my hand. The strike on my right foot was hard, and I felt the prick of its fangs through shoe leather. The penetration was shallow, and at first it was not painful. But then the venom hit my nervous system like a steamroller. I was paralyzed. At that point my vision began to blur—I could hear the voices of the American man and woman, but it was not good. Everything spiraled into darkness as the black curtain again fell across my vision.

When I awoke, I was sitting in the stone room, my back against the wall and the painting of *Kukulkan*. Dusk was threatening to descend over the ruins of *Q'uabaj*. Rocío and her grandmother looked at me, and Rocío, holding my hand, told me to drink some more water. I sensed something weighed heavily on the souls of the two women. They asked how I felt, and I said I was fine—just a little confused.

"It is time to walk back to the house, *señor* Odel. You traveled great distances on your voyage, and soon darkness will fall. Our trail is that of the jaguar; we should not be walking on it after the sun has set. We can talk as we walk, and over dinner tonight. You are a gifted traveler, with the ability to move though time and space. Perhaps the most gifted we have ever met." *Vamos a la casa.*

27

Cidabenque 3

June 1984

I hadn't heard Lieutenant Polyphemus's booming voice for an hour or so, nor had I heard the sounds of any soldiers. The sun was close to the horizon, so I guessed they'd given up looking for me. My whole body ached from being squeezed between the buttress roots of the ceiba tree, unmoving for so long. I stretched my arms and legs and slowly tried to stand. Just as I got onto my feet, I heard a single shot from an M16, followed by loud voices.

"*¡Puta madre, le disparaste a la maldita serpiente, José!*" Two men laughed.

Target practice! The soldiers were still around, just a couple hundred feet from where I hid. I weighed my options. There were only two—walk or stay put. If I walked, what direction would I go and to what end? In three directions, there was only the jungle, a green labyrinth in which I had no way of knowing what might lie ahead, or if I could even walk in a straight line. In the fourth direction was the village, the soldiers, and Polyphemus. I had to stay put—but I had no water, nor even a flashlight. I knew that a night in the jungle would be frightening. But not as frightening as a rogue band of crazed armed soldiers under the command of a psychopathic one-eyed monster. I had the lieutenant's handgun, but it would be of little use in the darkness of the jungle. Besides, if I fired the pistol they would hear it, and then it would only be a matter of time until they found me. And the handgun would be of no use whatsoever against three-dozen M16 semiautomatic rifles. I had no choice. I'd have to tough it out until morning and then see if I could sneak close enough to the village to check things out. The soldiers would likely leave at dawn. There were no civilians in the village, and they'd probably already taken what they wanted from the homes—food and water, maybe a few blankets or some clothing. These *campesinos* had nothing else.

I settled back down into my buttress niche and tried to psych myself up for the long night ahead. With the sun now low in the sky, a momentary breeze scrambled black shadows against gray-green foliage as the jungle's dank and gloomy mantle enveloped me. Great blue morphos drifted effortlessly in front of me and vast billows of mosquitos emerged and began to drink my blood. Thousands upon thousands of mosquitos. There was nothing I could do. My mind raced through the list of tropical diseases that mosquitos carry in this area: malaria, dengue, yellow fever, encephalitis. And then I heard a troop of howler monkeys approaching. Their shrill call, loud and nearly identical to the roar of a puma, was startling and could carry for several miles through the jungle. Though primarily herbivores, their incisors and canines were like knives and they could be ferociously aggressive. The group of a half-dozen moved toward me, staring and making menacing sounds. All I could do was sit very still and appear to be of no threat to them.

To the ancient Maya, the howler monkey was a divine patron of the artisans, especially scribes and sculptors. In some regions, the Maya venerated them as gods. Copán, in particular, is famous for its representations of howler monkey gods; the spiritual provider for their artists and musicians. Two howler monkey brothers also play a role in the myth of the Maya's third worldly cycle, and it is one of the oldest stories to be handed down by the Quiché Maya. Thus the demigods of the *Popol Vuh* known as the "hero twins," *Hunahpu* and *Xbalanque*, were sometimes portrayed as monkeys. They were complementary forces, yin and yang, their figures intricately carved in stone, the two simians separated by a symbolic effigy, representing life and death, sky and earth, day and night, sun and moon. Right now, I just wanted the howlers to move on, which they eventually did.

Exhausted, I began to drift into sleep, as a relentless rain of leaves, twigs, insects, spiders, spores, and moist organic particles began to coat my head and skin with a squirming biological powder. I woke every fifteen minutes or so to listen intently and then fall back into a half-sleep. The sun set, and I could no longer see my watch in the black of the heavy jungle air. I heard and felt the nocturnal creatures all around me and upon me. Multilegged arthropods crawled on my skin, and I tried to shake them off quietly. Tiny fur-covered night things crawled across my face. Aromatic black beetles dropped from dripping palmate leaves to burrow into my hair. Unknown flying insects landed on my face, crawled around my eyes and into my ears. Crashing sounds occasionally emanated from the foliage around me, and in my mind I ticked off the larger mammals of the lowland rainforest: armadillos, anteaters, sloths, howler and spider monkeys, porcupines, vampire bats, tapirs, peccaries, ocelots, margays, jaguarundis, pumas, jaguars. It was the last two that worried me the most.

And then I went through all the venomous snakes of the area that I could remember: fer-de-lance, several species of coral snakes and Viperidae, including a deadly rattlesnake and the eyelash viper. Not to mention the venomous beaded lizard. Deep in my subconscious, I felt a growing certainty that a snake was going to bite me in the dark of the night. I kept my grip on Polyphemus's handgun.

As the hours passed, I became increasingly desperate. The insects and spiders and other tiny creatures of the jungle had begun using me as a night roost and feeding station, and I was at their mercy. I barely resisted jumping up and running—but run to where? What was left of the rational part of my brain told me that in two strides I would crash face first into a tree in the black of the night. I couldn't stay awake, and I couldn't sleep. After four or five hours, I began to feel I was losing my mind. I had perspired away what little excess water my body had and was dehydrated. I sensed my skin had been transformed into warty purple leather from all the nibbles and punctures and stings of the night creatures, and I could smell the microbial rot of the soil penetrating into my clothes and my skin. I was certain that several hundred mosquito bites had turned my face into a corrugated baroque epidermal landscape.

I felt the weight of the handgun in my hand, sensing how perfectly balanced the weapon was. It felt like an extension of my own hand. I considered my lethal options. Would there be any point in shooting one or more of the soldiers? It would only make them torture me with more sadistic determination and force. Perhaps the best option was simply turning the gun to my own head.

A feeling of heaviness on my calves and feet startled me awake. The weight moved slowly; something long and heavy was slithering across me. My hand clutched the pistol tightly. In the dark, I lifted the gun quietly, leaving my wrist on the ground, trying to point the barrel of the weapon parallel to my leg; I didn't want to shoot myself in the foot. I was cautious, aiming the gun at a slight angle so the bullet couldn't possibly hit my body. The snake's strike on my foot was hard, and I could feel the prick of its fangs through the shoe leather. The penetration felt shallow, and at first it was not painful. I fired the Browning—a single shot. The beast jerked and moved away quickly. But then the venom hit my nervous system. It was excruciating. I involuntarily jumped up, tripped over the buttress root, fell and smashed my face on something hard. But all I could feel was the fire running up from my foot, through my ankle, into my calf, entering my thigh. It was unbearable. As I drifted toward unconsciousness, I had a vision of decaying corpses in army uniforms, their blood-stained hands gripping the souls of young Maya men and women.

28

A Mountain Ninja Warrior in Joyabaj

Guatemala, July 1983

As the three of us walked back to the house, the sun made its steady descent toward the mountaintops, elongating the shadows that ambled in front of us and pushed across the forest floor as the temperature began to quickly drop. Rocío and I chatted as we negotiated the *sendero*, which I now recognized as an ancient game trail. Although I'd seen the high pine forests of the Guatemalan sierras dozens of times, they had never looked and smelled as they did that day. The land seemed raw and elemental through my heightened senses, with an amplitude I had never felt before. I could taste the air that emanated from the giant conifers; it lifted my consciousness and stirred my imagination. The thick trunks of the ancient *Oyamel* firs burst with massive burls as big as Volkswagen Beetles, while the tops of the sacred trees had an incandescent glow. Silent scarlet macaws floated overhead. I sensed the hooves and paws of the thousands of animals that had walked this trail for centuries, as if they were there with us now as ghost guides. Gray fragments of mist coalesced in the woods, delicately floating up to the canopy where they merged, creating a growing cloud illuminated by the red-orange sun that danced just above the horizon behind us. Even through the soles of my shoes, I could feel the soft cushion of conifer needles beneath my feet on the forest floor. The moist green foliage of the drooping pine and fir branches, and the moss hanging from the limbs wordlessly spoke, offering obscure but reassuring symbols from ancient beliefs that had taken hold of me, perhaps were now guiding me forward.

Though not delirious, I recognized that I was in an altered state. My whole body was newly sensitized, as if awakened after months, years of torpor. But more, I felt something was happening to me, something rich and palpable but that I still didn't understand. The deep emerald hues and resinous fragrance of the forest assailed my eyes and nose, the sounds of the forest were sharp and clean, and Rocío's voice was like honey pouring out of a teacup—crystal clear, soothing, and compelling. I felt time was expanding and small bits of my journey clung to the edges of my mind in curious ways.

As we continued eastward, the long shadows grew, and on the horizon Venus threatened to defeat the glow of dusk as the sky began slipping into its black sequin evening gown. Rocío said the mist clouds around us were ascending spirits of the dead. She also told me that the dreams I had under *Abuela's* tutelage were gifts from the Maya god *Morphina*, known to the ancient Greeks as *Morpheus*. She explained to me that I'd experienced astral projections in the serpent room at *Q'uabaj*, traveling through time in the land of the Quiché and Lowland Maya. That I had described what I'd seen, including the long history of her people, from their beginning as a glorious civilization, to their subsequent suppression by European invaders, right up to today's civil war. I had also talked of the ancient Maya gods and told stories that she and her grandmother knew only from the *Popol Vuh*.

As we walked, it gradually came back to me. My "dream" had been explicit, rich and colorful, beautiful and bloody. It left me feeling deeply sad for the Maya, whose civilization was once on par with the greatest European nations, though with very different cultural underpinnings. The experience also left me feeling humbled and small. I recalled the words of the curandera in Barrio Esperanza who had told me of the Feathered Serpent—"human sacrifice can be the price he demands for sharing his knowledge." I pushed the thought out of my mind, though it left me feeling uneasy.

I asked Rocío what the amber amulet was that her grandmother clutched while I "traveled." She replied that it was an effigy of the heart of Princess *Ixkik'*, carved from the resin of a magical plant called *chik'te'*.

Rocío said, "*Ixkik'* is a goddess in the Quiché creation story; her life is described in the *Popol Vuh*. She is grandmother's chosen ancestral spirit. As you may know, our creation story tells of a number of worlds, or cycles, before mortal Maya walked the Earth. In those earlier world's, only gods and demi-gods occupied the universe, the Earth, and the Underworld. During the third cycle, *Ixkik'* gave birth to the Hero Twins, *Hunahpu* and *Xbalanque*. Like you, *Señor*, those twins endured a long and difficult journey, but it was in the land of the gods, before mortals existed and maize was harvested. At the end of their journey, the twins died but were resurrected. They then climbed into the sky, where *Hunahpu* became the sun and *Xbalanque* the moon. And that is how light first spread over the surface of the Earth, making it possible for mortal Maya to be born. As with the Hero Twins, *Abuela* thinks you, too, may have to 'die' to be reborn with a new light that will reveal your destiny."

I hoped Rocío was speaking metaphorically.

I asked her what the tea her grandmother gave me the previous night was made of, and she said it was *yerba de la pastora*. "What the mestizos called Salvia, or seer's sage."

As we approached Rocío's house I saw the *temescal* I had been in the night before with *Abuela*. I noticed that surrounding the small entryway at the front of the domed structure was a crude painting of the Maya god-creature known as *Sapo*, a frog-like being with limbs of both iguana and toad. The legs were positioned such that they enveloped the doorway, so that entering or exiting the *temescal* required crawling between the legs of the mythical creature. I asked Rocío about it, and she explained that the Maya do not differentiate between natural and supernatural, or between structures and living beings, as is done in Judeo-Christian beliefs. The supernatural dwells within the natural, and sacred buildings such as certain *temescales* must be "fed" with rituals and gifts. *Abuela's temescal* was first built by her own grandmother and gifted with blood, *copál* smoke, and sacred objects that now lie beneath its floor.

"*Abuela's temescal* is more than a structure," she said, "it is a place of our ancestors and a place of supernatural beings. And it is also the home of *Abuela's* grandmother. It thus has accrued great power. It represents the eternal and abiding grandmother who helps healers like *mi abuela* treat disease and allows her to see unborn children inside their mother's womb and fix them if they are misplaced. It is a place for healing and hygiene, and for care of new mothers and their children. When you entered the *temescal* last night, you entered through the womb of *Sapo*, the amphibian goddess; you allowed yourself to be consumed and then reborn, and that gave you a gift of perception. You see, you are learning that sometimes when things start to happen to us, it is best to just let them happen. Thus your path is made by walking."

We arrived at the house just as blackness enveloped the valley of Joyabaj, although the high edge of the mountain range in the west still shimmered with a silver afterglow. Kerosene lamps lit the windows of the house, and my rental car was parked in front. It looked like a silhouette of some arcane foreign creature to me. Delicious smells from the kitchen wafted out the front door. Rocío talked softly with her father and two brothers, while *Abuela* chatted with Mamá and helped in the kitchen. The tire repairman had patched the

371

spare and put it on the car, but the blown-out tire was ruined, and there were none to be found in Joyabaj. I would probably have to drive all the way back to Santa Cruz del Quiché to find a used tire of the right size.

Dinner that night was a delicious stew, and the meat tasted like nothing I recognized. It was sweet and succulent, dancing happily in big plastic bowl filled with broth and perfectly cooked garden vegetables. I asked Rocío what the meat was and she said, "Tonight we celebrate your visit and your journeys with abuela with a special dish, *estofado de armadillo*." It gave me pause, but I knew that fresh meat was rare in these homes, and I felt honored. I realized that Rocio's family lived a life of little margin, rarely being too hungry or too cold, but with nothing to spare.

After dinner, I thanked the family profusely for their hospitality and extended my gratitude to Rocío's father and brothers for their help with my car. I expressly thanked *Abuela*, for helping me travel to such extraordinary places and for being my guide, and Rocío for being our interpreter and for giving me the trust and confidence I needed to travel. Rocío's grandmother reiterated that I had a great talent for travel and large "animation of spirit." She told me that my own life's journey would soon become more challenging, but that I had trustworthy friends who would be there to help me through difficult times. And then she handed me a small jar filled with a clear liquid. I looked at the rusty cap. It read, GERBER PUREED PEAS—an old baby-food jar. With Rocío translating, *Abuela* told me it was an elixir of nepenthe, *un brebaje potente*. She said that great sorrow lie in my future. There was to be a dark time, so dark that even in yesterday's profound travels it had not been revealed to me. If I needed strength to cope with suffering, I was to put a teaspoon of the elixir in a cup of tea and drink it.

Rocío went on, "Abuela sees that you are a good person. My father and I also see kindness and honesty within you. Please know that you will always be welcome in our home."

In the flickering light of the kerosene lamps, I saw Rocío's father and brothers watching us closely, their faces strong with shadows, and I sensed the countenance of Maya royalty in their features.

As I drove away from Joyabaj the next morning, I knew I would miss Rocío and her family. They were extraordinary, each in their own way. I knew in my heart that I had received a great gift from them, one that would linger with me forever. I also knew that my experiences over the past two days had deeply affected me, changed me, that my life was truly on a new and different path. My mind was filled with the rich visions of the Maya worlds that I'd seen and the puzzle over how such "traveling" was possible. Perhaps it was purely hallucinations, but the details and accuracy were astonishing. My visions had flawless context and made perfect sense. Perhaps the two women used suggestive methodology to direct my hallucinations, if that's what they were, but I didn't think so. I felt the dreams I experienced came entirely from my own mind; not from any outside clues or impressions. And my new experiences with *curanderas* and mystics also had a consistency to them. I wondered, *Why now, and why me?* The empyrean time travel entrusted to me by the Feathered Serpent was not the time travel of an individual man. Nor was it in "my time." It was in majestic time, bold and venerable time, time in the age of gods and of monumental transformations. And I could feel it silently reordering my priorities.

Were these events somehow preparing me for the next juncture, the next chapter in my life? My curiosity and interests in the Maya civilization had been reenergized, and I felt a strong need to understand more of their history. And what did *Abuela* mean when she said I might have to "die" to be reborn with a new light that will illuminate my destiny. Have I somehow separated my years of training as a scientist from this new world of mysticism I've entered—like the Maya so comfortably separate their ancient gods from the modern god of Catholicism that dwells only in the whitewashed churches? I began to wonder what my brain might have to look like to comprehend these things. Or maybe it was already changing its neural topography to do so.

Parallel to these thoughts, another part of my brain told me I should drive straight to Santa Cruz del Quiché to try to find a used tire to put in the trunk as a spare. Driving these remote roads in the sierras without a spare was foolish. I wondered if the three-man checkpoint on the west side of Zacualpa would still be there. If so, they would certainly recognize me, and this time it wouldn't be so easy to slip by them. But there was nothing I could do about it; there was only one road through that village and on to Santa Cruz. I drove carefully on the bad road, not wanting to contend with another flat. As I descended in elevation from Joyabaj, the morning clouds lifted and sunlight broke through the tall conifers, illuminating the road ahead.

I got to Zacualpa, crept cautiously through the village, and exited heading west. Just a few miles down the road, I saw the orange road cones—the faux checkpoint was still in place. Again, there were the three men and no vehicle. They were wearing the same camo pants and dirty T-shirts. I decided the best thing would be to approach them slowly but then gun it at the last minute and drive as fast as I could past them and on down the road—and keep going fast until I got to Chinique. It seemed like a good plan, and things were going fine until they recognized my car, and two of them stepped out into the middle of the road. They stood there with their rifles pointed straight at me. There was no shoulder and the road was narrow. I was trapped. *Damn, I've got to stop.* I came to a standstill but left the car in gear and held it in place with my foot on the brake.

The guy in charge came to my window and immediately told me to get out. I shifted the car into park, left it running, and opened the door. As soon as I stepped out, he grabbed my arm and slung me around, facing the back of the car. He told me to put my hands on the roof and not to move. One of the other men walked to the passenger's side of the car, while the other stood in place in the road and kept his rifle pointed at me. The boss took my wallet out of my pocket, and the other man opened the side door and took out my backpack and duffel. He dumped them out on the road, no doubt looking for money or guns; he found neither.

"Este imbécil no tiene nada. Vamos a tomar su auto. ¡Y sus pantalones!"

Well, I guess this is the part where I walk in my underwear back to Joyabaj, I thought. *Rocío's going to get a big laugh out of that! Is this rental car insured for theft?*

But then the boss said, no, that I had seen them all twice now, and I could recognize them again. It would be best if I "disappeared." He told his comrades that I was alone, and probably no one even knew I was here. They could drive the car to Guatemala City and sell it quickly. They argued a bit, but the outcome was obvious. I would be disappeared. I broke out in a cold sweat.

The boss swung the butt of his rifle hard, smashing it against the side of my stomach—it was a perfect kidney punch. I doubled over in pain, sliding to the ground. I looked up just in time to see two things happen simultaneously. My assailant lifted his rifle to his shoulder and took aim at my head, screaming *"¡Muere, chingado gringo, muere!"* And in my peripheral vision I saw a person dressed all in black move rapidly from the bushes on the side of the road ahead where the third guy stood with his rifle still pointed in my direction. The man wore a black Italian cap, was short and small in stature, but was astonishingly fast, like a cat, and chillingly efficient. As he ran at the man in the road, his legs flew into the air and his right hand dropped to the ground. His left leg snapped out like a jackknife, smashing into the man's knee. I heard a loud pop-crunch as his tendons snapped and his knee buckled sideways. The man screamed, dropped his rifle, and collapsed in pain. The guy standing over me swung his rifle to fire at the surprise attacker, and as soon as he did I instinctively lunged at his legs to throw him off balance—his shot went into the air. But he didn't fall; he straightened up and swung the rifle to take aim again. I looked up the road, and the figure in black was now pointing the first gunman's rifle at my attacker. I heard the crack of the M16 and saw the thug's head jerk sharply backward. Small pieces of his skull and brains spattered down and across my face. He hit the road hard, a neat two-inch hole in his forehead and a larger ragged hole in the back of his head were draining blood and gray matter. I jumped up just in time to see the man in black aiming at the third man, whose eyes were like saucers. With his jaw hanging open, he dropped his rifle and ran into forest. The black-clad figure fired a few shots into the trees, but it was obvious they were just to keep the guy running. The whole thing couldn't have taken more than thirty seconds. One powerful karate kick and one perfect head shot.

Holy shit, what have I got myself into now? A mountain ninja warrior in the Guatemala highlands! I couldn't move or speak. I just stood there looking at the mysterious stranger in black, now walking slowly toward me.

He took off the Italian cap, shook his head, and down fell two and a half feet of the most beautiful black wavy hair I'd ever seen. *Coquette!*

Suddenly the pain in my kidney disappeared, and I felt suspended in time and space. I knew two things at that moment, beyond any doubt. First, that I truly was on a journey and great changes were at play in my life. And second, I was completely and unconditionally in love with this magnificent woman.

"No time for explanations now, Odel. Someone may come driving down the road any minute. Help me drag these brigands into the brush. By the time the guy with a broken leg gets back on the road and finds help, we'll be long gone. My guess is the group he's part of will put a bullet through his head when they find him; he's of no use to them now."

After we'd stashed the orange cones and two bodies, one live and one dead, off the roadside, we picked up my things and stuffed them back into my bags, throwing them into the rental car. Coquette said, "My car is just around the bend there. Drive on quickly now, and don't stop until you get to Antigua. I'll meet you where we'd planned." Then she gave me the most breathtaking kiss I'd ever experienced; neon lights went on in my brain, and fireworks exploded in my rapidly beating heart. She turned and ran around the bend. I could hear her car start up and head quickly back up the road.

29

Odel Gets Snoopy in Antigua
Guatemala, July 1983

I got to Antigua just as the purple dusk collapsed into darkness, in a state of total confusion but also feeling supercharged with adrenalin and high as a kite. I parked my car in the parking lot of Casa Santo Domingo and walked through the front door. Coquette was in the lobby, calmly reading a newspaper. She was dressed in a conservative but colorful dress and bright red Italian strap sandals. Her toenails were painted the same color as her shoes. She was still wearing the black Italian cap, which went flawlessly with her attire. *God,* I thought, *she's as cute as coconut crab.*

The Casa Santo Domingo is a beautifully converted, colonial-era Catholic convent; the walls inside and out are massive blocks of stone and the rooms encircle a large, lush courtyard garden. The roughhewn stone walls contrasted smartly with the overstuffed leather chairs, the polished mahogany tables, and the elegance of Coquette. Two or three other people were in the lobby, sipping drinks and chatting quietly. Coquette rose and strolled over to me. "I got us a room yesterday, registered under Mr. and Mrs. Pallas, and I can turn my rental car in here tomorrow. What took you so long to get here?"

All I said was, "Let's go to our room, my sweet little pistol of a wife."

She smiled broadly and led the way.

When we got to our room she said, "First things first, Mr. Pallas." She poured two glasses of *Flor de Caña* over ice, and we toasted to our "rather exciting visit to Zacualpa."

I said, "Would Mrs. Pallas care to explain to Mr. Pallas just what the hell happened back there?"

"I told you I was worried about you driving those back roads in Quiché Department. Things are so bad there now, it's bordering on anarchy. The whole of Quiché is now under the pall of Ríos Montt's henchmen. Apparently there are thugs like that everywhere these days. It was making me crazy. So I made the decision to try to find you. If you were determined to visit those villages, I wanted to be with you. Well, I found you all right, and just in the nick of time! Odel, I already lost my first love; I'm not going to lose you. Not now. I hope you understand."

"But how on Earth *did* you find me? Not even Nestor knew where I was going exactly. I told no one."

"My adorable but naive Mr. Pallas," she said, "it was easy as pie finding out what kind of rental car you had—there are only two agencies at the airport. A lady can be persuasive when need be. And you had mentioned to Nestor that you would likely stay at the Pan-American Hotel in Guatemala City. The people there seem to really like you, and they're very nice. They even shared with me the recommendations of places to stay that they'd given you. So I knew what road you were on—I just didn't know how far you'd driven. Looks like I was just a day behind you. You must have stayed in Joyabaj or Pachalum for a few days?"

"In Joyabaj, but that's a long story. So it was just coincidence that you and I met at that roadblock west of Zacualpa?"

"Not at all. I got to it about two hours before you this morning. I gave the thieves some cash and let them turn me back, acting frightened and saying I was going back to Guatemala City and staying there. But instead I just drove back up the road a ways until I could find a place to hide the car. I figured you would encounter these guys sooner or later, though I didn't know from what direction you'd be approaching. I made myself comfortable in the bushes off the road about thirty feet from them and simply waited. It was the best plan I could come up with. We did get lucky, though, because just a couple hours later, up you drove."

"Coquette, I don't think I could have gotten out of that one. You saved my life. And you risked your life for me. And I've never seen such beautiful moves or such marksmanship. That wasn't just luck; that is a skill set you've developed with a great deal of training. And, shit, you just killed a man—how are you feeling?"

"I feel OK. It wasn't fun, but I honestly had no choice. It was them or us. Those men are scum—ruthless sociopathic killers. I think those guys are part of a death squad out of Santa Cruz. They've apparently set up those roadblocks in many of the remote areas, robbing and killing people."

"How do you know this, Coquette? And if it's true, why didn't Nestor warn me about it?"

"I told you I was angry when I heard what they'd asked you to do. They might not have known about this latest activity in the area, though. They do need better Intel—that's why they wanted you to do this. There's so much pressure on them to get Ríos Montt to do something about this stuff. I have a good friend in the embassy in Guatemala City; she told me about these roadblocks springing up in the Quiché Department. But it still isn't right for them to send you into these places. I let him know how I felt about it all." She was agitated, pissed.

"What do you mean, you let *him* know how you felt?" I asked. "And who would that be exactly?"

"It doesn't matter; let's talk about that later. I just took things into my own hands. That's how I am. And, I once told you that I've trained in Shotokan karate since I was a child. My father insisted on it. I've also had a lot of marksmanship training, although that guy was only twenty feet from me, so it was no big feat. By the way, I hear you're a pretty good shot, too. Wanna have a contest some time?"

I chuckled at that thought and told her the only kind of contest I wanted to have with her would be an endurance test, in bed. She purred and smiled her amazing sweet-sexy Coquette smile.

"I thought karate was about self-defense—that's not what I saw. And what's with the black outfit? Is that part of Shotokan karate?"

"Oh, silly Mr. Pallas, it was just my black jeans and an old black T-shirt. Hey, do you like my Sicilian cap? It's from your family's homeland, and I think it's my new good-luck cap!" She tilted her head and pushed the hat back an inch or two. "Shotokan is a far more aggressive form of karate. Not many people know about it. I began my training when I was just fourteen."

All I could say was, "Wow!" And then I added, "Thank you for saving my ass. And for loving me."

We sat silently for a few minutes and then I asked her if she'd ever killed anyone before.

She responded unemotionally, flatly, "Does it matter?"

I didn't have a ready response to her tone or her question, so I said nothing. We talked for another hour or so, and I told her I'd decided to skip the other drive I had planned to make, out the even-more-remote northern route from Santa Cruz to the string of villages leading to San Andrés. She thanked me for having good sense, and she told me that she thought the

Agency was just going to keep asking me to do more things, and more dangerous things, and she was uncomfortable with it all. We realized we were ravenous, so walked to the hotel restaurant for a quick meal. Back in our room, Coquette asked me what my travels had been like and if my collecting trip was successful. "And I want to know what had happened to you in Joyabaj." I suggested we save that discussion for the morning. I could wait no longer to lie on the big queen bed with her, naked, exploring her perfect body, showing my gratitude in every way I could think of.

We made love for hours. Neither of us could get enough. We would explode, lie exhausted, cuddle, become aroused again, and then figure out something new to try. Coquette was an extraordinary lover, and I told her so.

She replied, "Odel, *you* are the extraordinary lover, and every time I see you, you help me discover new things about myself!"

"It's not me, Coquette—it's us! We're in tune with one another, on the same wavelength with everything it seems. You're a mindful lover, and you're perfect for me. I predict that many years of learning how to please one another lie ahead for us."

"You know, my love, it's because I trust you completely. It allows me to be fully open to you, to hold nothing back."

I asked her what she meant by "trust."

"Odel, I trust you in every way. First and foremost, I trust that you will always be honest with me. But I also trust that I can rely on you. And I trust that you'd never hurt me, emotionally or physically. And that you respect me, and respect what we have and our privacy and our feelings. Even if we disagree on something—and that day will come, I'm sure—I trust that you will respect my thoughts and ideas. And I trust my own feelings, too—my feelings that you are a good and honorable man. Honestly, I believe we are soulmates, Odel."

I thought she was probably right.

We spent the next four days exploring the old colonial city of Antigua, with its well-preserved Spanish baroque architecture, colonial churches, numerous ruins, and meandering tree-lined streets. We had amazing meals, met some wonderful people, played with kids in the plazas, petted stray dogs, and made love over and over in countless ways. One night, when we arrived back at our hotel, Coquette was tipsy from an hour or so we'd spent in a bar on the main plaza, laughing and drinking. When we entered our room, she stood in front of me in her long thin cotton dress and put my hands on her bosom. As I felt their perfect shape and played with her hard nipples through the thin fabric, she asked me if I liked her boobs. I told her they were the most exquisite and exciting tits I'd ever seen. I'd already discovered they were a major erogenous zone for her, and she loved all the attention I gave them.

She sighed and gave me a big wet kiss, attacking my mouth and probing deep with her tongue. I'd never seen her so aroused. She pressed my hands strongly against her breasts, whispering, "Harder, baby."

"Harder."

"Harder."

She let loose a little yelp and then dropped her dress to the floor. She took her left breast into her hands and played with it. Roughly. I got it.

I did the same, and her moans and quivers were hypnotic. She was in the mood to walk that fine, sensuous line between pleasure and pain, leaning toward the latter. It was galvanizing for both of us.

"Ohhhh baby," she moaned, climbing onto the bed and lying face down. She slowly raised her golden derrière high, leaving her shoulders and knees on the bed, her arms stretched wide across the mattress, her thin thighs spread wide, and said,

"I'm so hot for you, lover. Come take me . . . any way you want me."

And I did. Every way I could think of.

In the morning, as we snuggled like birds in a nest in the big queen bed in the centuries-old convent, I told her I hadn't realized she liked it that way. She replied, "Liked it? I loved it! But you're the first man to ever have me that way. I had no idea how good it would feel. Can we do it again soon?"

We both giggled, and I assured her that I was at her beck and call.

On our fifth day in Antigua, after a late dinner, I thought I'd better call Penelope. I knew she would be worried about me. It was around 11 p.m. Seattle time when I called on the lobby phone. There was no answer, so I left a message on our answering machine. I assured her I was fine and that all had gone well, but it would be a few days more before my return. In reality, I didn't want to return at all. Nor did Coquette want to leave Antigua. We were in a state of bliss in one of the most beautiful towns in Latin America.

Coquette asked me how Penelope was. I told her she wasn't home, and that I suspected she was likely in bed at Marjorie's house, or some other woman's house.

"Oh Odel, there are many other explanations for why she isn't home right now. Maybe you're just thinking that because it's what you *want* to believe. Be careful not to create your own narrative for your wife's story. You cannot be in her mind; you only know her through the filter of your own mind."

The next morning, sitting in the hotel's lovely courtyard garden after breakfast, I finally got around to telling Coquette about my experiences with the *curandera* in Joyabaj. I also told her about the others—the beggar at Teotihuacan and the curandera in Managua and her daughter. She listened carefully.

"And there's also the dream you had, presumably about me, for so long. Perhaps you do have prescient powers. That was your own creation, so it seems you don't always need a *curandera* to help you 'travel.' Perhaps, as the old woman in Joyabaj said, you truly are gifted?"

"Thanks for not telling me I'm nuts."

"Oh, you're not nuts. But you are a highly sensitive and talented man. And I think those people who told you that you are on a journey were correct. I just hope I'm on it with you!"

"Oh, you are, Coquette. I think you're at the heart of it!"

"No, Odel, I can't be at the heart of it. It's *your* journey—and your heart—and it is immensely personal. I guess I meant I just want to be there at the end, waiting for you, and still see love in your eyes."

"I can't imagine ever falling out of love with you."

"Odel, you know there are some things I cannot share with you because of my involvement with the Agency. But I'm going to our room now to freshen up a bit, and I'm leaving my purse here on this bench, right next to you. Will you please keep an eye on it for me? Of course, I know how boys are—sometimes they get a bit snoopy. It's possible you might peek into my purse while I'm away. And it's possible you might find a white envelope in it, and your curiosity could get the best of you. I'll be back in a few minutes."

I stared at her, not knowing what to say. She stood and walked away. I opened her purse and saw a white envelope, pulled it out, and read the printed words on the outside—MACDONALD PHOTOGRAPHY STUDIOS, LOS ANGELES. I opened the envelope, and inside was a very old and faded color photograph. I turned the photo over, and on the back was written *Buenos Aires, 1968*. Turning it over again, I studied the washed out and discolored image carefully. The photograph had an ageless quality to it. In it were two cute young girls holding hands, one of them was blond and fair-skinned, the other had long, wavy black hair and a darker complexion. The black-haired girl was dressed in an all-white karate outfit. Behind them stood four adults. As I stared at the girls, it hit me. Like a ton of bricks. It was Penelope and Coquette.

Then I studied the adults. Behind Penelope, I recognized her parents, young and rather serious looking. Behind Coquette was a remarkably beautiful dark-skinned woman, smartly dressed, with large eyes behind metal-rimmed glasses, and with an exquisite smile. Studying her face, her eyes seemed to be of two different colors, one appeared green, the other brown. Next to her was a handsome man with tousled hair, oversized ears, a Hawaiian shirt, and a big grin. It was John Thornton.

30

Odel Loses His Job
August–September 1983

My mind concentrated on the old photograph, trying to put the pieces together. Coquette had told me she'd known Penelope for a long time, and I'd guessed perhaps even since her college days. But these girls couldn't have been more than fourteen or fifteen years old. I remembered that Penelope lived with her parents in Buenos Aires when she was young. This photo must have been taken then, I reasoned, which means Coquette must have been there as well—wait, didn't Thornton once mention that he and his family lived in South America for a few years? It must have been then, in 1968. But did Coquette change her name? It should be Leilani Thornton, not Coquette Pallas. I was confused.

Coquette returned, with a mischievous look in her eyes. "Why, Odel, have you been snooping in my purse? Shame on you! I stopped on my way to the airport in L.A. and had a photographer make a copy of that old photo. He's going to clean it up and try to refresh the colors. It's wonderful, isn't it?"

I just stared at her. And then I began working through it in my mind, piece by piece. "Your name is Coquette Leilani?"

"No, but you're warm." She giggled.

"Leilani Coquette." I smiled back at her.

"Bingo!"

"The other great love in your life, who you lost some years back, was your husband. You took his surname, and you are still using it."

"Correct again."

"How did he die?" I asked the question, even though I remembered what Thornton had told me.

"He was killed in a horrible car crash south of Managua. He was sideswiped and his car swerved off the road; it ran head-on into a massive fig tree by the side of the highway. But he didn't die instantly; he died in the hospital hours later. If an ambulance had gotten to him sooner, he might have lived." Salty pearls escaped from her eyes, turning to gold as they slowly traveled down her caramel cheeks.

"Oh, Coquette, I'm so very, very sorry."

She couldn't speak as she slowly shook her head back and forth. Finally she whispered, "I'm doing OK now, in large part thanks to you, Odel."

We sat in silence for a while. And then I remembered the ancient fig tree near my own car accident south of Managua. I recalled seeing the large scar from where a car must have run into it. "How far south of the city was his accident?"

"Not far, maybe twenty miles or so."

I wanted to tell her that I thought my highway accident had been at exactly the same spot as her husband's death. But it was too surreal, and she seemed too fragile at the moment. The thought of it was crazy. *How could a coincidence such as that possibly be? Were it not for a broken tie rod on a crappy Russian-built sedan, I might have been forced off the road and hit that very same giant, immovable fig tree head-on. Damn it, there have been too many coincidences in my life lately.*

But then a strange and powerful thought washed over me—like some opaque and weighty memory, or perhaps an emerging prophecy. It dawned on me that the *Ficus*, easily half a millennium in age, was older than Managua, older than Nicaragua, older even than the time when white people first came to this place in the New World. It was a primeval fountainhead, a semaphore concealed in plain sight and predestined to take the life of one of Coquette's great loves. If it had not been her husband, it would have been me, and the story would have been very different all around. My inner scientist balked at the notion, but some emerging awareness in me knew, beyond a doubt, it was true. The thought passed through me like a bright light, and I wondered what other secrets that primordial tree held. I knew that my life, any human life, is but a blink of the eye compared to the life of this tree, which is a living telescope on time. Its memory—encoded in its rings and roots—stores a living history of this place on Earth over the past 50 human decades.

I went on with my questions. "So, I'm guessing your dad, John Thornton, and Penelope's dad, worked together at the U.S. Embassy in Buenos Aires?"

"I can't answer that question." She gave me a big smile.

"I see. And I'm guessing that's when you and Penelope first met and became friends."

"If you're asking me if Penny and I have been friends since 1968, my answer would be yes, that's correct." Another big smile.

I wasn't sure where to go next with my questions, so I went sideways a bit. "How soon do you think your dad will be retiring?"

"Retire? Dad? Why would you ask that?"

"Just wondering."

"An awful lot of people depend on him."

"You know, I think I've been pretty confused about your dad. And I also think I like him a lot."

"I told you, he's a prince! How could you be confused? He's one of the most transparent and obvious people I know. What you see is what you get with my old man."

"It was his idea for me to visit the villages in Quiché Department, wasn't it?"

"Now you *know* I can't answer that question!"

I smiled at her. "You don't need to. And I can just imagine you giving him hell when you found out what I planned to do." I went on, "Your mother, Isabella, was so beautiful. And darker skinned than you."

"Yes, she was a gorgeous woman—and charming and smart, too. Pure Miskito Indian, if there is such a thing. She and her sisters grew up in Bluefields. They all moved from the coast to Managua when they graduated from high school, to make better lives for themselves."

"Tell me something—why haven't your dad and Gabriela gotten married yet?"

"Good question. I think simply because it's too complicated. Dad travels so much; he's always in Panama or Florida or Virginia—as you might imagine. But there's also that element of risk in his job. I'm guessing he doesn't want to put Gabriela in a position where she might lose another husband. I know that sounds dark, but it's how my dad thinks about things. They've been pressuring him for years to move back east and take a desk job, but he's resisted. And I know he doesn't like the conservative culture of the Agency in Virginia and Washington. But really, I think it's because of Gabriela being in Seattle, and probably also because I'm on the west coast."

We decided to spend one more day in Antigua and then fly out. I'd been away from work for quite a while (not that I cared) and I was worried about my dad. We arranged for flights just a couple hours apart so we could go to the airport together, drop off my rental car, and walk across the street to the airport. Our goodbyes were bittersweet. Coquette shed a few tears, and my eyes grew moist. I told her I had decided to separate from Penelope, and I hoped we could see more of each other. She wished me luck and told me her heart belonged to me.

My flight home was melancholy but filled with a barrage of thoughts about Coquette, her father, Penelope, the unexpected journey I found myself on, and wondering what my mystical experiences really were and what they meant. Could it actually be possible that I had some talent for visions or traveling in time? Or was it all just imagination enhanced by drugs in tea and mushrooms and suggestive ideas from my "guides?" Would I ever know? Did it matter?

I called Penelope from the Dallas-Fort Worth airport, and she said she could pick me up at Sea-Tac. She sounded blue. As we drove home, she told me my dad wasn't doing well, and the family was very worried about him. She also said she'd heard from one of our friends at the museum that a couple more curators had gotten jobs elsewhere and quit, and that morale was at an all-time low. I was happy for them but sad for the museum. I asked her how Marjorie was doing, and she said they weren't seeing each other any longer. *So, that's why she looks so down in the dumps. So, am I supposed to say something like, 'Oh, I'm so sorry baby, but don't worry—someone else will come along'?* OK, it was a sarcastic thought, but really, what *was* I supposed to say? I said nothing.

As we walked into the house, I noticed that the pinhole in the door was no longer visible. It seemed symbolic of some kind of finality or closure—perhaps my decision to separate from Penelope and my admission to myself that I wanted to be with Coquette? It seemed to mark a juncture in my life, a turning point. That note stuck to our door was the beginning of a long and complex series of events that had redirected my life. I'd had so many stressful days and so much confusion, but now I felt I was through it and could finally see things clearly. Or so I thought.

When I got to the museum the next morning, the science-pool secretary told me that Acting Director Bligh wanted to meet with me as soon as I got back. I asked her to schedule a meeting time for us. She called him while I waited in her office, and I could hear his obnoxious, booming voice on the phone even six feet away. She hung up and said, "He wants to see you now."

When I walked into his office, he didn't stand up or even extend his hand for a shake. He told me to take a seat. I sat across from him in what appeared to be a new, expensive-looking leather chair, one of several I noticed in his office. "New chairs?" I asked.

"Yeah, I got rid of those old moth-eaten things that had been here for twenty years."

"Probably not a good time to be spending money on expensive furniture for your office." I realized as soon as I said it that it would piss him off, but I didn't care.

"What would you know about such things, Odel?"

I took the bait. "I know this looks like six $500 chairs, and I can think of a lot better places to invest $3000 in the museum right now."

Bligh just shook his head. "Where have you been these past few weeks?"

"On a collecting trip in Guatemala. I'm sure you saw my travel memo."

"Maybe I did—I don't recall. But why the hell are you collecting in Gua-tee-fucking-mala? I don't even know where that is!"

I took the bait again. "I'm sure you don't. It's right below Mexico, if you know where that is."

"Don't get smart with me, Odel. Who paid for that trip? Did the museum pay your expenses?"

"Of course not—it was covered by one of my grants. My travel is always paid out of my research grants."

"Well, we paid your salary while you were gallivanting around down there, didn't we? And I don't think *that's* a wise use of museum funds right now."

"Bill, it's my job. My research is tropical American Crustacea. It's what I do. It's what we all do—all the curators."

"I'm beginning to think you guys should be working here in Washington State, maybe in Puget Sound or something— you know, regionally. Our visitors aren't from Mexico, and they don't speak Spanish. They're from Seattle!"

It was all so ridiculous, I hardly knew how to respond. "Actually, Bill, our visitors come from all over the country, all over the world really. And many of them are Spanish speaking. As you may know, some of us have been lobbying to get bilingual signage on the public floors. As for us becoming a regional museum, I think it's far too late for that kind of an idea—the horse is already out of the barn. We've been recognized for fifty years as a first-rate worldwide research museum, with valuable collections and research papers in top-tier professional journals. We simply aren't some little regional museum."

"Do you think I can't change that? Do you think because you and your intellectual friends have fancy degrees that you run this place? You don't—I do."

It sounded like a challenge from a junior high school kid. I realized that all this guy wanted to do was argue with me. And he clearly didn't like academic types.

"Bill, this discussion is ridiculous, and I think you're upset about something right now. I suggest we talk about these things later in the week. In fact, what you're suggesting is so consequential, I think we should talk about it as a group—the science staff and all the rest of the senior staff of the museum.

If we agree some kind of change is needed, we can take a plan to the board of trustees to review."

I stood and walked out. He said nothing.

When I arrived the next day, there was an envelope in my mailbox. I opened it and read the message with a mix of sardonic humor, sadness, and anger. It was an "official disciplinary action" from "the Office of the Executive Director," accusing me of insubordination. *What the hell! Does this guy think he's an army sergeant or something?* I tore the note in half and put it in his mailbox. An hour later he walked into my office steaming.

"I have instructed our new HR director to give you a two-week unpaid disciplinary leave. I'll expect you to be out of this office within two hours."

I couldn't believe my ears. I lost it. "And I expect you to be out my office within two minutes, or I'll throw you out." I got up, walked to my office door and opened it, and stood there. He walked out.

An hour later he showed up again, this time with one of the museum's security guards. It was Carlo Scaredelli, another Sicilian who I knew well—we got along great. Bligh instructed Carlo to "escort me out of the building." Carlo said, "Sorry, Odel, the boss says you threatened him. I've got to ask you to leave the building . . . or he's going to call the cops." Poor Carlo looked like he'd been run over by a tractor. He looked at me sad-eyed and shrugged.

That was the last straw. I gathered my things into my briefcase and walked out. As I passed by Bligh, I looked him in the eyes and said, "Bligh, you are going to destroy this fine museum. In fact, you're well on your way to doing so already. You're a first-rate jerk and an ignoramus." I thought he was going to explode, his face got so red.

"Bernini, you're fired. Get out."

At that moment, I couldn't care less.

The next few weeks were crazy. I received a letter from Bligh; it was two sentences long. The first sentence said I'd been discharged for insubordination; the second asked me to sign a nondisclosure agreement that came with the letter. It was ridiculous. I hired a good labor lawyer who wrote long letters—to Bligh, to the president of the board of trustees, and to the museum's legal counsel. I wrote an op-ed piece for the *Seattle Times*, which they were happy to publish, about the demise of the museum under an interim director. And I brooded about things. Penelope was supportive, as were all my friends. Everyone thought I'd done the right thing. The Biology Department head at Northwestern Washington University offered to assign a fall semester class to me so I'd have some income. Carlo called to say that he would testify on my behalf if ever needed; he hated Bligh as much as the rest of us. My lawyer told me not to sign anything and said he felt we had an excellent case for unlawful termination.

I also got in touch with my old museum buddy, Audrey. I wanted to fill her in on things at the museum, including my situation, and see how she was doing. She was sympathetic; she said her new job at the community foundation was going just fine but things were a bit rocky at home, and suggested we get together for lunch one day soon. She was a good-hearted soul.

A week or so later I met with Nestor Papadakis and gave him my transcribed notes from the Santa Cruz–Joyabaj road. Although I described the thugs outside Zacualpa, I didn't mention the incident or Coquette's intervention.

"I know it's not much, Nestor, but things are so dicey in Quiché these days, I wasn't inclined to drive into any other areas."

"No problem, Odel. This is good stuff, and I really appreciate it. Around the same time you left, we started getting Intel from our guys in Guatemala City that things were getting loopy up there. I'm glad you didn't take any unnecessary risks."

Little did he know!

"I hope your collecting trip was successful too. By the way, Thornton wants to catch up with you soon, but he's out of the country at the moment. He'll no doubt be in touch in a few weeks. And you might have heard, there was another coup d'état in Guatemala—it just occurred. Ríos Montt is out, thank god, but the new guy might not be much better. It's the defense minister, Mejía Víctores."

"Wow, Ríos Montt didn't last long. What was that—something like a seventeen-month presidency? I know there was a lot of international pressure to get rid of the guy, but I'm not sure how much will change under Mejía Victores."

By mid-September I was feeling better; I was fully engaged in teaching an invertebrate zoology course at Northwestern Washington, and our garage was full of boxes of books from my museum office. And then I got a call from Lorenzo with another bombshell—Dad had passed away.

"He died in his sleep," Lorenzo said. "I think he just gave up. He'd pretty much stopped eating. The doctor thinks he probably had a massive heart attack."

The news hit me like a heavy body blow.

31

Splitsville

September–December 1983

For my brother Lorenzo and me, Dad's passing was just the opposite of our mother's death. It hit us hard. While we'd both developed only a minimal attachment to Mom, Dad was always our bedrock. In our youth, he was the one we turned to if we needed good advice. He's also the one who taught us so much about life—hunting, fishing, and survival skills in the wilderness, fighting skills in the inner city, how to use guns safely and sanely. He taught us to work hard and save our money, and not to go into debt. He admonished us to "wise up and go to college," to treat people fairly, to not be judgmental of others, and to follow the Golden Rule in life. He was the kind of person who later would have been called a "pragmatic progressive." He always voted the straight Democratic ticket, except when he didn't. Putting Dad in the ground was probably the hardest thing I'd ever done. At least, it was the thing that brought more tears to my eyes than anything else I'd experienced. Up until that point in my life anyway.

Because I was teaching a class at Northwestern Washington University, I couldn't linger in L.A. My brother and my cousin Marco stayed on after the funeral to deal with legal matters and estate issues. It wasn't complicated. Dad had the house we grew up in, his butcher shop, and one savings account at his bank—that was it. He didn't believe in the stock market or anything with associated risk. I suspected he might have cash stashed under his mattress (he did!). We decided to sell his house. We also decided to put Dad's meat market up for sale. We had no idea if it was worth anything, but he did own a sizable piece of property—the old market, a large parking lot next to it, and a vacant lot beyond the parking lot. But it was in a lousy part of central Los Angeles.

I got back to Seattle and my teaching job, but I felt myself slipping into low spirits. I hadn't yet mustered the courage to talk with Penelope about a separation. I was holding my own though, meeting my teaching responsibilities, writing and delivering what I thought were decent lectures, meeting frequently with the students to help them. And then the other shoe dropped. Penelope told me over dinner one night that she had a new "friend." She was a professor in the Department of Agricultural Economics at the university. I didn't know how to respond to her announcement, and I wasn't even sure I knew what "ag econ" was.

"Why are you telling me about this, Penelope? I presume that when you say a 'new friend,' it means 'new lover.' That's your business, not mine. And, honestly, I don't really want your female lovers, or any of your lovers, to be part of our marriage."

She'd had too much Jack Daniels, and her dark edgy side was coming out. "I'm not suggesting she be part of our marriage, Odel—don't put words in my mouth. I just thought you'd want to know. I'm trying to be open and honest with you. Isn't that what you want?"

She said it sarcastically, not sincerely. Her voice had a churlish roughness that I didn't care for.

"I thought you might want to meet her." Penelope went on. "She's very bright, just got tenure, and you might find her interesting."

"What's her name?"

"Frankie, Frankie Skylla."

"Frankie? Jesus, Penelope! Sure, bring Frankie around if you want me to meet her." I wanted to say, *Frankie, I don't give a damn, Penelope!* Maybe I should have. Instead I said, "Penelope, I think we should separate for a while. I think we both need some breathing room. I'm honestly not comfortable with a wife who leads two lives. Or three lives, or four, or however many you have." She said nothing. It was clearly time to tell her about Coquette. "I've met someone on my travels, someone that I'm very fond of." She stared at me with a blank look, a look I didn't recognize and that manifested nothing decipherable at all. She asked no questions, not even for a name. It was as if the whole thing were some unimportant little detail or afterthought to our discussion, which seemed to have run its course.

That night, lying in bed, she began to weep. I let her cry for a while and then asked her why she was crying. I meant it as a rhetorical question. Until she responded.

"Dad is going to kill me."

"What?"

"My dad is going to kill me. Marriage is so fucking important to him."

At that moment I felt like the biggest fool on the planet. The word *naive* began flashing neon in my mind. I knew our separation would be permanent.

One day the following week, I stopped by the University of Washington. I wanted to look for a good biology dictionary in their bookstore. But before I left campus, my curiosity got the better of me. I walked to the building that housed the Ag Econ Department, and, as I'd expected, on the wall outside the departmental offices were photos of the faculty with their names and a few words about each of them and their areas of research. And there was Dr. Frances (Frankie) Skylla. She was a cowgirl, wearing jeans, a red plaid shirt, and pointed cowgirl boots. Standing next to her was a beautiful, 2000 pound Belted Galloway steer, with black shaggy hair and a band of white around the middle of its torso. The bio noted that her family had a large ranch in eastern Washington State, outside Pullman, that they'd run for three generations. She was butch-cute, though it took a couple minutes to see that because she looked like she would break your arm if you said the wrong thing to her. And you probably wouldn't even know what it was when you said it. She had a menacing glare in her eyes, and her face wore a partial grimace, not a smile. *What the hell*, I thought. *Not my problem.*

On October 11, halfway through the semester, while I was teaching my students about the joys of echinoderms, I got a call from Bob and Beatriz in my new office at Northwestern Washington. They asked if I'd heard the news about the previous day's attack on the port of Corinto.

"No," I said. "Unfortunately, we just don't get news about that sort of thing in the States. What happened?"

Bob's voice was odd. "The CIA and U.S. Navy SEALs just destroyed all the fuel storage facilities. It was an incredible operation in the dead of the night completely taking our guys by surprise. Over three million gallons of fuel up in flames. More than eighty percent of our oil is supplied by the Soviets, and about half of it relies on the Corinto port for delivery. Reagan and the State Department are denying any American involvement, but everyone here knows what happened. It's going to seriously disrupt our petroleum supply for a while."

I had a pit in my stomach. In my mind I saw the sketch map of Corinto that I'd made for the Agency, the little penciled circles of where all the new storage tanks were emplaced. And I thought, *Yes, and it will also disrupt the import of weapons from Russia, and goods from Cuba and Russia, and any naval operations that might have been possible.* My mind was awash with mixed feelings.

"That's terrible news, Bob. Listen, as soon as my teaching semester is over, I'll come visit you two, and I'll bring you a stash of whatever you need. Light bulbs, toilet paper, whatever—just let me know."

I could hear Beatriz in the background saying, "Tell him to bring me some sewing needles and thread."

Bob asked how I was doing, and I admitted I was hitting some pretty low points these days. "Even my teaching has gone downhill. I'm just not on top of things like I should be. I know I can do better, but I'm simply not motivated."

"That's to be expected, *amigo*. You just experienced three of the primary change factors that precipitate depression—loss of a job, loss of a close family member, and separation from a spouse. You're dealing with a lot right now. As for doing better, the only person you should try to be better than is the person you were yesterday. Just keep putting one foot in front of the other. You really should come stay with us for a while down here. Chill out, give another seminar if you'd like—or not. Go visit your new friend, Violeta Chamorro!"

"I'll do that, Roberto. I'll do that."

I didn't take much when I moved out from Penelope, although she was happy to let me keep the bottle of '61 Mouton that her dad had given us. I knew it was likely the only opportunity I'd ever have to taste a Mouton, let alone the famous 1961 vintage. I found a little apartment close enough to campus that I could walk to work. We split what we had in the checking and savings accounts. We eventually agreed to get a no-contest divorce. We had each put twenty grand down on our house when we bought it, and she said she wanted to keep the place and buy my half out. I thought she had enough stashed away to do that, and I knew if she didn't her dad would help her out. We had the house appraised, and she ended up giving me my original twenty thousand dollars, plus another twenty thousand dollars in appreciation value. With the Cleia funds I had in the bank, I suddenly found myself with close to a hundred thousand dollars in cash. If I was frugal and clever, I could get by on my part-time salary and use only a little bit of my cash reserve for quite a while.

I drifted in to and out of the blues, but periodic phone calls and letters from Coquette kept me going. I just wanted the semester to end, so I could go visit her. We talked about her coming to Seattle to see me, but with my separation still so fresh, it didn't seem like a good idea. We were worried Penelope might find out she was in Seattle and that we were seeing each other. I thought it best wait until a few months after the divorce was finalized before Coquette visited me.

In mid-December, as things were winding down at the university, my labor lawyer called to give me the news. The museum's board of trustees was willing to settle my unlawful termination complaint by giving me twenty-four months' salary, if I would sign the nondisclosure agreement not to bad-mouth the museum in public, either in writing or in speech. My firing would be rescinded, but I would then have to resign, which would "look better on my résumé" they thought. My lawyer had gotten letters on my behalf from directors of several other natural history museums around the country, as well as from a dozen or so nationally recognized scientists. I concluded he was worth his price, which amounted to six months of my recovered salary.

Coquette and I talked about how to get together as soon as my teaching semester ended. She said she'd gotten an invitation from her Aunt Esmeralda to spend Christmas with her at her home in Managua. It was her mom's sister and one of Coquette's favorite relatives.

"Would you like to meet my Aunt Esmeralda? She's really sweet, and I know you'll like her. She's also beautiful; she was named after color of her eyes. And she'll love you!

Christmas in Managua can be so much fun. And if you're inclined, maybe I could meet your friends Bob and Beatriz?"

"That sounds wonderful, Coquette. I guess it's time we started meeting each other's friends and families. I'm ready if you are."

John Thornton finally called, and we agreed to meet for lunch at Gabriela's place. For once, I got to the *pupusería* before him. Gabriela and Corazón were there and welcomed me in their usual warm and friendly fashion. Gabriela brought me a beer and sat down to chat with me while we waited for Thornton. She told me Alma was engaged to be married to a fine young man from Mexico City, a *chilango bueno*, who had a good job in Tacoma. He was an engineer, and he was quite handsome. She said she'd seen my op-ed piece in the newspaper and read some other articles about the museum, and she offered her condolences. She was such a fine woman.

Thornton walked in looking exhausted. He collapsed into his usual chair and said, "Shit, what a freakin' month this has been."

I just stared at him.

"All hell seems to be breaking loose in Guatemala, man! Listen, Odel, I'm sorry about the Agency asking you to head into the Quiché region. We honestly didn't know how bad it was when you left. I heard what happened outside Zacualpa. I'm sure you're probably pissed about things right now. All I can do is offer my apologies. It's not the kind of thing we expect from cooperators. I owe you one, my friend."

I cut to the chase. "Do you know that I know you're Coquette's father?"

"Yes, a little birdie told me you did a purse snatching move and saw an old photograph." He had a crooked smile on his face. "You do understand why we couldn't tell you, right? And you also understand that, although many people know Leilani's my daughter, it's not something we want broadcast around. Especially not south of the border, where it could put her in a compromised position."

403

"Of course I understand, John. But you need to know something. I am in love with your daughter, and I'm serious about our relationship. I don't want her put in that kind of a situation again either. I will do everything in my power to protect her. And my intentions are wholly honorable."

"I know all that, Odel. Leilani and I do talk, you know!" We both chuckled at that remark. Corazón came over with menus but didn't hand them to us. Instead she just asked, "The usual?"

We both nodded our heads affirmatively.

"You know, the last time I heard the words *my intentions are honorable* was when I spoke them myself to Isabella's parents. That was so long ago." He got a faraway look in his eyes.

"John, I want to apologize for my earlier uncertainty. It's taken me a while to understand you, but I want you to know that I now fully trust you. And I hope you know that you can trust me."

"Ditto, *amigo*, but I've trusted you all along . . . or you wouldn't have been dating my daughter!" He laughed heartily.

We had pleasant conversation over our *pupusas chingónes* and polished off three beers each. Then Thornton said, "I hear you may be going to Managua for Christmas to meet the lovely Aunt Esmeralda with the captivating eyes. That should be just great. *Incluso a la edad de sesenta y cinco años, Esmeralda sigue siendo tan vivaracha.* Could you do me a tiny little favor while you're there?"

"Well, now, that depends on what it is, John. No more roadside hijackings, though."

He gave me his big crooked smile again and said, "No, I just thought it would be good for you to take Ms. Chamorro up on her invitation to visit her at the newspaper. She is someone who could be enormously helpful to us at some point in the future. If you had a good relationship with her, well, who knows how things might play out. Just seems like a valuable opportunity all around."

"I'd already planned to do that, John."

I called Bob and Beatriz to tell them my plans and to ask if their spare room might be available over Christmas. They were thrilled at the prospect of having Coquette and me stay with them. "We finally get to meet this mystery girl from your dreams," Bob said. Coquette and I would fly the same day—I from Sea-Tac, she from LAX—and we'd meet up in a bar in the Managua airport. The day before we were to depart, my brother Lorenzo called. He told me that Dad's house and his meat-market property had both sold.

"Hold on to your hat, brother, because you're not going to believe this. The house sold for $125,000. But the property Dad had the market on turned out to be worth far more than we'd ever imagined. It was bought by the grocery store chain, Safeway, and they paid just over $1.2 million for it."

I almost fell over when I heard the news. Two checks would be in the mail to me in few weeks, totaling $675,000.

"Jesus, Lorenzo, I had no idea. This is a real game changer for me."

"For both of us. God rest his soul, he was a smart cookie."

32

Just One Last Request

Early 1984

Christmas in Managua was magical. The elegant and charming Aunt Esmeralda gave us her blessings. She bore a considerable resemblance to Coquette and was slim but strong, though she had a somewhat darker skin tone. But it was Esmeralda's stunning eyes that struck a deep thread in me. They were slightly oversized, like Coquette's, and resembled two luminous emeralds on her beautiful cinnamon face. The emeralds were highlighted with the same tiny golden flecks that highlighted Coquette's ebony eyes; an uncommon and curious quality. In our conversations, it came up that Coquette's mother had two sisters, but Isabella and Esmeralda had lost track of the third one. She was apparently odd, not very sociable, and not concerned with keeping up the family ties. Coquette had only met her other aunt a couple times when she was just a child, and she could barely remember her. She described her as "a bit of a mystery woman; kind of spooky in my childhood memory".

Bob and Beatriz loved Coquette. One evening after dinner at their house, when Coquette was in the bathroom, Beatriz said, "Odel, she is so very different from Penelope."

Bob said, "And yet so similar—they're both drop-dead gorgeous women, Odel."

Beatriz replied crisply, "I wasn't referring to their looks, Roberto. I meant their personalities. Penelope was so guarded—or aloof or something. I never felt like I could get close to her. But Coquette is just the opposite. She is open and sweet and forthcoming. She's so easy to get to know. You are fortunate, dear friend; she is a prize."

"She's just like her dad," I said.

"Oh, and what does her father do?" Beatriz asked.

"It's some boring government job in Seattle. I'm not even sure what it is exactly. But he's a handsome man, comfortable in his own skin, and easy to trust—like his daughter." I thought about how my views of John Thornton had morphed over time. And about how dangerous first impressions can be.

"Well, Coquette must be a good writer to make a living doing freelance work. And, speaking of writing, have you thought about that memoir we've been urging you to write? Perhaps this would be an appropriate occasion to start on it. You might have time on your hands."

"Perhaps it would be a good time, yes. But first I need to figure out my next moves. I'm thinking of leaving the states, at least for a few years. Settling in somewhere agreeable in Mexico or Central America for a while. There have just been so many changes in my life lately, I feel like it's a sign—for a redirection."

"Excellent idea, compadre! Do you have some specific ideas where you might want to live?" Bob asked.

"Oh, maybe Mexico City. I don't know. I haven't broached the idea with Coquette yet."

"How about here in Managua? Take us up on that idea of professorship at the National University. It sounds like Coquette could do her work from almost anyplace. You two could get a nice cozy cottage in the Las Colinas barrio and live the life you both deserve. Daniel Ortega is really supporting higher education these days. The National University is constantly looking for new, high-grade professors to hire. Last year we even opened a new engineering college here in the capital."

"Thanks for the great suggestion, Bob! I'll get back to you . . . we'll get back to you on that one."

We flew back to the states on January 10. When I got home, the two checks from my dad's property sales were there waiting for me. The next day, I went straight to bank and put them in a short-term CD account. I would spend the next few weeks looking into how best to invest the money for a decent return but with an investment strategy that was conservative enough for me to not worry about losing the principal—short of a national financial collapse. From what I could tell, I should be able to draw thirty-five or forty thousand dollars a year without depleting the balance. Enough to get by in the States, and enough to live very comfortably indeed in Mexico. Or Nicaragua. Coquette and I began what would be a protracted and fun discussion, scheming and dreaming about how and where we might live together. I'd gotten through the bottleneck of sadness and my blues were turning to joy. I was in love with the most awesome woman I'd ever met, and she was in love with me. And we were both free to follow our dreams. Life was good again and there were only happy times ahead. At least, that's all I could imagine.

I visited Coquette in L.A. every couple weeks. She had a lovely townhouse just three blocks from the old Santa Monica pier. Our time together was emotional, romantic, red hot, and sweet. We cooked together, took long walks on the beach, and explored a thousand different scenarios for our future. She was open to moving to Coyoacán or Managua or anyplace else I wanted. She didn't care. She just wanted to be with me.

And she could work from anywhere, though she noted that it might be best if a U.S. embassy was nearby—a comment that gave me pause, but didn't trigger any warning bells. We even talked about trying out life in Cusco, Peru, for a while. We'd both been there, though many years ago, as it was the gateway city for visits to Machu Picchu and the Urubamba Valley, heartland of the most mysterious of all the ancient civilizations of the New World. She liked Cusco as much as me. So many options, so many dreams.

The year 1984 looked to be a political blockbuster. In mid-February, while I was at Coquette's place in Santa Monica, news broke that the CIA had mined the harbor at Corinto. The Nicaraguans, with help from the Cubans, had been quickly rebuilding the fuel storage facilities that the CIA-Navy operation had destroyed, and Cuban and Russian ships were again starting to use the port. According to the *New York Times*, the CIA had been laying mines since the beginning of the year. Small speedboats, launched from a clandestine offshore vessel, were coming in at night and dropping miniature mines known in the business as "firecrackers." They were designed to discourage boat traffic, but they did little damage to steel-hulled ships. Half a dozen fishing boats ran into them and sustained some damage, in addition to a Dutch dredge boat that was helping the Sandinista government with new wharf construction. A Soviet tanker ran into a couple of the mines, but they had little effect on it. Once the Sandinistas discovered how small the mines were, they quickly figured out how to clear them out of the harbor. It was a bad plan and the CIA looked foolish. Congress was furious. But the Washington bullets kept coming.

Over the coming weeks and months, President Reagan and Congress fought like cats and dogs. Congress demanded all funding to the Contras, both overt and covert, be stopped. The Contra counterrevolution was a stalemate at best. The Contras themselves were divided, and the CIA had trouble trying to coordinate them. The Sandinistas turned them back every time they made a military excursion into the country. The CIA and Congress came under fire from the public, both in the United States and abroad. Even Honduras, a key U.S. ally in the conflict, was getting nervous. Daniel Ortega gave the U.S. Congress a blanket invitation to visit and travel throughout Nicaragua without restrictions. He offered to put in place an indefinite moratorium on acquiring new weapons from the Cubans and Russians, as well as to send one hundred Cuban military personnel home. However, there were an estimated three thousand Cuban military in Nicaragua, and another four thousand nonmilitary personnel. The Nicaraguan standing army was approaching fifty thousand troops, with another fifty thousand reserves, draining the country's meager economy. This, in a country of only three million people. Ortega said he was willing to sign a regional security agreement, but he would not agree to negotiate away his ties to Cuba and the Soviet Union because he was "committed to their revolutionary ideals."

Reagan took to fiery rhetoric about the Sandinistas, trying to portray them as cruel totalitarians and warning that allowing the Nicaraguan government to continue as it was would lead to a "domino effect" throughout Central America, and country after country would fall to the commies. What he failed to understand was that if we had supported the fledgling government appropriately from the outset, they might not have turned to Cuba and Russia in the first place. Secretary of State George Shultz threatened that an all-out attack by the United States might be necessary if the Contras were unable to topple the Sandinista government. Rumors circulated that retired commercial and military pilots were being covertly recruited by the CIA, paid to become "secret soldiers of the Cold War." These freelance pilots were contracted to fly arms and ammunition to the Contras from secret bases in Honduras and Costa Rica. They mostly flew planes for Air America, a CIA-owned airline used for covert ops.

Another CIA defector, Ralph McGehee published his memoir, *Deadly Deceits: My 25 Years in the CIA*. Though McGehee's book focused on Southeast Asia, its central thesis was that the CIA has never really been a "central intelligence" agency. It is, McGehee argued, no more than the covert action arm of the president's foreign policy advisors. In that capacity, it overthrows or supports foreign governments while reporting "intelligence" to justify those activities. The book also argued that most communist movements in the world were actually grassroots crusades, typically with strong peasant support, with the primary goal of freeing people from a history of colonial and neocolonial oppression. He was, of course, correct in both assessments.

To everyone's surprise, Pedro Chamorro (son of Pedro Joaquín Chamorro) quit his job at *La Prensa* and joined the Contras. Even Edén Pastora, *Commandante Zero*, turned on Ortega and his Cuban-Marxist agenda to became leader of an anti-Sandinista force known as the Democratic Revolutionary Alliance. Based primarily in the far south of the country, it resisted any alliances with the Contras. In February, the first untethered spacewalk took place, while hardly anyone in the U.S. noticed that Ethiopia had slipped into the worst famine in the history of the modern world. The summer Olympic Games would take place in L.A., with the USSR and Soviet Bloc boycotting them. Sally Ride would become the first American woman in space, and a Union Carbide plant in India would leak toxic gases that would kill more than 3,500 people. A global recession in the early '80s would lead to more than seventy U.S. banks failing, while the movies *Indiana Jones and the Temple of Doom* and *Ghostbusters* topped the Hollywood moneymaker list.

On the first of June, I got a call from my old friend and colleague, Simon Jolly, at the University of California. He was incredibly excited. He told me he had finally determined the chemical structure of the active molecules in a Caribbean mangrove tunicate, *Ecteinascidia turbinata*, based on collections we had made scuba diving in the West Indies some years earlier. The tunicate had shown strong antitumor activity on tissue culture plates during the expedition. It was one of the Jolly lab's primary targets. Simon wanted to know if I would be available for an expedition to the Caribbean coast of Central America, steaming from Panama to Cancún. We would focus on the collection of other Caribbean tunicate species throughout the great Mesoamerican Barrier Reef, which is second in size only to Australia's Great Barrier Reef. Also known as the "Great Maya Reef," it stretches over six hundred miles from the tip of Mexico's Yucatán Peninsula to Honduras. Isolated reefs crop out south from there, all the way to the San Blas Islands on Panama's largely uninhabited Caribbean shoreline. In addition to the countless invertebrates and fishes of this massive reef system, there are manatees, four species of sea turtles, and two kinds of crocodiles. The water is warm and usually crystal clear. It's a marine biologist's idea of heaven, an oceanic Elysium. I agreed to join Simon and his chemist colleagues for the trip.

I called Coquette to let her know and suggested we might meet up in Cancún at the end of the expedition. She was excited and agreed to meet me. She said she knew of a little "undiscovered" beach village south of Cancún called Puerto Morelos, where we could rent a beach house for as long as we wanted. It was near the coastal Maya ruins of Tulum, so she thought I'd find it especially fun. I called John Thornton to let him know about my forthcoming expedition and also to let him know that his daughter would be joining me in the Cancún area for a couple weeks, or maybe more. He asked if we could meet at Gabriela's for lunch the next day.

Over *pupusas* and beer, Thornton told me that Secretary of State George Shultz had received a special request from UNESCO asking for some help.

"The UN is worried about the level of rogue and renegade banditry in Guatemala, and they have particular concerns about Tikal National Park, which is a UNESCO World Heritage Site. In fact, it's one of the first designated, back in the late 70s, and a crown jewel in the UN's worldwide system. They've asked if the U.S. can use its influence to get some assurances that the park is being protected and is safe for tourists to visit. They know we hold more sway over the present administration in Guatemala than anyone else. The State Department wants feedback from the Agency, but we don't have any of our people in that area. As you know, it's very isolated, deep in the jungle in a region with no major cities anywhere nearby. The closest city is Belmopan, across the border in Belize. We'd send someone from our embassy in Belize, but we don't want to risk exposure at the border crossing between the two countries. It's a particularly snoopy border because of the friction between the Guatemalans, who still claim Belize belongs to them, and the Belizean and British authorities."

Continuing, Thornton said, "I know you've been to Tikal; it's a premier Maya site. It occurs to me that your expedition ship will likely stop over in Belize City, as it's the only large port between Panama and Cancún. If so, perhaps you might be able to slip away for a day to take a look at a village for us, just across the border in Guatemala, called Cidabenque. It's close to Tikal; you could be a gringo visitor heading to Tikal, simply stopping over in Cidabenque for coffee, or maybe you get lost along the way and stop for directions . . . whatever. I know you might be a bit gun shy after that experience in Quiché last year, but this should be perfectly safe and something you could do with an easy day trip out of Belize City."

I agreed to help them out, but I made it clear to Thornton that it was a personal favor to him and that it would probably be the last thing I did for the CIA. He said he understood and

413

appreciated my help. It sounded straightforward enough. *What could go wrong*? I thought.

PART IV. FINDING DESTINY

Sadness is but a wall between two gardens.

Kahlil Gibran, *Sand and Foam* (1926)

33

Cidabenque 4

June 1984

I saw the Archangel Michael floating on a cloud before me. He had the wings of a white dove and was wearing a beautiful blue robe that blended seamlessly into the cobalt sky behind him. His brown cape danced in the breeze, merging inconspicuously with his long, flowing brown hair. Beyond Michael, the blue sky darkened gradually into violet and then into a velvet black night, with stars and planets floating like algae on a gently rolling sea—a slow-motion dance of the cosmos. I could see the distant constellations and celestial bodies; Mars blushed red and content just above the horizon. From the top of Saint Michael's head emerged a crown of beautiful multicolored soft coral polyps, alive and writhing slowly about like drunken snakes. Saint Michael smiled serenely at me, extended his open hand, and said, "Odel, come with me. There are some things I want to show you."

In the distance I could see the Archangel Gabriel, in a white gown, the deliverer of messages and Michael's frequent companion. In one hand he held a trumpet, in the other a lily.

As Gabriel watched, Saint Mike and I set sail over the great green Petén. Below us, we saw screaming macaws flitting above the canopy and silent jaguars walking on the moist dark ground below. The otherworldly calls of toucans and the roars of howler monkeys rose up from the verdant wilderness beneath us. Michael said, "Do you see the North Star, Odel? It is your guide, your touchstone. It is the one thing that you can always trust. It is the star that shines on the lives of everyone north of the equator; but each of us must find our own way to follow it." As we flew north, toward the bright Polaris, we passed over the great Maya ruins of the Yucatán, across Mexico City, and over the Temples of the Sun and the Moon in Teotihuacan. Then we flew above the vast expanse of northern Mexico's *Gran Desierto* and on to Los Angeles, where we paused. Below me were my mother and father and my brother Lorenzo. They were packing our 1955 Oldsmobile, hooking up the old aluminum-shelled house trailer behind it, preparing to drive north into the high country of Montana. We followed them and saw them camped on a lakeshore, Dad showing Lorenzo and me how to rig a trout pole, attach the hook and sinker to the line, thread the wriggling night-crawler onto the barb. He was teaching us how to assemble an old, oiled canvas tent and build a proper campfire.

We moved on, and I saw my cousin Marco and me. I was leaving to go off to college and Marco was telling me he'd always be there for me, giving me a big Sicilian hug. "Odel," he said, "if you're ever in a serious jam and need some help, call me. I have connections, you know." And then I saw Penelope—the beautiful, flaxen-haired Penelope. But she wouldn't allow me to get close to her, staying just out of my grasp. "I just want to understand you," I said. She shook her head back and forth in slow, silent refusal, no words spilling from her mouth. We turned and flew back southward, to Managua. I saw Bob and Beatriz, laughing and happy, full of love for life and the land. They saw me and Beatriz said,

"*Amigo* Odel, you will always be welcome here. And bring your friend Mike along too." And Bob said, "Remember the words of the *Tao Te Ching* Odel, 'Nothing is gentler than water, yet nothing can withstand its force.'"

And then I saw Coquette. She was dreamlike in her beauty and serenity. We swooped down to her, and she spoke to me as a Siren. I embraced her, and she said, "Odel, I love you so, and I promise I will always protect you."

But then, in front of us, there appeared the Maya Hero Twins described in the *Popol Vuh— Hunahpu* and *Xbalanque*. They were on a journey to the great Maya underworld known as *Xibalba*, to meet the lords of the dark realm. *Hunahpu* spoke, telling me not to stay with Michael but to go with them, and if I did all the secrets of the Maya would be revealed to me. He said, "We are travelers, like you, and it is here that our journeys cross. We will show you what you have been searching for. Trust us."

I moved toward the Maya twins, but then I heard Coquette's melodic voice, lilting and sweet, and it drew me back to my vision of a beautiful chocolate-colored woman with flowing black hair. She was standing on the bank of a river, and on her zephyr dress, over her heart, was a circle with a dot in the center. She said, "Odel, I'm afraid. I think my role here has been completed, and now I do not have long. But before I leave you, please tell me of your love once again." And I knew that a dozen years or five hundred years, for an archangel, was but a blink of the eye.

When I opened my eyes, all was dark. I was on the ground, heavy water droplets falling from the jungle canopy onto my face. In the silence all I heard was my heartbeat. Aromas of organic tropical soil, bifurcating white fungi, rotting jungle fruits, and my own body steamrolled over me, conflating me with the damp earth.

I tried to stand, but my right leg was numb and frozen. I could taste blood in my mouth. With my left leg and my arms, I dragged my body a foot or two until I ran into a tree trunk and pulled myself into a sitting position against it. I vomited, and my mouth filled with rancid blood from my stomach. Then I heard the first shot.

To my left and my right, there was sporadic gunfire. It sounded like both rifles and handguns. I could hear voices filtered through the damp jungle foliage, but couldn't make out was what being said. My head was a fog. I wasn't sure if I'd lost my vision or if it was just pitch dark. And then a light appeared, swinging back and forth but moving in my direction. From twenty feet away, it found my face.

"Over here. I thee him. Christ, he lookth like a thombie!"

And I heard a woman's voice. "I see him. I'll call in the location."

Together they tried to get me to my feet. I mumbled, "Snake."

"Thit, I see it. It lookth like a fer-de-lance."

She screamed, "We've got to get him out of here, now!"

They dragged me through the jungle. Another man showed up to help. More gunshots in the distance. I saw a clearing ahead and in it a sedan. As they dragged me toward the car, two men in Guatemalan army uniforms broke through the foliage about fifteen feet away. "Get him into the car!" the woman yelled, as she moved quickly toward the two men.

"Leilani, no—don't!"

She caught the first man in the throat with a lightning strike of her hand, and he went straight down, gasping for air. But the second man was fast, and he kicked her hard. She fell against a tree, sprang back up and lunged at him. But he'd already swung his gun in her direction. The muzzle of the rifle was just three feet from her chest. The bullet went through her with such impact that it lifted her off the ground and hurled her back against the same tree she'd bounced off,

419

shredding her sternum, exploding her heart into a dozen pieces, and leaving a massive exit wound in her upper back.

John Thornton's face drew into a grotesque and contorted grimace, and he let out a scream that reverberated through the jungle like a wild wretched beast from the Maya underworld. I couldn't speak or move. As the compass in my mind began to spin wildly out of control, my eyes closed and I felt myself collapsing in slow motion into the abyss of a black and bottomless cenote.

34

Gorgas U.S. Army Hospital
Panama City, July 1984

I had been unconscious for six days. When I opened my eyes for the first time, Thornton was there, staring at me. He said nothing, but the look on his face, the profound sadness in his gaze, brought it all back to me.

"Tell me it isn't true, John. Please tell me it was just a bad dream."

Tears rolled down his cheeks; he slowly shook his head back and forth and I could see the ghosts in his eyes. He looked old and demoralized. "Odel, I don't have words to express how sorry I am. But thank god you're going to make it."

I wanted details, but I didn't. So I said nothing, closed my eyes, and let exhaustion drag me back into unconsciousness. As I slipped away, I saw myself on Jacob's Ladder, climbing slowly, one step at a time, with Michael and Gabriel helping me on either side. The steps were carved with undecipherable glyphs of Mayan, Nahuatl, Egyptian, and other ancient languages that I did not understand. Lesser angels from the clouds above were descending the ladder toward the Earth, but when we met they passed through me as if I were vapor. Moving upward, it occurred to me that in the clouds there would be neither heaven nor hell, no seraphs of ardor nor depraved demons, but instead simply a place of transformation where I would be given a new life, a renewal or second chance to be.

Two days later, I opened my eyes again. Nestor Papadakis was there. He, too, had a look of profound grief.

"Where am I, Nestor?"

"You're in the army's hospital on Ancon Hill, in Panama. It's the closest place we could get you to that had antivenom. You're going to pull through, and it's likely you won't lose your leg, though the doc's not entirely sure yet. You may not feel like it right now, but you're lucky to be alive."

"What the hell happened?"

Nestor took a deep breath. "It's a complicated story, Odel. But, I think you know that we lost Coquette. And another man, from the British High Commission in Belmopan."

"Where's Thornton?"

"He's with the agency's liaison unit at Southern Command headquarters in Doral, Florida. He's a mess. Coquette was his only child. And he'd already lost his wife. It's all just fuckin' horrible, man. He feels so sorry about asking you to go into that stinking village."

I felt as if I were in a state of suspended animation, or in a dream, that I might wake up any minute and Coquette would be beside me in her big bed in her townhouse in Santa Monica. A hundred thoughts echoed in my head, but I couldn't pin any of them down.

"I want the whole story, Nestor. And I've got nothing but time."

Nestor told me it had been a seemingly innocuous situation. Just a little Intel gathering to help with a report the Agency was preparing for the State Department. But they had gotten bad information from Guatemala's Defense Department. And because my ship had been delayed getting to Belize City, it had given Polyphemus time to get from his encampment west of Flores, to Cidabenque. He'd kept his movements so secretive, no one knew where he was. But the peasants knew he was approaching. They almost always knew when trouble was imminent. They had fled the village just before I got to it. I just stumbled into the wrong place at the wrong time. But when Coquette had found out from her dad where I was headed, she immediately flew to Guatemala City, hooked up with an Intel analyst friend of hers at the U.S. Embassy there, and started looking into things on her own.

"About the same time your ship pulled into port, Coquette realized that Polyphemus and his private army were heading to Cidabenque. She got in touch with her dad, and they rendezvoused in Belmopan. They managed to recruit a few of the British agents in Belize who were jungle savvy and immediately headed across the border. They found you nearly dead, Odel, with a fer-de-lance bite, dehydration, and your face and arms covered with leeches and ticks and god knows what else. You were a goddamn mess. You'd become jungle fodder for the wildlife. You wouldn't have lasted much longer."

"Who dropped the bomb in the plaza?" I asked. "The timing was perfect on that—Polyphemus was about to pump lead into me when the explosion occurred."

Nestor chuckled softly. "That wasn't a bomb, Odel. It was a lightning strike on the church steeple. Took off the entire bell tower. Must have been providence; some higher force smiling on you."

I had to think about that one for a few minutes. "And what happened to Polyphemus? Did the SOB get away?"

"Coquette took him out before she and John found you. She broke his fat neck with her bare hands."

"She was much more than just a contractor with the Agency, wasn't she?" I asked.

Nestor simply said, "Yes."

It was the answer I suspected, but didn't want to hear. "How long am I going to be in here, Nestor?"

"We're not sure. You got a pretty good dose of venom, and it traveled in your bloodstream for a while before you got here to the hospital. You lost a lot of blood, bleeding through your nose, gums, and your gut. There was a fair bit of localized necrosis on your ankle and calf; they had to remove that, and now you need a little time to heal before they'll let you out. They might have to remove a bit more of your calf, but you'll be able to walk. You were close to renal failure when they got you here, but the docs have stabilized your kidneys. Thank god you didn't go into hemorrhagic shock."

My head was still foggy, and my brain was slow to put things together. "What's John going to do?"

"I'm not sure. But I've known him for a long time, and I know that girl was his pride and joy. I wouldn't be surprised if he just dropped out—retired or something. Right now, in Doral, they're probably trying to talk him out of it, though. He oversees every operation we run in Central America, and he's at the top of his game; he's probably the best talent the Agency has ever had in the region. Thornton's the kind of guy who thinks like a chess master, but imagine a game of chess with dozens of players; he's able to anticipate everyone's moves ahead of time. He's really irreplaceable. But . . . well, even Homer nods."

Nestor's eyes had a faraway look. He said, "John was my mentor. He and Coquette and I worked together on so many ops . . . they were like family to me."

I thought again about how far off my first impression of Thornton had been. "And, what about my colleagues on the *Double Helix* in Belize City?"

"Someone from the British High Commission went to the ship and explained to them that you'd be bitten by a fer-de-lance while you were knocking around some Maya ruins in the jungle and had been medevacked to Panama."

I tried to absorb it all, but grief overwhelmed me. "We had so many plans," I mumbled. "Why couldn't it have been me?"

Nestor had a faraway look in his eyes as he softly said, "In the end, time is the only currency that matters."

"Nestor, please leave me alone now."

"Sure, Odel. I'll be hanging around here until John gets back. Just let one of the nurses know if you want to talk anymore."

35

Nepenthe
Fall–Winter 1984

I decided to call Bob and Beatriz. They'd left voice messages for me, but I'd not returned any of them. Time is a curious thing. I hadn't had a serious conversation with anyone other than Thornton or Nestor Papadakis since I left the hospital in Panama five months earlier. I'd sunk into a depression, turning down a fall teaching offer from Northwestern Washington University and hardly leaving my apartment. The sum of all my losses felt beyond my grasp. A kind of opaque film settled over my mind and I didn't even think about my research, which now seemed inconsequential. Sadness hung on me like a wretched fog. I fell asleep with it, and I woke with it. A dismal melancholy oozed out of my pores and brought uncontrollable tears to my eyes at inconvenient times. When the tears came they seemed to uproot my sense of place, fragment by fragment, until I felt so ungrounded I hardly knew where I was, let alone what to do. I was adrift, with no anchorage in sight, struggling to suppress the recurring image in my mind of Coquette's body slamming against the tree, her shirt growing red with a large and grotesque amoeba of blood. Several times a day, I compulsively pulled one of her old sweaters out of my top dresser drawer, burying my face in it to breathe in her fragrances—scents of her skin, hair, and the light plumeria cologne she favored. Never before in my life had I imagined craving solitude, but now it was all I wanted, all I could deal with, even though it infused me with ennui.

I read books, struggling to concentrate. I read the *Tao Te Ching* again, but found it shallow and useless. I reread Hermann Hesse's *Glass Bead Game* and John Fowles *The Magus*. If Hesse and Fowles couldn't offer me some insight, no one could. It was good distraction. And I reread Thomas Mann's *Death in Venice*, which resonated with me in a way it hadn't when I'd first read it in college many years earlier. I sat for hours rethinking, reliving every moment Coquette and I had spent together, remembering the things she had said, the mysteries that will forever surround her, the feelings of both emotional and physical love that I had with her. I thought about my years with Penelope and concluded we had had friendship and erotic love, but it was probably never enough to sustain a marriage. But what I was unable to do, was to think about the future; where to go from here. I seemed stuck in place, even though my mind was imbued with a sense of inquietude. I felt Seattle had changed so much that it no longer held any attraction for me. Even Northwestern Washington seemed to have lost its charm. But eventually I realized, of course, that it was I who had changed, not the place.

As the months of my solitude drifted by, I began to re-read scholarly papers and books on the Maya and their cycles of life, their creation myths, their legion of deities, and the many manifestations of the Feathered Serpent. A commonality among the apparitions of *Quetzalcoatl*, or *Kukulkan*, or any of the dozen other names the deity went by, was its ability to transport humans through space and time, to be a link or bridge between human and godly worlds. As I delved deeper into stories of the chimeric snake, I remembered the beautiful carved stone bench uprights in *La Señora's* yard in Barrio Nueva Esperanza. And I thought about the woman and her daughter, Destiny, and my visits to their home. I suddenly had the thought that the stone carvings of Quetzalcoatl at their house might somehow provide a mythical, or even a tangible arch that could connect me from the past to what lay ahead. As more time went by, I began to obsess about the carved stones. And I realized that I'd developed an emerging ache or desire for something that does not actually exist; something other than the present, a turning toward the past or toward the future, not as active discontent or poignant sadness but a languid dreamy wistfulness. What the Portuguese call *saudade*. But of course, I could not go back, and knew not the way forward. Yet I needed to do something. I had to regain a sense of agency in my life. It's an odd thing, the way your mind begins withdrawing from circumstances it knows you must leave behind.

I had a limp and a bad scar on my right calf and foot where necrotic tissue had been cut away by the surgeons; now a permanent reminder of nearly losing my leg to a fer-de-lance bite. Nestor became a good friend, clement and caring, dropping by to see me every couple of weeks. On one visit, he told me that more than three thousand CIA personnel were now in Central America, most of them involved in the training of nearly twenty thousand Contras—even though CIA director William Casey publicly stated, "There is no chance that the Contras will be able to overthrow the Sandinista government." It all seemed like madness to me.

"Nestor, at this point, all Reagan's doing is destroying Nicaragua's economy and creating misery for the Nicas for decades to come. Ortega isn't going anywhere."

He agreed.

In September, and again in October, the CIA, with a handful of Contras as cover, attacked Nicaraguan patrol boats at Puerto Sandino. It amounted to little more than harassment.

On November 4, the first free general election to be held in Nicaragua since the revolution took place. A phenomenal ninety-four percent of eligible voters had registered, and seventy-five percent of them voted. Observers from the European Economic Community and a host of international organizations from the U.S., Canada, and Ireland were on hand to assure the elections were fair and legitimate. Daniel Ortega won by a landslide. But, taking a cue from the Marxist revolutionary playbook, his first move as a freely elected president was to declare a national emergency and suspend civil rights.

I called Bob's office phone number. He picked up and said, "Well, my long-lost *amigo*, Odel. Where the hell have you been?"

I recounted to him the story that Thornton and I had agreed on. Coquette had been on a research-writing project in the Petén, though I didn't know where exactly, and had encountered a rogue army gang. She got caught off guard and found herself trapped in gunfire between some army regulars and the gang, catching a stray bullet from the latter. Her dad had gotten a call from Guatemala City, where the army had taken her body.

"Oh my god, Odel—I'm speechless. I'm so very, very sorry, my friend. I know there's nothing I can do or say that will help, but please consider coming down and staying with us for a while. You've lost so much in the past year or so, you need to find a way to decompress and regroup. Maybe getting out of Seattle will help your psyche. You know Beatriz and I are here for you."

"Thanks, Roberto. I need to spend Christmas up here with Coquette's dad and also with my own family in L.A. But maybe in January I could fly down for a while."

"Yes, please do. *Nuestra casa es tu casa.* Stay for a while with us. Settle in here."

"I'll think about it. Thanks Bob."

John Thornton retired. He wanted nothing more to do with the Agency. Like me, he was buried under his own mountain of sadness. We both knew that the image of Coquette's death had been burned into our memory forever, and neither of us had any notion of how to grapple with it. He was staying with Gabriela and her daughters, and I ended up having Christmas dinner at their place. Thornton gave me a box that had been in Coquette's bedroom closet; in it were all the letters I'd written to her. It would be a long time before I could look at them. John had talked with Penelope and her parents, telling them the same story we'd agreed on. From what he could judge, they didn't know that Coquette and I had been lovers, or that we even knew one other. It seemed the best way to leave things. Even in death, secrets remain. As the old *curandera* from Managua had told me long ago, some secrets may be for the best.

Penelope had moved on to a new, overtly lesbian lifestyle, dressing more butch and seemingly having no interest in men at all. I hoped she was happy. I wanted to believe that I loved her, though it was surely misplaced love.

I spent some time with my brother Lorenzo and my cousin Marco, and a half-dozen of my aunts and uncles who I was never really close to. It was part of the closure I needed. Marco and I looked so much alike that, as children, people often mistook us for brothers. Even as adults, I was far more similar in appearance to Marco than I was to Lorenzo. Our aunts and uncles marveled at it and offered endless explanations, mostly based on the theory that Lorenzo had somehow gotten "short-changed in the Sicilian gene department." But of course, look-alike first cousins are common.

In January, I packed two large suitcases—one filled with sewing needles and thread, light bulbs, toilet paper, and other essentials—and headed to Managua. I decided to rent a car for a month, with an option to roll the contract over to six or twelve months. I made the familiar drive from the airport to

Bob and Beatriz's house. As I drove through the city, memories of driving to the old *curandera's* home in Barrio Nueva Esperanza flashed through my mind. I thought about Destiny. *I wonder what has become of those two unusual women.* Suddenly the name of the barrio took on new meaning for me. *Maybe I should try to visit La Señora again, if she'll see me.*

When Beatriz saw me, she said, "Odel, what has happened to you. You are gray as a ghost and thin as a rail. When was the last time you saw sunshine and ate a decent meal?"

I tried to formulate a response to her question, but my thoughts became entangled in the complex imbroglio of the past year and no words came out of my mouth.

They had fixed up the guest room for me, even putting an old used TV in it, as well as a small fridge and a well-stocked liquor cabinet with several different vintages of *Flor de Caña.* They told me I could stay as long as I wanted. I realized I was envious of them; they had what I had dreamed of having with Coquette. They were best of friends, two people who knew each other deeply, knew one another's strengths and weaknesses, wisdoms and foibles, and completely accepted each other for who they were. They had resolute trust and love.

The first couple weeks were suffused with painful discussions about Coquette and other sad matters. I slept terribly, waking to horrible nightmares in dark jungle settings. I was sure my maudlin ways were becoming a drag on my friends, but I couldn't seem to pick myself up. Beatriz did her best to reassure me, saying, "Odel, there *are* times in life when the best thing to do is nothing at all." Bob said, "If you must have a midlife crisis Odel, this is the place to have it. You're with friends here."

One night when I couldn't sleep, I remembered the baby-food jar of nepenthe that Rocío's grandmother had given me. I'd thrown it into one of my bags when I packed for the flight to Managua. I decided to give it a try. *Abuela* had said to put a teaspoon in a cup of tea. But when I removed the rusty cap of the jar, I decided to add the teaspoon to a double shot of *Flor de Caña. Couldn't hurt*, I thought.

That night I slept straight through and had no nightmares. In the morning, I felt good. Beatriz even commented on it. "You look particularly well this morning, Odel. Good night's sleep?"

The next night I did the same thing, and the night after that. In a week the nepenthe was gone, and I felt better than I had in months. The dark jungle nightmares had vanished, and I sensed they might not come back. Our dinner conversations began to turn to happy stories about the good times Coquette and I had had, what a character my dad had been, and how well things were going at the National University in Managua. I felt that perhaps I'd turned a corner. As if I was gradually being reinvented. Was it the nepenthe? Or was it Bob and Beatriz, or just the passage of time?

One night after dinner, I spoke of my period of solitude after Coquette's death. As I did, I was reminded of something Destiny had said to me long ago: *To find yourself, to be true to your nature and your innermost yearnings, cannot be achieved without solitude, which you need not seek as it will find you.* When I told Bob and Beatriz of this, Beatriz, the wise and beautiful Beatriz said to me, "I know that the loss of Coquette has left a deep wound in your heart. It will heal, though the scar will last a lifetime. You cannot erase the past. But, Odel, you are lucky in one very important way. You experienced the kind of deep and heartfelt love with Coquette that many people never glimpse in their lives. I believe that you and Coquette loved one another fully, as Roberto and I do, without limits. And that is such a rare and beautiful thing. But nothing is forever, and when great loss comes, I suppose it forces us to confront the ephemeral nature of all things, good and bad, especially those worldly matters we cherish most and that we wish would continue into eternity. Yet, even when love vanishes, we are left with an irrevocable personal joy that it had entered our lives and so profoundly animated us for the time it did. And no one can ever take that joy from us. Do not let your losses imprison your spirit, *querido amigo*. Instead, adopt your wound and let the scar grow to become a positive force in your life, a strong supportive spine to brace your spirit. Trust that memories are life's way of framing our future. You have always been an enthusiastic participant in life. I know you my friend, and I know there is a rainbow lurking in that dark cloud on your shoulders."

After a moment of contemplative silence, Bob said, "Perhaps you've been chasing your own shadows Odel, and now it's time to turn around and look in the other direction. You only get one shot at life *compadre*. Take the time you need for processing things, but remember that you'll never get that time back—it's gone. Let the past inform you, but don't be shackled by it. Every day you must live life as fully as you can." His comments made Beatriz smile, and he went on. "You've been down so long, but I sense you might be turning a corner. Maybe you should consider teaching a course here. When you're ready, I mean. The students would flock to your class. The pay isn't great, but you've got free room and board here as long as you want. The spring semester starts the first of February. I'll bet you could get a contract of some kind by then."

Addressing both of them I replied, "Thanks, I'll definitely think about it. You know, I so admire the day-to-day optimism you two have, even when the morning newspaper brings grim news, you remain so confident and positive."

Beatriz replied, "The way we spend our days is how we end up living our lives. The world is a beautiful and hopeful place, so when bad news appears we must avoid its gloom and focus on the good things around us, move toward higher goals and aspirations. And as Bob says, living with joy is essential to good health and long life."

It was then that I told them about the inheritance from my father's property and the legal settlement from the museum.

Bob said, "Dude, you could live like a king in Managua on thirty-five thousand dollars a year. Just move here! Take a job with us at the university. We could teach seminars together, take students to the coast on field trips . . . It would be a blast! They'd give you a full professorship, or a part-time gig, whatever you wanted, in a heartbeat. I'm tired of teaching the invertebrate zoology course; I've been doing it for ten years—teach that one, please!"

Beatriz chimed in, "And I'm tired of teaching the marine ecology course. Take that one too!"

I decided it might be a healthy thing to do. "But just one course," I said, "in the spring semester."

It was agreed. Bob and I met with the dean of science the following week, and we decided that I would teach marine ecology in the spring. It was a one-semester contract, but the dean made it clear that if things went well, we could discuss a permanent position.

Between then and the start of classes, only Spanish was spoken among Bob and Beatriz and me. I needed to polish *mi Español*. Beatriz gave me her lecture notes and slides for the course she'd taught for years, and I studied them intensely. It was distracting. It was a good thing.

36

Finding Destiny

1985

The year started off with more bad news from the Sandinista government. They decided to set up neighborhood "watch committees"—asking neighbors to spy on neighbors. They also instituted a press-gang draft, which immediately caused young men to begin fleeing to Honduras, or worse, to run to the Contras. Newspapers reported that five thousand civilians had died in 1984 due to the "Contra-Sandinista War." The country's economy was in shambles. Bob and Beatriz did their best to stay optimistic, but I could tell they were disheartened.

In April, about halfway through the spring semester, I resolved to try to visit *La Señora* again. I mentioned it to Bob and Beatriz over dinner, but Beatriz said she'd heard the old woman had died.

"What about her daughter, Destiny?"

"I don't know," Beatriz said, "I will give Dolores a call tomorrow and ask if she knows anything. But frankly, Odel, I don't think it is wise to see anyone from that family again."

On my way to the university the next morning, I decided to drive by the house in Barrio Nueva Esperanza. I could tell from the street that the place was deserted. The marigolds were all dead, the yard was littered with trash, and weeds were taking over. I parked in front and walked to the door. It was locked. I knocked, even though I knew the house was empty. The one-legged grackle was nowhere to be seen. The place had a sad, forlorn look to it, like a tired old black-and-white photograph. I walked to where the beautiful stone bench had been. The heavy, water-polished rock slab now lay on the ground, barely discernable beneath the dandelions and tall grass. But the two end pieces, the carved *Quetzalcoatl* uprights, were gone.

That night, Beatriz said Dolores told her that when the old woman died, the daughter had moved away. No one knew where she'd gone. The house sat empty and no one in the neighborhood wanted anything to do with it.

Something in the back of my mind told me I should try to track down the girl. I remembered her parting words, so long ago: *Perhaps we will meet again, farther along in your pilgrimage.* I decided I'd look for Destiny, though I had no idea where to begin.

By the time the spring semester was about over, my Spanish had improved considerably. My students congratulated me, some of them mentioning that I'd been rather hard to understand the first few weeks. I thanked them all for tolerating my language learning curve. Apparently, the course was a rousing success, and during final exams week the department head and dean asked if I would be willing to be considered for a permanent faculty appointment. I expressed my appreciation but told them I needed to think about it. Bob, of course, knew the offer was coming but he wanted the news to come from the administration, so he hadn't said anything to me.

That night, the three of us were sipping rum on the veranda and discussing the idea of me taking a position at the university. It was a warm and muggy tropical evening, but a soft breeze made it comfortable enough. There was a child's birthday party going on across the street, with music and laughter. A new street-taco vendor had recently set up shop on the corner thirty yards away, his bright gas lamp casting a happy glow. The neighborhood had a gay and lively look to it. It was a nice barrio, though not what you'd call upscale.

I told them I didn't think I was ready to make the kind of commitment necessary for a regular faculty appointment. A full-time job, with a significant teaching load, would be demanding—probably two courses each semester. I also felt I'd lost much of my former enthusiasm for teaching. And it would mean moving myself to Managua more-or-less permanently, and I wasn't yet convinced that was what I wanted. I still had thoughts of living in Coyoacán, or maybe even Cusco. Beatriz suggested I take a half-time position with the university on a year-to-year contract, just to try it out for a while. I agreed that might be a good idea.

Once final exams were over and I had more free time, I looked for a place to rent near the sprawling campus. As happy as Bob and Beatriz were to have me stay with them, I didn't want to wear out my welcome. I found an attractive place that was biking distance to my campus office. With two bedrooms, the house was larger than I needed, but the price and location were perfect, and most importantly it already had a phone line connection. Getting a new line to a house in Managua had become frustratingly difficult and could take up to a year. I planned to use the summer break to start on my memoir or autobiography, or whatever it might end up being, that Coquette and Beatriz and others had urged me to write. I would use my campus office as a writing venue, keeping the clutter out of my house and also keeping me in touch with the university community. I realized that between the letters Coquette and I had written to one another, my field notebooks, my research papers, and my memory, I could compile a fairly detailed diary of the tumultuous past five years. I could write that story first and then go back in time, should I wish to. Summer session began at the university and I started to write.

As I began writing my story a new consideration grew in my mind. It occurred to me that my prescient dreams of crossing the jungle river had even deeper significance that I'd thought. In making that crossing, I had indeed gotten to Coquette, the dark siren who had been calling to me. But it also had been a passage that opened the door to a new world for me, one that led me away from my previous life and into a journey of discovery, challenge, and perhaps even some wisdom. Coquette truly *was* a siren; one that offered me not just temptation, but new awareness and strength. Strength to recognize and follow a new path that I found myself on. And strength to let go of Penelope, to save a young girl from the razor-sharp slashes of a broken beer bottle, and to step out of my "science silo" and untether my mind for wondrous visions and travels.

Despite the lingering damage from the earthquake and the civil war, the National University's campus was a beautiful and peaceful place, with many gardens and tree-lined paths. One day in July as I walked to the cafeteria for lunch, I saw thirty feet in front of me a thin woman with beautiful long black hair. Her back was to me; she was standing in front of a kiosk covered with ads that students had stuck up with pins and staples, selling their bikes, looking for rides or roommates and such. She seemed rather old to be a student, and she wasn't dressed in the typical '80s college student garb of jeans and a T-shirt. Something about her seemed familiar, so I approached. When I was twenty feet from her, she turned around and looked straight at me as if she knew I was there. A streak of pure white hair cascaded down from her head like a mercurial waterfall.

"Hello, *señor*. It has been a long time."

"Destiny! Yes, it has. I . . . heard that your mother passed away. I'm so sorry. She was a lovely woman and an important person in my life. As were you. I hope you are doing well."

"Thank you, *Señor* Odel. I am fine."

I can't believe she remembers my name! "What are you doing on the university campus?" I asked.

"I am a student. After Mamá died, I decided to go to school. It is something I'd always wanted to do, but my mother was never very encouraging. I know I'm a bit old for such a thing, but I am determined to get my degree in psychology. As you might guess, it is an interest of mine."

Destiny was wearing a lovely dress that fell to mid-calf. The dress flattered her perfect body, and I was struck by how attractive she was. She bore that unique and innate beauty so often seen in multiracial persons. And it occurred to me that she was about the same height, build, and skin color as Coquette. In fact, I realized for the first time that she bore a striking resemblance to Coquette.

"I have been unable to sell my mother's house. People seem to think it is haunted or something! The people in that barrio are very superstitious. I was staying in one of the student housing projects but was just told that I would now have to find my own place. I am pretty new to all this, so I was looking at these postings to see if I might come across something. And how about you, Mr. Odel, what are you doing on this campus?"

"It's just Odel. Odel Bernini. I'm teaching part time in the Biology Department. Destiny, I was just on my way to lunch at the cafeteria. Would you care to join me? I would love the opportunity to chat with you."

Her generous, dyad, gold and emerald eyes looked directly into mine and seemed illuminated with a pure and joyous radiance. She smiled a familiar, serene, knowing smile and said, "Yes, it is time we talk, isn't it." I thought I was picking up the scent of plumeria, though I didn't see any plants in the nearby garden.

Her story was fascinating, and it did not jibe at all with the third-hand stories and rumors that Beatriz had heard. But she had indeed been the child of a difficult birth, and she had no siblings.

"By the time I started elementary school, the other children were already beginning to say bad things about me. My eye heterochromia and Mallen streak seemed to frighten them for some reason."

She knows the technical names of her conditions. She's obviously a self-educated woman.

"Of course, they also knew my mother was a *curandera*, and that I was somehow different. As I grew older, their teasing got worse. I began to feel I was cursed. By the time I entered high school, the girls were calling my mother and me witches, and the boys would frequently express obscenities at me. Children can be so cruel. I became reclusive, not wanting to go out of my house for fear of encountering more ridicule. Even my mother's neighbors gave us strange looks. I turned inward and to books. I read every book I could get my hands on, especially philosophy, psychology and medicine. I did not really understand my affliction, which made me insecure. I finally broke down; I just couldn't take it anymore and I refused to go to school. When I was fifteen, my mother sent me to stay with a friend of hers who lived in Los Angeles, and I was able to finish high school there. Kids in the U.S. didn't seem to mind my oddities. It was in California that I came to realize that there is no such thing as a "curse"—that concept is just voodoo nonsense. What I had been born with was actually a gift. I believe that many things we might think of as hardships or burdens are actually gifts in disguise. We simply need to alter our way of thinking about them, step out of the reality we're stuck in to see them in a new light." She said it all matter-of-factly, with a lightness of spirit.

Destiny's comment made me reflect on my hyperosmia, and how it had taken me years to learn to appreciate it—and to finally realize that it, too, was not an affliction but a gift.

"I graduated from high school and worked for a few years in L.A., but I missed my mother, and she was beginning to have frequent illnesses, so I came home. But I fell back into my old reclusive ways. That was when I met you. And it was when my mother was living the last of her days in this world. But my mother's death forced me to start changing my habits. And now, here I am!"

We had a long, leisurely lunch and shared much of our personal histories with one another, although I didn't mention Coquette. I was drawn to her candid ways, to her pellucid way of speaking. I enjoyed talking with her so much that, when she said she had to go to meet someone to look at an apartment, I didn't want her to leave. It was impulsive, but I blurted it out: "If you're free tonight, would you like to have dinner with me? I'm renting a house near campus; I'd enjoy showing it to you and preparing us a light supper. I feel we have so much more to talk about."

I was worried she might think I was being too forward. She did seem shy, perhaps even guileless. But she responded comfortably. "That is very kind of you. I would enjoy continuing our conversation over dinner. And we do have a great deal more to talk about."

We agreed on a time and I gave her directions to my place. As I walked back to my office, I chuckled to myself. *Wait until Beatriz finds out I spent most of the day with La Señora's mysterious daughter!*

I made a simple dish of roasted vegetables and a grilled red snapper I picked up at the fish market on my way home. For reasons I'm still not clear on, I wasn't certain if offering her a drink would be appropriate. But I bungled my way along. "Destiny, I don't know if you drink alcohol, but may I offer you a beer or a *Cuba Libre* or something while I cook?"

"Well, I'm not much of a drinker, but I'll try whatever you're having."

We sipped our *Cuba Libres*, and after dinner we sipped a *Flor de Caña*, and then we sipped another. My house had a small covered porch and some comfortable chairs, and we sat in the tropical evening air watching fireflies dance in the yard. Eventually I asked her to tell me about her special gift, hoping she didn't think I was prying.

"I knew from an early age that I was somehow different from the other children. At night in bed, I would have visions of my playmates—just little things, a few seconds or so in which I could see them playing in the schoolyard the next day, or several days in the future. Sometimes I felt a foreboding, as if something was hiding in the shadows. Like the slightest scent of wet copal wood even before a rain begins. I knew things before they happened, although I cannot explain how. My mother called them premonitions. And those little visions would always come to pass. As time went on I learned that, by focusing, I could see clear snatches of a person's future. And as I grew older, I discovered that by holding someone's hands and concentrating, looking deeply into their eyes, the visions could be extended and grow farther out in time. My mother said I was a conjurer. I had the ability to summon forth images in my mind, invoked by the spirit and feelings I sensed in another. And the deeper I concentrated on the vision, the greater it resonated, like little echoes bumping the boundaries back farther and farther until I had a clear vision of the person at some future point in time. But the farther into the future I pushed them, the more vague the visions became. The details would be fuzzy and they would appear as if through a filter or through gauze. I have no idea how it happens, but it seems to be a kind of prescience. I cannot engage with everyone, but you were especially open and easy to see into. I believe you, too, are a mystic, Odel."

With a slight smile I said, "I doubt that I am a mystic!"

But she replied, "You know, it is said that a mystic is simply one who is able to surrender completely to their surroundings, to let go of their everyday self and allow the universe to take over their thoughts and actions—take over their being. In doing so, they are able to see behind the human conventions that bind us, to see even beyond consciousness. From deep within, perhaps from a collective human unconsciousness, ancient images may surface. For some, this may be a religious experience. But for others, it is just a movement from one conscious world into another, parallel world. This can be a form of transcendence that allows one to see otherwise concealed connections and information. While your future does not exist yet, there are still clues that suggest the forward path of your life. Perhaps the sharing of my vision itself affects your course of being. And I believe you know, Odel, that some people are even able to see their own future in their dreams."

Her words made me hesitate. "But what exactly do you mean when you say you can 'see into' another?" I asked.

"When I can connect with someone—deeply connect, as I did with you—it is as if I see into their brain . . . or deeper, into their soul. I don't concentrate on the center of what I see; I focus on the edges, for it is there that their future is emerging. In the penumbra of their thoughts, I feel their emotions, their pains, and their joys. I see them following a trajectory, or path forward, and I sense things about it. It's hard to explain. Perhaps it is no more than a form of extreme empathy. But I do know that when fully aroused, the brain becomes receptive to all manner of ideas and details. Sometimes a small shift in perception is all that is needed. You see, I trust myself, and time has proven me correct. It seems I was correct about you. You have been on a journey, and it has brought you here. It has brought you back to me."

I suddenly had the feeling I'd known Destiny for a very long time, or perhaps even in a former life. She had a beguiling and peaceful smile on her face, and her words hung in the air. The look in her magical bicolored eyes told me all I needed to know. And then she said the words before I could get them out of my own mouth.

"Odel, I sense that you have a desire to make love with me. I feel the same stirrings in myself. But I must tell you, I am not so experienced with such things. You might have to show me the ways and be patient with me."

And together, we yielded to our sweet surrender.

We spent the next five nights together at my house. It was divine. She wasn't experienced, but she was curious, open-minded, and relaxed yet with an adventuresome spirit. Her naiveté only heightened the sensual and playful aspects of our lovemaking. Her empathy was strong, her desire to learn was boundless, and her energy extraordinary. And Destiny had a delightful sense of humor. On the sixth day I suggested that, since she still hadn't found anyplace to move in to, she take the spare bedroom in my house. I told her she could stay there until she found her own apartment. I also told her she could stay for as long as she wished.

As time passed we became very comfortable together, and as more time passed we found the bond of our friendship growing stronger and stronger. She taught me how to cook some new Nica dishes, and I taught her some gringo kitchen tricks. She told me hilarious stories of her mother's clients, and that her mom used to proclaim, "The Virgin of Guadalupe is my business partner!" Our sex was more fun than it was steamy, more relaxing than exhilarating, and more comfortable than I'd have ever guessed it could be. There was no drama around it; just trusting, happy contentment. We seemed a natural fit in every way. There wasn't anything she didn't enjoy in the bedroom. She was like a kid in a candy shop for the first time in her life. And Destiny had a unique ability to anticipate my desires that made her giggle with satisfaction. I tried to reciprocate in every way I knew how, and she happily helped me learn what she found most enjoyable and what she desired.

But perhaps most startling, her body was uncannily similar to Coquette's; the tone of her golden-bronze skin, the flow of her hair, her high cheekbones that spoke to Native American ancestry in her bloodline, her classically slender arms and legs. Even the extraordinary gold sprinkles that dusted her emerald-colored right eye. And, most remarkably, her scents were even the same as Coquette's—her hair and body aromas, and her delightfully sweet herbal bouquet when we made love. It seemed a preternatural similarity.

We concluded that we were compatible, and we enjoyed each other's company in a peaceful and fulfilling way. Destiny was also a candid and reliable woman. She was sincere and genuine; I trusted her, and she trusted me. Sometimes, in the middle of the night, waking to find Destiny lying next to me, I felt I saw a saint in her sleeping face. I came to believe she was truly an old soul, born with a wisdom that takes most people decades to learn, if ever. She was artless, natural, and seemed to have no deep or dark secrets; she was just who she appeared to be. We became best of friends and contented lovers. As the weeks turned into months, we established our routines and found strong compatibility in the daily patterns and pleasures of our lives. Our most enjoyable times were when we were alone together, reading books as we snuggled on the couch, preparing a meal in the kitchen, and, of course, rollicking in the bedroom.

One night I asked her to tell me more about her family, and I apologized for not remembering her mother's name.

"My mother was Circe. It's an unusual name; most people just called her *Señora*. I never knew my father and know nothing about him. My mother did not speak of him—it is as if he simply never existed. She died of an aggressive cancer called liposarcoma. Her family was from the Miskito Coast, near Bluefields. She was the oldest of three daughters that my grandmother had, and all three of them moved to Managua as they finished high school. One of them went to the university and eventually became a professor here. That was long ago, of course. The other became a successful businesswoman. But Mamá was different. She followed the ways of her mother, my *abuela*, and decided to help people with her gift. That is why she inherited the cards. Her sisters distanced themselves from her. I met them only a few times, when I was very young. Eventually they just lost track of one another, I guess."

"Do you know what kind of classes your professor-aunt taught here at the university?" I asked.

"I'm not sure, but I think she was a biologist, like you. Perhaps something to do with birds. Hummingbirds, I think."

I felt my mind stutter for a moment, and a chill ran down my spine. "What was her name?"

"Isabella."

My skin had goosebumps, and I stumbled with my words. "And . . . what was your other aunt's name?"

"Esmeralda."

Suddenly the uncanny likeness between Coquette and Destiny made complete sense. I recalled Destiny's words from so long ago: *What you might think are coincidences are actually the crossings of your life's threads on your journey from the past to the future—they are connections between the warp and weft in the growing tapestry of your being.*

I would say nothing about it for some time. As was my way, I had to think about it all for a while.

As Beatriz came to know Destiny, her concerns dissipated and she accepted her—maybe she didn't *embrace* her, but she became comfortable around her. However, one day she mentioned that she'd never known a person with as much empathy as Destiny. I replied, simply, that it was a key element of her special gift. I could see Beatriz contemplating this, but she chose not to pursue it. I signed a half-time teaching contract with the university, and Destiny and I often rode our bikes together to campus in the mornings. In the fall semester I taught the invertebrate zoology course that Bob was tired of teaching. It was easy because it was basically the same course I had taught many times at Northwestern Washington University. My Spanish continued to improve, Destiny was enjoying her classes, and we were happy together. Our relationship was growing in an organic fashion.

As time passed, my appreciation and respect for Destiny continued to flourish, and there was no one I more enjoyed spending time with. I looked forward to being with her every evening. I knew she felt the same way about me. We trusted one another deeply and connected in an elemental, natural way. And as still more time passed, I came to realize that I was deeply in love with Destiny. At last, I had the kind of relationship that I had envied for so many years in Bob and Beatriz. And it had happened so naturally, so easily, growing out of a deep and abiding friendship. I thought about how little I had known of love when I'd first met Penelope so many years ago, and how easy it had been to confuse love with passion.

One night Destiny said, "Odel, I know there is much that you have not told me of your journey. Of course, it is your private matter. But I see lingering in you a profound pain. I know that you experienced great challenges on your pilgrimage. But our losses, all our misfortunes, mistakes, and disappointments—they are all part of the raw material from which we shape ourselves to become the person we might be. Time can be our friend. I also know that you are a strong man, and like Siddhartha, wisdom has emerged out of your suffering. No heart passes through life unravaged by loss. Sooner or later, grief comes; usually unpredictably and sometimes mercilessly. Deep grief can undo the very fibers of our existence. Loss of a great love can result in loss of part of oneself, our confidence and clarity, our plans and our future. Yet out of those ashes, loss can eventually give rise to strength, as the spark in the cinders of our life slowly begins to grow again, turning first into an ember, and eventually into a new flame that burns with a clear raw light and a new understanding of ourselves and the universe. It is a curious thing that grief can add to a person, make them more. I sensed much of this for your future the day we met at my mother's house long ago, though I could not see the details. Through your struggles and losses, you have come to know yourself more deeply, and you have also become the man I now love. I believe that at the bottom of your pool of sorrow you found a surprising thing—the coalescence of compassion and courage. I see this luminous in you today. Should the time ever come that you wish to share more with me, please know that you can trust me to understand and to hold your words and feelings in confidence. I will always be your friend."

Her words were soothing and pressed lightly on my thoughts with a gentle melancholy that made them seem as beatitudes. I realized that Destiny embodied a natural kind of grace. And as she spoke with such a full heart, she could see the small tears of joy well up in my eyes.

Late in 1985 I got a letter from my old museum pal Audrey Arente. We hadn't talked in some years, but she tracked me down through some mutual friends. It was a chatty letter, but near the end she mentioned that her husband had left her for a younger woman, and three months later she'd lost her job at the Seattle Community Foundation. I guessed she might have a case of the blues, or worse. I decided to give her a call. By the time she'd finished telling me about her situation, she was bawling into the phone.

"Audrey, I'm so sorry. It sounds to me like you need a break. Come down and visit me here in Managua for a few weeks. My partner, Destiny, and I will treat you like a princess—good food, lots of fresh fish from the Pacific, great rum. We can go to the beach and visit some volcanoes. There's plenty of room in this house we're renting."

She replied with alacrity. "God, that sounds great, Odel. I just might take you up on that offer. However, I don't speak a single word of Spanish, so I'm not sure how well it would work out."

"No worries, Audrey. The university crowd we hang out with all speak some English. And you might even decide you want to learn a bit of Spanish; it's a lovely language, and there are several language schools near our place that have excellent reputations." I told her to look into flights on TACA or Copa, which would be cheaper than any of the U.S. carriers.

A month later, we were picking Audrey up at the airport. We had spruced up the spare bedroom and told her she was welcome to stay as long as she wished. On one of the bedroom walls, Destiny had hung the beautiful painting of Saint Michael the Archangel from her mother's house. Destiny had also taken the two stone carvings of *Quetzalcoatl* from her mom's yard when she'd moved away to start school at the university. These, too, were now in the guest bedroom, incorporated into a makeshift bookcase. They were indeed authentic. Something her grandfather had taken from an unexcavated Maya ruin on the Caribbean coast of Honduras long ago. On the bottom shelf of the bookcase, between Carmen Pettersen's book of Maya village paintings, and Ann Parker and Avon Neal's *Molas: Folk Art of the Cuna Indians*, was an old pair of hiking shoes. The right one had two snake fangs embedded in the leather, gifted by a fer-de-lance in the Petén jungle of Guatemala.

When Audrey saw the stone carvings, she asked what they were. I told her they were two-thousand-year old Maya figures of the great god *Quetzalcoatl*, the Feathered Serpent, one of the most powerful deities of pre-Hispanic America. I explained that in the sacred Mayan text called *Popol Vuh*,

Quetzalcoatl is known as the "Wind Guide," capable of traveling through space and time, the firmament and the underworld, to reveal great visions normally hidden from mortals.

"That sounds fascinating," Audrey replied, "You must tell me more about this Feathered Serpent one day, and how you know so much about him!"

"I will one day, Audrey. Or perhaps you will discover him on your own, if you linger in this part of the world. It is, as they say, the land of the Feathered Serpent."

On her first night in Managua we had a pleasant dinner of grilled steak, black beans, rice, and yucca, with a special plantain bread pudding that Destiny's mother had taught her to make. And we drank *Flor de Caña* into the night. Around ten, Audrey thanked us for our friendship and, looking at me, said, "Odel, I'm so happy for you. You seem to have found your place in the world. You are more content than I ever saw you during those years we worked together at the museum in Seattle. In fact, you almost seem like a different person."

"What do you mean, Audrey?"

"Well, you just seem more at peace with the world. But at the same time, you have more depth. Oh, I'm sorry, I don't mean to say you lacked depth in the past, just that . . . your views and your thoughts on things seem so much more nuanced and expansive . . . your life seems richer and more fulfilled. Honestly, all you used to talk about at the museum was science."

The three of us laughed at her comment.

Audrey continued. "And you and Destiny are so wonderfully happy together. Who would have ever guessed you'd end up here! You must tell me your story tomorrow—how you got to here from there."

Destiny watched me closely as I considered a reply.

"Everything you say is true, Audrey. When I was working at the museum, I *was* trapped in my science tunnel. And I had little imagination. But over the past few years I've made the wonderful discovery that the world is blessed with parallel realities. We seem to need a jolt to our sensibilities to bump us out of the one we're stuck in, that we've lived our life in, before we can see another that might be right next to us, hiding in plain sight. I'm still a scientist, but now I've also stumbled into another world, one that is even older than science itself. Five years ago I wouldn't have been able to see this parallel universe; it hides behind symbols, coincidences, and seemingly mystical experiences. But now I know it exists. And even though I lack a scientific explanation for it, I'm certain it is just as real as the world of science. Imagination, I've discovered, is the critical element needed to reveal hidden relations between things. With imagination we can see beyond the symbols and recognize that coincidences are actually where these parallel universes intersect; we become aware of the little knots where the warp of one gets tied around the weft of the other."

Audrey looked at me inquisitively, and I continued.

"These past years have been quite a journey for me, and I'm sure I've changed in many ways. I've come to believe that boundaries are simply human contrivances, even the boundaries of our knowledge. I've learned that life can be illusionary, certainty deceptive, and trust capricious. And almost nothing is simply black or white. I've discovered that even truth itself can be intangible and, like beauty and poetry, often best recognized by indirect illumination. And there is a truth, Audrey, that lies beyond what we see. I've also learned that wisdom, true wisdom, often comes at a cost. A cost greater than most hearts would wish to pay. But it's a long story. Actually, I've written it all down."

"Written it down?"

"Yes, I've just finished writing a book about my journey. I don't know if I want to try to publish it or not, but I wanted to write it."

"A book? Really? Can I read it? I have time on my hands now!"

"If you wish, of course." I went to my desk to retrieve the manuscript and handed it to her.

She looked at the cover sheet: *In the Land of the Feathered Serpent*. "What an interesting title, Odel."

"I hope you enjoy reading it. But, Audrey, I want to invite you to spend some time with Destiny tomorrow evening. She's very perceptive, and she's told me that she sees in you a troubled path forward. I know that you are a strong and intelligent woman, but she might be able to help you. She has a unique gift, an ability to estimate one's direction of travel and to provide some guidance."

"Well, that sounds interesting. Sure, I'm game."

I glanced at Destiny and saw her smiling serenely at the two of us.

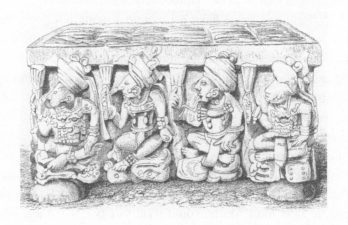

EPILOGUE

Odel and Destiny

Destiny completed her psychology degree at the university in Managua but decided she wanted to practice psychiatric medicine. She and Odel agreed that the outstanding medical school at Mexico's National University (UNAM) was the best option for her. Thus it came to pass that, with Destiny's intervention, the arc of Odel's journey took him back to Mexico City's charming neighborhood of Coyoacán. They found a house on a quiet street, Avenida Ithaca, not far from *Iglesia San Juan Bautista*, and Destiny began working toward her medical degree. In their little patio, they had a vegetable garden that was recipient of their most passionate care and enriched some of their most intimate moments together.

Being in the heart of Mexico's rich archaeological landscape, Odel's interests drew him to the National Institute of Anthropology, where he eventually was offered, and accepted, a research position as bioarchaeologist. He helped excavate Maya ruins on the Yucatán Peninsula and, eventually, in newly discovered hidden chambers beneath the enigmatic Temple of the Feathered Serpent at Teotihuacan. His identifications of insects, snails, and other invertebrates trapped for millennia in ancient ruins pioneered an entirely new field of paleoecology based on animal remains found in archaeological sites. And by the turn of the century, Odel would be using molecular genetics and ancient DNA to understand the entombed invertebrates he recovered during his excavations.

Destiny finalized her medical degree and became a clinical psychiatrist at Mexico City's National Institute of Neurology and Neurosurgery. However, her unorthodox patient protocols eventually led her to open her own private practice.

In time, of course, Destiny read Odel's story of his journey, learning of Coquette and the curious twist of fate that they were first cousins. Destiny and her long-lost Aunt Esmeralda were subsequently reunited, and as the years went by she and Odel would often visit Esmeralda and Bob and Beatriz in Managua.

Looking back on his experiences of the past few years, they seemed to haunt, rather than live among his memories. Odel sometimes thought about his youthful naiveté and recklessness, and how, were it not for the help of friends and acquaintances he met along his journey he might have perished on more than one occasion. And he frequently reflected on how he had been unable to fully subsume the pain of losing Coquette until he had shared it with Destiny, for in doing so he surrendered to that great loss. Destiny told him, "You have learned that loneliness can be the loudest voice in your head. That you miss the life you might have had with Coquette is *la añoranza*, divine nostalgia, one of our most powerful and important emotions. It honors your time with her, and it will only give it increasing depth as years go by. Let it illuminate your memories and your heart."

And then, on occasion, he would even wonder if everything that had come to pass between his first meeting with *La Señora* Circe and his encountering Destiny on the campus of the university had been but a dream or altered state of consciousness—time spent in the wilderness of his own mind.

Odel was thrilled when, in 1990, the great Russian Mayanist Yuri Knorozov made a visit to Mexico and Guatemala. The famous anthropologist and linguist had cracked the Mayan hieroglyphic writing code; the only fully developed writing system invented in the New World. It was the first time Knorozov had been allowed to leave his home country to visit the archaeological region he had studied from afar, in Leningrad, for decades. Knorozov's visit was at the invitation of Guatemalan President Marco Vinicio Cerezo, near the end of his term in office. The president presented him with a medal of honor, and Knorozov was able to visit several important Maya sites, including Tikal. However, shortly after Vinicio Cerezo left office, Knorozov received threats from extreme, right-wing military groups who were hostile to the Maya, and he was forced to go into hiding and then flee the country. This was, of course, just as Odel has visioned in Joyabaj during his Maya temple travels with the Feathered Serpent seven years earlier. His prediction of Knorozov's visit to Guatemala, and the reaction of anti-Maya militants in the country, now seemed a perfectly reasonable conjecture to him. A few years after Knorozov's return to Leningrad, the government of Mexico awarded him the *Orden del Águila Azteca* (Order of the Aztec Eagle), the highest decoration awarded by Mexico to noncitizens, which was ceremoniously presented to him at the Mexican Embassy in Moscow on November 30, 1994. Just two years earlier, K'iche human rights activist Rigoberta Menchú had received the Nobel Peace Prize, and in 2010 she would also receive the *Orden del Águila Azteca* from Mexico.

Occasionally, Odel would have dreams in which he was living happily with Coquette, but they would argue about her work with the CIA. He would struggle to explain that he could never fully trust her so long as she worked for the agency and had to keep so many secrets from him. But the harder he tried to make her understand, the more she would respond in Penelope's voice, and after a while the two women began to merge into one, leaving Odel feeling dispirited and confused. He would awake from these dreams overwhelmed with sadness until, seconds later, he would see Destiny beside him, her silver streak running like mercury through the river of her long black hair. He would reflect on how happy he was, and how Destiny was the trusted and reliable partner he'd always desired. He would curl up against her and fall back into a peaceful sleep, remembering Beatriz's musings on love and with the joy of knowing that he and Destiny had many years in front of them, during which time their relationship would develop an even deeper patina of trust, devotion, and friendship.

One morning after this dream Odel told Destiny of it, and of his thought that when Coquette tempted him to cross the river of his dreamworld it not only took him to her, but it helped him take the first steps into what was to become a transformative journey. Unbeknownst to him at the time, that river had been his Rubicon.

Destiny replied, "Odel, your journey is within yourself. Coquette, your river crossing, the many friends and strangers you've met along the way, even I—we have been here to offer you support and counsel in your passage. This is how it is for those who seek, for pilgrims and those who strive to lead a purposeful life. People, places, events . . . these are but guideposts for those who are mindful enough to see them and to learn from them. But as the great German polymath Nietzsche said, '*No one can build you the bridge on which you, and only you, must cross the river of life.*' Your wisdom comes to you through your own inner reflections. You know, I believe you have always been a passionate man; but passion is such a strong emotion that it can prevent us from seeing important clues that may lie in the periphery of our vision. Perhaps the exhaustion of passions can open one up to the first step on a path toward wisdom."

And then, after a pause, she continued. "You know, your life is an unfolding story being written day by day. But the story does not end with you. Just as others along your journey have shared their wisdom, revealed mysteries, helped you through difficult times, you will do the same for others before you die. And those who you influence will thus carry the tale forward. This is the way humankind's continuing story unfolds."

Odel would also dream of his father, in the woods teaching him and his brother tricks of survival, and how to be a good person and to have strength of character. Though these dreams would become less frequent over time, they would last the rest of his life.

On his fiftieth birthday, Destiny gave Odel a beautiful little rescue puppy. They decided to name him Argos. That same night they had dinner at their favorite steak restaurant not far from *Casa Azul* and took along the bottle of '61 Mouton from Penelope's father. Even with over thirty years of age, it was an exquisite Bordeaux. After dinner, Destiny said this to Odel: "I cannot see far enough into our future to know if we will be together forever. But I can tell you this— so long as I am alive, I will love you." Odel reciprocated in kind and with a joyful heart. As the years went by, Odel and Destiny built a happy and enduring life together, frequently spending evenings strolling Plaza Hidalgo in the beautiful barrio of Coyoacán.

John Thornton

The wedding of John Thornton and Gabriela López took place in San Juan Bautista church, in Coyoacán. Odel Bernini and Nestor Papadakis were the two best men, and Corazón and Alma were the two maids of honor. Aunt Esmeralda wore a beautiful emerald gown that matched the color of her eyes. Odel thought she looked like Glinda the Good Witch, from *The Wizard of Oz*. For five days, Nestor and Corazón flirted with one another and took long walks together in Plaza Hidalgo. As the years went by, John and Gabriela would frequently enjoy Christmas in Mexico City with Odel and Destiny, and the angels would sing a sweet refrain.

Penelope

In 1989, Penelope was offered a two-year internship as an information officer at the U.S. Embassy in Panama City. She accepted the offer and took an unpaid leave of absence from the University of Washington. Eighteen months into it, she was offered a permanent position at the embassy, as a Cultural

Attaché.   With her father's blessings, she let go of her university position and went to work full-time for the government. Just three years later, she was offered the station head position in Panama for the Central Intelligence Agency. Taking the post, she became the agency's first-ever female station chief in Latin America. She brought in Antin Morales to head up her intelligence analysis team. Penelope earned a reputation as a brilliant and cunning CIA officer, and one not to be trifled with.

Dr. Simon Jolly

In 1990 Dr. Simon Jolly was able to isolate the bioactive compound in the tiny Caribbean mangrove tunicate, *Ecteinascidia turbinata*.   He named the compound ecteinascidin, or ET-743. It proved to be effective against soft-tissue sarcomas and lung, breast, and ovarian cancers. The effectiveness of the compound led to bulk collections of the tunicate from various locations in the Caribbean to supply material for preclinical research studies. However, collection of sufficient quantities proved impossible. Jolly decided to let someone else take over work on his "silver bullet."

The University of California, who owned the patent on Dr. Jolly's compound, licensed it to the Spanish pharmaceutical company PharmaMar. They gave the compound a commercial name, Trabectedin, and hoped to grow the little tunicates in aquaculture ponds along the Mediterranean coast of Spain. But one ton of animals was required to isolate just one gram of Trabectedin, making the farming process unfeasible. This prompted Jolly and a Harvard chemist colleague to develop a synthetic method of making Trabectedin in 1996. A key breakthrough was achieved in 2003, when the synthetic process was refined enough to manufacture Trabectedin in large quantities. The method was patented by Harvard and subsequently licensed to PharmaMar, who now produces the drug.   Trabectedin succeeded in clinical trials and was launched as a highly effective treatment for soft-tissue sarcomas. Had Trabectedin been available in the early 1980s, it might have saved both Isabella and her sister Circe from their premature deaths from liposarcoma.

Professor Jolly died on June 13, 2005, at the age of seventy-six, after a long and difficult illness. He had been elected Fellow of the American Association for the Advancement of Science and was also a Sloan Fellow and Guggenheim Fellow. He was an active (and reckless) scuba diver, mountain climber, and skier. He was also a brilliant scientist and extraordinary gentleman.

Flor de Caña Rum

Ron Flor de Caña has been made since 1890. *Compañía Licorera de Nicaragua* developed sugarcane plantations and built the first distillery in Chichigalpa (about 120 kilometers north of Managua) at the base of *Volcán San Cristóbal*. The company was founded by the great-grandfather of the current president, who moved from Italy to Nicaragua in 1875.

In 1959 *Ron Flor de Caña* began to be exported to other Central American countries. During the 1970s a second distillery was constructed in Honduras. In the 1980s, during Nicaragua's Contra War, *Flor de Caña* was stored in large quantities in various hiding places. Thus, by the 1990s, *Flor de Caña* had the largest reserve of aged rum in the world. The distillery in Chichigalpa was finally renovated and modernized in 1996.

Flor de Caña rum is distilled five times during its production. It is aged in charred white oak barrels that had previously been used to mature bourbon whiskey. The company's finest vintages are aged for up to twenty-five years. *Flor de Caña* is renowned as one of the best rums in the world, having won more than 150 international awards since 2000. Today, *Flor de Caña* rum is distributed in forty-three countries, and on each bottle are images of *Volcán San Cristóbal* and medals won by the legendary rum. *Flor de Caña* is also made to comply with kosher standards.

Matins for the Virgin of Guadalupe

Jerusalem's matins have rarely been recorded, but at least one version of this stunning composition still exists—*Matins for the Virgin of Guadalupe*, 1764, by Chanticleer (Teldec/Warner Music 3984-21829-2). And for excellent covers of *Into the Mystic*, check out the incomparable Lavelle White's R&B/funk version and Marc Cohn's sweet refrain version. And try the powerful, soaring, 10-minute electric version of *Fanfare for the Common Man* by Emerson, Lake & Palmer (Works, Vol. 1).

ACKNOWLEDGMENTS

I carried this story around in my head since the 1980s. So many people helped me experience, explore, and understand Central America and Mexico since then that I cannot possibly list or even remember them all. Most important has been my wife, the wonderful Wendy Moore, who helped me keep this idea alive and schlep my boxes of notes and books from house to house as we moved around the country, always encouraging me to start writing it down.

I owe much of my inspiration to the writings of Hermann Hesse, Joseph Campbell, and Kahlil Gibran. While those are the books most of us read in our youth, I have found returning to them in adulthood a wise use of one's time. My writing also has been influenced by the insightful autobiography of Trappist monk Thomas Merton (*The Seven Storey Mountain*) and by John Fowles' classic novel, *The Magus*, which I find myself returning to every few years for the astonishingly nuanced plot and mind-bending story. My perspective on writing (and life) is strongly grounded in the 1960s and 1970s when, for a decade or so, I experimented with hallucinogenic drugs. Those experiences offered me new ways to see the world and explore ideas, made me unafraid to take risks, taught me mindfulness and deep concentration, and convinced me to keep my mind alive and open and not get trapped in the silo of academia that so many of my university professors seemed trapped in.

Jeff Hartman and Linda Brewer, ace writers and editors, gave me sage advice and help for the couple of years I worked to get my story onto paper. Wendy Moore and Carlene Brusca read an early version of the story and provided criticism and editorial help. Amanda Krause did an outstanding job of copy and content editing on the penultimate draft (and relieved me of comma fatigue). Ricardo Rodriguez Estrella and Lloyd Findley checked and improved my Spanish. The superb artist

Alex Boersma (alexboersma.com) created the cover design and chapter dividers. I also want to thank my friend and consummate dreamer John Gregg, who invited me to stay in the old house at his boatyard in Moss Landing, California, in 2018 when we were working on the *Western Flyer* project—a summer of intense writing when I finished this story. And special thanks to Jay Savage and Peter Raven, for turning me on to Flor de Caña rum one wild night in 1980 in San Jose, Costa Rica.

In Mexico, Guatemala, Nicaragua and Costa Rica, many friends, colleagues and strangers made my travels in the 80s informative and exhilarating. The wonderful people of those magnificent lands always made me feel welcome and valued, as is typical of the vibrant Latin American culture. Very special thanks to the congenial staff at the Pan-American Hotel in Guatemala City, which, 40 years later, still provides a peaceful respite in the heart of a clamorous and congested city. Infinite gratitude to Manuel Murillo and the Universidad de Costa Rica for hosting my research throughout the 1980s. And an exceptional note of appreciation to a certain *abuela* and her granddaughter in Oaxaca for an unforgettable temescal experience.

In recent years, my visits to Mexico City have been hosted by the remarkable family of Rodrigo Medellín and Clementina Equihua Zamora, and their delightful children Alejandra and Rodrigo. Special thanks to Clementina for an extraordinary visit to the remote *Oyamel* forests of Michoacán in pursuit of Mexico's magical migratory monarchs, and to Rodrigo and INAH archaeologist Sergio Gómez Chávez for a personalized tour beneath the Temple of the Feathered Serpent at Teotihuacan by way of the underground tunnel sealed 2000 years ago and rediscovered by Sergio in 2003.

The opening image of a stela and closing image of an altar from Copán are by Frederick Catherwood, in J. L. Stephens's 1841 classic *Incidents of Travel in Central America, Chiapas, and Yucatán* (Harper & Brothers). The image of Quetzalcoatl below is adapted from the *Codex Borgia*.

To learn more about the author, the novel, and Central America please visit: **www.featheredserpent.online**

REFERENCES AND FURTHER READING

Agee, P. 1975. *Inside the Company: CIA Diary.* Penguin Books, London.

Agee, P. 1982. *White Paper Whitewash.* Deep Cover Books, New York.

Aguilar Mora, J., J. Salmón and B. C. Ewell. 2017. *Anthology of Spanish American Thought and Culture.* University of Florida Press, Gainesville.

Amnesty International. 1981. *Guatemala: A Government Program of Political Murder.* Amnesty International Publications.

Anaya, R. A. 1987. *Lord of the Dawn. The Legend of Quetzalcóatl.* University of New Mexico Press, Albuquerque.

Anderson, T. P. 1988. *Politics in Central America: Guatemala, El Salvador, Honduras, and Nicaragua (Revised Edition).* Green Wood Publishing Group, Rochester, New York.

Baldwin, N. 1998. *Legends of the Plumed Serpent: Biography of a Mexican God.* Public Affairs New York

Cabezas, O. 1982. *Fire from the Mountain: The Making of a Sandinista.* New American Library, New York.

Canuto, M. A. and 17 others. 2018. Ancient lowland Maya complexity as revealed by airborne laser scanning of northern Guatemala. Science 361: 1355-1355.

Carballo, J. L. and 4 others. 2000. Production of *Ecteinascidia turbinata* for obtaining anticancer compounds. Journal of the World Aquaculture Society 31: 481-490.

Carlsen, W. 2016. *Jungle of Stone: The True Story of Two Men, Their Extraordinary Journey, and the Discovery of the Lost Civilization of the Maya.* HarperCollins Books, New York.

Carothers, T. 1993. *In the Name of Democracy: U.S. Policy Toward Latin America in the Reagan Years.* University of California Press, Berkeley, California.

Ceballos, P. A., M. Pérez, C. Cuevas, A. Francesch, I. Manzanares and A. M. Echavarren. 2006. Synthesis of ecteinascidin 743 analogues from cyanosafracin B: Isolation of a kinetically stable quinoneimine tautomer of a 5-hydroxyindole. European Journal of Organic Chemistry 8: 1926–1933.

Central Intelligence Agency. 1973. National Intelligence Survey: Guatemala Armed Forces. 14 pp.

Chapman, P. 2007. *Bananas: How the United Fruit Company Shaped the World.* Canongate Books, Edinburgh.

Coe, M. D. 1992. *Breaking the Maya Code.* Thames & Hudson, London.

Coe, M. D. and S. Houston 2015. *The Maya.* 9th ed. Thames & Hudson, London.

Colle, M.-P. 2003. *Guadalupe: Body and Soul.* The Vendome Press, New York.

Cullather, N. 2006. *Secret History: The CIA's Classified Account of Its Operations in Guatemala 1952–54 (Second Edition).* Stanford University Press, California.

Díaz, del Castillo, B. 1496-1584. *Historia verdadera de la conquista de la Nueva España.* Translated and with an Introduction by J. Burke and T. Humphrey. 2012. Hackett Publishing Company, Indianapolis.

Dosal, P. 1995. *Doing Business with the Dictators: A Political History of Untied Fruit in Guatemala, 1899–1944.* Roman and Littlefield, New York.

Fauriol, G. (ed.). 1985. *Latin American Insurgencies.* The Georgetown University Center for Strategic and International Studies and the National Defense University, Washington, D.C.

Forster, C. 2001. *The Time of Freedom: Campesino Workers in Guatemala's October Revolution.* University of Pittsburgh Press, Pennsylvania.

Fried, J. L. 1983. *Guatemala in Rebellion: Unfinished History.* Grove Press, New York.

Gallenkamp, C. 1985. *Maya: The Riddle and Rediscovery of a Lost Civilization. 3rd ed.* Viking Penguin Inc., New York.

Garcia Ferreira, R. 2008. The CIA and Jacobo Arbenz: The Story of a Disinformation Campaign. Journal of Third World Studies 25(2): 59.

Gleijeses, P. 1991. *Shattered Hope: The Guatemalan Revolution and the United Sates, 1944-1954.* Princeton University Press.

Goetz, D. and S. G. Morley. 1950. *Popol Vuh: The Sacred Book of the Ancient Quiché Maya. From the Translation of Adrián Recinos.* University of Oklahoma Press, Norman.

Gomez, M. C. 2015. Maya Religion in, *Ancient History Encyclopedia.* www.ancient.eu/Maya_Religion/.

Grandin, G. 2007. *Empire's Workshop: Latin America, the United States, and the Rise of the New Imperialism.* Holt Paperbacks, New York.

Grandin, G. and N. Klein. 2011. *The Last Colonial Massacre: Latin America in the Cold War.* University of Chicago Press, Illinois.

Guatemala National Museum of Archaeology. 2001. *Popol Vuh: The Sacred Book of the Ancient Mayas-Quiché.* Translation by David B. Castledine. Monclem Ediciones, Mexico, D.F.

Hanson, P. M. 1949. *In the Land of the Feathered Serpent.* Herald House [of the Mormon Church], Independence, MO. [A curious tale of travel by Paul M. Hanson (president of the Council of the Twelve Apostles, Mormon Church), Apostle Charles R. Hield, and Elder Harold D. Smith, to Mexico, to build support for the Mormon belief that Native Americans did not come from Siberia by way of the Bering Strait and that Jesus himself evangelized the first Americans shortly after his resurrection. The dramatic conclusion seems to be that the Mesoamerican deity *Quetzalcoatl* was, in fact, Jesus Christ.]

Hoepker, T. 1998. *Return of the Maya: Guatemala—A Tale of Survival*. Henry Hold, New York.

Holland, S. and D. Anderson. 1984. *Kissinger's Kingdom?* Bertrand Russell House, Nottingham, England.

Homer. 1998. *The Odyssey. Translated by Robert Fitzgerald. Introduction by D. S. Carne-Ross*. Farrar, Straus and Giroux, New York.

Iannone, G., B. A. Houk and S. A. Schwake. 2016. *Ritual, Violence and the Fall of the Classic Maya Kings*. University of Florida Press, Gainesville.

Immerman, R. H. 1983. *The CIA in Guatemala: The Foreign Policy of Intervention*. University of Texas Press, Austen, Texas.

Jamail, M. and M. Gutierrez. 1986. *It's No Secret: Israel's Military Involvement in Central America*. AAUG Press, Belmont, Massachusetts.

Kinzer, S. 1991. *Blood of Brothers: Life and War in Nicaragua*. Putnam Publishing Group, New York.

Koeppel, D. 2008. *Banana: The Fate of the Fruit that Changed the World*. Hudson Street Press, New York.

Lafaye, J. (translated by Benjamin Keen, with a Foreword by Octavio Paz). 1976. *Quetzalcoatl and Guadalupe. The Formation of Mexican National Consciousness, 1531-1813.* The University of Chicago Press. [An extraordinary, scholarly work describing development of the collective social-spiritual consciousness in Mexico during and after Spanish colonial rule. Originally published as *Quetzalcóatl et Guadalupe*, 1974, Éditions Gallimard.]

LaFeber, W. 1993. *Inevitable Revolutions: The United States in Central America*. W. W. Norton, New York.

Lathrop, J. P. 2016. *Ancient Mexico. Cultural Traditions in the Land of the Feathered Serpent*. 11th ed. Kendall Hunt Publishing, Dubuque, Iowa.

López Austin, A. (translated by Russ Davidson, with Guilhem Olivier). 2015. *The Myth of Quetzalcoatl. Religion,*

Rulership, and History in the Nahua Word. University Press of Colorado, Boulder.

Loveman, B. and T. M. Davies. 1997. *The Politics of Antipolitics: The Military in Latin America (Third Edition).* Rowman & Littlefield, Lanham, Maryland

Lowenthal, A. 1991. *Exporting Democracy: The United States and Latin America, Themes and Issues.* Johns Hopkins University Press, Baltimore, Maryland.

Luís de Rojas, J. 2012. *Tenochtitlan, Capital of the Aztec Empire.* University of Florida Press, Gainesville.

McCleary, R. 1999. *Dictating Democracy: Guatemala and the End of Violent Revolution.* University Press of Florida, Gainesville, Florida.

McCreery, D. 1994. *Rural Guatemala, 1760–1940.* Stanford University Press, California.

McGehee , R. W. 1983. *Deadly Deceits: My 25 Years in the CIA.* Sheridan Square Publications, New York.

Menchu, R., E. Burgos-Debray and A. Wright. 1984. *I, Rigoberta Menchú: An Indian Woman in Guatemala.* Verso, London.

Montejo, V. and L. Garay (translated by D. Unger). 1999. *Popol Vuh. A Sacred Book of the Maya.* Groundwood Books, Toronto, Canada.

Nicholson, H. B. 2001. *Topiltzin Quetzalcoatl. The Once and Future Lord of the Toltecs.* University Press of Colorado, Boulder.

Orsini Dunnington, J. and C. Mann. 1997. *Viva Guadalupe. The Virgin in New Mexican Popular Art.* Museum of New Mexico Press, Santa Fe.

Parker, A. and A. Neal. 1977. *Molas: Folk Art of the Cuna Indians.* Barre Publishing, Barre, Massachusetts.

Pérez-Maldonado, R. 1966. *Tales from Chichicastenango: Legends of the Maya-Quiché.* Unión Tip, Guatemala City.

Pettersen, C. L. 1976. *The Maya of Guatemala: Their Life and Dress.* Ixchel Museum, Guatemala City.

Poelchau, W. (ed.). 1981. *White Paper Whitewash: Interviews with Philip Agee on the CIA and El Salvador*. Sheridan Square Publications, New York.

Poole, S. 1995. *Our Lady of Guadalupe. The Origins and Sources of a Mexican National Symbol, 1531-1797.* University of Arizona Press, Tucson.

Richards, M. 1985. Cosmopolitan world-view and counterinsurgency in Guatemala. Anthropological Quarterly 58(3): 94.

Ridenour, R. 1986. *Yankee Sandinistas: Interviews with North Americans Living and Working in the New Nicaragua.* Curbstone Press of Northwestern University Press, Evanston, Illinois.

Rinehart, K. L. and 24 other authors. 1981. Marine natural products as sources of antiviral, antimicrobial, and antineoplastic agents. Pure & Applied Chemistry 53: 795-817.

Rudolph, J. D. 1982. *Nicaragua: A Country Study*. Secretary of the Army, U.S. Government, Washington, D.C. 278 pp.

Schele, L. and D. Freidel. 1990. *A Forest of Kings: The Untold Story of the Ancient Maya.* William Morrow and Company, New York.

Schirmer, J. 1988. *The Guatemalan Military Project: A Violence Called Democracy*. University of Pennsylvania Press, Philadelphia, Pennsylvania.

de Sahagun, Fray Bernardino. 1950-1959. *General History of the Things of New Spain*. Monographs of the School of American Research, Santa Fe, New Mexico. [English translation of the Franciscan Padre Bernardino de Sahagun's monumental, 12-volume *Historia General de las Cosas de la Nueva España*, 1558-1569.]

Streeter, S. M. 2000. *Managing the Counterrevolution: The United States and Guatemala, 1954–1961*. Ohio University Press, Athens, Ohio.

Striffler, S. and M. Moberg. 2003. *Banana Wars: Power, Production, and History in the Americas*. Duke University Press, Durham, North Carolina.

Tedlock, D. 1996. *Popol Vuh. The Definitive Edition of the Mayan Book of the Dawn of Life and the Glories of Gods and Kings (revised and expanded 2nd edition)*. Touchstone, New York.

Time Magazine. 1986. Numerous essays on Time's cover story: "Daniel Ortega: The Man Who Makes Reagan See Red." *Time Magazine*, March 31, 1986.

Tzu, Lao. 2018. *Tao Te Ching* (paraphrased by Sam Torode). Ancient Renewal Books.

U.S. Army Special Operations Command. 1964. Case Studies in Insurgency and Revolutionary Warfare: Guatemala 1944-1954. 119 pp.

Walker, T. W. and C. J. Wade. 2011. *Nicaragua. Living in the Shadow of the Eagle (Fifth Edition)*. Westview Press, Boulder, Colorado. [Note that the 4th edition was titled, *The Land of Sandino*.]

Webb, G. 1999. *Dark Alliance: The CIA, the Contras, and the Crack Cocaine Explosion*. Seven Stories Press, New York.

Woodward, R. 1987. *Veil: The Secret Wars of the CIA, 1981-1987*. Simon and Schuster, New York.

Zgryziewicz, R. 2018. *Violent Extremism and Communications*. NATO Strategic Communications Centre of Excellence, Riga, Latvia. 50 pp.

"I think that if there is one truth that people need to learn in the world, especially today, it is this: the intellect is only theoretically independent of desire and appetite in ordinary, actual practice. It is constantly being blinded and perverted by the ends and aims of passion, and the evidence it presents to us with such a show of partiality and objectivity is fraught with interest and propaganda. We have become marvelous at self-delusion; all the more so because we have gone to such trouble to convince ourselves of our own absolute infallibility. The desires of the flesh—and by that I mean not only sinful desires, but even the ordinary, normal appetites for comfort and ease and human respect, are fruitful sources of every kind of error and misjudgment, and because we have these yearnings in us, our intellects present to us everything distorted and accommodated to the norms of our desire."

The Seven Storey Mountain. Thomas Merton, 1948

"Self-discovery is above all the realization that we are alone."
The Labyrinth of Solitude. Octavio Paz, 1961

"There lies a green field between the scholar and the poet; should the scholar cross it he becomes a wise man; should the poet cross it he becomes a prophet."

Sand and Foam. Kahlil Gibran, 1926

Made in the USA
Las Vegas, NV
28 February 2023

68312504R00288